New

A FLAME FOR THE FIRE

A FLAME FOR THE FIRE

Nigel Tranter

Hodder & Stoughton

First published in Great Britain in 1998 by
Hodder and Stoughton
A division of Hodder Headline PLC

10 9 8 7 6 5 4 3 2 1

British Library Cataloguing in Publication Data

Tranter, Nigel, 1909–
A Flame for the Fire
1. English fiction – 20th century – Scottish authors
2. Scottish fiction – 20th century
I. Title
823.9′12 [F]

ISBN 0 340 69670 2

Typeset by Hewer Text Ltd, Edinburgh
Printed and bound in Great Britain by
Mackays of Chatham PLC, Chatham, Kent

Hodder and Stoughton
A division of Hodder Headline PLC
338 Euston Road
London NW1 3BH

Principal Characters in order of appearance

David Kennedy: Eldest son of the second Lord Kennedy.

Janet Kennedy: Younger sister of above.

John, Lord Kennedy: Head of that family, styled "King of Carrick."

James the Fourth: King of Scots.

Archibald, Earl of Angus: The Red Douglas, known as Bell-the-Cat.

Patrick Hepburn, Lord Hailes: Later Earl of Bothwell.

Alexander, Lord Home: Later Earl of Home and High Chamberlain.

William, Master of Borthwick: Later Lord Borthwick.

Agnes Borthwick: Sister of above.

Sir Andrew Wood of Largo: Admiral.

MacIan of Ardnamurchan: Great Highland chief.

John Macdonald of Islay: Great Highland chief.

John, Lord Drummond: Powerful noble.

Perkin Warbeck: English Pretender, styling himself Richard, Duke of York.

Lord Maxwell: Important noble. Warden of the West March.

William Elphinstone, Bishop of Aberdeen: Noted cleric and statesman.

Don Pedro De Ayala: Spanish ambassador.

Richard Fox, Prince-Bishop of Durham: Important English cleric.

Andrew Forman, Prior of Pittenweem: Later Bishop of Moray.

James Stewart, Earl of Moray: Illegitimate child of the king and Janet Kennedy.

Margaret Tudor: Queen of James and sister of Henry the Eighth.

Lord Dacre: Cumbrian noble. English Warden of the West March.

George Vaus. Bishop of Galloway

Quintin Agnew of Lochnaw: Sheriff of Galloway.

Alexander Kennedy: Younger brother of David and Janet.

Robert Borthwick of Ballencrieff: Master of the Ordnance.

De La Motte: French ambassador.

Elizabeth, Lady Heron: Wife of Sir William, imprisoned English Warden.

Earl of Surrey; Earl Marshal of England: Heir to the Duke of Norfolk.

1

David Kennedy drummed his fists impatiently on the parapet of the wall-walk of what was known as the Laigh House of Dunure Castle, gazing out to sea. This waiting! He had promised the master-mason, Dod Johnstone, from Ayr, to be at Cassillis, seven miles eastwards, well before midday. And here that wretched Red Douglas, Archibald Bell-the-Cat, had arrived again, and was closeted with his father and sister. And Janet wanted to go with him to Cassillis, being almost as interested as he was himself in the building progress there. He could go on alone, of course; but he wanted to have her with him on this occasion. And he did not want to leave her with that Earl of Angus, whatever their father thought and planned. David was fond of his sister.

How long could he wait? The man would almost certainly go back to Ayr again if they did not arrive at the building site after a couple of hours or so, for he was working on another project, more important for him, as he was also building a castle at Skelmorlie for the Earl of Eglinton, the Montgomerie chief, who was his own laird. And he, David, particularly wanted to see the man to explain his plans and wishes. His coming to Cassillis today had been difficult to arrange.

And now Archibald Douglas, Earl of Angus, had arrived just as they were going to set out, and Janet was detained.

Was there any way in which he could contrive his sister's escape? She would thank him for it, even if their father would not. David Kennedy was perhaps an impatient young man. At twenty-five years, he chafed at his father's

1

autocratic ways. He was Master of Kennedy, after all. But his sire, the second Lord Kennedy, self-styled King of Carrick, was not to be thwarted by any of his sons and daughters. This dominant and peremptory attitude was indeed why David was building the new castle for himself at Cassillis, his personal property as Master and heir to the title, and where Janet was volunteering to come and keep house for him in due course – if she was not married first, she also desiring to distance herself somewhat from their commanding father; but not by wedding the Red Douglas!

In a way, of course, he, David, would miss dwelling here at Dunure, where he had been born, for it was a most notable stronghold, perched on top of a great column of rock thrust up out of the waves of the lower Firth of Clyde, some eight miles south of Ayr, in Carrick; at least the ancient keep was, oddly shaped to conform with the summit limits of the crag, although the Laigh House, more commodious and built by their grandfather, was sited on slightly lower ground on the little peninsula linking the rock with the shore, itself cliff-sided but less lofty, with steps leading up to the keep, which meant that all who would enter this last must climb up afoot, leaving horses and any numbers of men down in the inner courtyard, a defensive measure. David could look down on the Atlantic rollers smashing themselves in spray on the rocks below, with the recurrent but unending sigh-and-roar, a sound which had been in his ears all his days, and which undoubtedly he would miss at Cassillis, where there would be only the chuckling murmur of the River Doon to hear; but that would be a small price to pay to be out from under the immediate sway of the King of Carrick.

At length he heard the swish of skirts above the noise of the waves, as his younger sister by two years came running along the parapet walk to him from the stairhead caphouse.

"I knew that you would be here," she cried. "You could

not go without me, and I could not get away until now. That man! His paws on me! Stroking. Feeling. I am not his yet! Whatever our sire says."

"No. I pray that you never will be."

Janet Kennedy was a sight to be seen, even by her own brother. Tall, lissome, shapely, spirited, she was a beauty, indeed the most beautiful woman David had ever seen, long of neck, fine of feature, with flashing, laughing eyes. But it was her hair that struck most viewers first, vivid and plenteous red hair, flame-coloured and cascading down. She was known as Flaming Janet Kennedy all over Carrick and beyond. They were very close, these two.

"Can we go now?" he went on. "Before they call you back. Our horses are saddled, waiting."

"Yes, yes. I am scarce clad for riding. But I care not. Off with us, yes. And quickly."

They hurried down the winding narrow turnpike stair, past the door to the first-floor hall where Lord Kennedy was entertaining the Earl of Angus. The groom waiting with the horses, a little apart from the group of Douglases with the earl's mounts, grinned conspiratorially and helped the young woman up into her saddle, she agile and with a flash of long white legs, caring nothing for the stares of the Angus men. Then they were off, kicking their horses' flanks urgently, even there on the cobbles of the yard, out through the gatehouse-arch, over the drawbridge and moat, and so down the hill towards the more level ground amongst the cattle. Due eastwards they rode, at a canter now, up the Dunure Burn's little valley and on through the Brown Carrick Hills, heading for the River Doon.

As they went, when the terrain allowed them to ride side by side, David asked about what had taken place and been said with their father and Archibald Bell-the-Cat of Angus, that notable and unscrupulous chief of the Red Douglases who had engineered the notorious slaughter, at Lauder Brig, of the late King

3

James the Third's minions and familiars, whence he gained his by-name.

"They were chaffering over lands," he was told. "Lands in exchange for *me*! Angus was offering two baronies. In Lanarkshire: Braidwood and some property called Crawford-Lindsay. For these I was to become his third Countess of Angus, wed to a man older than our father. He was not satisfied, wanting more. I will not have it, I will *not*!"

"We must stop it, yes. But how? There must be something that we can do."

"I am of age now. Twenty-three years. No longer some child to be used, bought and sold . . ."

"I fear that an unwed woman's age does not prevent her father giving her in marriage. Wrong as it is. Different with a man. I am of full age, and cannot be forced to do this and that. But, unfair as it is, with a woman it is different."

"I would flee, run away, go into hiding, rather than be wed to that man! Would Father be able to take me out of *your* house? Cassillis?"

"I deem that he would. In law. Although he could scarcely besiege us! But sooner or later he would grasp you, outwith it."

"Why is he so eager for this? Why Angus, a man older than himself and of ill repute?"

"He is the Red Douglas. Chief of the second branch of the greatest family in the land, after the king's own. And rivalling the king in power. Angus has been given control, since his Lauder affair, of all the Borders and Lanarkshire. How he can offer these lands for you! And he now dwells at Douglas Castle, none so far away, so we see the more of him. Our sire is ambitious. He would be more than King of Carrick! He once told me that he should be an earl. Power he wants – and Angus could aid him to that. For the new king seems to esteem him highly. King James needs Douglas support also . . ."

They rode on, swinging southwards by Garryhorn towards the Doon valley, well above Maybole. Soon they were into David's own lands, Grange and Milton of Cassillis, and so to a quite dramatic area. The Doon, a major river flowing north-westwards out of the Galloway hills, had here channelled for itself a steep-sided trough, up to one hundred feet deep, where trees and bushes clung precariously. And on a strong site above the river, on the south side, was Cassillis Tower, their destination.

There had long been a small and simple tower-house here, the heritage of the heir to the Kennedys of Dunure. But David wanted something better, more commodious, where he could live in fair comfort away from his father. But strong, for strongholds were necessary in the Scotland of the late fifteenth century, with the nobles and lairds aggressive and the central government weak, although the new king, James the Fourth, was seeking to improve that. So a new fortalice had risen, incorporating the small tower, massively built with walls a dozen feet in thickness. It was complete to the wallhead, and the roof timbers were in place, but the stone slates were not yet on.

After fording the river at a brief shallow reach downstream, with relief David saw that three shaggy garrons were tethered nearby, which meant that Dod Johnstone, the master-mason, would still be there. Janet and he rode up, to dismount from their very different, taller and better-bred horses, to go within.

They found Johnstone, a heavy, slow-spoken man, talking with the four builders employed on the construction work. It was not for the Master of Kennedy to apologise to a tradesman, however skilled, for keeping him waiting; but he did explain that the arrival of the Earl of Angus had delayed them at Dunure. They moved over, to discuss the object of this visit.

It was, strangely enough, a staircase, not the usual preoccupation of a laird at his house-building. But this was to be a very special stair. The old one, for the previous tower, was still there, a typical narrow winding ascent, even more limited than that they had descended at Dunure. It had been on an earlier visit, when they were

5

having great difficulty in getting the new fourteen-foot-long lintel for the hall fireplace up to the first floor, that the matter had arisen. They just could not manoeuvre that length of solid stone up the twisting constrictions of that stairway. They had had to devise and erect a hoist up at the window-opening of the hall, and with great labour, and some danger, heave the lengthy and so weighty piece of hewn sandstone by means of ropes and tackle, and in through that aperture. Janet had pointed out that this would also apply to required furnishings, such as a long hall-table and benches, indeed to bedroom plenishings for the upper rooms also, hereafter. What was needed was a much wider stairway. David had accepted that, and told the builders to consider one at least twice as wide.

It was the next day that Janet had come up with the idea. She had been thinking about it all before sleeping that night, and had a suggestion to make. Since the stairway was to be so much wider, could they not have a much wider, thicker newel also, that is the central pillar from which the steps and treads of the twisting stair projected? These turnpike stairs were necessary for defence; that is why they were shaped and twisted that way, so that one man, or two, with swords, could hold up and keep out attackers, however many, themselves safely hidden behind the said newel, only the sword-arm and weapon in evidence. That was fair enough. But these narrow turnpikes were highly inconvenient for normal living, not only for the carrying of burdens up, but for mothers with children in their arms, elderly folk unsteady on their feet, and the like, especially as the public rooms, halls and bedchambers were always on the upper floors. So – a wider stairway. But also, a great inconvenience was their lighting, by night, when no light came in from the narrow arrow-slit windows in the walling, and one had to carry a lamp or candle up the circular ascent, and many had been the falls and minor disasters in castles by the hundred over the years.

Janet's notion, simple as it sounded once it was propounded, was that a wider newel such as she suggested

6

could be hollow down its centre, built that way; and this, with slits in the sides of it, would allow lamps to be lit and placed therein, which would give light to folk going up or down, steady and reliable light. A hollow newel, that was the answer, with little shelves for lamps and candles.

David was much taken with this idea, and wondered why nobody had thought of it before, at least not that they had ever heard of. Praising his sister's ingenuity, he agreed to have such built. It must be possible. Hence the master-mason from Ayr.

Johnstone, considering it all, said that he thought it could be done, indeed might well be something that he could recommend to others. David foresaw Skelmorlie Castle perhaps getting a similar innovation. But the mason thought that the present narrow stair in the thickness of the walling should be left intact. A wide one replacing it would inevitably project into the floor space at each level, making for awkward angles into the rooms and difficult access. Much better to build a little extra wing to house the new stair at a corner of the keep, making the whole L-shaped. This would be less difficult, less costly and more convenient than replacing the old turnpike. And shot-holes in this extra extension would give improved defence by allowing flanking fire along the two sides of the main walling.

This all commended itself to David and Janet. So be it.

The pair lingered on at Cassillis long after Johnstone and the builders departed, in no hurry to return to Dunure in case Archibald Bell-the-Cat was still there. He had left his men and horses in the courtyard unstabled and waiting, so it had looked as though he had not intended to remain for very long. If he was going back to Douglas Castle he had a lengthy journey ahead of him, although he had a nearer property at Garvellton. David and his sister spent the time examining all the new construction, noting where improvements could be made, and admiring the handsome great fireplace in the hall, with its ingleneuks under that

7

noteworthy lintel. Thereafter they went walking up the side of the River Doon, in its picturesque glen, beside the cataracts and minor waterfalls and deep pools, so very different a scene from the surroundings of clifftop Dunure.

At length they set out on their return to the coast, hoping for the best.

Best it might be, with Angus gone, but that did not mean any pleasant reception by John, Lord Kennedy. Their father was a tall and sternly handsome man, in his late forties, with a somewhat hawk-like stoop. He was waiting for them, less than warmly.

"Your behaviour, Janet, in absenting yourself like this, with our distinguished guest here, was ill-done, and an embarrassment for myself," he greeted them. "I expect better of my daughter. *And* my son, who went with you! It was ill-done, I say. Earl Archibald was much put out, as well he might be, seeking your hand in marriage as he does. What have you to say for yourself?"

"As well to let him know, then, that I am not for him!" his daughter returned, nowise abashed. "I much mislike the man. Whoever I wed, it will not be him."

"You will wed whom I tell you to, girl!"

"Why so? I am no child now. Twenty-three years. I have a mind of my own. That Douglas is all but old enough to be my grandsire! And he has had two wives already and seven children, all older than am I. Why have me to marry such a man?"

"I have my reasons. Our families linked could be to much advantage and worth."

"For whom, sir?" That was David.

"Quiet, you! Where did you take her? To Cassillis? That, in despite of my wishes."

"Father, I would remind you, we are no bairns! You forget it at times. Our brothers and sister may still be subject to your charge, but Janet and myself are not. We have our own lives to live. You cannot trade Janet, like cattle or merchandise, for lands or repute or influence. As this would be."

"When I require you to tell me what I can or cannot do, David, I will ask you!" the King of Carrick jerked. "In my house, what I require will be done."

"Then the sooner that Cassillis is ready for us to occupy, the better for us all."

Father and son glared at each other.

Janet had her say. "I perceived, before I left you, Father, that you were less than satisfied with what that man was offering you for my hand: these baronies in Lanarkshire, Braidwood and the other? Did he raise the price that you desired for me?"

"I do not like the style of you, girl! If I say that you will wed the Earl of Angus, wed him you will. But, yes, he did speak of Bothwell. Which he won from that sawnie whom the late king made Lord Bothwell, that Ramsay. But that is no concern of yours. I shall be seeing Angus again before long, and we shall come to agreement, I judge. Now, go to your room. And you, David, I'll thank you not to encourage your sister in her undutiful behaviour, of which there has been over-much of late. Or you will pay for it!"

"There are duties and duties, sir! I see mine somewhat differently than evidently do you!" And the Master of Kennedy tooks his sister by the arm, inclined his head briefly towards his father, lips tight, and led her from that hall.

2

The matter of the Red Douglas's marriage prospects was rather put in abeyance for a space, at least as far as the Kennedys were concerned, by an unexpected, indeed exciting, happening very shortly thereafter: no less than the arrival at Dunure of the King of Scots himself. James Stewart, fourth of his name to be monarch, had now reached full age, six years after the defeat and death of his feeble father, James the Third, at Sauchieburn, a battle in which the son, aged fifteen, had been on the other side, led by the nobles in rebellion against the misgovernance and the unstable rule, not so much of the weak king as of his low-born favourites. After that battle, shown the corpse of his father at the Mill of Bannockburn, where he had been slain, fleeing the field, he, the son, acknowledging unfilial guilt, had sworn to do penance all his life for his share, however nominal, in the deed, and there and then, in the stable of the mill, had taken down a harness chain from where it hung on a hook on the wall, and girded his loins with it, this ever to be worn, to remind him of his guilt. This he still wore always.

He had instituted other penances, including a yearly pilgrimage to the shrine of St Ninian, he who had first brought Christianity to Scotland, or what was to become Scotland, about the year 400, at Whithorn in Galloway, the famed Candida Casa. James was on the way to Whithorn on this occasion, and having been already at the royal castle of Dunbarton, on the Clyde estuary, was heading for Galloway down that coast with a small group of personal attendants.

The unannounced royal arrival at Dunure created a

great stir, inevitably, that May evening of 1494, with James, King of Carrick only too eager to show his loyalty to James, King of Scots, he who had fought on the other side at Sauchiburn. So it was every effort to be made to provide the young monarch with hospitality and cheer, and, for the moment at least, all signs of disagreement and resentment in the family banished.

James Stewart, despite his preoccupation with guilt, was a cheerful and amiable young man, scarcely handsome but personable, pleasantly open of countenance, frank and anything but stiffly aloof. And from his first sight of Janet Kennedy he was most clearly much impressed. Unlike his late father he was known to be in favour of the opposite sex; indeed he had had a son born the year before to a mistress, Mariot Boyd, and was known to be presently interested in Margaret Drummond, daughter of the Lord Drummond, while King Henry the Seventh of England was making moves to have his young daughter Margaret Tudor wed to him. But all this by no means inhibited the royal interest in other attractive women. And Flaming Janet, finding him to her taste, was nowise concerned to repel him.

Her father, of course, like the rest of the family, could not fail to perceive this attention and admiration, and whatever his ambitions with regard to alliance with the great house of Douglas, recognised that royal favour could have its advantages also. So no instructions were issued to reject the king.

James was entirely frank in this, as in almost all else, that evening concentrating his attentions on the young woman, kissing her goodnight when she retired, and lingering next morning when his party was clearly expecting him to be on his way. He was not aggressive nor cavalier about it, but clearly appreciative. Janet could not but feel flattered; and she perceived this royal interest as perhaps not unhelpful in her battle against Angus's intentions.

When the king's group was gone, her father made no comment on the monarch's attitude towards his daughter, but did remark on his great improvement on the previous king, and left it at that.

So, for a few days there was comparative peace and ease in the Kennedy household, although Janet was dreading a return of Archibald Douglas. But instead of that, on the fourth day, James Stewart it was who again appeared at Dunure, on his way back to Stirling, even though this was scarcely on his direct route. It was fairly evident to all what had brought him again.

The family could not but welcome the royal attentions, and, since his party arrived at midday, Lord Kennedy suggested that perhaps His Grace would care to go hawking up in the Brown Carrick Hills, amongst which there were three or four small lochs apt to provide good sport, in wild duck, the occasional goose, herons and even swans. The king, glancing at Janet questioningly, agreed when she nodded.

She went off with her sister Helen to dress suitably for riding and hawking, her brothers Alexander, John and William, as well as David, not requiring to do more than improve their attire for royal company. Helen was the youngest of the family, a plain-featured lass compared with her sister, but pleasantly smiling and buxom for her fourteen years. Apart from David, her brothers were all under twenty.

With the king's entourage they made over-large a party for effective hawking. Also they had insufficient trained falcons to provide all with birds; so Lord Kennedy divided up their numbers. David found himself put in charge of the less important group, Janet of course staying with their monarch and her father.

David took his section by the more southerly route into the hills, to the less productive Loch Drumshang area where wildfowl was concerned. Nevertheless they made quite a successful day of it, their four hawks bringing down no fewer than eight mallard, three widgeon and a heron, their two tranters being kept busy retrieving both the hawks and their prey.

12

The royal party was rather later in getting back to Dunure, and actually had not done so well. Perhaps some of them had been otherwise preoccupied on occasion.

That evening, after a worthy repast, considering the visitors were unexpected, there was music and dancing, King James, who had an excellent voice, contributing to the former, and entering into the latter with vigour and enthusiasm. He had one round with the young and bouncy Helen and devoted all the rest to Janet, whom he did not fail to hold close to him on every available occasion. Later, he undoubtedly would have conducted her up to her room had not Lord Kennedy carefully engaged him in talk just as she was leaving the hall.

David was amused, but also just a little concerned by it all, whatever his father might be.

In the morning James Stewart, taking his leave, told his host that he desired to repay his excellent hospitality in some measure. "Come you to my house of Stirling, my lord, and soon," he said. "You shall have good sport there, in the Flanders Moss and the Tor Wood, stags and roe-deer, even boar. And wildfowl aplenty. And bring your daughter with you. And the Master, to be sure. And such other of your family as you wish." He turned to Janet. "Do not delay overlong. Wiser to send me word, lest I be away – which I would not wish. It would be grievous indeed to miss you, lass."

'Is this a royal command, Sire?" she asked, smiling.

"Why, yes, you could make it so! Although *I* might be yours to command!" And he kissed her heartily before remembering to salute her young sister also, but less lingeringly. There was no other female thus to embrace, the Lady Kennedy having died some years previously.

The royal party mounted and rode off.

When they could be alone, David tapped his sister on the shoulder. "You have much affected our liege-lord," he said. "I do not wonder, for you are . . . very lovely. But, remember: he is the king. And a man of some thirst

13

for women, I think. Indeed, we know it. And kings can be . . . demanding!"

"I like him," she said simply.

"Aye. But you must watch how you go with James Stewart, Jan. That one will not be content with a mere kiss or two. And his demands cannot lead to any fulfilment. Kings must marry into their own kind. James is all but promised, is he not, to that English princess, Margaret Tudor. So, watch you!"

"His interest, may keep Angus at a distance!"

"There is that, yes. But, at a price, perhaps."

"Our father appears none so ill-pleased."

"But he will still want those Douglas baronies!"

"We shall see . . ."

See they did, for although Lord Kennedy decided to take the king at his word and to go to Stirling shortly thereafter, Archibald Bell-the-Cat did arrive again at Dunure before they made a move. It was not to be known if the monarch's visits had anything to do with this, or whether word of the royal regard for Janet had reached his cars; but he came, and almost the more eager to claim the young woman as bride, and now made his offering the greater. Not only the large Bothwell Castle was to be added to the price but also a town-house in the capital, Edinburgh.

Being such a notably beautiful female had its advantages, undoubtedly, but also its problems and handicaps. Janet had a trying interlude with the earl, but on this occasion David made a point of remaining at her side, with his father and the visitor, somewhat inhibiting the Douglas in his advances. James Kennedy himself was clearly in something of a dilemma.

The entire situation was as difficult as it was unusual, for all concerned – save perhaps James Stewart.

3

James Kennedy took only his heir and elder daughter
with him to Stirling, although escorted by a sizeable
train of mounted men-at-arms, as became the King of
Carrick. They went, all wondering, with their different
preoccupations and questionings.

It made a long ride, fully seventy-five miles, going
by Kilmarnock, Eaglesham, Glasgow, Cumbernauld and
Falkirk, but all, necessarily, good on horses and their
mounts of the best. Passing Bannockburn, beyond the
great Tor Wood, it was David who gestured towards the
mill thereof, to his sister, not their father. For this was
where, near the scene of Bruce's great battle, James the
Third had been murdered, and Lord Kennedy had been
on the side of the defeated. That unhappy king, no hero,
had fled the field of Sauchieburn, alone, this a mile or
so to the west, and at the burn of the Bannock, crossing
here, his horse, misliking the rushing water, had reared
and thrown him. Clad in armour as he was, he had been
stunned. The miller had witnessed it, and not knowing
who it was, had dragged his monarch over to the stable,
fearing that he was going to die, when presently a group
of the victorious rebels, including the Lord Gray, had
arrived. The miller had told them that he feared that
the unconscious man in his stable was going to die,
and perhaps he should be shrived, this the blessing of
a priest before death. Gray had declared that *he* would
shrive him, and there and then, drawing his dirk, had
stabbed James through the heart. So ended an inglorious
reign. The dead monarch's eldest son, on the side of the
rebels, arriving then, uneasy about this sudden ascent to

15

the throne, had taken down that harness chain and begun his penances. All this David told Janet as they rode by, their father silent.

Another four miles and they came to the town of Stirling, its royal castle soaring dramatically on its great rock and dominating all, this above the first, vital and indeed only, bridge across the Forth, with the wide estuary to the east and all the equally wide and marshy wastes of the Flanders Moss to the west, almost less crossable since it could not be by boat, providing the most strategic locality in all Scotland, in the centre of the kingdom, its castle-palace all but impregnable, and for long the favoured seat of the monarchy, this despite Edinburgh being the nominal capital, thirty-five miles away. Hereabouts, at the junction, as it were, of Lowlands and Highlands, had been fought some of the most significant battles of the realm's bloody history, not only Wallace's Stirling Bridge and Bruce's Bannockburn, the said Sauchieburn itself, but also Malcolm the Destroyer's defeat by King Knut of Denmark, Canute.

Up through the narrow streets of the town they rode, the higher they went the larger the dwellings, these the town-houses of the nobility, and the nearer to the castle.

At the tourney-ground in front of the fortress they were challenged by the royal guards, but presumably the king had given orders to look out for them, for at the name of Kennedy they were admitted and escorted up and over the moat and drawbridge and through the gatehouse arch to the rock-top citadel. In an inner courtyard, after a brief wait, they were approached by Patrick Hepburn, Lord Hailes, the Master of the Household, who eyed Lord Kennedy distinctly sourly as one who had been on the other side at Sauchieburn, but Janet much more interestedly, informing her that His Grace was just back from hunting in the Moss, and would accord them audience in due course. Meantime, one of his underlings would conduct them to their quarters in the West Tower. He would inform His Grace.

"That man," the King of Carrick muttered as they were led off. "An up-jumped rogue! Laird of only a small property in Lothian, now *Lord* Hailes, Master of the Household, Captain of Edinburgh Castle, even Lord High Admiral of Scotland! Home, his friend, little more than a Borders mosstrooper, likewise Lord Home and High Chamberlain. So much for rebellion against the late king. Treason!"

His offspring made no comment.

At least Lord Kennedy had no complaint to make anent their accommodation. The West Tower, living up to its name, was perched on one of the highest crags of the castle rock, overlooking the vast panorama of the Flanders Moss, twenty-five miles of it by five in width, that impassable barrier that had held up even the Roman legions as so many other armies, flanked on the north by all the blue mountains of the Highland Line, and beyond the far western end, the challenging mass of Ben Lomond in the MacGregor country. Their rooms were notably fine, a small hall in which to dine, three bedrooms above, all hung with tapestries, and servants to wait on them.

Exclaiming at the magnificent prospect, Janet demanded details of all that she saw, David able to inform her, for he had been to Stirling before although she had not. Lord Kennedy chose the lower and larger bedchamber, and brother and sister went to the lesser rooms above.

King James did better than accord the visitors the promised audience. Quite soon he came personally to welcome them in their tower, running up the twisting stairway to the upper rooms when he found only Kennedy in the lower one. Janet was greeted fairly comprehensively, hugged and kissed when he found her brushing that long red hair of hers, and David had a twinge of concern, almost jealousy, as he saw it. This visit was going to be a testing time for his beloved sister.

As Janet sought to coil her hair up in a suitable fashion,

James told her to leave it hanging loose and long; he liked it that way. And he stroked and rippled it to prove his point. He declared that he had never seen the like and that she was even more beautiful than he had remembered, she making the required modest disclaimers. He announced that they were to dine with him within the hour in the main hall of the royal quarters.

When he had gone, David put it to his sister. "Janet, what are you going to do about this? James is going to seek to take you, here. That is evident. How are you going to deal with it? Are you going to try to fend him off? It will be difficult, with that one, I know. He will want to go . . . far."

"Do you think that I do not know it, David?"

"Then . . . what? And he the king."

"What choice have I? It is either him or Angus! Or, in time, some other. It is my lot, it seems. And I do find him . . . pleasing. He will be kind, I think. As well as demanding. No?"

"Who can tell? Men, in their desires, can be . . . exacting. And forceful."

"I know it. I have discovered that, have I not? John Dalrymple of Stair. He was very . . . urgent. Gordon of Lochinvar also. I am not without some experience, David."

"But these were not the king, used to having his own way. Able to command, indeed. And with other mistresses. How will you cope with him, lass? For nothing is more sure than that you will have to! These others – none has had his way with you, however eager to. You have told me so."

"Yes. But I am no artless innocent, even though I am still my own woman. One day, it seems, I must learn the price women have to pay for being women! Or most of them. And it may not be so hard a bargain in the end? You should know, brother – *you* have had your women."

"So long as you are not . . . hurt, lass. That I would have you spared."

"My kind brother . . ."

Their father came up to them. "We are to dine with the king," he said. "Are you ready, girl? We must not keep him waiting."

"James Stewart would wait, I think! On this occasion." That was David.

"We must not displeasure him."

"How much pleasuring would you afford him, sir? Your daughter's, in especial?"

Their father frowned. "Watch your words, boy! And see that you behave aright in the king's presence. We want no trouble with His Grace. He could grievously harm us in Carrick. Mind it." Actually it was at Janet that he looked as he said that.

They followed their sire downstairs and over to the royal apartments.

The great hall was already crowded, and musicians playing from the minstrels' gallery. Many men, and a few women, were sitting at the two long tables which stretched down from the dais platform, but the table on that was still unoccupied.

One of Lord Hailes's minions was waiting for them. He conducted David to a comparatively lowly place at one of the lengthwise tables, where he seated him between an elderly man and a young woman. But he took Lord Kennedy and his daughter up to mount the dais. There were nine chairs at this smaller table, in the centre one high-backed and throne-like. To the immediate left of this Janet was escorted, while her father was led to the last chair on that side. There they were left, turning to eye each other.

Presently six men came through a doorway behind the dais, led by Hailes himself. One came to sit on Janet's left, a man of middle years, who introduced himself as the Lord Home, High Chamberlain. The others seated themselves as directed, a tall and handsome man on the other side of the royal chair.

Then the musicians stopped their playing, and one of

them beat a long rat-tat roll on a drum. And in at the dais door strode James Stewart, as everybody stood, to wave cheerfully right and left, smiling – the same hand to drop and linger on Janet's shoulder as he pressed her down into her chair. All could sit.

"I see that you have put up your hair again!" he said to her. "We will have to improve on that! Later." And he laughed, and patted her hand.

"As Your Grace prefers," she murmured.

He leaned over, frankly to admire the cleft between her breasts just visible in the not particularly low-cut neck of her gown. "You have a handsome bosom, I judge," he added.

She shrugged, which stirred those breasts. "I am as the good God made me!"

"He knew what He was at, in forming women," was the royal reply. "Or, some of them!"

David watched all this from his more lowly seat – as of course did others – and tightened his lips. The older man on his left chuckled.

"He fancies that one," he said. "She was with you, no? Not your lady-wife, I hope?"

"Sister," David jerked briefly.

"Ah! Then perhaps you will be the gainer!"

David turned his shoulder on the man, and this brought him into eye contact with the young woman on his right. She smiled.

"The king, he is well accompanied this night," she said. She undoubtedly had seen Janet's arrival with David and their father. "Did I hear the name of Kennedy?"

"Yes. I am David, Master of Kennedy. Janet is my sister."

"And a remarkably lovely woman. I am Agnes Borth-wick." She half turned to her own right. "This is *my* brother, William, Master of Borthwick."

The young man at her side nodded easily. "I have heard of Flaming Janet Kennedy," he said. "I have not been misled! She is a sight to see."

"Yes." This sort of talk scarcely pleased David, however much he admired his sister.

The girl at his side possibly recognised this, from his rather abrupt answers. "Have you come far this day?" she asked. "You are from Carrick, south of Ayr, are you not? We came yesterday. But only from near Edinburgh." Her words were melodiously unhurried.

David had hardly looked at her until now, preoccupied as he was with the dais-table situation. He saw now that his companion at table was fair rather than beautiful or handsome, but good to look at, attractive in a gentle, calm way, with a strange serenity about her eyes and bearing.

"I have seen Borthwick Castle, on the Gore Water, but have never visited it," he said, less curtly. "A mighty hold, tall indeed. It was named otherwise once, was it not?"

"The lands were called Lochorwart, yes. Until our grandsire built the castle. Our family had come from the Borthwick Water in Teviotdale. So he changed the name. Next time that you pass that way, do not." She smiled her gentle smile again. "Call on us, instead."

Her brother leaned forward. "Do so," he said. "And bring your sister."

The servitors intervened meantime, bringing the notable choices of meats, venison, wild boar, duck, goose and beef.

The elderly man on David's left introduced himself. "I am Boyd of Bonshaw," he announced gruffly. "So, grandsire of His Grace's bairn Alexander. Your sister, Kennedy, would best heed the same!" That had a grim note to it.

David did not anwer. All knew of Mariot Boyd, the young king's first mistress, who had borne him a son at twenty years. Presumably her father was warning anent discarded courtesans.

Up on the dais James was personally selecting choice pieces for Janet's plate, and making something of a show of it. This monarch was not one to hide his feelings.

21

Agnes Borthwick sipped her wine. "I have heard your father termed the King of Carrick," she said. "Was not that the great Bruce's style, before he gained the throne?" She sounded interested, not critical.

"Yes, he was Earl of Carrick, in right of his mother, as well as Lord of Annandale, through his father. My own father is not the first Kennedy so to style himself, however foolishly. It all started as a mockery by less successful folk who envied them the lands they gained in Carrick partly by the sword and partly by well-chosen marriages! So they sought further to earn that title over the years."

"So you are the Prince of Carrick!"

"No one has ever called me that, lady. I am content to be David Kennedy of Cassillis."

"A modest man?"

As the repast, banquet indeed, progressed, David got on well with the Borthwicks, less so with Boyd of Bonshaw, who clearly thought that *he* should be sitting up at the dais-table instead of some of the others.

When the dining was over, even though the drinking was not, the long tables were pushed over to the walling to clear space for dancing. Waving to the musicians in the gallery to change their tunes and tempo, James conducted Janet down, to lead the way. For a while they had the floor to themselves, an eye-catching pair. Then others joined in, at the king's gesturing, and soon the floor was crowded, some cavorting rather than actually dancing, there being insufficient women present to provide partners for all, and the wines and spirits having their effects. David felt that he could not do other than ask Agnes Borthwick to step out with him, she inclining her fair head and proving most graceful in this activity as in all else, good to feel in his arms, indeed causing him to decry himself as a clumsy yokel.

In one of their circlings they passed near to the monarch and Janet, she held a deal closer than was his own partner. Sister raised her eyebrows eloquently at brother as they went by, and James released a shapely breast momentarily to wave. Agnes smiled, but did not comment.

She partnered her brother thereafter, but presently came back to David for one final dance before she retired, he appreciative. It was when this was ended, and she said goodnight, serene as ever, that he noted that the Borthwicks were not the only ones who had thought of retiring. There was no sign of James Stewart any more than of Flaming Janet. Nor, indeed, of Lord Kennedy.

David made his way back to their West Tower. His father was not there, nor, upstairs, was Janet.

David waited and waited in his own room, gazing out over the dusky levels of the Flanders Moss as darkness grew. No sound came from the next-door chamber.

He kept thinking of Janet, and what was happening to her this while. But also, occasionally, another image came into his mind, that of a quietly calm and comely face, so much less animated than was his sister's, but by no means listless or stolid.

For how long he sat there waiting, he could not tell, before he heard voices, and the door next to his own opening, a man's voice but not his father's. The door shut, but he heard no footsteps descending the stairway. So still he waited. At length the door did open and close again, with a laughing goodnight called.

David rose, drawing a deep breath. Now, strangely, he was almost loth to do what he had been waiting to do. He paced his floor to and fro, set-faced, before he went to open his own door and knock at the other, then entered.

In the semi-darkness he saw Janet on her bed, not in it, her clothing disarranged. She lay on her back, gazing up at the bed's canopy. She did not turn to look at him.

He went to her side. 'Janet, lass," he said. And could think of nothing else to say there and then. He did reach out, to touch her arm.

She did not speak, for a little. Then she sighed. "That was it, then."

"You . . . he . . . James? Was it . . . grievous? He, he took you? All?"

"All, yes. But . . . grievous? I do not know, David. I do not know. If it had to be . . ." She reached to take his hand. "Tell me. Should it have been so grievous? It was painful, yes. At first. But . . ."

He shook his head. What were words in such circumstances?

"He was strong with it. But not, not . . . It was . . . strange. And that chain! He wears it always, he says. That was, was awkward! He never takes it off."

"He wears it at night? We have all heard of the chain. But not . . ."

She pressed his hand. "Leave me, David. I must be alone. To think. I am no longer a virgin. You see?"

Long David Kennedy lay awake that night, or what was left of it, wondering. His thoughts, however, were not entirely on his sister.

In the morning David came late to the lesser hall downstairs for his breakfast, but not as late as his sister. Their father was waiting, with some impatience.

"The king has sent word," he announced. "We ride for the hunt within the hour. Janet, what of her?"

"What think you? She is in her bed – her *own* bed!"

"Then go fetch her, boy. His Grace will not wait overlong. He expects us to join him."

"The joining was done last night!"

Lord Kennedy did not answer that, leaving the room.

Janet appeared presently, and although David searched her features he saw no evident signs of distress.

"You slept well?" he asked, somewhat fatuously.

"Sufficiently well," she answered. "Should I not have done?"

"I know not," he admitted. "My knowledge of woman-kind is . . . limited!" He shrugged. "Our sire is concerned that we do not keep the king waiting. We are to hunt with him. Father is much concerned for His Grace's favour."

"And you are not, David?"

"Say that I am a loyal subject, and leave it at that!"

"He is none so ill," she said.

Eyeing her thoughtfully, he told her to eat her breakfast.

In due course, changed for riding, she accompanied her brother over to the courtyard before the royal quarters, where men and horses were already assembled, their father amongst them; two or three women also, Agnes Borthwick included. David went over to greet her and her brother – and it was Janet's turn to do the thoughtful eyeing.

Whether or not James Stewart had been waiting for them within, he arrived very promptly thereafter, waving genially to all, and coming over to clasp Janet in his arms and kiss her frankly. All were to be left in no doubt as to his esteem for her. He clapped David on the shoulder, but firmly pushed him aside when he moved to assist his sister to mount her horse, and performed that service himself.

"We hunt boar in the Moss," he told her. "With spears. But no spear for you, my dear. I would not have you risk your beautiful neck to a boar's tusks." And on an afterthought, added, "Nor any other fair lady's."

David was provided with a long spear, at least fifteen feet of it, like most of the other men.

They moved off behind the king and Janet, David electing to ride beside the Borthwicks rather than with his father.

They proceeded down through the town streets for some way until they could swing off on to a fairly steep track, which led down around a bluff of the castle rock, to reach more level ground in the vicinity of a strange feature known as the King's Knot, a geometrically shaped and stepped mound, grassed over and terraced in extraordinary fashion, over four hundred feet square

25

and rising to a central elevation, this alleged to be King Arthur's Round Table.

Westwards they rode, following the course of the River Forth, but soon they were more than a mile inland from its south bank, this because of the ever-widening marshland, reed beds, pools and scrub woodland of the Flanders Moss. There was an area of over two hundred wet, square miles of this boggy terrain, the Gargunnock and Fintry Hills, with the Campsie Fells, to the south, and the Mounth of Teith, outlier of the Highlands, to the north, this the haunt of wild creatures in plenty but not of mankind, no single dwelling amongst it all. The streams running off these flanking hills, and more or less trapped here, were responsible for it all, as well as the frequent flooding of the river itself, this on account of the bottle-neck of rocky land in the Stirling vicinity, so that the river was not able to drain all the water off effectively. James explained to Janet as they went that, had the almost parallel and indeed larger river to the north, the Teith, not been diverted in curious fashion by the same intrusive ridges, its stronger waters could have drawn off all this plain's wetness, and the Firth of Forth would have been the Firth of Teith, and his realm's history changed, for this barrier between Highlands and Lowlands would not have been there.

They trotted on for almost eight miles until, crossing the incoming Goodie Water, the king led them off into the reedy levels of what he called the Poldar Moss, part of the greater morass. He said that there was slightly firmer ground here, and they could see more of stunted trees, birch as well as alder, scrub oak and bushes, these in patches. There were pools and mires here also in plenty, and care had to be taken as to where horses could safely go; but it was a good area for wildlife, roe-deer especially and the occasional boar. All had to watch out for these last, dangerous animals in dangerous terrain, especially for those unused to it all, the ladies in particular.

They divided into three parties, right and left, with the king's group in the centre. Soon they saw roes, graceful creatures only half the size of the red deer of the hills, bounding off into leaf cover, and one or two crossbow arrows were loosed at these, bringing two down, the tranters attached to each party going out to collect them. Today James was not really interested in these however; he wanted to display his prowess with the boar-spear before his new lady-love.

It was in fact some time before they met with any challenge, with plenty of deer, hares and wildfowl in evidence, but no boars. But at length, as they were passing a clump of alder and thorn, James held up a hand, reining in. Then they could hear a sort of snuffling growl coming from the tree cover. The king was telling Janet to go warily when out hurtled a massive tusked creature, dark brown, almost black, head down, to charge the horsemen, grunting loudly as it came, swiftly indeed for that heavy body, as large as a small pony, on such short legs.

James grabbed at Janet's arm to have her pull aside out of harm's way, risking danger for himself in the process, and all but cannoning into the Earl of Montrose, who was already lowering his long spear, as indeed were most of the men. It was chaos for moments, perilous moments. But perhaps the confusion of rearing and turning alarmed horses and shouting men also confused the boar somewhat in its growling dash, for it slightly changed direction once or twice in covering the hundred or so yards from its recent cover.

Montrose, in fact, seemed to become the creature's target, and he had his spear down and levelled before the king did. But he recognised that this first test was James's privilege, in the circumstances, and jerked his mount up on to its hind legs in an urgent turn aside, and the brute plunged past, heading for the next nearest horsemen who happened to be the Lord Kennedy. Janet yelled her alarm and warning, and her father in his haste to get out of the way dropped his unwieldy spear. This proved to be no misfortune, for the tusked creature ran into the shaft of it, tripping slightly. David, just behind his father, with the Borthwicks, had his own spear levelled, but was uncertain just how to wield it, never before having hunted thus, boars not being prevalent in Carrick. His sire's horse cannoned into his own, all but unseating him. But the menace tore past, close enough for him to smell the stink of it, and now headed straight for the monarch and Janet.

James Stewart proved his courage, gallantry and expertise, for instead of pulling aside, he jerked his frightened steed round in front of the young woman's, and reining it up so that its forelegs pawed the air, drove his spear down on the charging animal as it came directly below. The creature all but brushed his horse's hind legs as the spear struck into the massive shoulder, and was thereby wrenched out of its wielder's grip as the boar plunged on, long lance affixed and trailing, no further target ahead of it.

The king was shouting now, and, pulling out, grabbed the earl's spear out of its owner's grip, and spurred his horse round to go dashing after his quarry. The boar, hampered by that dragging shaft, and seeking to shake it off, slowed its pace, and James came up behind and, before it could turn and face him, drove the borrowed weapon deep into the brute's rear, unprotected compared with its heavy thick-skinned shoulders. Snorting loudly, the animal's onward career came to a slithering end. It collapsed, its legs twitching and jerking, the two spears still embedded.

Waving his proud satisfaction, James came back to Janet's side. "A tough tusker!" he exclaimed. "Hard of hide, but excellent sport!"

"Sport?" she asked. "You name that sport?"

"To be sure. The fiercer the brute, the better. So long as *you* were not endangered."

Janet shook her red head and refrained from comment.

The monarch rallied his male companions on their performances, spears were retrieved, and the tranters were left to attend to the still twitching carcase. Massive as it was, it would have to be dragged behind a garron to wherever a farm cart could be brought for it. James announced that he would have the tusks made into a trophy for Janet.

They rode on, more warily now, shot more roe-deer, and tried their hands at shooting fowl in the air, but gave it up as a wastage of arrows, with hawking the way to deal with such.

The flanking party on the right rejoined them at an open space beside a lochan, complaining that they had seen no boars.

They all dismounted there to refresh themselves with oatcakes and wine from flasks. Agnes and Janet disappeared together into bushes, exchanging views on boar-sticking, David and Will Borthwick agreeing that it was not a sport for the ill-prepared.

In the afternoon, they did see and kill another boar, but this one a deal less aggressive, a female which, after a mere token charge, turned and fled, but fell to Montrose's spear.

Thereafter it was the long ride back to Stirling, not all the sportsmen as pleased as was their royal host.

That evening's feasting was a repeat of the previous night's, with the king and Janet waiting only for the first dance and then disappearing.

James had planned a tournament for the following day, but the rain poured down, and even the royal enthusiasm was discouraged. Instead, games were played indoors, and later an impromptu masque was staged in the great hall, and here the ladies came into their own. They contrived a display on the theme of Helen of Troy, with Janet playing the name-part as the most beautiful woman of ancient Greece, daughter of Zeus, with Agnes Borthwick as her sister Clytemnestra, and the Countess of Montrose their mother. James himself acted as a acantily clad Paris – although there was little of acting in it all, gesturing, posturing and parading to music being the way of it. There was much applause and hilarity.

The visitors learned that the next day the king was due to visit Fife on his way north to inspect the building of two new war-vessels, one at Dysart and the other up at Aberdeen, this work under the supervision of Sir Andrew Wood of Largo, a master-mariner as well as a laird and merchant-adventurer. Wood had advocated the creation of something that the Scots had hitherto lacked, a fleet of fighting-ships, a national asset that the English had had in some measure for long. At his own expense Wood had built two large war-vessels, although useful also for trade with the Low Countries, the *Flower* and the *Yellow Caravel*, and used these against English piracy of Scots shipping, this with such success that King Henry Tudor sent up five war-craft of his own to counter Wood's activities. That sturdy character had accepted the Tudor challenge, and had in fact won a sea battle with the enemy, under an admiral named Stephen Bull, two ships against five, capturing three English vessels to bring in to Leith and present to young King James. That over-chivalrous monarch, to keep the peace with England, sent the ships back to Henry, and allowed Bull to return with them, without ransom. The Tudor's response had been to offer the huge sum of £1,000 sterling for Sir Andrew Wood, dead or alive. Now James was encouraging more of this useful warship-building, hence his present mission. And while up at Aberdeen he would also inspect progress on Bishop Elphinstone's notable institution of a university in that city, to be the third in Scotland, after St Andrews and Glasgow.

So it was an end, meantime, to dalliance at Stirling, and a return home for many there, including the Kennedys; but not, strangely enough, of the King of Carrick himself, who elected to accompany his monarch on this northern journey, presumably determined to demonstrate his new-found adherence to the royal cause and to wipe out his previous allegiance.

His son and daughter made no objections, indeed Janet favouring a fairly prolonged absence from Dunure as helpful in keeping the Earl of Angus at bay. After an undoubtedly passionate night, and an openly demonstrative parting in the morning by the king, Janet, with the Borthwick brother and sister and David, set off southwards, while the royal train rode eastwards for Fife. It had all been a lively and significant interlude.

At the Borthwicks' urging, they travelled by the longer route, to Edinburgh and then south from there by Borthwick Castle, to spend the night. The two couples got on well together, although all so very different in temperament, William being a quietly studious young man, slow of speech but nowise lacking in character.

Borthwick Castle lay, or rather stood, some thirteen miles from the capital, on a spur jutting into the Gore Water valley before that stream joined the South Esk. It was quite the tallest tower-house David had ever seen, six storeys of it, in the shape of an E, before the parapet and wall walk with a garret above, the walls thick indeed, the whole a frowning, defiant strength. It would be a hard hold to capture.

The Lord Borthwick was now in late middle years, a widower. He eyed David doubtfully at first, whatever he thought of Janet, for the Kennedys had been on the other side in the late troubles, and the Scots nobility tended to have long memories. But he thawed in due course. He obviously doted on his daughter.

They spent a quiet evening, compared with the Stirling ongoings, but pleasantly and without any stress, in the magnificent hall with its great hooded fireplace, the visitors learning much as to the antecedents of the Borthwicks from earliest times, more ancient than the Kennedys, or so was claimed.

Agnes made an excellent hostess, and had a tuneful if slightly husky singing voice, accompanying herself on the lute, the others joining in when she offered them ballads.

She conducted the guests upstairs on retiral, and David offered a goodnight kiss at his room's door, which was not rejected. That young woman's serenity was having a growing effect on him, something that he had never known in any other.

The two girls went together into Janet's allotted bedchamber, no doubt to share female confidences; so David still had no word alone with his sister.

In the morning, when they took their leave, Agnes it was, after kissing Janet goodbye, who offered her lips to David – and cool as that young woman might be, those lips had a warmth to them.

Thereafter, as they rode, south-westwards now, by Tynehead and the Morthwaite Hills to Peebles and the upper Tweed, over into Clydesdale and so to Ayrshire, David had opportunity at last to discuss the situation with his sister.

"The king?" he asked. "How is it with you and him, Janet? The truth of it?"

She shook her head. "I, I do not know. I like him. He is demanding, yes. But kind also. I do not find him . . . displeasing. Even if he is something . . . importunate. It is strange, but I do not feel used by him!"

"Yet you are being so, lass. For nothing can come of this. You know that. No future in it for you."

"Think you that I have not considered this? Considered it much. What is my future? Our father will seek to marry me off to someone, to his own advantage, even if I escape Angus, nothing more sure. But if I am linked in some fashion with the king, I may be spared that."

"James will marry. That is certain. If not to this daughter of King Henry, then to some other princess. And then, what?"

"I do not know. But kings have . . . mistresses."

"And would you be content to be that? Mistresses can be discarded. Have you sufficient liking for James Stewart to face that, sooner or later?"

"That I have asked myself also. I think that I could . . . *love* him! And so . . . ?"

He turned to gaze at her, silent now.

"Do you wonder at me, David? Can you understand? We have always been close, and . . ." She left the rest unsaid.

"I will try to, lass, try to . . ."

4

They had over two weeks on their own before Lord
Kennedy returned, most of the time spent at Cassillis,
just in case Archibald Bell-the-Cat turned up at Dunure.
They had their brothers and sister also there frequently,
for the same reason. However, they were spared the
earl's attentions; possibly he knew of their father's
absence, and might well have heard of the king's concern
with Janet. What effect would this have on the Red
Douglas?

They were glad to see that the new tower with
the hollow-newel staircase was progressing satisfactorily, being more than half built indeed, with no serious
problems developing. Roosting in the unfinished castle
was scarcely comfortable, but there was its home-farm
nearby where supplies and help were available. David
turned his own hand at the mason-work and joinery; and
Janet saw to furnishings and decoration. The subject of
James Stewart was not avoided but not dwelt upon.

It was good to be closer to the younger members of the
family, for these were more in awe of their father and in
consequence less involved with their elder brother and sister, whose defiant attitude they could hardly share, the age
gap contributing. Alexander, the eldest at seventeen, was
fair of feature, almost too much so, without being actually
effeminate, but less than positive. His twin brothers, two
years younger, John and William, were more lively, but
still only boys; while the baby of the family, James, was
only twelve. Helen, their sister, was fourteen and just
beginning to blossom towards womanhood; she seemed
unlikely to rival Janet in looks.

Those two weeks were pleasant for them all, even though Janet had her spells of introspection and contemplation.

Them, at the end of the month, their father came back, and all was changed. He was never a communicative man, but on this occasion appeared to be fairly well pleased with his circumstances. His attendance on the king had evidently paid off. He had been reappointed to the Privy Council, from which he had been dismissed, with others, after Sauchieburn. No doubt his being Janet's father had told with James Stewart.

He brought back two significant items of news which he imparted, however abruptly, to his offspring. The first was that the king, arising out of this association with Sir Andrew Wood, the admiral, and the shipping situation, had decided to make an expedition into the western Highlands and Isles, this by sea necessarily, to impose his royal authority on the turbulent Lordship of the Isles, the chiefs of which had long been in all but open rebellion against the crown, and were becoming increasingly aggressive against the mainland areas, ravaging as far south as Kintyre, as the eagle flew no more than fifty miles from the Clyde at Dumbarton. So Wood was to collect his various ships to form a fleet, and bring them right round Scotland, north-about, to Dumbarton, where James would be waiting with what it was hoped would amount to an army, to sail off in them to teach the Islesmen a lesson. Kennedy had promised to send his son David with a contingent of Carrick men to join this expedition at Dumbarton. He was to be there in ten days' time. And the king had indicated that he would be pleased to see Janet there before he set sail.

The second item was very different, and rather extra-ordinary. It referred to the individual who was being called Perkin Warbeck by his ill-wishers, although he claimed to be Richard, Duke of York, one of the two princes allegedly murdered in the Tower of London by the Lancastrian Richard the Third, his brother indeed having died. This claim was being supported by his aunt,

Margaret, Duchess of Burgundy, sister of the Yorkist Edward the Fourth. He was now asserting that he was the rightful King of England instead of the usurping Henry Tudor. It seemed that the Wars of the Roses were not yet over. He had gone from Flanders to Ireland three years before this, gained acceptance there, and then repaired to Versailles, where the King of France had backed him, also the emperor, and had been promised armed aid against King Henry. An Irish–French force had landed in England, had suffered repulse, and the Pretender, as he was being styled, had returned to Ireland. Now he had sent an envoy, Hugh, Earl of Tyrconnel, to King James, seeking his co-operation.

There were grave doubts as to the authenticity of this claimant, a Flemish nobody, despite his aunt's acceptance. But James Stewart appeared to be considering his support as a means of bringing pressure to bear on King Henry, ever menacing Scotland, even though offering his daughter to James as bride, this possibly a sort of back-door entrance to the northern kingdom. Lord Kennedy was somewhat alarmed by all this, since he, and others, felt that it could lead to open warfare with England.

So David found himself recruiting men for the king's force for the Isles venture from the Kennedy lands of Dunure, Bargany, Auchindrone, Culzean, Blairquhan, Kirkmichael, and the rest, as well as his own Cassillis. Since it was to be a seaborne expedition, it was not the usual mounted following that he sought. So boats were needed to sail them all up the Firth of Clyde from the little harbour below the cliffs of Dunure, fishing-vessels and such larger craft as could be got from the port of Ayr.

In the next few days he mustered some two hundred men, few actually unwilling but many hoping that this enterprise would not last overlong, with harvest-time looming ahead, for most were workers on the land.

When all were assembled, Janet came to join them in the boats, herself nowise reluctant.

There was quite a flotilla of boats of varying sizes

36

waiting for them down at the harbour, some having to lie off, unable to enter the limited space. So getting all the men embarked took some time, especially as most had come on horseback from a distance, and their mounts had to be taken back up to the castle precincts to be collected and removed by other men. David led Janet on to one of the larger Ayr craft, and in this eventually led the way up-firth.

They had quite a long way to go, almost forty miles; but fortunately the prevailing south-west breeze allowed them to use the sails to good effect, to the relief of fishermen-rowers.

They went midway between the Ayrshire coast and the Isle of Arran, its mountains dominating the scene; then up the narrows between the southern tip of Bute and the Cumbrae islands and so to the great band eastwards of the estuary, off Gourock, whereafter it was only a few more miles to the town of Dunbarton, with its upthrusting conical rock crowned by the royal castle. Below this they found the anchorage already full of shipping, the trading vessels of the port augmented by Sir Andrew Wood's fleet, the large and handsome *Yellow Caravel* and *Flower* outstanding. The newcomers had to berth where they could.

David left the Carrick men to join the large numbers of the other contingents camped around the town, and with Janet climbed the steep ascent to the castle, busy with folk going up and down with stores and weaponry for the fleet.

The castle itself was as crowded as was the port, with a great assembly of the nobility rallied for the king's sally up into the Sea of the Hebrides. There would almost certainly not have been so large a response had the assault been on some Lowland target, with family and district alliances involved; but the Highlanders were considered to be fair game, in especial the Islesmen, whose depredations were notorious, and whose leaders, the Lords of the Isles, looked upon themselves as independent princes, indeed the present Lord John having made his own private treaty with the King of England. He was now, in consequence, something of a prisoner in a monastery near Stirling, captured and held as a hostage for the better behaviour of his chieftains and clansmen; but this precaution had not had the desired effect, and a still more aggressive son, Angus Og, now styling himself the new Lord of the Isles, not only refusing to pay homage to the king but setting all the west alight with his depredations, ably assisted by another MacDonald, Alexander of Lochalsh.

A strange atmosphere prevailed, nevertheless, at Dunbarton Castle. This was Lennox country, and the Stewart Earl of Lennox was its hereditary keeper. An elderly man, he was head of the secondary and non-royal branch of the Stewart family, and had been disappointed when, after Sauchieburn, he and his friends had been left out in the high appointments process of the new reign, this on the advice of Hailes and Home. He had actually risen in rebellion the next year, and with the Earl of Huntly and the Lords Forbes, Lyle and others, had taken to arms in protest, and attempted to capture the young monarch. James had personally led an assault on this royal castle, and it had taken three months for it to fall, although Lyle's castle of Duchal nearby had capitulated earlier. The rising had gone on, however, and the king had sustained his first injury in battle in a royal victory at Gartalunane, at the west end of the Flanders Moss. Thereafter he had found it diplomatic to forgive the rebels, for the sake of the realm's peace, against the advice of some of his intimates, and Lennox was still keeper of Dunbarton. But there was no love lost between the two Stewarts, and that atmosphere up on the rock-top hold reflected this, even though now some of the former insurgents were to take part in this Isles expedition, suspicions remaining. James had a difficult kingdom to rule.

The arrival of the Kennedys however did improve matters, at least as far as the monarch was concerned, his welcome of Janet manifest, indeed demonstrative. His eagerness to get her alone in that crowded establishment was almost as difficult to assuage as it was comic. There appeared to be practically no other women present, save for servants.

The newcomers learned that they were to sail the very next day, with two or three ships left to bring on late-comers. Accommodation at a premium, David, along with others, elected to go back down to pass the night in their vessels rather than try to sleep half a dozen to a room. Janet, needless to say, was left behind. She did not seem to be upset over this.

In the morning it was for off, and with Janet coming down to bid them farewell, David found himself inevitably taking leave of his sister in the near company of the king. With no certainty as to when the mission would be over, that young woman, having no urgent desire to go home to Dunure in case of the arrival of Angus, decided to avail herself of an invitation by Agnes Borthwick, with whom she had become very friendly, to go and wait at Borthwick Castle, James having demanded that she should be nowhere very far away from Stirling when he got back.

David was taken by the king thereafter on to the large vessel, the *Flower*, which proved to be Sir Andrew Wood's flagship. Hepburn of Hailes, now created Earl of Bothwell by James, and who amongst other offices held that of Lord High Admiral, took over command of the *Yellow Caravel*. Other large craft there were under Home and Drummond and Montrose. Lennox remained behind, as did Argyll, the Chancellor, who probably did not wish to get too far wrong with his West Highland neighbours. There was no sign of the Earl of Angus, nor of his ally the Lord Gray. As well as these fighting-ships there were at least a dozen other, smaller vessels, trading-craft taken over for the occasion, and all provided with cannon of varying calibre. James had scoured the land, or the fortalices thereof, for artillery pieces, including the great Mons Meg itself from

Edinburgh Castle, this aboard the *Flower*. He judged that cannon would be very valuable in this enterprise, for artillery was something that the Highland chiefs and Islesmen lacked, indeed had little use for, however well supplied with armed clansmen, Angus Og boasting that he could put forty thousand men in the field given one week.

They sailed without undue delay, the *Flower*, flying the Lion Rampant banner of the King of Scots, leading.

Much tacking to and fro was necessary on this first part of their voyage, for they had to sail southwards and then westwards for almost one hundred miles, down the Firth of Clyde and beyond the tip of Arran, before they could round the mighty Mull of Kintyre and turn up northwards into the Hebridean Sea, with the south-west wind at last in their favour. All this tacking added almost half as much mileage again to their journey. So it was nightfall before they could round Arran. Fortunately, in this early summer it was never really dark, so the ships could sail on, even in the fairly dangerous waters, in a lengthy column behind *Flower*. James remained up half the night, with Wood, interested in the navigation. David sought a bunk much earlier.

By morning they were passing the mouth of the Sound of Jura. There had been much debate at Dunbarton as to the best strategy, and therefore route. The decision had been to avoid all the narrow waters, the sounds as they were termed, between the multitude of islands, this because the Islesmen chiefs possessed great numbers of long-oared galleys or birlinns, the descendants of the Viking longships, greyhounds of the seas; and if the word of the royal ships' approach had reached these parts, as was not unlikely, then these restricted channels could readily be blocked and the fleet more or less ambushed and possibly cut up into segments and so vanquished. So it was to be the open sea for them, west-about round the large islands of Islay and Jura, of Colonsay and Oronsay, to great Mull itself, passing near to Iona, the only one of them all known to most aboard, where the High Kings of Scots had formerly been buried and their successors elected.

Angus Og was thought to be based on his headquarters on Islay; but the objective was to separate him from his northern allies under Alexander of Lochalsh. James's Highland adviser, present with them on the *Flower*, MacGregor of Glenarklet, said that Lochalsh, far to the north at Skye, in present circumstances was likely to be at his secondary seat of Mingary, on the mainland-jutting peninsula of Ardnamurchan, just north of the tip of Mull, if not actually with Angus Og already. From Mingary he could call on many mainland clans such as MacIvers, MacRaes, MacInnes, MacIans, Camerons and Mathiesons. A wedge, then, between Mingary and Islay. And the former apparently had a strong castle, rather unusual in the Highlands, where the chiefs tended to rely on their clansfolk for protection rather than stone and lime. The cannon, then, for Mingary.

Off Mull, twenty-five miles of it, they were in the open ocean, with powerful seas rather than islets and reefs and skerries to contend with. The second night, the wind behind them now, they passed near outlying Staffa, that legendary isle with its extraordinary columnar formation and caves, the greatest known as the Uamh Binn, the Cave of Melodies, from the strange music that the waves made therein, that and the crooning of seals. So far they had seen no war-galleys, only fishing-boats; but these would have given warning of the fleet's presence undoubtedly.

Passing Staffa, thereafter they threaded their way between a scatter of smaller islands fairly wide apart – Little Colonsay, the Treshnish Isles, Gometra and others – before they able to round the northern tip of the great Mull itself and enter its sound, this one of the largest and most important waterways of the innumerable channels of the Inner Hebrides, separating Mull from the mainland peninsulas of Ardnamurchan and Morvern. For almost everyone aboard the fleet's vessels this was all new territory, not only the lie of the land but the utter difference of it all from anything they had previously known, as much water as land, mountains soaring everywhere, the impossibility of distinguishing what were lesser sounds and sea lochs opening on all sides, the usual skerries and islets, traps for the unwary navigator, waterfalls, stretches of white cockleshell sand intervening, these making the shallows brilliant with colour, azure blue and emerald green, many-hued seaweeds so different from the darker brown weed of the eastern and southern coasts, all adding to the strange mixture of enchanting loveliness and sheer dramatic threat and challenge. For anyone with an eye for scenic beauty, this all was enthralling, including James Stewart, who kept exclaiming and pointing. But most there, undoubtedly, were much more concerned with the dangers of navigation, to say nothing of possible attack by hidden galleys coming out from some or many of the bays, sounds and inlets.

Mingary Castle was not hard to locate, at any rate, it soaring conspicuously above a rock jutting into the mouth of the sound, on the north, the mainland Ardnamurchan side. Below it some half-dozen galleys were seen to be moored. But were there others, many others, hidden, waiting? This was the danger.

James and Sir Andrew between them had concocted a strategy, hopefully to deal with this anticipated situation, and had sent orders to all the other vessels of their fleet. They were to form up in a long line, some three hundred yards out from that castle, and at a given signal from the *Flower* of one cannon-shot, all were to open fire with their many pieces, but with blank shot, no ball. This barrage of noise was to inform MacIan of Mingary, and anyone else who might be within hearing, of the power and threat waiting out here. They could not fail to recognise that cannonballs were available, if required.

The king's force had not long to wait. Their line of ships was barely in position before out from bays and inlets on both sides of the sound, appeared galleys, long-oared, shield-sided, sails and banners bearing the devices of the clans, in twos and threes and tens, score after score of them, sufficient to make the royal flotilla seem small in numbers, although none, of course, could rival the size of Wood's great warships. This concourse of vessels, scattered as it was at first, quickly coalesced into a disciplined whole, and came along westwards in double file to line up in a crescent-shaped formation not far seawards of the king's ships. Their threat was as manifest as had been the royal gunfire.

James, tense now, looking from the galleys to the castle, where the craft there were commencing to move out from under the shadow of the rock, glanced at Wood, who nodded. The king raised a clenched fist towards only two of the *Flower*'s cannoneers. Promptly the waiting men applied their smouldering fuses to the powder scoops on the gun barrels. Explosions erupted deafeningly – but this time it was not only powder and smoke. Two cannonballs sped, to throw up great spouts of water either side of the castle's ships, sufficiently near for the warning to be entirely clear.

James waited for moments, until the cannon-fire ceased to re-echo from the surrounding mountains. Then, once again, he raised his fist, to shake it. And, however raggedly, all the fleet's guns belched smoke, flame and din, but only that, no balls. The message was reinforced.

There followed another period of waiting, longer this time. Then, with a sigh of heartfelt relief, not only on the part of James Stewart, they saw a white flag rise to flutter amongst the banners on Mingary's topmost tower. Presumably all the galleys saw it also, even if they showed no reaction.

At David's side, the king did. He called to Sir Andrew Wood for a boat to be lowered.

"I wouldna trust these Hielant scum, Sire!" that man exclaimed. "They are savages, just."

"Not so," James declared. "And they are all my subjects, see you. I will go speak with them, with MacIan." He looked round him, and waved to Sir Robert Bruce, MacGregor of Glenarklet and David himself, who all stood near. "Come, you," he commanded.

The three of them followed their young monarch down the swaying rope-ladder to the boat that had been lowered, with its oarsmen, James waving back others who would have joined them.

It was a strange experience, for David Kennedy at any rate, to be rowed landwards to that grim stronghold on its rock-top, just the four of them, no longer protected in any fashion, galleys bristling with armed men just ahead of them, and with a host more behind the ships they had just left – and all because of a piece of white cloth hoisted up on a pole. He saw the whites of James's knuckles as they tightly gripped the thwart on which he sat. No words were spoken.

Their boat was rowed on between the birlinns, from which tartan-clad men, swords and axes in hand, stared at them silently, anything but welcomingly. None moved.

On they went, for their boat to ground on a small stony beach below the castle rock. It was none so very different from Dunure, David noted at the back of his mind.

James vaulted over on to the shingle, followed by the three others. Pausing there, he felt into the inner pocket of his royal lion rampant doublet and drew out a simple gold circlet, which he raised to place over his plentiful reddish hair, the symbol of the crown. Then, leading his companions, he started to climb the steep zigzag track up the cliff. At the top they could see many men gazing down, but none came to meet them.

They took their time to make that ascent, not only to retain their dignity, for it was all but precipitous. The king paused more than once to adjust the chain that he always wore round his waist and which the climbing seemed to make the more uncomfortable.

Up at the summit quite a crowd of clansmen stood watching, in their ragged kilts and plaiding. None responded when James waved towards them. There appeared to be no chiefly characters amongst them.

Walking on towards the castle itself, they perceived that it was defended on this landward side by a deep ditch and moat. And the drawbridge to cross that was upraised. David and Bruce exchanged glances at the king's back. They could see armed men watching their approach from the gatehouse parapet walk.

Reaching the edge of the ditch, they had to stand and wait, humiliating as this might be, deliberately so no doubt. James bit his lip, but stood there silent.

Then the ringing blare of bagpipes sounded from within the walls. This went on for some time. Still they waited. Another noise presently competed with the piping, the creaking, clanking sound of the drawbridge being lowered. A royal sigh of relief was just evident.

When the bridge thudded down into position, James strode forward on to its timbers. Then he paused. They could see beyond it, hitherto hidden, a group of men standing under the gatehouse arch, no clansmen these but all wearing eagle's feathers in their bonnets, some three, some two. They made no sign, but stood there. The pipes played on.

Drawing a deep breath, James paced forward over the bridge, his companions at his back, but not so confidently as appeared to be their monarch. A few yards from the waiting chiefs then James halted once more, waiting for that piping to cease. He was not going to shout above it.

At length it wailed into silence, and a royal hand was raised high. "Greetings, friends and subjects!" he called. "I am James Stewart, King of Scots, your liege-lord. Which is MacIan of Mingary?"

An elderly man, fine-featured if grey, clad in a saffron kilted tunic and tartan plaid over one shoulder, answered. "I am John mac Alastair mac Ian of Ardnamurchan and Sunart." He had a lilting all but musical Highland voice at odds with the less than friendly expressions of himself

45

and his companions. "Why come you, James Stewart, into the Isles, with ships and guns?"

"I come to receive you, and your friends and neighbours, into my peace and goodwill. And my guns are to salute you, Islesmen."

There was silence at that, although one of the chieftains hooted.

"I see your welcoming ships," James went on, waving seawards. "A notable array. I esteem it."

"Esteem it with cannon!" a younger befeathered man exclaimed. "I, Ranald mac Alan of Uist, would name it otherwise." He too had that sibilant voice.

"Cannon can speak loudly, yes – but for good as well as ill, sir. You would note that the only balls fired were in token of friendship, to greet the movement of your vessels." James paused. "Although we have no lack of cannonballs on our ships, to be sure!" That was pointedly said.

The chiefs stood, expressionless.

The young monarch changed his tone. "I bring you greetings from your former Lord of the Isles, John of Islay, now dwelling in peace and goodwill in the monastery of Paisley. He has yielded up his lordship to me, and would have you know that from henceforth the King of Scots is also Lord of the Isles, and you my supporters. This to my much satisfaction and regard, and the well-being of my realm. Hence my greeting to you all, my friends."

Silence.

"In token whereof," James went on – and David could detect the slight tremor in the royal voice – "I would do you honour, and express my favour and further salutation. Step you forward, MacIan of Ardnamurchan."

That man stared, clearly at something of a loss for so dignified a chieftain. But when the king moved forward two or three more paces, with a glance at his fellows he did pace a little way on to the bridge, and there halted.

James had to advance further to reach him. There he reached out a hand to grasp the plaid-clad shoulder.

"Good, my friend," he said, managing a tight smile. "See you, I have come unarmed, in friendship. I have no sword. Lend me yours, John of Ardnamurchan."

That had the other staring the harder. At his side was hung a two-handed blade, hilt adorned with jewel-stones amidst Celtic carving. When the man made no move, James changed his grip from shoulder to sword hilt, and drew out that blade from its sheath with the skreich of steel.

"Kneel, John mac Alastair mac Ian," he ordered.

That man shook a perplexed head. He half turned to look back at the others watching. But when James repeated the order to kneel, and reinforced it with the pressure of his other hand, he did sink down, if only on one knee, grey head anything but bowed.

The king had to be careful with that heavy sword, to avoid the upturned head and tall feathers of the bonnet, before he brought down the blade on the tartan shoulder. "John MacIan," he intoned, "with this sword I, James Stewart, name and create thee knight, as is my right, in the sight of God and these present. Be thou good, true and faithful knight until thy life's end. Arise, Sir John!"

The older man rose, still uncertain – and he did not look the sort who would know much of uncertainty. Oddly, when the young monarch actually took the sword by the blade to hand it back, hilt first, this gesture seemed to have more effect on the man than what had gone before. He took it, and bowed wordlessly.

Smiling, less tensely now, James raised his voice towards the watching chiefs. "My friends," he called, "who next would have the accolade of knighthood? To seal our accord and regard?"

The array of Highland notables eyed each other. Then one, a burly man of middle years with an air of authority to him, stepped forward. "I, John of Islay, would be so honoured," he said.

David, for one, all but gasped. Here was success indeed, for this was a much greater personage than MacIan, known

47

to all, one who had claimed the forfeited lordship of the Isles of his namesake, and the earldom of Ross. Moreover his grandfather had been a son of another John, seventh Lord of the Isles, who had married the Princess Margaret, daughter of King Robert the Second. The visitors had not known of his presence here.

"Ha, Islay!" James exclaimed, obviously greatly surprised by this totally unexpected presence and development, elation scarcely hidden in his voice. "Cousin! Here is a pleasure indeed, kinsman! I knew not . . ." He held himself in, with an effort that was all but evident. "Greetings! We have never met. But I have heard much of John of Islay!"

"None so ill hearing, whatever, I hope," the big man said. And he inclined his head, and added, "Cousin!"

Everywhere men all but held their breaths. This changed all. If John of Islay, that island the caput and chapter of the entire lordship of the Isles, accepted knighthood from James Stewart, who could be in any position to refuse it? Another chief made that recognition clear, stepping out.

"I, Alexander of Lochalsh, would be so declared," he said, a tall hawk of a man.

David, of course, had heard of him also. He was likewise a MacDonald, a sister's son of the last Lord of the Isles, and powerful to a degree in the north-west mainland, few more so.

James acknowledged his appreciation of this by a welcoming wave of the hand. He sought John of Islay's sword, ordered him to kneel and again went through the formal procedure of knighting. And when this second Sir John rose, he smilingly asked if he might retain the weapon meantime, gesturing towards Alexander of Lochalsh. These two, related to each other as they were, it was known were not on the best of terms; but the sword was lent, with something between a bow and a shrug. His second cousin became Sir Alexander.

That established the direction, none in a position

to discountenance these two, and there was all but a queue of applicants thereafter seeking the accolade; but it was noteworthy to the Lowlanders that these Highland dignitaries had their own precedences and formalities, for it was only the three-feather men who advanced towards the king, all chiefs of the name, no two-feathered chieftains venturing forward. But those who did made a resounding file: MacDonald of Dunivaig and the Glens of Antrim, MacDonald of Sleat, MacNeill of Barra, Maclean of Duart, Macleod of the Lewes and Cameron of Lochiel.

James made no protest at having to knight all these. For here was victory indeed, and not a drop of blood shed. David was rather surprised that the bestowal of knighthood should clearly mean much to these Highland chiefs.

As all stood back from the monarch now, MacIan bowed. "Lord James," he said, "my house is yours. Honour it by your presence, and come dine at my table."

Inclining his head, the king turned to look seawards. "My friends, many out there wait, and no doubt wonder. I would have all to know of this accord and happy outcome. Those in my ships and in your galleys. All cannot join us here – but some few may? With your permission, Sir John, I would so invite them. Two or three, no more."

MacIan nodded. "So many as you wish . . . Sire." That was the first expression of the royal address at Mingary.

"I thank you." James turned to David. "Master of Kennedy, will you go out to Sir Andrew and my lords of Bothwell and Drummond. Have them come ashore. Give them the word. As to the galley fleet . . .?" He looked at the group of chiefs. "They must be . . . informed. By one whom they will heed."

"I will go, Sire." That was John of Islay. "I am known to all." He gestured towards David. "My own birlinn lies below there. We shall use it." That was in the nature of a command.

"That is well," the king said. "Now, Sir John of

49

Ardnamurchan, I shall gladly accept your hospitality."
And he turned towards the gatehouse, all this having
taken place on the lowered drawbridge.

John of Islay beckoned to David to follow him, and strode
off towards the cliff track to descend to the waterside.

Some of the castle galleys still waited a little way
offshore, but two were at the beach, beside the *Flower*'s
rowing-boat. Ignoring this last, the big man waved
to one of the other craft, the largest there, and had
the dragon-prowed galley run up on to the shingle so
that he could board it without wetting his feet, not
concerning himself to see that David climbed in after
him. He promptly had the great square sail hoisted on
the single mast, this blazoned with the design of the
bannered Galley of the Isles and red lion of chiefship –
this indeed the symbol of the Lord of the Isles himself.

In the sixteen-oared craft they were rowed out towards
the two waiting crescents of ships.

It was perhaps significant that John of Islay directed
his oarsmen half right, to skirt the western end of the
king's vessels and make for the further lines of galleys.
There he headed for one fairly centrally placed in the
great fleet, this flying three boar's heads banners. On
to this he transferred himself, and waved David away
dismissively.

That man, frowning, turned and pointed the birlinn's
steersman back in the direction of the Lowland ships and
the *Flower*; and without comment he was rowed thither,
in no very confident frame of mind.

When he reached Wood's flagship and climbed aboard,
the birlinn promptly pulled away to return to the galley
it had just left. David found Bothwell and Drummond
with Sir Andrew on this vessel's afterdeck. They eyed
him enquiringly.

"It is success," he announced, although less than elat-
edly. "His Grace has gained the day, won them over.
He sends me to summon you, Sir Andrew, and you my
lords, to yonder castle. To sit in at table there. They, the

chiefs, have accepted him. He has indeed knighted some of them. Including that John of Islay, who brought me out, and who is informing the galley fleet that there is to be no fighting, that all is now well."

"And is it?" Bothwell jerked. "*Knighted* them?"

"Yes. James has won them over. He talked them into favouring him most, most ably. Told them that *he* was now Lord of the Isles, with the agreement of the captive at Paisley. He was now their monarch, lord and friend. All to retain and hold their lands and positions freely of him. Knighted five or six of them there and then. Now they would have him sit down to eat with them at MacIan's table. And he would have you, my lords, join him there. And you, Sir Andrew."

"No' me!" Wood declared. "I bide here, with the cannon! I'm no' trusting these cut-throat Hielantmen!"

"The king believes them assured," David said. "Proud, but not false. He said that once you sit at meat with a Highlander, partake of his hospitality, you are safe from any evil or betrayal."

"I have heard of that," Drummond agreed. "If the king commands us, then we must go. Support him."

Somewhat more doubtfully, Bothwell nodded.

"Go you, if you will. I stay with the guns," Wood repeated. "And if there is any sign o' treachery, knavery, I open fire!"

The others did not seek to dissuade him. They sought a rowing-boat from the *Yellow Caravel*, lying nearby, to take them ashore. David told them more as they went. None of them was entirely confident as to the situation.

Climbing up to the castle, they found the crowd dispersed. A minor chieftain was awaiting them at the gatehouse to escort them within. This stronghold was of a different contruction to the general run of Lowland fortalices, basically a great high-walled square, topped by parapet and walk, enclosing what was almost a little village of turf-roofed huts and buildings, cothouses, storehouses, byres and sheds, with a central hallhouse, this last of timber, clay-coated, extensive and roomy. In the great hall of this they found the king and the chiefs already at table, sipping the fiery spirits of these parts, *uisge beatha*, the water of life, whisky, in apparent good fellowship.

Bothwell and Drummond were introduced to their host and other notables as servitors came in with laden dishes from the kitchens, no lack of provision here, despite the numbers of guests. There were only two or three women present, one of whom was sitting beside James, a slender, willowy, dark-haired creature, to whom the impressionable monarch was already clearly attracted. This proved to be Marsala MacIan, their host's daughter.

John of Islay arrived back with three other chieftains from the galley fleet, these presented to the king as Mackenzie of Kintail, MacQuarrie of Ulva and MacDuffie of Colonsay. It was noticeable that, although the Islay lord was given a seat near the king and next to Alexander of Lochalsh, these two turned shoulders on each other, although kinsmen, and did not converse. David was seated in a much more lowly position.

The repast proceeded to the accompaniment of piping, clarsach-playing and an exhibition of Highland dancing. David found the whisky, stronger than the wines and ales to which he was used, going to his head, and refused to have his goblet recharged, although all around him his fellow guests seemed to be able to quaff quantities of it without evident effect.

Whether it was otherwise or not with James Stewart, presently he rose from his seat, bowed to the young woman at his side, and then raised her up to lead her out to the cleared area beyond the tables, and there, after a somewhat stumbling start, performed a quite energetic and graceful dance with her, she partnering him with no least reticence nor reluctance. This obviously much pleased the company, applause demanding more, before others came out to join the pair.

This was scarcely how David and his Lowland colleagues had expected this occasion to end.

In time, finding himself bleary-eyed, and blaming the whisky, David sought a bed for the night. A servitor was detailed to lead him to one of the outside hutments, where he found bunks with folded plaiding awaiting the weary, with more whisky to assist sleep. Before leaving that noisy hall, he had noted that the king had disappeared, the young woman with him – Highland hospitality? He would have to tell Janet about Marsala MacIan.

It had been a day to remember.

5

The days that followed were memorable also, different as they were. James decided to wait at Mingary for the other Isles and Highland leaders to be brought in, to enter into bonds of amity with the new royal Lord of the Isles. This entailed the Lowland fleet dispersing to anchor itself in sundry sheltered inlets and havens, such as were not already occupied by the chieftains' galleys, a situation deplored by Sir Andrew Wood. Alexander of Lochalsh departed, ostensibly to send in his lesser chieftains and *duin'-uasals* from further north, Muick, Eigg, Rhum and Skye, although some doubted his commitment to the new regime, knighthood notwithstanding. John of Islay, his rival, stayed on to ensure that all went satisfactorily, or so he said. Bothwell opined that he intended to make himself the king's deputy in the Isles; with James necessarily absent in the south for almost all the time, he would lord it in all respects save in the title itself.

As they waited for absent chiefs to appear, the time was passed with a variety of sports and recreations, largely new to the visitors, MacIan proving an excellent host. Hawking was a pastime known to all, although in the Lowlands it was done on horseback, here not. But the game was plentiful, wild geese in especial, and herons much in evidence. There was tinchelling, that is hunting deer, again not mounted but the sportsmen waiting hidden behind deer dykes while regiments of clansmen rounded up vast numbers of the animals, such as never seen in the south, and these driven in herds through gaps in the dykes, to be shot by crossbow. There were archery competitions, tossing the caber – that is individuals raising and throwing what amounted to lesser tree-trunks to see how far they might be heaved – something at which the Highlanders much outdid the king's people; the same with putting the weight, when a heavy stone was tossed instead of a caber. In all this James joined in, and proved himself no laggard, to the approval of the Highlanders, who clearly found him acceptable as a man, as perhaps distinct from a monarch – as did the MacIan young woman very obviously.

The missing Isles chiefs duly appeared, some having had to come from quite far off, and whatever they all thought of the developments, none refused to give his bond of amity in return for freeholding under the crown. King James was well content, whatever Wood declared.

Four days of this and a move was made. Most of the Lowland fleet would head for home ports, many going north-abouts to reach the Tay and Forth estuaries, others south, for Dumbarton on the Clyde. But James, in *Flower*, would make a number of visits briefly to various of the Hebridean islands to announce his assumption of the Lordship of the Isles, John of Islay accompanying him with an escort of galleys; this also as something of a warning, if such was needed, to Alexander MacDonald of Lochalsh.

So there was a great parting at Mingary, with Marsala MacIan all but in tears. David went with the king, Bothwell and Drummond. They sailed first for Coll, only a score of miles westwards, which was one of the isles under Alexander's control. At Arinagour there they made an appearance, but not finding the MacDonald, they set off northwards for small Muick and the larger Eigg and Rhum. Still there was no sign of Alexander. Skye, just ahead, was huge of course; but calling in at Armadale on its southern Sleat peninsula, they were informed that the man they sought had not come there either. So presumably he had gone on further north to his great territories of Torridon and Gairloch. This quest could go on and on, and with John of Islay less than eager to continue with it, the king decided to turn back. They would visit John's own isles of Scarba, Jura and Islay, and make that serve.

Actually David quite enjoyed this cruising up and down the Hebrides, undoubtedly the most scenic and picturesque area of all Scotland, all blue mountains, beetling cliffs, sea lochs, sounds and bays, the water as colourful as all else because of the underlying white cockleshell sands, azure and pale green and sparkling. In this summer weather it all held a dream-like quality, although it would be very different in wintery conditions, all recognised. James Stewart revelled in it, beauty in scene, as in women, much affecting him.

Between Scarba and Jura they passed near to the notorious Strait of Corryvreckan, scene of tragedies innumerable, where an enormous whirlpool could draw ships to their doom, this caused by an undersea conical mountain round which the fierce tides of the isles swirled in roaring menace, the sound of which could be heard for miles. This greatly intrigued the monarch, who was all for venturing nearer than Wood or John of Islay judged wise. They did win close enough to see the white rim of it, perhaps a mile off, but that was as much as Sir Andrew would risk.

The long, narrow island of Jura, with its shapely, breast-like mountains, led them down to Islay itself, a mere mile-wide sound separating the two. Down this channel they probed, to Askaig, where they landed, to make for Loch Finlaggan. Islay proved to be very different from all the others; large, yes, but not mountainous, many low hills but fairly fertile and populous. It was not so strange, once visited, that it should be the caput, all but the capital and main seat of the Lordship of the Isles, at the southern extremity of the vast watery domain as it was. Here they landed, then.

They had to walk a couple of miles through rolling slopes to Loch Finlaggan, past Pictish standing stones and an ancient cross, to no very impressive sheet of water, at the very north end of which were two small islands, side by side, on which rose a large hallhouse and a little chapel. The former was no defensive strength, for what need had such as its lord for the like here on his island sanctuary amidst so many of his clansfolk? John of Islay made it very clear that he was monarch here, and none other.

But, whatever his plans for the royal visitor might have been, they were negated promptly by circumstances. For waiting at Finlaggan, sent there by MacIan from Mingary, was none other than Boyd of Bonshaw, father of Mariot who had borne the king's child, on the orders of Argyll, the realm's Chancellor, to inform James that he should return to Stirling just as soon as possible. A grievous plot had been uncovered, hatched by Archibald, Earl of Angus and James, Earl of Buchan, in collaboration with King Henry of England, to get rid of the king and replace him on the throne by his young brother, the Duke of Ross, with Henry Tudor accepted as Lord Paramount, or overlord, of Scotland, with meantime these two earls to rule the land for the boy. Swift action was essential.

Astonished and appalled, the royal party, without any delay, took hasty leave of the bemused John of the Isles, and hurried back to the *Flower* for the sail to Dunbarton.

Aboard, James held a conference with his advisers, David Kennedy included. This so unlooked-for crisis called for urgent and drastic measures, most clearly. But what was the first priority? The Earl of Buchan, Hearty James as he was known, was in fact great-uncle to the king, son of Queen Joan Beaufort by her later marriage to the Black Knight of Lorn, so was not in the royal succession, but very influential. Angus, of course, had ever been a questionable character, but powerful as chief of the Red Douglases. Both had been on the losing side at Sauchieburn, supporting James's father. But so had many another in high position, inevitably. Would these two be able to call on support for their traitorous embroilment with Henry the Seventh? Was the realm to be faced with a major uprising, civil war, with English involvement?

Bothwell said he did not think that there would be any large-scale defection against James. He was proving an excellent monarch and popular with all classes of the people, in the way that his late father had not been. Some few lords might back Buchan and Angus, if they seemed to be gaining ground, but not many. So it must be dealt with, and speedily. A parliament should be called, but that required forty days' notice. Meantime the Privy Council must take swift and strong action.

Lord Drummond agreed with that. The Douglas power was, in his opinion, the most dangerous factor. Buchan had nothing like the manpower that Angus could field. But he was close to his kinsman, the Earl of Atholl, who could be a threat if he joined them. He also had fought on the other side at Sauchieburn. A move should be made, if possible, to ensure that he did not join any rising. That was the first priority, in his view.

Sir Andrew Wood wondered about King Henry's involvement. Was he not seeking for his young daughter to wed James? This barely seemed to match with that project. Unless he was thinking to transfer the proposal to the Duke of Ross?

David had little or nothing to contribute to the discussion, save the obvious need to summon all leal men either to muster maximum force in arms at once, or to have their strength ready to move at shortest notice.

The king declared that much depended on how far this plot had developed before Argyll got word of it. If it was still in an early stage, it might be possible to bring it to naught without recourse to arms. So much would depend on the Douglas power, and whether the Black Douglases joined the Reds. Together they could prove a menace indeed. So, much more information was needed than Bonshaw had been able to give them. But it was galling indeed, apart from all else, to have hopefully solved this Highland and Isles situation, only to be confronted with potential revolt in the Lowlands. How long until they could reach Dunbarton, *en route* for Stirling?

58

Wood judged it some forty-five miles to the Mull of Kintyre from Askaig, then sixty more on up the Clyde estuary, wind largely against them for the first but for them in the second; say just over twelve hours' sailing for *Flower*. With that, impatient men had to be content. On horse to Stirling from Dunbarton, some forty-five more miles, would take most of a day. They must sleep while they could, however unlike sleep they might feel.

Thanks to good conditions they made Dunbarton in slightly better time than assessed. And there not far from midnight, David saw little point in riding on to Stirling with the king. Nothing that he could usefully do there, whereas down at Carrick he could seek to have the Kennedy strength ready for action, given the word. He wondered about his father. What would his reaction be to this of Angus? Would his new-found support for the king remain firm, if indeed firm it was? Here would be test.

Like the others, David hired a horse at Dunbarton, and in the June half-dark set off southwards by west, to cross Clyde at Glasgow and head down through Cunninghame by Eaglesham and over the Fenwick Water to Kilmarnock and so to Ayr and Dunure, some sixty-five miles. It had been vexing to pass within a few miles of the Carrick shore in *Flower* on their way north, but he could scarcely have sought to delay the king on his urgent way by desiring to be set ashore there.

Would Janet be at Cassillis or Dunure? Or even still at Borthwick Castle? For how long had he been away? Surely she would not have remained with Agnes Borthwick all that time, nearly two weeks? Himself, he would have quite favoured a visit to Borthwick, but that would mean considerable delay, far out of his shortest route, and was not to be considered.

He rode all night and well into the forenoon, his hired mount not so fast as one of his own beasts.

He did call in at Cassillis before Dunure, and was glad

to find Janet there, as he had rather expected, sister Helen with her. Avoiding their father had become a concern of Janet's. He was welcomed warmly, and weary as he was, he did not delay with his news, in especial of course the matter of Angus's treacherous plotting. They had heard nothing of this in Carrick.

Janet's always lively eyes widened. "Is it true?" she demanded. "If it is, then, then . . . ! This could change all! If that man becomes a rebel against the crown, then I may be free of him! Would our father still wish to tie me to him?"

"Of that I am unsure, lass. Angus is rich in lands, and powerful. Already he has placed properties in your name, as pledge . . ."

"But in revolt against James! The king. High treason! If it is true."

"The Chancellor, the Earl of Argyll, says that it is. And he should know. But our sire, if he thinks that the plotters could possibly win, might elect to turn away from the king. His loyalty has never been firm, I would judge. Only a matter of policy. If he sees James possibly unseated, slain perhaps, he could well decide to, if not actually support Bell-the-Cat and Buchan, at least not support the king."

"James slain! No, never will they do that! Even Angus. Dear God, not that!"

"Argyll said as much. To put young Ross on the throne. And wed him to Henry Tudor's daughter, the plotters to rule Scotland for the boy. And for Henry! Angus in power indeed, and the richer!"

"Will Father know of this?"

"I think it unlikely. From the Chancellor's message it is all at a very early stage. But who can tell?"

"It must be stopped. What is being done to bring this evil to naught? And to punish the scoundrels?"

"That is what will be being discussed and decided at Stirling now by James and his council. The loyal forces of the realm to be readied. And myself to seek to raise the Kennedys. Whatever Father may say!"

60

"And I will come with you! I will!"

"Think you that will help, lass? With either Father or his lairds and landed men?"

"I do. With Father I know not. But with the others, yes. Even if I have to shame them into it. I could become Flaming Janet indeed! Help to set Carrick alight for the king!"

David mustered a smile. "I am tired, girl. Ridden all night and slept little before. Give me an hour or two of rest, and we shall go to Dunure."

"Yes. I am sorry. We go whenever you are rested."

By midday they were on their way the seven miles to the coast, and not dawdling, David mounted on a better horse now.

They found their father and brothers at home, the latter at least glad to see them and demanding details of the Isles expedition. David shook his head.

"It was successful, yes, the king most able. Bringing the chiefs to terms without any warfare. But there are less good tidings. A conspiracy against His Grace. Treason! In league with Henry Tudor. And it is led by the Earls of Angus and Buchan!"

Quick breaths were drawn. Lord Kennedy stared.

"Angus? Conspiracy? What, what is this?"

"A dastardly plot. Uncovered by the Chancellor. He sent word to the king at Islay. Angus and Buchan in league with King Henry to bring down James, possibly have him slain. To put the boy Duke Alexander of Ross on the throne, with Henry as overlord. And Angus and Buchan to rule the land."

"I have heard nothing of this. How true is it all? It may be but a canard. Argyll deceived. Or jealous . . ."

"The king, Bothwell, Drummond and Wood believe it. The Privy Council is to take all necessary steps. A parliament to be called. The forces of the realm to be rallied – for the Red Douglas power could be rising to aid the plotters. And I am sent by James to raise Carrick and the Kennedys."

Their father opened his mouth to speak more, then shut it again, and began to pace the floor back and forward, his older son and daughter watching him, his younger ones chattering excitedly.

Janet raised voice. "Kennedy must prove its loyalty. The Red Douglas, whom you would have me to wed, is traitor!"

Her father did not so much as glance at her. He made for the door, swinging on his heel, and went out.

His family eyed each other.

"So much for the King of Carrick!" David jerked. "*We*, at least, know our duty!"

"Where do we start?" Janet demanded.

"Culzean first, I judge. He is senior in the line. Our cousin. If he makes good response, that will help with the others. Then inland for Maybole, Baltersan, Dalquharran, all the Girvan Water seats, and up to Dalrymple. It will take time . . ."

"Then what are we waiting for!"

David glanced at that shut door. "He . . . he will not say us nay, think you?"

"If he does, we are deaf of ear!"

He nodded, turning to the younger ones. "I would keep out of our father's way, see you," he advised. "He will take all this less than kindly. Be . . . absent! *We* do what he should be doing."

Followed by Janet, David went to the other door, and out.

They wasted no time, fearful that their sire might try to halt them. Seeking their horses again in the stableyard, they mounted and were off, southwards now.

They had some four miles to ride down that cliff-girt coastline into wide Culzean Bay, passing the little fishing-haven of Isle Port behind its rock-stack shelter, to reach Culzean Castle, similarly situated to Dunure on a precipitous headland above the waves. Kennedy of Culzean, in cousinship, was the next most powerful of the Carrick lairds, a youngish man. He proved to be out

fishing in a boat, a favourite pastime, time, his wife able
to point out his craft from the tower-top. He might be long
enough out there, so there was nothing for it but to go down
to the shore, where there was a small shingle beach nearby
on which two or three other boats were drawn up and nets
hung to dry beside two fishermen's shacks. Dismounted
now, there they requested an elderly man and his son to
row them out to the laird's craft, half a mile away. One
of the boats was pushed down into the water and all four
climbed in. Janet was used to boat-fishing at Dunure,
and made no bones about this. The sea was not rough.

Culzean, with another of his fishermen, watched their
approach interestedly, as he held his baited line, for he
could scarcely mistake the striking red hair of the woman
approaching, even at some distance. He was a stocky man
with reddish hair of his own, but nothing to rival Janet's.
He hailed them, waving.

"To what am I indebted for this honour?" he called.
"Are you so short of flukies at Dunure?"

"It is time that we are short of, Pate," David gave
back. "For we have to visit many another this day.
Let us hope that they are not all afloat!" And as the
boats drew alongside, he explained. "We come on King
James's command. The Kennedy strength is to be readied
for service in the royal cause. Archibald Bell-the-Cat and
the Earl of Buchan are serving the King of England to
unseat our liege-lord. The realm's leal forces are to be
prepared for action. How many men, horsed if possible,
can Culzean raise?"

"Lord!" the other exclaimed, astonished. "Angus?
Against King James? In rebellion? The Red Douglas."

"Yes. We all must be ready for the word. How many?"

"Sakes, I do not know. I have not thought on the like."

"Well, think now, Pate," the young woman added.
"James needs us."

"Aye, I heard that the king was seeing something of
you, Janet! But this is—"

"You have many men." David cut him short. "It will

63

be the horses that are the trouble. Fisherfolk do not have horses. But you have farms aplenty."

"Aye." Patrick Kennedy drew up his line, with a flapping flounder hooked at the end of it. The detaching of this gave him moments to think. "I dare say that I might raise thirty or forty, horsed," he said. "How soon is all this to be? It will take time."

"To be sure, but as little time as possible. Who knows when the word will come. So, to ready your people. And bring them to Cassillis when I call."

"Do not fail His Grace," Janet charged him. "The Kennedy honour is to be upheld."

"My lord is friendly with Angus, we hear . . . ?"

"Not to the king's cost!" David said. "So, see you to it, Pate. Now, we must get back. On our way."

"I will return with you."

So it was back to the boat-strand with both craft, and the climb up to the horses with the flounder catch, Culzean promising full cooperation.

On, then, inland for Maybole, for brother and sister, another four miles. They came first to Baltersan, a smaller house belonging to the Laird of Row, who actually was Lord Kennedy's brother, but out of favour with him. It seemed that he was, however, at his larger establishment of Maybole itself, Egidia, Lady Row telling them. So they moved on thither.

Maybole Castle was a strange laird's house, for it was situated in the middle of the town of the name, this more or less the ancient capital of Carrick, no true town-house but a fortified strength, however surrounded by dwellings which had grown up about it. James Kennedy thereof, their uncle, was not in the best of health and took little part in affairs in Carrick. But he had three strapping sons, James, Robert and John, and these responded heartily, especially when Janet all but challenged them. Once again horses would be the problem, for only the better-off townsfolk possessed such. But there were good farms at Baltersan.

Leaving uncle and cousins, it was on to Kirkmichael, where the laird was a mere youth, his father having died young; but the mother was a stout character in more ways than one, and she assured that she would have a score of mounted men ready within a day or two. Not only so but she would send the word to her brother-in-law at Blairquhan, who ought to do even better, and this would save the visitors some extra mileage.

Down the Girvan Water now they rode, heartened by their success thus far. Dalquharran was their next objective, a large property and impressive fortalice. But it had a moody owner, another David Kennedy, notable as a ladies' man despite, or perhaps because of, his very plain wife, who had in fact brought him this Dalquharran. So here Janet had to play her part, and with some judgment and discretion, seeking to beguile the laird without offending the lady. She proved to be successful enough at this to win not only a promise of fully forty men but generous hospitality as well from their hostess, welcome indeed, for it seemed a long time since David had eaten. They would return home by Dalrymple, and that would be enough for one day. On the morrow they would cover the northern and eastern districts of Carrick, which the Kennedys tended to share with the Cunninghames and Dalrymples, although with generations of intermarriage their influence there was strong.

That night, back at Cassillis, tired but reasonably content, brother and sister wondered about their father. Would he react in any positive way to their activities? He could, of course, if so he decided, send out messengers to command cancellation of their torch-bearing, and, lord of them all, he would not go unheeded. But they hoped, in that case, that some at least would put their loyalty to the King of Scots before that to the King of Carrick. And David thought that he might well choose to do nothing, as it were wash his hands of the mustering effort, so that, in the event of the plotters' efforts succeeding, he could blame it all on his son, to Angus; and if the king won the day, no blame would attach to the Lord Kennedy.

That evening, Janet became quite emotional over the danger to James Stewart, admitting to her brother that she loved the man, no mere girlish infatuation nor romantic dalliance with royalty. It was deep in her.

David was understanding, but concerned also. What was there in all this for the sister he loved?

6

They waited at Cassillis day after day without word from the north, word from anywhere – and that at least included no hint that Lord Kennedy was taking action in the present situation. David reckoned that, if the call came for mustering, he could count on almost four hundred men, horsed. Carrick would not be ashamed of its contribution to the royal cause.

It was ten days before they learned of the position, and then, in most extraordinary fashion, from the mouth of the King of Scots himself. For brother Alexander arrived hot-foot from Dunure, to announce that James Stewart was there, come from Ayr, he said, with a host of men, and was demanding the persons of David and Janet. They were to come at once, for the king was on his way southwards for Liddesdale.

Astonished, they were riding in mere minutes.

They had to pass through a great number of armed men and horses before they reached the cliff-top castle. There they found the place crowded with the leaders of the army, including Bothwell and Drummond, with many other lords, knights and notables, Lord Kennedy playing less than happy host to them all. James they reached in the withdrawing-room off the hall with, amongst others, the Earl of Atholl, his distant kinsman, who at least seemingly had not joined his friend Hearty James of Buchan.

The king rose to embrace Janet entirely frankly in his arms before saluting David, while their father looked on expressionless. Talk was somewhat incoherent at first, but eventually the situation became clear. The conspiracy had been proved to be fact, the Earl of Buchan had been arrested, one or two lesser men arrested likewise, and Angus was said to be presently in Hermitage Castle in Liddesdale, where he could conveniently communicate with King Henry's emissaries at Carlisle, the West March border being only a few miles therefrom. Angus happened to be senior Warden of the Marches, and so had authority to use this stronghold, which was a very powerful one, had to be. It would demand a strong force to take from him. How large a company of Douglases Angus might have with him was not known, but James had brought this army, in person, to deal with it. He would teach Bell-the-Cat his lesson. He had come by this, his old pilgrimage route to St Ninian's Whithorn, from Stirling by Glasgow and Ayr, to pick up the Carrick contingent in the by-going. He did not need to add that he had hoped to see Flaming Janet in the process.

David told him, glancing at his father, that he had four hundred available, but that it might take all day to assemble them. The king nodded.

"I will send on the force that I have brought," he declared. "Down by Loch Doon to Nithsdale and so over into Eskdale and Hermitage, picking up Maxwells and Johnstones on the way. Gather you your men, Lord Kennedy" – although it was at David that he looked – "and I will bide the night here, and catch up with the others on the morrow." The thinking behind that was not difficult to assess. David wondered what Bothwell, Atholl and the other lords thought of it.

"There is Douglas country to go through, Sire, on the way to the Nith," he pointed out. "*Black* Douglas, not Red, but still a danger. Morton, Drumlanrig, Penpont, Thornhill . . ."

"I know it. I have sent word to Lord Maxwell and others. They will be ready to threaten the Douglas rear. But we may need all that we can raise, *your* people likewise. So, see you to it . . ."

David bowed himself out, leaving Janet there.

He sent his brothers to inform some of the Kennedy

lairds, himself going to others, all to assemble at the soonest at Maybole, suitably central. There by noon on the morrow.

It was late before he got back to Dunure, to find the assembled force gone on, the king already retired for the night and no sign of Janet. He did not go seeking her. Nor did he exchange more than a word or two with his father, who seemed distinctly preoccupied.

He was up betimes in the morning, and off to Maybole before James showed face, or Janet either. This would be his first experience of marshalling a force of armed men to lead personally in possible battle.

The king and some of his closer nobles duly arrived at Maybole by midday, where David had about three hundred and fifty horsed men awaiting him, with some from the eastern areas of Auchinleck, Sorn and Cumnock still to come. He left word for these to follow on, making south-eastwards for the hilly passes of Loch Doon and Carsphairn, and so to the headwaters of Scar and Afton and Nith, with all speed.

As they left Maybole and rode on in that direction, James had David ride beside him for some way through Carrick country, the latter very much aware that his sister's favour with the monarch was of no disadvantage to him. He was emboldened to enquire as to the third aspect of this conspiracy, that of King Henry Tudor's involvement. He was told that this side of it all had to be handled with care indeed, for outright war with England was to be avoided if at all possible. But he would let Henry know of his displeasure. He had a card to play in this: the matter of Perkin Warbeck, whether he was indeed Richard, Duke of York, as his aunt the Burgundian duchess claimed, and which he doubted; at least Henry, informed that the man's claim to the English throne was being considered in Scotland, making the Tudors usurpers, ought to have pause, for there was still a strong Yorkist faction in England, and in any warfare this could rise in Henry's rear. So he, James, was intending to find a bride for the young and quite personable visitor, some high-born lady who could sound like a suitable bride for a would-be king, and let the Tudor take note. David forbore to ask about the proposed betrothal of Henry's young daughter, the Princess Margaret, to the King of Scots.

Riding faster than could the main army, the royal party caught up with this before nightfall in the hilly area of Loch Doon where they were encamped. So far there was no word of any Black Douglas rising in support of Angus, and they were nearing Douglas country here.

David found William, Master of Borthwick, amongst the camped host, and was able to ask after his sister Agnes, whom he often thought of. He got on well with the brother, and they shared a shelter in a hay barn that night.

Next day they were into the hills, all but mountains these, with Cairnsmore and Corserine and Carlin's Cairn soaring majestically, difficult country for an army to traverse, with high, stony passes and defiles to thread, dangerous for ambushes. If the Douglases did intend to back Angus, this might well be where they would strike. Scouts were sent out well ahead, prospecting.

No trouble developed however, and they made fair progress considering the terrain. An army could never rival individual riders as to speed, and the king fretted.

They reached the Nith by evening, a major river, to encamp at the far side beyond a ford, between Drumlanrig and Thornhill, with no signs of Douglas uprising. By his admittedly somewhat vague calculations, David reckoned that they had still some sixty-five or seventy miles to go to Hermitage on the Ewes Water and Liddesdale. With this host it would take them two days. Did Angus keep a watch well afield? And if so, he would have all too much warning of their approach.

They won out of the high hills thereafter, and down to Duncow, where they swung eastwards for Lochmaben of Robert the Bruce fame. Then still east to Lockerbie on the Dryfe Water. Their route became ever less direct, with so many rivers coming off the high ground to be forded, bridges being all but non-existent. All the Border Marches were thus awkward for travel, this west one in especial, one reason why it was notoriously lawless, its moss-troopers all but ungovernable. So seventy miles of travel for an army represented major challenge, even without any fighting.

They got as far as a ford on the oddly named Water of Milk for the next night. James was becoming ever the more agitated at the time being taken, fearing that Angus, aware of their approach as he might well be, would be enabled to make himself the more secure, even perhaps summon English aid from over the border. He decided that a fast-riding group must go forward to present a challenge and discover the situation, the major body to follow on. None with him here knew the terrain intimately, if at all; and David was deemed to be the best guide, disclaim it as he would. He was to lead, with the king himself with him, on the morrow.

Using his own four hundred Carrick men as this advance party, David, with James and Drummond, set off at first light, through more quite high hills again, still eastwards, making the best time that they could. From the Water of Milk they came to the Esk in time, seeking a ford. They were all eyes alert now, fearing scouting parties out from Hermitage. David thought it unlikely that Angus would not somehow have heard of the approach of a large army by now. He would have his links, as a warden, with the local moss-troopers. But if being watched they were, they themselves saw no sign of it, this territory being most apt for small groups to remain hidden.

Over Esk they approached the valley of the Ewes Water, wild country indeed, not far above Langholm. David had only visited Hermitage once and had approached it from the north, by Teviothead, not thus; so he felt very inadequate as guide. It was on a lesser Hermitage Water, he knew, but how far from the Ewes Water he was uncertain. They did call in at a small hill farm, which must have much alarmed the family there, where, warily eyed, they were told that the castle was still some ten miles away, to the north-east. The farmer was not informed that it was the king who asked, nor why they were heading to Hermitage.

The final leg of that long journey took them over more heights to a narrow, twisting valley, in which they were uncertain whether to turn upstream or down, David unsure just where they were, although he must have come this way those years before. He decided down, southwards probably, for Hermitage was said to be none so far from the greater Liddesdale, which in part marked the Debateable Land of the Borderline.

He was proved right in this, at least, for rounding a bend in the valley, there ahead of them abruptly towered the mighty stronghold, grey, menacing, amongst the green hills.

They drew rein, staring at this sudden confrontation which they had come so far to seek, stared and exclaimed. For they had expected to see something very different from this, men encamped around it, banners flying. But no, it seemed all but deserted, although blue smoke did rise from one of its many chimneys.

"This is Hermitage?" James demanded.

"Yes, Sire. None others look like it, with its four great towers linked by those arched curtain walls."

"Then, then . . . ? Has he gone? Are we too late? Hermitage it may be named, but the Red Douglas is no hermit, to shut himself up, alone, in such a place."

"He has, I fear, heard of our coming, and fled. Perhaps over the border, to the English."

"A curse on it! Come, we shall go discover it."

They rode forward to the castle. No obvious sign of alarm developed.

They were close to the gatehouse before there was any reaction. Then a voice hailed them. "Who comes? Who comes to Hermitage?"

"I, James, King of Scots, come!" was shouted back. "Who speaks me here?"

"I, keeper of this hold, speak. Dod Armstrong o' Sorbietrees. What seek you here?"

"Speak more respectfully to His Grace the King!" That was David Kennedy.

No response.

"I seek Archibald, Earl of Angus," James called. "Is he here?"

"He is not."

"He *was* here, no? Where is he, then?"

"Should I ken? Belike by now he will be back at his ain Tantallon, in Lothian."

James drew a deep breath. "Do not seek to cozen me, Armstrong," he cried. "We know that he was here."

"Aye, he was. Twa days syne. And he can ride fast, yon one."

"Damnation!" James thumped fist on saddlehorn. "Gone! All our coming for nothing!" He raised voice again. "You are sure that it was Tantallon? Not . . . England?"

"Tantallon he said, aye. And he rode north."

"So-o-o!" The king looked at David. "We have wasted our time."

"Perhaps not, Sire. After all, if he has fled north to Tantallon or other, not to England, then you may still lay hands on him."

"Tantallon is a strong place. Even stronger, I deem, than this."

"Cannon? Artillery?"

"Perhaps, yes . . ."

"What then, Your Grace? Back to the others? No sense in besieging this hold."

"No. Back it is. Too late . . . by two days!"

The return to Carrick, with something of a sense of anticlimax, David for one remembering those two days of James's dalliance with Janet, was only for a temporary interlude and short dispersal, for his force would be required for the next stage in the pursuit of Angus, like the rest of the army. But not immediately, for Tantallon Castle, on the eastern Lothian coast, was recognised by all to be a hard nut to crack; and the necessary artillery had to be collected from various citadels such as the castles of Edinburgh, Stirling, Dumbarton and Blackness; and oxen-drawn cannon made but slow journeying, ten miles in a day being very good going. So it would be at least a couple of weeks before any siege could be commenced. An assembly, then, in Lothian, after such interval.

There was some grumbling amongst the rank and file at this delay and renewal of mustering, with harvest-time approaching. The king left Dunure with the declaration that he could give no very accurate timing for the move against Tantallon, for he wanted, as well as the cannon, to ensure that Sir Andrew Wood's warships would be able to play a part, if possible to make attack by sea, and he was not sure just where the vessels were based now, *Flower* possibly at Aberdeen. Therefore it would be best if the Carrick contingent came up to some area of Lothian, where it could wait, in readiness for swift action when called for.

The only links David Kennedy had with Lothian were at Borthwick, and he would quite relish a little wait there, with Agnes and William, the master. Would it be too far away from Tantallon on the coast for His Grace's purposes? His Grace thought not; no more than a score of miles perhaps. Indeed they might well make the assembly point for the entire army on Middleton Moor nearby, this far enough away for Angus not to be kept informed of it, and make urgent preparations. So he himself could possibly bide at Borthwick Castle for a short period. He understood from Janet that she was friendly with the Borthwick daughter? So . . . ? The point was taken. Janet would accompany her brother northwards in due course.

The feminine influence on even national events was not to be overlooked.

Two weeks waiting, then, and the Carrick men reassembled for the ride to Lothian; and there was no doubt considerable comment on having a spectacular young woman riding amongst the lairds at their head. What the Borthwicks would think of this influx of armed men into their territory was not to be known.

Fortunately Middleton Moor was sufficiently distant, a mile from the castle, for it not to be embarrassed by a host of idle men. There was a small village there also, which could help to supply the encampment, whether willingly or otherwise.

It made a ninety-mile journey, but through no very difficult country compared with the West March, and they covered it, by Cumnock, the Douglas Water to Biggar, skirting the southern end of the Pentland Hills and so on to Temple and the headwaters of the Gore Water, in two days, having spent the night at Carmichael, where Janet had found a bed. They discovered some troops already encamped on the moor, close to the village of Middleton.

David was faced with a problem here. He could not seek to fill Borthwick Castle with his Kennedy lairds, especially as the king would be arriving presently with his nobles, and these would expect accommodation there. Not to cause offence to either the Borthwicks or his own people, he decided himself to camp on the moor with the latter. There was nothing to prevent him spending considerable time at the fortalice however, after he had deposited Janet there.

Meeting Agnes again was good, the better for her being obviously pleased to see him, even though she was somewhat apprehensive about having to play hostess to the monarch and many of his lofty ones. Her mother had died some years before. She had three sisters, but these were young, and the responsibility for entertaining the visitors fell on herself and brother William. However, Janet's arrival was a help, for she would make a competent assistant. David recognised that he was unlikely to see as much of the young woman as he would have wished.

But at this stage Agnes was not over-busy, stocks of provender having been accumulated, the castle ice house full of meats and fish, the cellars of wines and ale, and the larders of flour, meal and honey for sweetening. So she did have some little time to spare.

With all the busyness at the castle, it seemed evident that any companionable association would have to be achieved outside. He proposed, at the first suitable opportunity, that some horseback exploration of the Borthwick vicinity, little known to him, would be a welcome break, Agnes acceding. He felt it only tactful to suggest that William went along also, but that young man, equally tactfully, said that he would keep Janet company, and take her round some of the nearer environs and down the Gore Water, she probably having had a sufficiency of riding, these last days, in reaching here. David, in fact, got the impression that his friend was much smitten with Flaming Janet, however hopeless might be his chances of making any headway with her in present circumstances.

So Agnes and he set off on their own, the first time that he had been alone with her, in fact. She said that she would take him due southwards into the Morthwaite Hills, uplands of which she was fond and of which he knew nothing.

This range of hills, not so high as the Pentlands nor so

extensive as the Lammermuirs, although situated between them, were nevertheless picturesque enough, with steeper slopes, deeper valleys, rushing streams and some hidden lochans, all producing some quite notable passes, not comparable of course with the great West March heights and dales of Nith, Annan, Dryfe, Ewes and Liddell which David had so recently been traversing, but excellent for riding in pleasant company, and Agnes was certainly that. She was a very happy-seeming young woman, calm and serene perhaps, but very given to quiet laughter, as companionable as she was comely and with an essential warmth which greatly appealed to David Kennedy. The fact that she was the reverse of pushing or forward in her attitudes did not mean no ability to offer her own challenges, however differently from Janet.

They chatted in easy fashion as they rode up Middleton South Burn and through a quite steep escarpment by a deep defile which the girl named Whitelaw Cleugh, and so on to the rolling hills of Hunt Law and Broad Law. It was quite some time before the man realised that he had been giving her not a few minor confidences – she was that sort of young woman. But she seemed to take it all as perfectly natural, and he discovered no urgent need for caution.

This ease of association did have its side effects, at least for David, and when they halted beside a small, lonely lochan amongst wind-blown birches, under Broad Law, to give their mounts opportunity for a drink, and David, aiding Agnes to dismount, held her to himself rather more closely and for longer than was necessary, she smiling at him and shaking her head, but hardly censoriously. He turned his attention to the horses, and when they had drunk their fill, hitched them to a dead tree.

"Shall we sit here awhile?" he suggested. "It . . . it offers a fair prospect."

"Why not," she said. "That is, if the prospects are for the scene, rather then . . . !" She left the rest unsaid, but her little laugh held but no hint of admonition.

They sat themselves on the deer-hair grass, and were silent for a while. With nothing to lean against, it seemed quite natural, presently, for the man's arm to encircle the woman's shoulders. She did not shrug him off.

"I like you, Agnes," he declared, a little abruptly.

"I was beginning to suspect it, David," she said. "We females learn to perceive such . . . overtures."

"You mean . . . ? You think me . . . presumptuous?"

"No, no. Merely manlike."

"Yes. I think that such as yourself, fair, so pleasing, and kind, will have had many men seeking your favours."

"Is that what you are doing, David? Seeking favours?"

"I . . . no. Not that. I but would have you to know that you, you much please me. That I deem you a joy to be with."

"I am glad of that, then. For I like you also, David."

"You do! Then, then . . . ?"

"Would I have come riding with you had I misliked you? Women are allowed to like men, some men, without necessarily offering themselves to them, no?"

"M'mm."

"Poor David Kennedy! Do I confuse? Disappoint? I would not wish that."

"And *I* would not wish you to, to mistake me. I am your brother's friend. And yours. I would not wish to harm that friendship. But I would have you to know that you are . . . much in my thoughts."

"Then I hope to be worthy of your thoughts. I am a simple, less than exceptional young woman, unlike your sister Janet, and I value your caring. Now, shall we be on our way? There is much for you to see yet."

Aiding her up into the saddle, David was more discreet.

When, later, it came to him having to say goodnight and return to the encampment on the moor, he wished that he was staying the night at the castle. For, on a previous occasion, Agnes had shown him up to his room, and this could have been an opportunity for a possible, if modest, demonstration of intimacy, and the caring which she had mentioned. However, she did accompany him to the castle door, along with her brother, to see him on his way, and there he risked giving her a kiss – and she did not jerk her lips away from his.

Next day, the king arrived, with all his train of lords, and there was little occasion thereafter for any close contact with their hostess, however much better James fared with Janet. A quite large force had now converged on Middleton Moor, and it was decided that the move to Tantallon should be made two days hence, by which time it was hoped that at least some of the cannon should be thereabouts. Actually, since something of a siege was anticipated, and a horsed force was not called for at such, fewer men had come with their lords to Middleton, larger contingents being sent afoot direct to Tantallon, these also being necessary to protect any artillery which might be there early; the last thing wanted was for Angus's people to sally out from the stronghold and capture cannon.

The ride to the North Berwick vicinity, a mere twenty-five miles or so, took only three hours, after a somewhat anxious send-off by Agnes and Janet, for the Red Douglas power was not to be taken lightly, and this Tantallon venture could be as much battle as siege. With Janet kissing her brother as well as James, the other young woman at her side could hardly do less, which did offer opportunity for appreciative reaction.

They went by Crichton and Ford, Ormiston and Bolton, to Haddington, the main town of the area, and then northwards to the shores of the Firth of Forth at North Berwick. This was very much Douglas country, and they rode warily, for there were many places where they could be ambushed, especially crossing through the minor Garleton Hills, and at the ford of Athelstaneford where, nearly seven hundred years before, Scotland might be said to have been born, at the bloody battle where the St Andrew's cross in the sky foretold victory and the uniting of Picts and Scots, this duly remarked upon to James Stewart by the knowledgeable. But no opposition developed on this occasion, and they reached salt water in time to meet up with a lumbering oxen-train of artillery, well escorted, which had come all the way from Blackness in the west of Lothian, near Linlithgow.

Off North Berwick's tidal harbour they were glad to see two warships lying at anchor, presumably *Flower* and the *Yellow Caravel*. James sent messengers out in a fishing-boat to inform Wood that action was imminent, and that he should sail the couple of miles eastwards to Tantallon, where the land curved away southwards and became the Norse Sea coastline.

After North Berwick, with its high conical law, the scene was dominated by two other features, the vast rock-stack of the Craig of Bass out in the mouth of the Forth, and the tall and massive towers of Tantallon Castle on its high cliff-top at the very bend of the land. All gazed thereat more than heedfully.

As they approached the mighty hold they came first to where their advance party of troops had cautiously camped above a steep-sided little bay, a good mile short of the castle, the cannon from Edinburgh amongst them, including the famous Mons Meg, which first had been used to pound another Douglas castle, Threave in Galloway, by the king's grandfather, James the Second, forty years earlier. Its guardians here greeted the royal arrival thankfully. They had, needless to say, been much concerned over a possible Douglas attack.

James, with his advisers, David and William Borthwick included, rode forward another half-mile, to prospect and to gauge their task. Halting when they could gain a good overall view, they were scarcely heartened by what they saw. And it was not only the vast towers and curtain walls rearing high on the cliff-girt headland that preoccupied them, but the landward series of deep ditches and ramparts thrown up, which had been created on the level ground before the fortress, in enclosing semicircles, three of these sealing off the entire headland and forming barriers which emsured that cannon would be kept outwith range of fire. It was this that had the visitors looking grim indeed. How was it to be overcome?

As the lords discussed this, the Master of Borthwick told David that he had had occasion to visit Tantallon twice, and that there was more to it than even appeared from here. In fact, that menacing front of towers and high parapet walling was but a sort of forward barricade cutting off a quite large projection of the cliff-top behind, allowing space not only for subsidiary buildings, barracks, stabling and storehouses, with a courtyard, but also leaving open ground on which could be quartered quite large numbers of men, this before the sheer drop to the waves below. So the fact that they had not seen Douglas forces on their way here did not mean that none were assembled. There could be many behind that frontage.

All rode back to the camp thoughtful.

A conference held thereafter came to the conclusion that all would depend on getting artillery sufficiently close to be effective against those massive walls. As it was, it was to be doubted whether even Mons Meg would have the range to damage the masonry. This must mean seeking to fill in some part of those deep ditches and levelling portions of the ramparts. They had plenty of manpower to effect this; but if Angus had cannon of his own, even modest in calibre, at the castle, this could be made impossible. And unfortunately they had word from Sir Andrew Wood that he had sailed past the stronghold previously and discovered that the height of the cliffs prevented cannon on his vessels from elevating their muzzles sufficiently to bombard the castle, save at such a distance as would make their ball quite ineffective.

This awkward situation produced the decision that any ditch-filling attempt would have to be done at night – and, in late July, the nights were short and never very dark. Someone suggested that if, while this was being attempted, the warships were to open up a barrage of fire, however ineffective, it might help to distract from possible attention on the landward side. This was accepted.

So James sent a messenger back to North Berwick, to be rowed out to Wood, to order this for that same night, for the sooner a bombardment could be started, the better, before all the Douglas country was roused against them.

They awaited darkness.

It was the boom of the warships' artillery that had all in very humble action for an armed force, hundreds of men hurrying forward to dig at earthen ramparts, without the benefit of spades and shovels, having to use swords, dirks and axes and bare hands to remove turf and soil, and cast this into the ditches, and all the time fearing attack from the castle so nearby. But the cannonade from seaward continued, and presumably diverted attention, however little it would damage the stronghold, and no reaction developed on the landward side. Fortunately it was a fairly cloudy night, and presumably the labouring behind the barriers remained unseen. It was, of course, only gaps in the ramparts which were to be created.

They did not risk digging into the third and nearest barrier to the castle, that being probably too close to escape detection. But they judged that the gaps in the other two would allow their artillery to get near enough, and up on to the final rampart, to be well within range. So, before dawn, with Wood's gunfire beginning to tail off, running out of powder and ball no doubt, the army's cannon were in position and the crews ready.

What reason to wait now? James gave the signal to open fire. At least the cannoneers could scarcely miss their target.

The barrage that followed was deafening, however ragged, and continuous. On and on the fusillade went. Whether Wood kept up his contribution now they could not hear in all their own din. What effect it all was having on the castle masonry there was insufficient light to see, peer as they would, amidst the smoke.

But surely much damage must be resulting, with eleven cannon repeatedly firing.

James began to be concerned that they too would run out of ammunition, for cannonballs and powder barrels made for heavy transporting, and less had arrived than he would have liked. He ordered the rate of fire to slacken somewhat, but not too obviously.

When at length, with sunrise, they were able to see more than just the looming mass of the castle walling, and details became apparent, it made encouraging viewing, at least for the attackers. The havoc wreaked on the great building was evident, gaps in the masonry, parts of towers demolished, parapets collapsed. Men cheered. And still there was no return fire. Presumably Angus had no artillery therein, or perhaps no powder and shot. The gunfire from the sea had ceased.

The king, after consultation, decided to, as it were, strike while the iron was hot. Under the royal lion rampant banner he and some of his lords went forward some way on foot to the final barrier, to mount it and have a horn blown for attention, and then to hail the fortress.

"Hear me, James, King of Scots," he shouted. "I require the submission of Archibald, Earl of Angus, to my royal authority. Yield now, and I will spare this hold further bombardment. Yield, I say."

There was no response.

"Heed me – or pay sorely for it!" James went on. "I can destroy this place and all within it if need be. I require answer."

He got that, in the shape of a ragged flight of crossbow arrows. None found a mark, perhaps was not intended to, but the response was clear.

Glancing at his companions, including David and Borthwick, who were already urging withdrawal, the king shouted once again.

"So be it! Defiance will serve you nothing, only a greater price to pay. I will give you one day to come to your senses. If not, thereafter this Tantallon will be reduced to rubble!" That day might give opportunity for more powder and ball to arrive.

They returned to their men, and promptly sent off horsed messengers to hasten the arrival of ammunition which they hoped was on its way.

All that day they waited, mainly in sleep, since few had done so during the night. It was evening before two more cannon came, from Stirling, and fortunately with a fair supply of gunpowder and shot.

There was, however, still not sufficient for any night-long bombardment. James decided to let his day's grace include the night, twenty-four hours, no sign having come from the castle. It made a strangely peaceful interlude.

In the morning, the king went forward again, and ordered Mons Meg to be fired, one single shot, and this well to the south of the castle, as token. The reverberations had barely died away, amongst screaming of seafowl from the cliffs, when a white flag was run up on one of the battered towers.

"God be praised!" James declared. "They yield. It is enough. Now, for Angus!"

Eagerly they all waited. At length the clanking of the portcullis being raised and the drawbridge chains being lowered heralded the appearance of a small party, which came over towards them. None waiting, who knew Angus, could identify him in the group.

James frowned.

When they came up, the king said, "I called upon the Earl of Angus to yield to me. I do not see him."

"My lord of Angus is gone, Sire," a tall man of middle years replied.

"Gone! How mean you, gone?"

"My lord left. By night. By boat."

"Boat! How that? Do not seek to cozen me, sirrah!"

"It is the truth. We keep a boat at the foot of our cliff. Descend to it by ladder, rope-ladder. In the darkness, my lord left. This past night."

"A curse on him! Where? Where has he gone?"

"That I know not, Your Grace."

James turned to those with him. "Escaped us!"

"It may be but a device, Sire, a ruse," Bothwell said. "In hiding. Still in this castle."

"No. He is gone, I say. With his son, the master. They will be in Dunbar by now," they were told.

"Ha, so he went south! For England?" the king demanded.

"I know not."

"I still say that it could be a ruse," Bothwell insisted. "We should search this hold."

"We shall do that," James agreed. "Who are you, sir?"

"I am Douglas of Kilspindie, keeper here, Sire."

"Then you will conduct us round your castle. We shall see . . ."

Summoning forward a strong escort of armed men, just in case any attempt was made to hold them in the fortalice, James and some of his lords accompanied the Douglas back to the massive gatehouse tower and over the drawbridge. In through the tunnel-like access they went, watched by scowling men-at-arms, to emerge into a spacious area of courtyard flanked by lower buildings, and even open greensward beyond. Men were everywhere, some injured, and bodies lay, casualties of the bombardment. The visitors could now see the warships lying off at some distance.

James detailed some of his people to search the premises, the damage to which was very evident. He himself went to the very edge of the cliff-top, to gaze down. There some steps led to a ledge, and sure enough, two long rope-ladders hung, right down to the water far below. There was no sign of any boat, but it could be seen how one could slip away in darkness, keeping close to the cliff-foots, in accordance with Kilspindie's statement.

No trace of Angus or any other notables was found by the searchers, and James had to accept that his quarry had escaped him. He told Douglas of Kilspindie that

85

Tantallon was now forfeited to the crown, and he would send his commands as to what was to be done with it in due course. Then they went back to their army and encampment, in various states of mind: disappointment, questioning whither Angus would have gone, and whether the conspiracy could be said to be disposed of; that and thankfulness that there had been no battles.

All were not long in heading back westwards by south for Middleton Moor, for dispersal of the host. Also for some female company, for those fortunate enough to obtain it. David's Carrick men would get home in fair time for the harvest.

8

On the way back to Ayrshire, Janet revealed to her brother that a royal command had been issued. She was to attend court at Stirling. David would take her when he attended the parliament now called for in two weeks' time.

Riding side by side, David eyed his sister. "Attend? For how long?"

"He did not say."

"So-o-o. You understand what this means, lass?"

"Oh, yes. He would have me with him, biding with him, not just on his visits."

"His mistress-in-residence, as it were!"

"You could call it that, I suppose."

"And you are prepared to be that?"

"I love him."

"You are not hoping that he will wed you?"

"No. I see that as impossible for the king. He will have to have a loftier bride than Janet Kennedy. But I still can have his love."

"Is it love on his part? Not mere . . . desire? He has had a child by Mariot Boyd. And there is talk of his fancy for Drummond's daughter Margaret."

"I know it. But I believe that his fondness for me is . . . deeper."

"I would not have you disappointed, girl; used and then rejected. You must recognise that it may come to that. But, you are your own woman."

"Or James Stewart's! I believe that he will not mistreat me."

"I will have a word with him, when I take you to Stirling, then."

"Need you?"

They left it at that meantime.

Back at Cassillis and Dunure, their father was fairly urgent, for that man, in his questioning as to the Angus situation and the royal forfeiture of Tantallon. If such forfeit was to be extended to include all the earl's properties, what would be the position of those he had put in Janet's name as token and pledge for their betrothal? That young woman made it very clear what her wishes were with regard to that. He was interested also in Janet's summons to Stirling. Evidently he judged that if Archibald Bell-the-Cat was not to be a source of revenue, the monarch's infatuation might be turned into an alternative benefit. But wondered why David had been instructed to take her and attend the parliament at Stirling? *He* was Lord Kennedy and entitled to sit therein. His son could only shrug at that.

The neglected reconstruction of Cassillis Castle occupied them fully during the interval until the journey north to Stirling. They did not ride with their father, who in fact set off two days earlier.

David would have liked to go via Borthwick, although it was far from their most direct route, but decided that, since he could scarcely do it again on the return journey, it would be best to do it then, when he was alone, rather than on the way up, Janet possibly tending to distract Agnes overmuch. So they went the shortest route, east of Glasgow by Cumbernauld and Falkirk and through the Tor Wood, managing it in one long day.

They found the great citadel on its rock above the town full to overflowing, and the latter's houses in great demand for accommodation. David wondered where he would find quarters, in all this crowd for the parliament, although he had little doubt that Janet would find suitable lodging. But when, at length, they won into the royal presence, it was to discover favoured treatment for himself as well as for his sister.

After embraces, somewhat prolonged, for the young

woman, James turned to David. "I looked for you two days back, when your father arrived," he declared, all but reprovingly. "What delayed you?"

"We, we esteemed that Your Grace would be much occupied, engaged with all the preparations for the parliament," David said. "And we did not judge ourselves as important, nor required in this."

"There are more sorts of requirement than one!' It was at Janet that the monarch looked. But he turned back to her brother. "Forby, *you* are to advance in importance, my friend. You have proved to be of value to me in my efforts against Angus. On the West March, in especial. I have decided to appoint you to my Privy Council, so you will be attending this parliament in that rank. Moreover, since you it was who rallied much of Ayrshire to my cause, not your father the Lord Kennedy, who calls himself King of Carrick, I am making you *Bailie* of Carrick, to act for me there. I see no room for *two* kings in Scotland!"

David blinked his surprise, temporarily at a loss for words. Janet it was who spoke.

"You are kind, James," she said. "David will serve you well, that I know." So she was calling him James now.

"I hope so. I require sound men on whom I can rely."

"That you can be sure of, Sire. I am . . . grateful. And undeserving. But – I am unsure of what Bailie of Carrick means? What my duties as such will be?"

"Act my representative there, that is what. Ensure that my interests prevail, rather than any others."

That fairly evidently referred to Lord Kennedy. David wondered what his father would think of this. And a seat on the Privy Council, which *he* had not. Also it occurred to him that this royal favour would make it the more difficult for him to speak to the king about Janet's future. Could that have something to do with it all?

James went on. "The castle is full. I fear that you will have to share a room with Rob Bruce and Lord Maxwell. Come, Janet," and he took her arm.

Clearly that was dismissal. But at the door the king turned. "There will be a council meeting tomorrow. Before the parliament. Attend you it."

That evening, at a banquet in the great hall, David found himself ushered by one of the Lord Lyon's heralds to a seat, not on the dais admittedly, but much nearer to it than he had occupied hitherto, and higher than his father, whom he saw eyeing him stonily from further down the table. This was not going to improve relations between them.

When, to a trumpet fanfare, and all rising, James led in the dais party, with Janet close behind him, it was to be seen that Perkin Warbeck, alias the Duke of York, and the Lady Catherine Gordon, daughter of the Earl of Huntly, were amongst the select group, with her father. So here was another young woman to be used for political ends. Janet sat at the king's left, with Warbeck and his bride-to-be on the right, and the young Duke of Ross next, he seldom seen at such functions.

David found the company of Sir Robert Bruce congenial, less so the Lord Maxwell's. He had no contact with his sister that night.

In the forenoon he attended the Privy Council, feeling something of an interloper and eyed distinctly questioningly by the score or so of other members, including the Lord Maxwell. James did not introduce him in any way, and got down to business without preamble.

That business was mainly in preparation for the parliament the next day, and largely dealing with the late conspiracy situation. The word was, via Maxwell and his West March moss-troopers, that Angus was now over the border at Carlisle, in touch with Henry Tudor's emissaries. So the threat of uprising was by no means over. And he had been joined there by Sir John Ramsay, formerly Lord Bothwell, James the Third's unpleasing favourite, and a Sir Adam Forman, who were presumably replacing the arrested Earl of Buchan. That man, elderly, was waa reported to be ill at his Kinneddar Castle. What were they to do about Hearty James?

It was decided that, since he was the king's great-uncle, son of the late Queen Joan Beaufort's second husband, he ought to be left under house arrest and no further steps taken against him. But Angus was a different matter.

The councillors were almost unanimous in declaring that a major demonstration should be made of Scotland's anger over the ongoing threat and the English involvement, King Henry to be left in no doubt about it. A large army should muster and cross over into England, Cumberland preferably, Warbeck with them as claiming the English throne. They probably would not be able to capture Angus, but at least they should make the message clear: no meddling in Scotland's affairs, and no favours for traitors.

James accepted this, and all judged that parliament would almost certainly agree it on the morrow. Let the harvest-gathering-in be over, and then they would obtain the fullest turn-out of men.

Another matter arising was the replacement of Angus as Chief Warden of the Marches. Almost inevitably James proposed the Earl of Bothwell for this important position, none making other nomination. This gave him control of Hermitage Castle, also the stronghold of Lochmaben.

The third and final item for consideration was that of the coinage of the realm. The king's father and his favourites, particularly William Sheves, Archbishop of St Andrews, had grievously corrupted this for their own gain. It had to be rectified, and national confidence in moneys and trading restored. To end the discredit, bullion had to be imported, and this inevitably would be a costly matter, demanding taxes and levies, always unpopular for any parliament to pass. James promised a major contribution from the royal coffers. Reluctantly the other privy councillors acceded that they would have to follow the royal example, Bishop Elphinstone of Aberdeen, a man of great character, clearly anxious to restore the credit of Holy Church after the Sheves scandals, declaring that he would seek, from his fellow clergy, a substantial donation, possibly as much as two-thirds of the total cost. This at least went down well. David wondered what his father would say to it.

The meeting broke up, David not having contributed one word, although he had nodded not infrequently.

For the afternoon, James led some of the loftiest magnates on a boar hunt in the Flanders Moss, a favourite activity, David electing to stay with Janet and pay a visit to Cambuskenneth Abbey nearby, where Bruce had accepted the surrender of the captured English nobles after the victory of Bannockburn. It was a magnificent edifice, one more of David the First's foundations, having, unlike any other in Scotland, a tall and free-standing belfry tower and campanile of five storeys, dominating all that level terrain of the River Forth's serpentine meanderings. Here they encountered Bishop Elphinstone in consultation with the Augustinian abbot, apparently an old friend from college days in Glasgow, over the new university he was establishing at Aberdeen, which he was going to name King's College in salute to Scotland's young monarch, for whom he was Keeper of the Privy Seal. It was thought-provoking that they should be standing beside the burial place of the king's scholarly but feeble father, James the Third, and his Queen, Margaret of Denmark. The younger James, with his feelings of guilt over the death of his father, tended to avoid Cambuskenneth. The bishop congratulated David on his appointment to the Privy Council, and was courteous towards his sister, whatever he thought of her association with their liege-lord.

On the way back to the castle, Janet urged her brother not to pursue his suggested enquiry with James as to her future.

The parliament next day, the first David had attended as a member, he again sitting in a loftier seat than his father, as privy councillor, much interested him. It provided him with an insight into how the government of Scotland worked, as King-in-Parliament. This was where decisions were taken, whatever propositions were put forward or advised. What parliament voted for was to be enacted, whatever the Privy Council, the officers of state, the Convocation of Holy Church, earls or other influential bodies put forward. But the king had to be present or it was no parliament, only a convention, and, as the latter, could only recommend. Usually, to be sure, the advice of the Privy Council was accepted and passed, but by no means always.

The business was conducted by the Chancellor, presently the elderly Colin, Earl of Argyll, although it was the king who presided, from his throne. On this occasion there was in fact little of dispute amongst the ninety or so members. The situation anent England, despite its dangers and challenge, for a gesture in strength over the border, with Warbeck, once the harvest was in, was agreed to all but unanimously. The coinage revaluation and improvement aroused much more contention, few disagreeing that such was necessary but many doubts expressed as to how this should be implemented – not unnaturally, since this implied hands into pockets and purses. The king's proposed princely contribution was accepted without comment as suitable, in view of his father's depredations; but it was Bishop Elphinstone's urgings that the Church should provide two-fifths of the cost which engendered the most heat, the other bishops and mitred abbots, apart from that of Cambuskenneth, protesting. Holy Church, admittedly, owned almost half the best land in Scotland, and therefore the wealth, but its individual representatives were much concerned that *their* coffers should not be unduly burdened – and a quarter of the attenders there were senior clergy. But Elphinstone was eloquent, diplomatic and persuasive, but firm; and Sheves, the unpopular archbishop, did not put in an appearance, for reasons of his own. So the thing was eventually accepted, however dubiously. It remained for the earls, lords, and shire representatives, to commit themselves, this arousing still more debate and

93

protest, until the Provost of Edinburgh, speaking for the commissioners of the royal burghs, offered to put in half of the Church contribution, that is one-fifth of the total calculated cost. The lords were shamed into agreeing to play their part. So the matter was dealt with.

The issue of Bothwell's appointment to the wardenship of the Marches was not contested; but Sir William Douglas of Glenbervie and Braidwood objected to the Red Douglas lands in Dumfries-shire and elsewhere in the Borders being forfeited because of Angus's defection. This engendered much heat and some little alarm, on account of any possible combined Douglas uprising of Reds and Blacks. It was James himself who smoothed this out by agreeing that he would compensate for the forfeiture with other lands, notably the lordship of Kilmarnock.

Thereafter there were moves put forward by various individual members on such subjects as unfair taxation, trade monopolies, merchant-guild privileges, harbour-dues and the like, which all had to be voted upon. This took considerable time, and it was late before a hungry parliament adjourned, for another banquet at the castle. The voice of Scotland had spoken.

David had only a brief word with his sister before bed-going.

In the morning it was parting, for Janet was remaining at Stirling. He had not spoken with James, as he would have wished, but at the final leave-taking, with the king present, he did venture a careful word or two.

"My sister, Sire, is dear to me," he said. "Her welfare my concern. Since it seems that I am to leave her in Your Grace's keeping, I do so the more contentedly in the assurance that she will be well cared for and . . . esteemed." He had spent some hours of the night compiling that little speech.

"Have no fears, my friend. Janet means much to me also. You have my royal word that she will suffer no ill here. Go with an easy mind."

"I thank you, Sire. Her fondness for Your Grace is great, I know. Or, or . . ."

"It scarce can rival my fondness for her, then, Master of Kennedy!"

With that David had to be content, and took his departure. His father had already gone.

9

Needless to say, despite the call of the harvest at home, David did not take the direct route thither, Borthwick Castle his first objective. Lord Borthwick, little concerned with politics, had not attended the parliament, and Will had no cause to do so; but they were both eager to hear of the decisions made thereat, and the attitudes taken by the various magnates. Agnes was less so, more interested in Janet's situation and feelings, although her enquiries were tactfully put, for which David was grateful, as he found it difficult to discuss his sister's intimate association with their monarch.

But later, when the young woman went out into the small orchard between castle and church to collect plums, which were beginning to fall, and David took the opportunity to follow her and assist, she it was who returned to the subject, and quite frankly.

"Your sister, how does she see this interest in her by King James?" she asked. "Is she flattered by it? Or concerned that it will bring advantage? Or just unable to refuse a royal demand? Although, from what I have seen of Janet, she is not one to lack spirit, if so she feels it. Or is it just a useful device to escape the Earl of Angus's claims?"

"No, it is none of these," he told her. "The fact is that she has developed an affection for James Stewart, indeed she confesses that she loves him. It is a strange situation . . . but there it is."

"Loves? To love a king is not an easy road to follow, I think."

"She knows it. But love, true love, is not a matter of

96

reasoned thought, of careful choice, is it? She can be impetuous can Janet. But this, I think, is otherwise. Deep of feeling."

"It must be. For she must know that her love cannot bring her what true love merits, and craves. In a woman, at least. It is customary for kings to marry princesses."

"She knows it, yes. She is not looking for marriage."

"Her love must be deep indeed, then. Can she hope that he feels similarly? There is talk of this Margaret Drummond. And he already has a son by Mariot Boyd."

"Aye. James is . . . fond of women. But Janet accepts that. However much it concerns *me*."

"It does, David? You and your sister are notably close, I know."

"We always have been. Our father, a strange man, has seen to that!"

She eyed him, and touched his arm, unspeaking.

"I have spoken with James," he told her. "As best I could. He knows of my concern. And answered me that Janet meant much to him. And will no-wise suffer for her warmth towards him."

They picked their plums for a little in silence.

David wondered whether this might be the moment to express something of his own feelings, in an alternative direction.

"You, Agnes, will well understand another woman's feelings towards men, or for one man? You, so fair and, and desirable as you are, must have had many men at your door. I have told you of my caring. Do you, could you find some caring for me?"

"Did I not say that I liked you, David? That day on the Morthwaite Hills."

"Yes. And I was glad of it. But I seek more than liking, Agnes."

"How much more?" She did not even look at him as she asked that.

"All!" he said simply.

She went on picking the fruit. "All of what, is it? All

97

of my concern? My attentions? My person and woman's body? My own satisfaction and my desires? It is a large demand!"

"Large, yes. I know it. But . . . that is what I ask. However boldly, although I feel less than bold! It is *you* I seek. All."

She turned to eye him now, with that serenity of looks and bearing that he found both so compelling and attractive, and yet testing and unsettling.

"Is this a proposal of wooing? Or of marriage, even, David?" she asked quietly.

"It is. If, if you will consider it, yes. Or – am I over-bold?"

Still she stood there, plums in hand, seeming to study him. "Consider, indeed," she said at length. "This I will have to consider. Well. But, I thank you, David Kennedy, for your . . . esteem."

She picked two more plums, put them in her basket, took it up, and turned back for the castle.

They walked together, in silence, he relieving her of the basket.

But in the courtyard, mounting the steps to the first-floor doorway, she patted his wrist as she took back that basket.

That evening seemed endless to David, even though the talk was of vital matters, such as the forthcoming invasion of England, how far they would go in it, and the Borthwick contribution in men thereto, the likely reaction of King Henry, whether the Princess Margaret Tudor betrothal was still to be considered a possibility, and the like, men's talk, Agnes needleworking and, when it came to time for the night-time drink, helping this down with a lilting song accompanied on her clarsach.

Then it was bed-going, and the young woman, lighting an extra lantern, escorted their guest upstairs to his chamber, he wondering, wondering.

At the door he took a quick breath for, opening it, she preceded him within, not pausing there to wish him a goodnight as previously. Was this a good sign? Or the reverse: a preparation for a gentle rejection of his plea?

She went over to inspect and test the water of the steaming tub for his ablutions, setting down her lantern. Then turning to him, she stood for moments. Then held out both her arms towards him.

No words were needed, that gesture saying it all. With something between a panting of joy and a groan, David flung himself forward into those arms and clasped her to him, all but shaking her in his surge of emotion.

For long moments they stood there, embracing each other, unspeaking. Then the man pushed Agnes at arm's length from him, to gaze into her eyes.

"My dear one, my heart's darling!" he got out. "You will have me? You will? Agnes, love – here is joy! Joy!"

She nodded, still wordless, but her eyes were eloquent enough.

"You are to be mine. And I yours. One. One, to love and live, to hold and abide. To share each other, to keep each other, and to go on our way together, always! When I feared . . ."

"Dear David! Was there so much of fear? Did you not know, in your heart, that I was to be yours? Come to you for always. Would I have allowed myself to be with you, alone, trusted myself with you and to you, as I have done, had I not? Not felt more than friendship for you? That my love for you was there, waiting . . ."

"Love! You have said it! You love me, as I love you? How was I to know? But, but . . ." He pulled her back to him, and used his lips to better effect than to jerk ineloquent words. They kissed and kissed, she nowise averse.

Presently he led her over to the bed, where he sat her down. "I want you! I need you!" he declared. "When shall we wed?"

"Be not in over great haste, man of mine," she told him, but smiling. "We are promised, yes? So we can savour our gladness while we wait, wait for a little time . . ."

"Why wait, girl? *I* have waited sufficiently long!"

"Impatient! Are men ever so? There is joy in anticipation also, see you. Besides, are you not off to England with the king any day now? And who knows how long that going may last, alas? I wish . . . ! It may be *my* impatience that will be the sorest. While you men go blithely off to your warfare! Impatient and anxious. The women's part! To wait at home and dread . . ."

"I will come back to you, never fear. I have all to come back for, and will be no valiant fighter!" While he spoke, David's arms had been around her, and his hands not inactive, stroking, gripping, cupping her breasts. "James Stewart will have to seek fiercer warriors!"

"Perhaps he too will be anxious to get back to his woman, and so be the less warlike?" she suggested. "Let us hope so. As will your Janet." She turned a little, within his arms. "You have roving hands, David Kennedy!"

"I, I find much to, to discover! To enjoy. To treasure. You do not . . . mislike it?"

"Not . . . thus far. But I am unused to this, see you."

"Then learn not to be, lass." His busy hand had found that the neck of her bodice was less than tight, and fingers slipped within to the warm and generous roundness beneath, even as his lips sought hers again.

"You do not delay in claiming what will be yours one day," she managed to mumble through this demonstration of appreciation. "*One* day!"

"You mean . . . ? Not now? Not yet?"

"I mean that patience, my dear, can have its rewards. And the promise is assured. Leave something for the marriage night, no?" But she did not remove his hand from her bosom, which did stir beneath it.

So they sat together for some time which was indeed timeless, in close togetherness, while the washing-tub water cooled, even though the man's fervour did not, and his hands and lips found other enticements. At length Agnes rose, to rearrange her clothing. She held out her hand to have him on his feet also.

100

"The hour is late," she said gently. "We both have much to think on, ere we sleep. And you have much riding ahead of you on the morn. Or is it today? So . . ."

Reluctantly he rose, to follow her out, and up a further few steps to her own chamber, at the door of which David took a while to let her go.

It was indeed a long time before he slept that night.

10

David had little time, nor care, for his duties as Bailie of
Carrick – over which his father most certainly would be
gravely offended – what with the harvest being the all-
important concern, before the mustering of the Kennedy
support for the royal venture over the border. Fortunately
this year's was a good harvest for almost all Scotland, a
vital matter, since on its yield prosperity depended in a
land where there was very little of industry other than the
agriculture, stock-rearing and milling, fishing inevitably
only a coastal activity, and spinning and weaving being a
very minor preoccupation and mainly left to womenfolk.
So even the nobility and lairdly ones were much involved
in the harvesting process; and both Dunure and Cassillis
properties had many farms and rig-lands, and there was
much to supervise and direct in the score of days
before the coming of the king's messengers requiring
a sufficient rallying of Carrick men, horsed, and this
promptly, whatever the corn-cutting and ingathering.

Actually the word brought was unexpected, when it
came, in that the army was not to come through Ayrshire
on its way to the West March and Cumberland, as was
anticipated, but to assemble at some quite far-off place
called Ellemford, near to Duns, in the north of the Merse.
This was apparently because it was reported, through the
Lord Maxwell's informants, that Angus had left Carlisle
and was said to be at Durham, where an English force
was massing to contest any Scots invasion; word of that
had evidently reached King Henry, who no doubt had his
spies near the Scottish court. This news came from Janet
Kennedy, who had come south with James's courier to

await the royal return at Cassillis. She was in good form, and obviously happy, although, like Agnes, anxious about this military venture. She rejoiced with David over his betrothal, admitting that she could have foretold it.

She announced that there had been developments at Stirling. The King of Spain, Ferdinand, had sent an ambassador to suggest a marriage for one of his three daughters with James, this envoy, one Don Pedro de Ayala, a lively character who had stirred the rather solemn Scottish court and made a marked impact on James; indeed he had left to accompany the king on this English venture. James seemed nowise upset by this notion of a possible Spanish match – nor was Janet, for she understood that the eldest of the Infantas was only of fourteen years, which would pose little threat to her relationship with the monarch for some considerable time.

She also informed that James had sent heralds ahead of him over the border, since Henry apparently knew of the invasion intention, to proclaim that he desired no harm to any in England who would accept Richard, Duke of York as rightful monarch, and would pay allegiance to him. The crossing of the borderline had been changed from the West March to the East, because of the Durham rallying. Hence this assembling at Ellemford, on the way thither.

So David had to muster his busy harvesters at Maybole forthwith, which took a couple of days, and to set off with some two hundred of them north by east, to head by Cumnock for the headwaters of the River Ayr, and so over into Douglasdale on the long road to this Ellemford, a strange place, he judged, for a nation's army to gather. For the Carrick force it was a case of avoiding or circling ranges of hills all the way, crossing the entire southern uplands of Scotland from the west coast to the east, fully one hundred and thirty miles, three long days' riding.

The first night they reached the upper streams of the Douglas Water, amongst the Tinto and Culter Fells, near

Carmichael. Thereafter, rounding the southern extremities of the Pentland Hills, by Carnwath and Biggar, they won as far as the foothills of the Morthwaites, near where David had ridden with Agnes. There was no avoiding this range, but steep as were its slopes and narrow its valleys, there was no great width to it all, unlike their next challenge, the Lammermuirs, which although more rounded and less demanding, covered hundreds of anything but square miles, sheep-strewn.

It was on the upper headstreams of the Whiteadder, in this green wilderness, that they came upon the lumbering train of cannon, making but heavy going of it behind plodding teams of oxen, David for one surprised that artillery was being brought to this endeavour, and which would greatly delay progress. Presumably there was reason for this, although the grumbling cannoneers did not know what.

They left these behind and pressed on down to the Whiteadder itself. Why that river was termed white water they did not know either, for it was more peat brown and not particularly fast-running as to create foaming falls.

It was at a major widening of this river, where another joined it amongst the south-facing foothills, that they came to the ford at Ellem, where there was a sufficiency of levellish ground to allow a large host to assemble and encamp. Here indeed was the army, but not all of it, for James himself had gone on ahead with perhaps a quarter of the total. Will Borthwick was there with his people, and informed that this was not just impatience on the king's part but a desire to be seeming to head for his force to cross Tweed at Berwick, and so to have the English massing to hold that difficult passage, whereas the Scots would really cross much further up-river, at Coldstream, twenty miles west, towards which he and his company would swing off, unseen, to take that ford and ensure an unopposed crossing for the main army. This sounded good tactics. But what were the cannon for? Will explained that these were to go on towards Berwick, and there set up a bombardment, mainly mere powder and noise, this to preoccupy the Berwick defenders and prevent them from heading off westwards, with the Scots army presumably following the cannonade. This too seemed to make good sense. David's third question was why had this Ellemford been chosen as assembly point in the first place, to be told that a remote and unexpected venue was desirable in order that the Tudor's spies should not be able to learn details as to numbers, routes and intentions.

They waited there for two nights, with companies arriving from far-off areas, even the cannon-train. The Lindsay Earl of Montrose had been left in charge of this gathering, and in due course he gave the order to march.

Now, out of the hills they went, past Duns town into the Merse proper, due southwards by Gavinton, reaching another river, the Blackadder, on to Swinton and Hirsel for Coldstream, leaving the cannon to go on towards Berwick. This made comparatively easy riding, after all the hill country, and they covered the thirty miles or so in good time. They found the king's party already there, on both sides of wide Tweed, and so were able to cross the long ford into England without any other problems but watery ones. Whether it was all James's own notion, or his advisers', it made for excellent strategy.

In the morning of 20th September the army moved on into Northumberland. David was interested to meet the envoy, Don Pedro de Ayala, a big and burly character, quite unlike his preconceived ideas as to Spaniards, dark admittedly but genially hearty, jovial, all but rumbustious, and looked on somewhat askance by some of the Scots nobles. But James obviously found him to his taste; and David got the impression that he was shrewder than he seemed. Presumably King Ferdinand had thought so also. Compared with him, Perkin Warbeck appeared a mere nonentity, however lofty his ambitions. It seemed that he had promised to cede Berwick-upon-Tweed back to Scotland if he gained his objective, the English throne.

The advance through Northumberland, avoiding the great castle of Wark, by the River Till, had James's heralds going ahead to announce to the local folk that here came the King of Scots, with their own rightful monarch, Richard, Duke of York, no harm intended to any so long as they paid due allegiance to him instead of to the usurping Welshman Tudor. Despite this, however, the people, in the main, fled before the advancing army with such of their flocks and herds as they could quickly gather, to take refuge in castles and towers such as Twizel and Duddo and Etal and Ford. It was no part of James's intention to assail such strengths, lacking artillery; they could do little harm at his back without major English reinforcement. To ensure that this did not happen, he detached perhaps one-third of his strength, under Montrose again, to head eastwards, roughly in the Berwick direction, to form a barrier to protect his rear, and his return in due course, and to keep an eye on those castles. Will Borthwick's company were sent with the duke, but David's remained with the main body, which pressed on southwards.

That first night in England they camped near Wooler. So far no blood had been shed, however much cattle had been slaughtered to provide food. As well as heralds, scouts were sent out well ahead to spy out the land. James at least was satisfied with progress. But some of his nobles were not, declaring that this was no way to challenge the Tudor. They ought to be attacking towers, sacking villages and townships, using good steel on the Auld Enemy, not parading as though on a friendly progress through their own land.

In the morning, a messenger came from Montrose's force, to announce that they had managed to take and destroy Twizel and Duddo Castles, and had made an example of their occupants, to warn off any enemy attack from eastwards, so the king's rear was safe. This pleased the more aggressive lords, but it had the unexpected result of much upsetting Warbeck, who declared that death and destruction was no way to win him the favour of his would-be subjects, and this must stop. James tended to agree with him, but few of the leadership did, and the two attitudes were less than advisable for an army invading hostile territory.

This conflict of views was the more emphasised when, having to avoid the high and intrusive ground of Cheviot, the army made a detour from the Till and reached Heaton, a community with the same name as that of the Scots village near Kelso, none so far to the north. And here they met with their first real opposition. Presumably these Heaton people had had time to be warned of the Scots approach, and to gather; or it may have been that the master of Heaton Castle was of a warlike character. At any rate, his folk attacked and slew some of the small advance party which James ever maintained ahead of the main force. The survivors hastened back to report. And vehement was the impact on the more militant of the royal company, especially on the Border moss-troopers, permanently in a state of war with their opposite numbers. Vengeance and assault on village and castle resulted, not at the king's behest, who had pressed on with some of his leaders. This tower-house was no great strength, and was taken, sacked and burned, some of its people being hanged from its shattered windows as example to others who might be like-minded.

The effect of this incident, in itself no unusual happening in the Borderland, was extraordinary. For Perkin Warbeck was enraged, claiming that it made a mockery of all that he stood for, the slaughter of his subjects-to-be on their own property. He had come for a demonstration of his rightful claims to the throne, not combat and destruction. And when most of the Scots nobles laughed him to scorn, the Pretender there and then turned and rode off whence they had come, accompanied by a few of his supporters. James was astonished and put out by the entire proceedings, and Pedro de Ayala laughed uproariously.

It was not for the King of Scots, of course, to hurry back after the offended Warbeck and seek to placate him.

So he was left to go where he would. The royal army moved on, in mixed wonder, displeasure and amusement, David Kennedy not alone in finding it all astonishing. Warbeck he would have expected to be less critical and more appreciative.

They got as far as Coupland by next noon, where there was another castle that looked sufficiently strong to warrant avoidance, when a messenger arrived from the north-east, from Montrose. This was to announce that the earl had warning that a large English force was advancing from Newcastle, presumably that which had been assembling at Durham, many thousands strong; and if it maintained its present direction it was come between the two Scots forces, which could be disastrous. What did His Grace desire? That he and his should come south-westwards to join the main army? Or the king to come back north-eastwards to him? James did not take long to decide. Probably affected by the disharmony amongst his leadership, he declared that he had made a sufficient demonstration towards the Tudor, and that they should forthwith turn back to rejoin Montrose, and then home. This also provoked some criticism, although not from most of the rank and file.

So it was a prompt return to the Till valley and on towards Berwick, that messenger guiding them to Montrose's present base in the Shoresdean area. It was something of a relief, to David at any rate, to join up with their colleagues, especially when they learned that the English army was reported to be none so far off, in the Belford vicinity. Although some of his lords urged James to find a strong position on some hill, possibly Branxton Edge, and wait for the English to come to grips, not to scuttle away, the king felt that he had done all that he set out to do. They would return northwards, cross Tweed where they had done so earlier, and wait on the far bank in case the enemy thought to make some counter-invasion. If nothing such eventuated, then home, their gesture made.

Will Borthwick reported to David that this sector of the army had been considerably more militant than had the main body, having destroyed quite a number of tower-houses and small communities and not spared hostile inhabitants. As well that Warbeck had not remained with them.

Northwards all went, then, and crossing Tweed in due course, halted on the Scots side, drew up in strength and sent parties east and west to watch out for possible attempts at English crossings elsewhere. Two days they waited, with no sign of the opposition, and it was reckoned that no invasion was envisaged into Scotland. All could retire northwards – but be prepared for a sudden recall should circumstances demand it.

David elected to take his Carrick contingent home by the most direct route from Coldstream, namely on up the great river for many a long mile almost to its headwaters on Tweedsmuir, and so over the Culter fells into upper Clydesdale, and west by south to Ayrshire, a two-day journey not three. James charged him to see that Janet was returned to Stirling at the earliest, suggesting that he should bring her himself, for he was very welcome at court; and, after all, if his father was King of Carrick he could surely look after that lordship adequately for a while, lacking his eldest son. So much for being Bailie of Carrick.

It had been an odd invasion of England, but at least there had been no Carrick casualties, and very few of other Scots.

11

At Stirling, in due course, they found that Perkin Warbeck had already departed, for Ireland apparently, whether of his own choice or of the king's will was not clear, possibly both. At any rate, few regretted it, for he had become something of a liability, was less than popular, and with so little prospect of future advancement. He had left announcing that he would raise an army in Ireland, then invade England, probably through another of the Celtic areas, either Cornwall or Wales, and he trusted that the Scots would again, then, cross the borderline in his favour.

Despite the monarch's welcome at court, and Don Pedro's urgings for David to remain, he seeming to find him companionable, he did not remain long at Stirling, with other matters on his mind. Borthwick called.

He had left Will with a message for his sister, that he would be back just as soon as he might, and he was not going to fail in that. Agnes was not to be left in any doubt as to his need for her.

Her greeting of him was warm, and although less demonstrative than his own, had a calm assurance about it which in no way disappointed his eager masculinity. She was his and he was hers, this accepted by them both, and she made no objections to his prompt enquiries, indeed all but demands, as to marriage. When? How soon?

"How soon do you desire it, David?" she asked. "What preparations are you to make? Are weeks required? Or months?"

"Days!" he declared.

"Ha, impatient, still! And I must heed the masterful

Master of Kennedy! Time, delay, is not to be considered? But women, see you, have to consider times and seasons for any wedding, even if men do not. Especially months."

"Months, girl? *Months*, you say!"

She smiled. "Not delay for months, no – never fear. But women have monthly problems, as you must know. And such should not spoil a marriage night, no? So, we must heed it."

"M'mmm. I . . . yes, I see it. And, and . . . when?"

"Well, demanding one, since you ask, I can be your woman in, shall we say, five or six weeks. Or—"

"Five or six! Save us, all that? But . . . monthly, you say. So, why not before? A month is only *four* weeks, is it not?"

"Before the five or six? That would mean, if I calculate aright, all but at once. Within the week!"

"Why not? Days, I said. And meant it."

She shook her fair head over him, but not exactly negatively. "Are you always impatient, David my dear? Am I to wed such a hasty man? Not only demanding but headstrong, rampant?"

"Impatient for *you*, yes, lass. Can you not understand? You are promised to me. Must I wait and wait? All the time since last I saw you, all the time away with the king, I have been waiting, wanting you, needing you. And now you speak of five or six weeks!"

"Poor David. You think me cruel? I would not have that. But, within a week? Is that possible?"

"Why not?" he repeated. "You have a parish priest here at Borthwick. And a church. Your father will not say me nay? What more do we need? Only the will. *I* have it. Have not you?"

She eyed him with that calm regard, so steady yet so gentle, warm. "In this your will must be mine," she said. "Yes, then; if so you would have it, so be it. Hasty weddings are apt to be for . . . different reasons! But let folk think what they will! My father esteems you, so he will not seek to deny us, I judge. And Will, of course, rates you highly."

"Then I will ask Lord Borthwick this night, my love." He drew her to him. "You are the most wonderful creature that the good Lord ever fashioned!"

"Scarcely that, I fear . . ." Then her lips were sealed.

Later, Lord Borthwick raised his eyebrows when presented with David's so urgent request, but voiced no actual objection nor displeasure, so long as it all could be arranged in time.

While most of these arrangements considered necessary for a wedding appeared to be required on the female side, with David wanting it all to be as simple as possible, on enquiry he did admit that he would like to have his sister Janet with them on this so special occasion, if that could be contrived. The rest of the family would not be greatly interested, he judged, and their coming take a deal of organising; but Janet was different. So, with the event proposed for five days hence, he decided to ride to Stirling on the morrow, and seek to fetch her back, James surely not objecting. Will Borthwick agreed to return her to the king thereafter, the bridegroom being by then otherwise preoccupied.

That night, at bed-going, David was even more eager than heretofore, asserting at his chamber door that betrothed and all but united in will and spirit as they now were, some further recognition of the fact was surely not only allowable but suitable. Agnes saw it rather differently, pointing out that four more nights, alone, would only make the fifth the more significant, joyful and fulfilling. However, compromise being accepted, they entered the room together; and that young woman did not get out again for some considerable time, after much fondling and caressing and exploration, her submission thereto being amusedly tolerant while yet retaining the ultimate controls. For a reasonably moderate and considerate man, David Kennedy was, in this respect and situation, distinctly importunate, aware of it himself, yet mastering some of it only with an effort. Nevertheless, when Agnes managed not so much to escape as to remove herself from his embraces not unkindly, she went to her own room in no state of apprehension for the future, the reverse indeed.

Leaving her busy, David's fifty-mile ride had an unexpected end to it, in that when Janet heard about the wedding and declared herself more than ready to attend it, James Stewart himself announced that he would accompany her on this occasion, and be glad to. Astonished that the King of Scots should consider being present at his nuptials, David was a little disconcerted, even though it was probably only an unlooked-for opportunity for the monarch to get away with his lady-love for two or three days without the ever-present collection of courtiers and attendants. Hoping that this royal presence would not in any way interfere with the bliss he was looking forward to, he indicated his wonder at it, even though his sister did not. James, however, told them that it was entirely right that he should present himself at Borthwick for this notable event, for had not the present lord's grandsire, those sixty years ago, done a great service to his own great-grandsire, James the First, by acting as hostage for his ransom, being held as prisoner in England for two years while the great sum of money was collected and paid? The crown owed the Borthwicks some recognition of this, to be sure, apart altogether from him being present at a friend's marriage.

Oddly, Don Pedro de Ayala, obviously now very close to the king, asked to be allowed to come also.

So the next day, the return journey to Lothian was made in very different style. However much James might wish to have Janet to himself, the King of Scots could not ride all that way without the required royal guards as escort. He, with David and Janet and the Spaniard, could proceed ahead some distance, but always behind came the escorting troop. What the Borthwicks would think of this invasion, at such a time, was uncertain.

The four of them, however, made a cheerful ride of it,

Janet very much setting the pace, in more ways than one, David noted.

Their evening arrival at Borthwick did produce something of an upheaval, needless to say, amidst the preparations for the day after the morrow. But Agnes had evidently inherited something of her serenity from her father, who took it all with a calm acceptance, however excited were the four younger members of his family. If his elder daughter was likewise affected, she did not show it. She declared herself delighted to have Janet as her bridesmaid. Looking after the royal escort and arranging a day's hawking in the Morthwaites for the royal entertainment kept brother Will busy.

There were no private bedtime intimacies that night for the betrothed couple, Don Pedro keeping the men at least up until a late hour with his lively and intriguing anecdotes and revelations about life at the courts of Christendom, with which he was apparently familiar.

Janet and Agnes did not accompany the sportsmen next day, with other unspecified matters to see to. David for one wondered what.

The hawking proved very successful; but James was more interested in the landscape, he never having been in these Morthwaite Hills before, or nearer than Middleton Moor. They got as far as the Heriot and Gala Waters, he surprised that this modest stream should be the same as gave name to the typical Borders town of Galashiels almost a score of miles away.

Again there was no opportunity for David and Agnes to exchange confidences that last evening of their single state, she having to act hostess to the distinguished visitors. It was October now and chilly of an evening, with all glad to sit round a blazing log fire in the great hooded fireplace of one of the finest halls in all Scotland, while being entertained from the minstrels' gallery aloft, Don Pedro contributing. The parish priest, a young man only recently appointed, and distinctly diffident over the company he was now keeping, was one of the guests.

114

So the great morning for David dawned, after a wakeful night. The ceremony was not to be until the early afternoon, and the bridegroom at least was uncertain as to how to fill in the time, with hunting, hawking and the like scarcely suitable. However, Will suggested an archery contest, and the men accepted this as fair enough, with Don Pedro, when David failed to register the most accurate shots, shouting jovially that he would have to get closer to his target that night.

The waiting seemed endless, but at last it was over, and a move made by the menfolk to the church, this only a few hundred yards from the castle. There was no large company present, a few Borthwick cousins from Crookston, Soutra and Glengelt arriving, much impressed to see the monarch there. Will was to act groomsman. The young cleric was even more nervous than he had been the night before.

They had not overlong to wait for the bridal train, with David and his friend standing up at the chancel steps, little more assured than was the celebrant. Lord Borthwick led Agnes up to stand beside the young men, she looking anything but apprehensive, the picture of tranquil and fair femininity, clad in white satin trimmed with gold lace to complement her yellow hair, the upstanding collar of her gown rimmed with Tay pearls. David caught his breath at the sight of her, even though the visiting Borthwicks were apt to be distracted by Flaming Janet, looking dazzling and more challengingly beautiful, just behind. Agnes's small smile for her groom was warmly reassuring.

It is to be feared that despite all the glamour and excellence, or partly because of it, the priest made a less than confident ritual of the nuptials, at first at least, although he recovered his poise somewhat as the brief service proceeded, perhaps the bride's aura of quiet confidence in him and in it all having a calming effect. At any rate, all the essential features of the service were got through without more than occasional verbal stumbles.

As for David, he was scarcely aware of all this, his mind

going partially blank, critical faculties suspended. All he knew was that here he was being made one with Agnes, somehow or other, his heart's desire fulfilled even though his body's was not yet so. The means thitherto were not of his concern.

With the ring-placing fumblingly effected, and with a little squeeze of female fingers to acknowledge it, they were proclaimed man and wife. It was all but in a daze, after the final benediction, that he led his new-made other half arm-in-arm down the aisle of the quite small church, and out, to the congratulations of all, his sister foremost and the king supporting her heartily. There, in front of them all, Agnes kissed him lingeringly, as her own seal and promise, and David Kennedy more or less returned to normal control of his wits. It was done. She was his and he was hers, for now and for eternity. He laughed aloud, for the first time that day.

The day, however, was by no means done, although he could have wished it so. There were hours, many hours, to get through before he could claim his new-found husbandly rights. If the forenoon had seemed endless, the afternoon and evening appeared more so, the feasting, the speech-making, the entertainment and the jollifications interminable. But David could not seek to curtail it all, in the bride's father's house, so suffer it he must. But he did have his say, in the end, when Don Pedro proposed the bedding exercise. This David had heard of, and in no way would have it carried out, however popular it might be elsewhere; for it consisted of the wedding guests conveying the bride and groom to their bedchamber, the men then undressing the wife and the women her husband, and then carrying them on to the bridal couch, there to ensure that the unity was duly enacted if not actually consummated, before leaving the couple to their own devices. Here the line was to be firmly drawn, David made entirely clear, and undoubtedly Agnes's relief was great.

They said their goodnights to all, to the accompaniment of much good and even detailed advice, and hand in hand set off up the tall, narrow stairway, wordless now. The night was their own.

The door closed on them, Agnes went over to the fire which blazed welcomingly, with the usual tub of steaming water for washing nearby, and stood, looking down into the flames. At her back, David drew a deep breath.

"At last!" he said thickly.

She did not turn. "At last, yes; for myself also, my husband. We are joined together now, to our betterment, surely? I think none the worse for the waiting? Although . . . although however much I rejoice, I still have some doubts, my dear . . ."

"Doubts, woman! You doubt it all, now? Our marriage?" He came over, to clasp her to him, almost fiercely. "After . . . all!"

She turned in his arms. "Not you, my love. No doubts there. Only that I may . . . disappoint. You have waited for this for so long. And I, I may not come up to your expectations. I am a simple woman, ordinary, and inexperienced in the matters of men. So . . . I wonder."

"You! Ordinary! Simple! Lord, lass, do you know what you are saying? You are the most wonderful, most desirable, most adorable woman ever created! I have told you so, have I not? *You*, to doubt yourself!"

"It is, I think, your sister Janet! She is so beautiful, so remarkable. And I know how fond you are of her, how close. I fear that I may not measure up to her, David." She sighed; but even as she said it, she showed a poise and innate assurance such as to belie her words.

Words – he had had enough of words. He all but shook her, standing there by the fire, before his hands began to run over her warm person.

Agnes nodded understandingly, and easing herself from his grasp, began to undo her bodice, eyes on his.

"No!" he jerked. "No. It is *my* privilege this night. To do this." And he pushed her hands away, to take over the delectable task, she shaking her head over him

117

but not denying him, indeed aiding him where expertise failed him.

It did not take long before all her fine clothing lay dropped on the floor and she stood naked, there in the flickering firelight, sheer loveliness personified. Holding his breath, he stepped back to gaze. She did not seek to hide any of herself, though by no means making any actual display, just stood there for him, his for sight and for taking.

David did not delay overlong, delight in what he saw notwithstanding. Wordless, he went to her, to hug all that soft but firm delight of warm femininity to him, hands touching, feeling, stroking, caressing, while he kissed her hair, her brow, her lips, her long graceful neck, hungrily at first and then more lingeringly, appreciatively, as he moved down from her fine shoulders to those full and shapely breasts, the nipples firm to his lips and tongue, the division between their rounded symmetry its own warm concern for him. Then further, to areas that he had not hitherto reached, to the gentle swelling of her belly with its demanding navel hollow asking for his attention, and so to the reddish-gold triangle between her loins, that especial area for men which, in contrast to all the soft, smooth, enticing flesh, was yet the very key to ultimate bliss, and to be relished accordingly.

He was down on his knees now, however masterful he seemed, on her discarded clothing, and turning her round, he stroked and savoured her moulded buttocks, firmly flexible as was the rest of her, before his lips moved on down her long thighs and calves, both sculptured to his relish, right to her feet. All the while Agnes stood, a hand stroking his hair, her person not exactly heaving but stirring a little at his attentions, the murmured word now and again far from discouraging him.

When at length he rose to his feet, and his busy lips sought hers, she moistening them with her tongue after all their activity, he abruptly half stooped to pick her up bodily and to carry her over to the bed awaiting them, a luscious armful without being any mere featherweight.

"The water!" she gasped, her first protest. "Washing, no?"

"No! That can . . . wait!"

Placing her on top of the blankets, the sight of her lying spread before him in the lamplight and firelight, had him bending for comprehensive kissing, until he felt her hands groping for the buttons of his doublet. He nodded, unspeaking, and straightened up, to start wrenching off his garments, she, after the merest token of assistance, lying back and shaking her head at his haste and at the difficulty he was having over the getting rid of his breeches in these circumstances. Inexperienced Agnes Borthwick might be, but she was all woman, and was intrigued and responsive to what she saw, and by no means looked away. Kicking off the last of his clinging gear, David flung himself on to the bed beside her, grasping, fondling, possessing, and quickly was on top of her, that so warm and enticingly available person.

It is to be feared that the man, as so frequently is the case, and despite the best of intentions, found his masculinity more forceful than his will, and did not exhibit all the gentle care which circumstances really called for with a woman who had told him that she was inexperienced. Not that she made complaint at his so urgent seeking of entry into her most intimate self, gasping a little as was not to be avoided when he achieved it. And thereafter accepted the vehemence of the all too brief assault on her femininity with even signs of tentative reaction of her own. But it was all too hurried for any real satisfaction, even for the man, as with a groan he collapsed on her, suddenly spent and muttering apologies.

Agnes stared up at the bed canopy and bit her lips. Had she failed him somehow?

When, thereafter, as he lay at her side now, deep breathing, and she put her doubts into halting words, he was not so physically and emotionally spent as not

119

to be able to assure her that the fault was his own, by no means hers, that he had just been overlong in the waiting and his male body had foiled him. But, give him time, just a little time, and he would do better, give *her*, and himself, some satisfaction. It would not be long, he thought that he could promise.

She squeezed his arm, and lay there silent.

He was as good as his word, in this at least. After only a few minutes of quiet his breathing became more normal, and David's hand came over to gently touch and finger the moist area he had so recently invaded. Then, as she stirred, he was on top of her again, murmuring fondnesses.

And now he was able to take his time and to nurse her into not only compliance but sympathetic response, he kissing her breasts and stroking her variously the while. And presently her breathing became deeper, faster, and he felt her fingernails digging into his back. And then, with a moaning shudder, as he maintained his rhythmic attentions, Agnes achieved fulfilled womanhood, heaving under him in an access of attainment, eyes shut, lips parted. So he could let go of his own held-back reserves, thankfully.

Soon they were able to kiss, deeply, and she opened her eyes and smiled that serene smile which he loved.

"Sleep now, my heart," he told her. "Sleep awhile. And we shall savour each other again. When we have rested. The night is young yet. And we are only at . . . the beginning."

Before that October dawn, they proved that David spoke truth again. And Agnes Borthwick proved that she was all woman indeed.

12

In the morning, with the happy couple deserving of some privacy to celebrate their union, Lord Borthwick had arranged for them to go off alone to one of his smaller properties, Hartside, near to Oxton, none so far off, where they could be reached readily if need be, for the king was very much aware that their recent incursion into England might well result in reprisals, and it might be necessary to summon his forces to arms again at short notice, and Carrick was a useful and reliable rallying ground.

At least David did not have to escort Janet back to Stirling.

So the pair of them, exchanging formal wear for more casual gear, headed off thankfully, with a plentitude of good wishes and more good advice, for the area where the Morthwaite foothills linked with those of the Lammermuirs, some ten miles to the south-east, under the fairly prominent Hartside Hill. This was to be only a brief interlude, for David was eager now to introduce his wife to her new home at Cassillis, and which, as he told her, required a woman to manage it now that Janet was gone.

Hartside proved to be no castle, only a smallish hallhouse, remotely sited but on the original Roman road of Dere Steet, in very much upland country. Agnes knew it well, and David not at all. They would have four days of quiet togetherness and leisurely exploration, then off to Ayrshire.

It turned out to be the happiest time of the man's life, to date, sheer joy, time utterly unimportant, doing what they would, often nothing at all save loving each other, being looked after unobtrusively by a motherly creature who confessed to being the illegitimate offspring of a former Borthwick, this all in golden October weather, crisp of morning and evening up in these hilly parts, but the slanting sunlight bringing out the rich autumnal colours of bracken and fading heather, birch and rowan leaves. Agnes took David to see the remains of the great and far-flung hospital area of Soutra, now but open plateau, he astonished at the size of it all. Also to the isolated ruins of what was known as the Resting House, nothing to do with the hospital, on an extension ridge of Clints Hill, which she explained had formerly been the monks' halfway house on their frequent journeys from Melrose to Edinburgh's abbey of the Holy Rood, and back, using the Roman route before the lower Lauderdale road was created; long walking for the brothers, the legend being that such of these as deserved punishment for clerkly failings got sent here by the Abbot of Melrose to keep this outlandish halting place in good order. They inspected various Pictish settlements and stone circles, discussed the reasons for their sitings, sometimes mounted but more often afoot, for Agnes proved to be good at walking – but none of all this in any sort of hurry or of effort, save for the act of hill-climbing itself. And time mattered nothing.

But time, in the guise of four blissful days and nights, did send them away on the long road to Carrick, after a call back at Borthwick for sundry items of clothing and personal use which Agnes would require at Cassillis. Thereafter they had to halt overnight at Carmichael, somewhat delayed by the pack-horse carrying their luggage, but they had a friendly reception there below Tintock Tap. Agnes had never been to Ayrshire, and next day was interested in all that she saw, observing that it was somehow very different from Lothian, even though a similarly placed county, with a firth shore, the Clyde instead of the Forth, seamed with river valleys widening into vales from the enclosing hills. What made the difference? Something to do with the background of

Arran's great purple mountains, the western light, the warmer Atlantic seas and the richer woodlands?

Cassillis Castle, when reached, much impressed her, so different also from that of Borthwick, less tall and massive, yet strong enough, solid, challenging in its own way. The alterations and additions work was now all but complete, and the young woman was greatly taken with the extraordinary wide stair newel in especial. She had been told about this, but she had not clearly visualised it, with its slits and internal little steps and lamp brackets. David was rather absurdly proud about this.

After a couple of days, he took her to visit the Kennedy family at Dunure, she exclaiming over the cliff-top hold above the waves, and the savage coastline and screaming seafowl. Lord Kennedy was civil but nothing more, expressing no surprise at his heir's wedding; David had made no secret of his intentions in the matter. The young people greeted their new sister-in-law much more kindly, obviously liking what they saw. Agnes had been interested, even concerned, over this odd family with its divisions, and was determined in no way to exacerbate the separation. Her quiet composure had its effect here also.

They did not stay at Dunure overnight, however.

Agnes proved herself to be more of a housekeeper than had Janet, and was soon making her mark on the Cassillis establishment, not assertingly changing things but unobtrusively rearranging, adjusting, improving, David only vaguely aware of this although sometimes noticing and acclaiming. He had much to see to himself, outwith the house, with his farms, herds, tenants, mills and the like; also the visiting of the lordship's lairds and landholders, to warn them of possible demands from the king at any time.

As well that he did, for only ten days after their arrival the word came from Stirling. The English had made a major sally over the border, into the East March from Berwick, burning, slaying and ravaging much more savagely than had been their own incursion into Northumberland, coming as far north as Duns, which town they had sacked before retiring. So now retaliatory measures had to be taken, and another assembly at Ellemford was ordered.

Agnes, shaking her head over all this, wondered what good this sort of ding-dong raiding and aggression was doing for either side. Must it be like this? Would not a truce, peace, benefit both realms, especially the common people of the assailed areas who had to bear the brunt of it? David acceded that it all seemed counter-productive; but the English had all down the ages sought to dominate Scotland, even take it over, and this reaction seemed to be called for, inevitable.

Home-coming for him, then, was short-lived indeed, with the royal call to answer. He felt that probably it was too soon to leave Agnes alone at Cassillis, but she insisted that she remained. This was now her home, as well as his, and her duty and pleasure was to keep it well looked-after and secure for his return to it, not so? She did accompany him as far as Maybole, however, for one more assembly of disgruntled Carrick men, before they parted. Ellemford did not exactly call aloud to them all.

Inevitably they were amongst the last of the contingents to arrive at the muster, James impatient to be off, although he welcomed David in friendly fashion and regretted that new-wed bliss had to be thus interrupted. Don Pedro, again with him, made intimate enquiries.

Lord Maxwell's Galloway people arrived next morning, and the move southwards was made forthwith. They were heading not for Coldstream this time but for further west, to be able to cross Tweed, which could now very well be guarded on the English side, but where both banks were in Scotland, and the borderline swung away south-westwards along the line of the Cheviot summits. They would penetrate and thread those heights by the long Bowmont Water valley, and so into Northumberland by the back door as it were. James was wondering whether, if further raiding was still called for, he might make use of his accord with the Islesmen and have them make a sea assault on the Cumbrian coastline, something which the English would find it difficult to counter or retaliate to. John of Islay or Alexander of Lochalsh might well find this to their taste.

From Ellemford to Edenmouth, where they were to cross Tweed, was only some thirty miles, avoiding shattered Duns, by Longformacus and the Dirrington Hills to the edge of the Merse at Polwarth Moss, and then by Greenlaw and Hume. They made it easily in one day, shorter as these were getting. Edenmouth, where that river joined Tweed, was a mere five miles east of Kelso, and a couple, at the other side, from where the greater river became the border. There was a wide ford here, shallowed by pebbles brought down by the Eden, and over this they crossed unopposed, indeed the terrain on the south side all but empty. They were able to get as far as Lempitlaw before darkness halted them, James well satisfied. Word of this advance could scarcely have reached Berwick or Tillmouth by this time. So they ought to gain a clear access through to the Kilham and Kirknewton areas of Northumberland.

They entered the valley of the Bowmont Water next forenoon. This was quite a major river, unusual in rising in Scotland but ending up in England, where it joined the Till, meantime threading its round-about way through the high Cheviots. They joined it at Yetholm, still in Scotland, two villages, one on each side of the river, with steep hills flanking both. Here the army turned almost due north, strange as this might seem, for the Bowmont did not make its great bend eastwards for another six miles, by which time it was well into England. Owing to the narrowness of the valley, inevitably now the Scots force became much strung out. Scouts were well ahead, however, and no surprise or ambush was to be anticipated.

Two miles on, and under Shotton Hill, they rode into England, although there was nothing to mark the borderline, and conditions remained the same, save for the feeling that they were satisfactorily now into the Auld Enemy's territory, and without having had to fight their way.

This gratification however lasted only for another three miles or so, when a couple of their scouts returning to them in haste brought news that changed all. The Prince-Bishop of Durham, more warrior than divine, had been sent north by the Tudor to his own fortress-castle of Norham, to make it the rallying point for a large-scale invasion of Scotland. Already there was a sizeable gathering there, presumably largely from Berwick; but they were waiting for the Earl of Surrey, England's foremost commander, to arrive with a major host.

These tidings had the king and his advisers much concerned, needless to say, plans having to be drastically changed. Next to Berwick itself, Norham was the greatest English stronghold of the Borderland, with its own ford of Tweed, this hitherto avoided by the Scots for good reason. And Surrey was a name to fear. This, then, would be no mere gesture in the manoeuvring between the two nations, but outright warfare. The scouts had been unable to glean from informants how far off was the Surrey army; but since this was the first that they had heard of it, if it was coming up from London, then it might still be fairly far off, with three hundred miles to be covered.

Action then was called for – swift action. No mere raiding now but a concentrated attack on Norham before the new host could arrive. They ought, with their numbers, to be able to dispose of the force already at the castle; but that powerful citadel itself was not one that would fall easily, and there was probably no time for any prolonged siege to starve out the bishop's garrison. Artillery would be needed. So, send in haste for cannon. But it was a long road to come from Edinburgh, the nearest base for the like, home of the mighty Mons Meg. How long would it take for such to reach Norham? The shortest route, by the Lammermuirs and Duns, across the Merse by Swinton, say sixty-five miles. At best, six days' journeying. Had

126

they time for that, for cannon to arrive? Norham to be battered into submission before Surrey reached there? It was questionable. But what other effective action was open to them?

James and Bothwell and Drummond, the last proving to be an able strategist, wasted little time on their decision, at least. Messengers were sent off for Edinburgh, at all speed, with orders that Mons Meg, the greatest Scots cannon with the longest range, and sundry lesser pieces, be sent south forthwith, using horses instead of the usual and slower oxen to draw them, fast, even if they had to kill the beasts in the task; they could always purloin other plough-horses from farms on the way. Meantime the royal army would head north, in equal haste, for Norham, and seek to disperse the force already gathered there.

They reckoned that it was about a score of miles from their present position, near the hamlet of Mindrum, north by east, once out of the Cheviots fairly level country. They could be there by nightfall. An attack in the darkness, then? Unexpected, on a sleeping encampment. They could not hope to take the castle that way, but could probably destroy or drive off the assembled company outside.

Out of the hills by the little valley of the Howtel's burn they went, and on past Flodden Edge and Branxton, riding faster now, and so to cross Till at Heaton where they had destroyed the lesser castle on the former occasion, this with the light beginning to fail. Scouts sent well ahead reported no enemy presence between them and their goal, Norham another seven or eight miles.

On Grievestead Moor they settled down to rest briefly, to be ready to make the assault around midnight, their destination now barely three miles off.

David, like most others there, had never been involved in a night attack, and wondered how effective it would be. After all, the night would be just as dark for the attackers as the defenders. Moreover, they had to find their way first, in these conditions, over unknown country. Also

127

the English might well have guards, sentries, well out from the camp, who could give warning.

But once started again, doubts were to some extent dismissed. Night-sight proved to be better than expected, after a little adjustment. Inevitably the host rode but slowly, picking their way; but it was remarkable how much they could see ahead, although lesser details were vague, but larger features such as hillocks and woodland, dips and ponds, were apparent as darker masses in the gloom. The same would apply to the enemy; but so long as there was surprise, a sleeping company would be slower in adapting, also in being effectively commanded by leaders.

Presently, still at a walking pace, the Scots saw pinpoints of red ahead of them, as the land began gently to slope down towards the Tweed. It was hard to tell just how far away these were, camp-fires no doubt; but as they moved on, these grew little larger or brighter, and it was evident that they were not blazing bonfires to provide light, but cooking-fires dying down, embers only.

James and his leaders discussed tactics now, as their mounts paced onwards. If the enemy were based round the castle, as seemed probable, it would be in something of a semicircle, for the Tweed would be directly to the north, with no room between the stronghold's mound and the river. So the assault would also have to be in crescent formation, a wide half-moon advance, and the approach slow still, no beat of hooves to arouse the guards or sleepers. Probably, too, the English leadership would be spending the night in the castle itself, so the chances were that there would be little coherent command, at first at least, which would be a help.

It was difficult to know just how close they were to those fires, when the signal was given quietly to halt. Would jingling bits and bridles, and the occasional snorts of horses, reach the camp? Everyone was well aware of the need for silence, except their mounts.

James gave his orders. David found himself allotted to

the far right wing, with his Carrick men. He was to sweep round to the river, although sweep was hardly the word in their careful pacing. The king, in the centre, would be unable to give any further signals, by sight or sound, when the final assault was to begin; all would just have to judge for themselves. If and when outcry from the enemy arose, of course, it would all be different, haste and fury. This was no chivalrous warfare such as the monarch preferred; but it could be effective enough.

David led his people off eastwards, regretting that Will and his Borthwicks had been ordered off to the left wing.

Very much aware now of the clop of hooves and the clink of harness, even the squeak of leather of saddles and stirrups, they walked their beasts in the required semicircling advance. Actually, soon they could see the river ahead of them, not the water itself but the darker line of the channel. The castle also now became visible, a towering black mass on its mound to the left, no shapes and details, but of sufficient bulk. Those fires were not evident from here.

David was wondering when to commence the inward movement, and whether he had given time enough for the left wing to get into position, when the issue was settled for him. Noise suddenly erupted to the west, shouting and clash and the thin ring of steel, with a hunting-horn ulalating above all. That would be the royal signal, need for silence past. He shouted aloud for the advance.

Still they could not charge, much as they might feel like it, for however good their night-sight had become, they could not risk fast riding over the shadowy, uneven ground. A trot was the best that they could do, swords drawn now, lances and axes ready.

The noise ahead of them grew to pandemonium, yells and shrieks, horses neighing, such arising above the clashing. Lights appeared at some of the castle's slit windows.

The first that the Carrick contingent experienced of

actual fighting was fleeing men on foot coming towards them, twos and threes at first, then many in bunches and groups. These presumably English, the horsemen slashed at, amidst more screams and bellows. Then some mounted men came, and David was uncertain whether or not to assail them also. Could these be Scots chasing the fugitives? Night-time warfare was full of dubieties, but undoubtedly much worse for the recently awakened attacked than for their attackers. He found himself almost sympathising with these, no state of mind for a commander of cavalry.

In fact, this of intercepting and cutting down panic-stricken runaways was all the fighting that his men had to do that night; for when they arrived at the encampment it was all over but for mopping-up processes, dead and dying lying around, riderless horses milling, men variously shouting, little sign of order and discipline anywhere. After gazing about him, at something of a loss, David left his people to do whatever they thought best, and went in search of his liege-lord for orders. He found James presently, with a group of his lords, staring up at the castle from the edge of an outer moat at the foot of the mound, its drawbridge raised. There was really nothing of any worth for him to report, and he just joined the others, to gaze upwards.

The citadel appeared to stand strangely aloof from all the chaos, misery and triumph below. Undoubtedly men therein were looking down on it, but such were unseen, and the great mass of towering walls and battlements soared dark above all, proud, impregnable – and somehow distant. That was what concerned the watchers. This water-filled moat was only the first; there was another, nearer the mound, to keep cannon at bay. James was shaking his head. Only Mons Meg, with its longer range and heavier ball, would have any real effect here, he feared.

However, the attack on the camp had clearly been a success, with practically no casualties on the Scots side, surprise complete, and lack of leadership confounding the enemy. Undoubtedly many English had escaped, mostly without horses; but it was not worth seeking to chase these fugitives. There were still hours of darkness ahead. It was just a case of taking over the abandoned encampment, piling up the dead, and allowing the less seriously injured enemy to look after their worse-off colleagues – if so they felt inclined. They must have captured a few hundred horses.

Success it might be, but David for one felt less than jubilant, even satisfied. It had all been too easy, somewhat unfair even, although he was thankful that his own men had suffered nothing. James himself seemed in a doubtful frame of mind, not entirely over the castle's evident ability to withstand onslaught. But Bothwell, Drummond and the others were well enough pleased.

They found a sufficiency of food and drink at the camp, and soon the fires were blazing again, for roasting beef now, while the winners consumed the fruits of victory. No surprise attack from the castle was anticipated, but a sufficiency of wakeful guards was established before the majority consigned themselves for what was left of the night. It had been a long day.

The groans of wounded men did not keep David Kennedy awake for overlong.

In the morning, a council of war was held. Some were for heading for home now, some for proceeding further into England while they were at it, and victorious; but James was determined that they must seek to make an example of Norham Castle, not leave it unharmed as a symbol of English strength and dominance of the borderline. They would besiege it, and hope that the cannon summoned would arrive in time to bombard it and hopefully destroy it before Surrey's host could get this far north. Not all saw this as wise, but the royal decision stood.

So it was a settling down in the former English encampment, after James made a formal call to surrender from the outer moat-side of the castle, a long distance for any

131

shouting to be heard, and in darkness. No answer was forthcoming. It was waiting, then, in the chill November weather.

It was not to be all idleness, for parties were sent out in various directions, to patrol the area in case of counter-attacks, and to emphasise the Scots presence to the Northumbrians, this in addition to scouting groups well to the south watching out for Surrey's approach. David and Will Borthwick were quite glad to go on these round-about missions, for siegery can be a very dull business, especially when no evident reaction came from the castle, which might have been empty were it not for the gleams of light at night. Presumably they had no artillery therein. A lot of sleeping was done, and some bickering amongst the bored followers of some of the lords.

Two days passed, and three, and then, on the fourth evening, they were surprised and James delighted at the arrival of the cannon and ammunition train across Tweed, sooner than anticipated, Mons Meg amongst them. It was the horse-drawn transporting, instead of the oxen, which had effected this, even though it seemed that Meg's gun-carriage had in fact collapsed at some stage and had had to be repaired.

James wasted no time now, having the guns lined up at that moat edge and fired off just as soon as they could be manned, primed, loaded and aimed. Action and noise suddenly replaced the idling and boredom.

It was to be doubted whether the smaller cannon had any real effect on the thick walling of Norham Castle, although all the banging and smoke may well have had an impact on the minds of the besieged. But Mons Meg was different. Her balls did register, gouging great dents in the masonry, smashing window openings and knocking tops off turrets. The king shouted his praise, and blessed his grandsire, James the Second, who had acquired this splendid piece of ordnance.

They kept up the bombardment well into darkness,

when the flashes, smoke-clouds and din seemed even more daunting. But this did mean that they were using up their ammunition supply at a great rate, and possibly to no great destructive effect. They had been told that more powder and ball was on its way, but it was uncertain when this would arrive. James felt that he had to call off the gunfire, so that it could be resumed in the morning, this when more selective aiming was possible.

Next day the cannonade had not long started when a white sheet appeared hanging over the battered castle parapet, clearly a white flag for either parley or surrender. To the cheers of his supporters, James halted the gunners.

Soon figures appeared from under the gatehouse arch, and came down to the first drawbridge. They had it lowered and moved forward to the inner edge of the second one, where they could call across without straining voices. This drawbridge remained lifted. One of the party was dressed as a cleric.

"To whom do we speak?" this portly individual cried. "Who assails this my hold so grievously?"

"You speak to James, King of Scots," he was told. "Who will assail it more grievously still unless you make surrender forthwith."

There was a pause, and then the same man spoke again. "Your Majesty, I say that there is no call for such sore threats. When speech could effect aught of controversy between us and make for harmony."

"I make no claim to majesty, sirrah! Grace is what I would claim and how we render it in Scotland. What speech could effect aught between us, other than your fullest surrender and submission? Are you the Bishop of Durham?"

"I am, Sire. And I can speak with a voice of some authority, at King Henry's royal will."

"Indeed? And what has Henry Tudor to say to me, through yourself, my lord Bishop? Since he can know naught of this assault on your castle." James pointed

133

to that drawbridge. "And, sir, if we are going to be exchanging more speech, would it not be best for this bridge to be lowered, so that we can do so without this unseemly raising of voices?"

The other did not comment on that last, but continued to call over the moat. "His Majesty does not desire a state of war with Scotland, Sire," he declared. "He has sent me word to this effect, before ever Your Highness made this incursion into his realm—"

James interrupted. "Yet he sends the Earl of Surrey north with a great array, I am told. I think that the Tudor, or yourself, sir, speaks with a forked tongue!"

"Not so, Sire. My lord of Surrey comes merely to ensure that King Henry's negotiations may be conducted in worthy and suitable fashion between the kingdoms. To support my own humble advocation."

"I think that you are deft with words, my lord Bishop! A man of eloquence. Your trade, perhaps? But, in this, I require more than flowing talk! What is Henry Tudor's purpose, Surrey's part, and your own mission?"

"His Majesty's message to me, before this of your onset and assault, was that there should be peace between the two realms. Which requires that Your Grace ceases to support the impostor and dissembler Perkin Warbeck in his shameful and ridiculous claims to the crown of England. That you surrender the said deceiver to him, and agree to make no more incursions into this realm. And either your royal self come to have personal word with His Majesty, or else send worthy ambassadors to negotiate a lasting peace."

"Ha! Honeyed words again, sir! So it is to be peace?" James looked at the lords at his side. "But, I fear, somewhat misdated! The Duke of York has departed my realm. Gone to Ireland, I am told. He no longer seeks my support. So I cannot surrender him, even if I would. Henry Tudor will have to deal with him . . . otherwise."

There was a distinct pause from across the moat, but

134

no sign of the drawbridge being lowered. Clearly this was news to the bishop. Presently he spoke again.

"This is welcome tidings, Your Grace. Why, then, may I ask, are you thus invading the realm of England?"

"Sufficient reason, sirrah! Did not your English invaders burn and sack my town of Duns but weeks ago? Under a Lord Daubeny. As well as make other armed assaults on my kingdom. And give shelter, refuge and welcome to the rebellious subject of mine, the Earl of Angus?"

Again a pause. "This of the man Warbeck changes all," the bishop said at length. "Does Your Grace say that there will now be no further Scots aid for his wrongous claims? And no further attacks on English soil?"

"Ask Surrey that last! No, I shall no longer support the Duke of York. And if there is no English invasion of *my* realm, I will refrain from assailing yours, meantime."

"That is well, Sire. Good news. I will inform King Henry so. And the Earl of Surrey, that peace may be established. And Your Grace can return to Scotland, assured of English goodwill."

"My Grace shall return to Scotland when he is ready so to do, my lord Bishop!" The king looked over again at his nobles. Heads were nodded.

"And I shall send word southwards forthwith," the bishop declared. "Be assured, all will now be well. And . . . I give Your Grace good-day!"

As he turned away to go back to the castle, the king stared at his companions, at something of a loss.

Bothwell hooted. "So now we know!" he exclaimed. "We have been given our lesson! His Eminence has spoken!"

There were growls from some of the lords.

"Aye, but we have gained what we wanted," Drummond pointed out. "Even if we have not brought down Norham Castle."

"We could still do so."

"What point so to do? Would it serve aught? The bishop, I say, is not mocking us, making but false words . . ."

"To save his castle? He goes back to it. See, that

135

drawbridge is being raised again. He will not have us in. He thinks to sit secure now."

David ventured a word. "He cannot go south, or send others with his message, while Your Grace besieges him. And that is what we want, is it not? For him to tell King Henry that Scotland no longer supports Perkin Warbeck. And seeks an end to this cross-the-border warfare? As he, the bishop, says."

"The proof will be if Surrey turns back," Drummond added.

James nodded. "It is a strange encounter. A strange ending to our assault. But I believe that we have gained what we require, what we came for. And at little cost indeed, if any. No need to remain here, to bombard this hold further."

"That man's name is Richard Fox," Bothwell said. "And he *is* a fox, if ever I saw one! Do not trust him, Sire."

"Not altogether, I do not. But, in this, I judge that he cannot be seeking to deceive us. He says that he speaks in Henry's name. And he, the Prince-Bishop of Durham as he is, is the most important man in this north of England. As Drummond says, the proof will be if Surrey turns back."

"So what do we do, Sire? Wait here?"

"No point in that. Blocking his going, sending to Surrey. No, we will return across Tweed. Wait there, on our own ground. Leave a small party hereabouts, to see if this bishop rides off. And whether Surrey turns back. If they do, then we have peace of a sort. Something to build on. What we desire and need."

"And if not? If Surrey comes on?"

"Then we will keep him from crossing Tweed. Better than fighting him here, on open ground. Use our cannon to better effect. When more powder and ball comes."

There was general agreement.

They turned, then, to order a packing up and retiral across the river into Scotland, leaving only a group to keep an eye on the castle and its occupants' activities,

136

and scouts to go further south to watch for Surrey's movements.

It made a strange situation.

For four days thereafter the king and his army remained encamped on the other, Scottish, side of the great river. They could watch departures from the castle; whether the bishop himself was amongst these it was impossible to tell at that distance. But no word came from their scouts to that effect, or of any approach by a large army. Whether Surrey had actually turned back, or merely halted, they could not know; but at least, had he been coming on, he would have been at Norham before this.

It was agreed that further waiting was scarcely necessary, with every lord's contingent more than ready to get back to their own parts and lives, the Carrick men very much so.

David took his farewell of the king, and led his people off up Tweed, for the second time.

13

It proved that James and his supporters were over-optimistic and speedy in returning from Norham when they did, for in fact the Earl of Surrey, although he had delayed his advance northwards, presumably at Bishop Fox's urging, did not abandon it, but, without seeking outright battle with the Scottish army, came on to Berwick, and further, for he marched over the border into the Merse, some seven miles, and there assailed and destroyed the Home castle of Ayton, no great stronghold admittedly; this evidently as a retaliatory gesture and warning, for he did not proceed onwards but returned to Berwick and there waited meantime with his twenty thousand men, no doubt for further orders from King Henry.

This much annoyed James Stewart, of course, but did not concern him sufficiently as to order one more muster of the nation's forces and to march south again for further battle. He saw it indeed only as a gesture, which did not invalidate the bishop's declaration and mission, but as intended to emphasise the need for a truce on the Scots part. Even so, James could not let it go without some positive reaction, especially as apparently Surrey remained at Berwick. So with his fairly typical preference for old-fashioned chivalrous behaviour, as distinct from downright military action, he sent a deputation under Don Pedro, as a neutral spokesman, but with a party of the injured Homes under Fastcastle, to Berwick to protest, and to challenge Surrey personally to a duel with himself; or if the other did not accept this, then to stage something like a tournament between equal numbers of Scots and English knights, this as token and dare. If this also was refused, then the English army should retire forthwith from its threatening proximity to Scots terrain, and return whence it came, in compliance with the prince-bishop's pronouncement.

Needless to say, Surrey made no response to this proposal, and the envoys returned to report.

The news of this singular succession of events reached David Kennedy in further unexpected fashion, by word of mouth of his sister Janet herself, who arrived at Cassillis alone save for two members of the royal guard from Stirling Castle, and in a fairly resolute state of mind. The Earl of Surrey was not the only one who had decided that James Stewart should be taught a lesson, she declared. *She* felt the same way, although for rather different reasons. She was pregnant by him, she was sure. And he knew it. But whether because of this, or otherwise, he had gone off northwards to Drummond Castle in Strathearn, ostensibly to consult with its lord over the Lennox situation and the possibility of enrolling the Isles lords in a sea-going demonstration down the English west coast, to emphasise Scots power; and not only had not taken her with him, but, she was reliably informed, was spending the nights with the Lady Margaret Drummond. Janet had known that he had been attracted by this young woman, as he could be by others; but to be conducting an open affair with her, immediately after learning of her own, Janet's, conception, was most unsuitable, and deserving of some demonstration of her displeasure. Hence this return home for a spell.

Her brother did not know what to say to all this; and Agnes was sympathetic but scarcely surprised. After all, James had behaved exactly in this way towards Mariot Boyd, and when she fell pregnant by him, transferred his attentions to Janet herself. Men, or some men, were like that apparently. She must have known that this was a possible outcome of her romance with the king?

Janet declared that her position was different. She was not just one more female dallying with the monarch; she

139

was deeply in love with him, and he had claimed to be equally so with her. Some indication of her affront was called for, and in no uncertain fashion.

David asked, what now? Was she ending her liaison with James? Distancing herself from him? Leaving him to Margaret Drummond? If so, what was to be her future? He could hardly say that she was not welcome to settle back into her life at Cassillis with her bastard child; but fond as he was of Janet, he could not greatly look forward to sharing his house between a new wife and his sister.

Her answer to that was no. Her love for James remained. And she thought that soon he would in fact greatly miss her. She would be glad and proud to bear his child; but he had to be taught his lesson. She was not going to share him with the Drummond woman. An occasional flirtation and play with other females was one thing for a man like James Stewart, especially with many so apt to throw themselves into his arms. But not an ongoing association with another of his lords' daughters; that was different, he was to learn. She believed that he could be brought to see it. He would, of course, be having to marry some child princess in due course, whether the Tudor one or the Infanta of Spain; that was, and always had been, a fact of the royal situation. But love was otherwise. She would make that clear to him.

So, a period of two women sharing his castle commenced for David Kennedy. Fortunately, Agnes and Janet got on well together, and the latter was helpful in recognising that the former was now mistress of the house, even though it had been her own former home. There was no suggestion of her going to Dunure. There was no friction either, Agnes being very understanding, which was as well, for this November was a cold, wet and blustery month, and outdoor pursuits at a minimum

They were into December, when there were developments, in the form of a royal visit, no less. James, with Don Pedro and Sir Rob Bruce, the king's personal attendant, arrived. There was no question but that it was Janet whom the king had come to see, even though he paid due attention to his host and hostess. The visitors stayed for two days. All saw that James and his mistress were given sufficient privacy, although this did not extend to them sharing the same bedchamber. Janet behaved heedfully towards him, suitably deferential to his monarchy, by no means distant or obviously at odds, but not offering any endearments either, he clearly desiring such. It made an odd situation for the others. Agnes behaved excellently in the circumstances, managing to ensure that the atmosphere was not too obviously fraught.

For his part, James had much on his mind beside matters of the heart. He had to tell David of the situation regarding England. Before coming here to Carrick, he had had a meeting with the prince-bishop, who had come as far as Melrose for it, sent by King Henry. The prelate had come offering more than any mere truce, but a pact of peace between the two realms. Apparently the need for this, for the Tudor, had been made the more evident and urgent by an uprising in Cornwall to support Perkin Warbeck, who had landed there, in traditional Yorkist country, with the Earl of Tyrconnel and an Irish force. Just what the Cornwall men's complaint against Henry was remained unclear, but evidently they were ready to revolt, and began a march on London. So Surrey had been recalled in haste, with his army, and had managed to defeat the rebels at Exeter, and captured Warbeck, who was now in the Tower of London. But there was still unrest in the English south-west, and Henry wanted no trouble with Scotland to complicate matters. Hence the bishop's embassage.

The Tudor terms for peace, an enduring peace, with the promise of no further English invasions of Scotland, were these: James to complete the years-old proposal of betrothal by marrying Princess Margaret of England, and this without undue delay. A substantial dowery of £30,000 Scots to be paid when the girl came north. James was to end the unsuitable alliance with France,

141

which endangered England. And a final and strange requirement: that Archibald, Earl of Angus, at present at the English court, should be received back into King James's favour, and all charges against him in Scotland dropped. What was behind this last demand was not clear, but presumably Bell-the-Cat had some especial influence with the Tudor.

When Janet heard this last, she was concerned, needless to say, the more so when it appeared that James was prepared to accede to the earl's return, since it seemed to be an integral part of the peace process. If his restitution was necessary, it ought at least to remove any threat to the crown of the Douglas power, something always at the back of the royal mind. When David, as well as his sister, wondered at this acceptance of Angus's return, James had to admit that some pressure had been applied by the Lord Drummond, whose other daughter Euphemia was, it seemed, to be wed to George, Master of Angus, the earl's son. This revelation by no means reassured Flaming Janet Kennedy.

The king told them that despite the time of the year and difficulties of travel, he was going to make a progress into the north-east of his realm, as far as Moray and Inverness his intention. It was long since he had visited these parts, and it was more than time that steps were taken to bring the unruly clans up there to order, the English situation having fully preoccupied him of late. That difficult great-uncle of his, Hearty James of Buchan, should be shown who ruled in the land, and that the king's peace applied even north of Aberdeen. Lord Drummond, who knew the area well, was to accompany him with an escort of his men. And Sir Andrew Wood would sail some of his ships up as far as Inverness, making calls at such ports as Dundee, Arbroath, Montrose, Aberdeen and Peterhead should horse-travel prove over-difficult, and take them on by water. This information aided Janet to decline the royal suggestion that she should return with him to Stirling, especially that mention of the Lord Drummond, which conjured up visions of his daughter making her presence available.

So James left Cassillis less than satisfied, but declaring that he hoped that Janet would join him at Stirling for the festive season of Christmas and the New Year, by which time he should be back from the north, she not committing herself. David noted that their liege-lord was not issuing royal commands now to his sister.

In fact, once the king's party was gone, Janet admitted to her brother and his wife that she had no intention of going back to Stirling for Christmas so long as James was seeing such a lot of the Drummonds. She was concerned to make him fully aware of her feelings in the matter. With their permission she would remain at Cassillis for this festive season. They could not say her nay, and Agnes was sympathetic. Privately she wondered, to David, whether this was the method to bring the king to Janet's way of thinking. James was clearly a man for no one woman – as she esteemed her husband to be – and it was a pity that Janet was so evidently in love with him. He might be in love with her – obviously he thought much of her – but that would never make a man of his temperament a faithful partner, she feared, especially as there could be no hope of him marrying her. But how to make Janet accept this?

The three of them spent Yuletide together, with the other young Kennedys joining them for Christmas Eve and Day, but not their father. Agnes was popular with them, and it looked as though David was going to see more of his brothers and sister than in the recent past.

Twelfth Night had just passed when they had a further unexpected visit, not from James Stewart but from his friend Don Pedro and the good Bishop Elphinstone of Aberdeen, these on their way to Richmond, apparently Henry Tudor's favourite abode, to complete the final details of the peace treaty, in especial to consider the proposed marriage arrangements with young Margaret Tudor. It seemed strange indeed that Don Pedro should be

143

entrusted with this mission, he who had come to Scotland seeking to promote a different marriage altogether, to his own monarch's daughter. But James obviously trusted and relied upon him. The king had asked him to call in at Cassillis on his way south, to urge Janet to come back to Stirling without delay, not a royal command so much as a royal plea. But when questioned about Margaret Drummomd, the two envoys could not honestly declare that James was seeing no more of her; and Bishop Elphinstone revealed that her father had been made Justiciary of Scotland north of Forth and Clyde, and also Constable of Stirling Castle.

Janet wished them well on their mission of state, but left them in little doubt that she would remain at Cassillis meantime.

14

A royal command did arrive at Cassillis a week or so later, but this was addressed to David, not his sister. There was to be a meeting of the Privy Council in four days' time, and he was to attend. No doubt the king hoped that he would bring Janet with him, but that was not stated in the message.

So the two young women were left alone for a few days.

At Stirling, the council meeting had much to attend to, not having met for a considerable time. James reported on his expedition to Moray, Inverness and the north, declaring that it had been successful and that he had, he thought, brought the Highland chiefs to heel, although one or two were still defying the royal will and prosecuting dire clan feuding, and such, of course, always provoked retaliation. Most of the day's business, however, was concerned with finance, or the lack of it. The Treasury was empty, all the troubles with England having cost it dear, and it had never been over-full, the king informing them that he had even had to melt down various gold chains of office and the badges of foreign orders to turn into coinage. Something had to be done. Taxes were unpopular and difficult to collect, but moneys had to be raised somehow. The crown could not be in debt, especially with the expenses of the forthcoming royal marriage looming. Linlithgow Palace had to be refurbished as the queen-to-be's traditional dower-house, and it was in poor state, having been unused for long.

Suggestions as to fund-raising were meagre, with all noble eyes turning on the churchmen there, who tended to be looked upon as the source of most of the wealth of the nation, thanks to their tithes, legacies and the rents of vast lands. But James, diplomatically, declared that certain matters regarding Holy Church should probably be dealt with first, as having some relevance. The Archbishop of St Andrews, in name if only that, William Sheves of ill memory, had died at last, a very old and unworthy man, who had long been retired but could not be replaced without the support of the Vatican, with which he had considerable influence. So now a new Primate for the Scottish Church was required; and although this was a matter for the College of Bishops to decide upon and to recommend to the Pope in Rome, the King-in-Council had interest and concern in the issue, in view of the great impact on national affairs. Also in the inevitable reallocation of bishoprics. He, James, had had discussions with Bishop Elphinstone and others on this subject, and had certain recommendations to make, first to this council and then to the College of Bishops. He, the king, in his capacity of Honorary Canon of Glasgow Cathedral, had petitioned the Pope that the promise of the previous Pontiff be implemented and the see of Glasgow be raised to an archbishopric, this not equal with St Andrews but complementary, as was York with Canterbury in England. This had been granted, and Bishop Blackadder of Glasgow, here present, was now archbishop thereof. This had largely been effected through the good offices of Andrew Forman, Prior of Pittenweem, their good secretary. A new Primate was therefore required for St Andrews. Archbishop Blackadder, so recently elevated, could scarcely be so promoted. Therefore he, the king, proposed that his own royal brother, the Duke of Ross, be so appointed, *ad interim*, to fill the vacancy until such time as Robert Blackadder, or another, should suitably take over the Primacy. Meantime, Prior Andrew Forman to be appointed to the vacant see of Moray.

Men gazed at each other, especially the clerics present. Here was an extraordinary development, with the monarch taking an all but unprecedented stance in the affairs of Holy Church. When, a year or two before, he had got himself made an honorary canon of Glasgow, folk had wondered why. Now they understood. Here he was more or less ensuring his own dominance in Church as well as realm, and so being in the position to gain no little hold over the great ecclesiastical wealth. The nobles on the council, at least, looked well pleased; it would probably save them much in financial contributions. And presumably James and Bishop Elphinstone had come to agreement on all this, he the most influential of the nation's clerics. But an eighteen-year-old prince to be Archbishop of St Andrews!

Into the silence that greeted this announcement Prior Andrew Forman, their clerk, spoke. He declared that he would be honoured to be Bishop of Moray, not adding that it was one of the richest sees in the land. David, for one, now knew why James had made that recent expedition up to Moray and Inverness. If the other two bishops on the council with Elphinstone, Blackadder and Andrew Stewart of Caithness, had any doubts about it all, they did not voice them. There was little question but that the College of Bishops hereafter would not dispute it.

Few there failed to recognise that here was a very major step taken by the monarch in the nation's affairs, and one which ought greatly to assist in the replenishment of the Treasury, whatever was the effect on the realm's quality of worship.

Seeming not to dwell overmuch on this aspect, James said that Bishop Elphinstone had a suggestion to make as to revenue-raising. This astute prelate then declared that duties on foreign shippers using Scots harbours, both for their exports and their imports, could produce a useful source of moneys, with the wool trade ever growing, especially to the Netherlands, and the Scots salted and smoked fish and meats in great demand in some countries. A levy thereon could produce considerable gain for the nation's coffers. None saw this as in any way objectionable.

147

Other proposals were put forward, again mainly by clerics, the nobility tending to consider such matters as little concern of theirs.

There were routine matters arising to be discussed, taking up much time such as the appointment of law officers, sheriffs and sub-justiciars, the promotion of royal burghs, the erection of baronies – at a due price – petitions to the council, and the like. All this could not be completed in one day, and the meeting was adjourned until the morrow.

James had a word with David Kennedy that evening, a difficult word, with Janet's attitude behind it all, even though not in any detailed fashion, more implied than specified. The fact that the Lord Drummond was very much present did not help. David had hitherto got on well with this man, and admired his abilities as a soldier. He was now very close to the king obviously, and this did not make the matter of female preferences any easier.

At next day's renewed meeting, after the distinctly boring but necessary further details concerning the government of the realm efficiently were dealt with, the matter of the return to Scotland of Archibald, Earl of Angus, was raised by Bothwell, who had, of course, profited by gaining some of the Red Douglas's forfeited estates. What was to be done about that miscreant? He was known to be back over the border. How were they to deal with him and his Douglases?

James had to be somewhat on the defensive over this question. He had by no means wanted Angus back from banishment; but the Tudor had made an express point of it as one of his terms for peace. Why was still not clear; and Bell-the-Cat might well be seen as working for Henry here, something of a spy and traitor in their midst. A close watch would have to be kept on him, and on some of his friends like the Lord Gray and the other Douglases, Black as well as Red. But he would probably lie low for a while.

Bishop Elphinstone suggested that it might be sound

148

policy not exactly to seem to favour him but to make use of him in some degree, and so nullify the ever-dangerous Douglas power. After an interval, if he did not make himself obnoxious, appoint him to some position wherein he could do no great harm, and in which they, the council, could oversee his actions, keeping him, as it were, always under their eye. Muzzle the cat-beller, by seeming to smile on him?

There were doubts expressed over this, but all recognised that Elphinstone had shrewd wits. James agreed to keep this in mind.

When the meeting broke up and David was for home, the king frankly urged him to try to persuade Janet to return to Stirling. Margaret Drummond was no longer in residence at the castle but was back at their house in Strathearn. David could only say that he would inform his sister of this.

But back at Cassillis he was faced with a situation that precluded anything such, the report of an occurrence that left him appalled as he was astonished. Agnes, in great distress, announced that, the day before, Angus himself had arrived at the castle, with a large troop of his Douglases, and had taken Janet by force away with him, where she knew not. There had been a dire scene, Janet having to be physically constrained and carried off. There had been nothing that she, Agnes, could do, the few men available at Cassillis being in no position to contest the Douglas strength. Angus had declared that he was but exercising his undoubted right. Janet Kennedy was betrothed to him, of long standing; he had endowed her with the lands of Bothwell Castle in Lanarkshire, as well as others, as dowery. Now he was taking what was lawfully his.

David, dismayed, was of course for rescuing his sister. But how? Where had she been taken? Angus had come in strength, and even if much of Carrick was to be roused against him, that would not compete with the Red Douglas power. What, then? The king? That was the only answer – if he would act.

That very evening, then, David turned and rode back through the night whence he had just come, on a fresh horse, mind in chaos. His beloved sister . . .!

At least, at Stirling Castle, he had no complaints as to James Stewart's reaction to the news. The king was utterly dismayed, and furiously so. This had to be dealt with at once and in no uncertain fashion. His Janet in the clutches of that treacherous scoundrel! Possibly being raped by him! Where? Where had he taken her? Tantallon was in ruins. But he had many other houses. She could be at any of these. And she was pregnant. By himself! Where? He must find her. His royal guard to be readied. Others summoned to help.

Elphinstone and others warned about provoking outright war with the Douglases. If the Blacks came to support the Reds, they could field many thousands, raise half Galloway, Lanarkshire, the Lothians. All for a mistress!

James would hear none of that. The wretch was to be brought to book, and forthwith. Gather men.

Conferring with those close to him over where to look for Janet, it was Bothwell who suggested that it might be worth trying Bothwell Castle itself first – where his own title came from although he himself had never owned it, only the earldom so styled. Angus had put it in Flaming Janet's name as marriage token. It was a strong place. She might well be there.

With no better proposal as to starting the search, it was agreed. Bothwell Castle was none so far off, eight miles south of Glasgow, on the lower Clyde, near to Hamilton and Blantyre, perhaps thirty-five miles from Stirling. They could be there this very day.

By noon a sizeable company was on its way, others to follow. Down they went by Falkirk and Cumbernauld and Airdrie to the Clyde, riding fast, Bothwell with the king and Drummond also, odd as it might seem for that man to be seeking to aid in the rescue of his daughter's rival. They came to Bothwell Castle in the late afternoon, and saw the Douglas banners, of the silver stars on blue above the red Bruce's heart, flying from its three towers. It was one of the largest fortalices in all Scotland, with an enormous circular keep, or donjon, and two angle towers flanking the large rectangular courtyard, all built in red stone, its windows pointedly arched.

James wasted no time. The drawbridge over the inner of three moats was in place, although the iron portcullis was down, barring entry. He rode right on to that bridge, under his royal standard, his companions just behind, including David Kennedy. A blast on his hunting-horn, and he raised voice.

"Heed me, whoever keeps this hold. I who speak am James, King of Scots. I seek Archibald, Earl of Angus. Tell him so."

There was no delay in replying, at least. "My lord is not here, Sire," a voice called.

"No? Yet his colours fly yonder. Do not seek to cozen me, sirrah!"

"My lord *was* here. But left this day."

"Left? Whither?"

"For Glasgow, as I understand it, Sire."

"Glasgow? What to do there?"

"That I know not, Your Grace. He did not say."

"No? Did he go alone?"

"Yes, Sire. Save for his guards."

"Ah! Glasgow is but a few miles. He will be back?"

"I judge so, yes."

"And his men? Where are they?"

"Encamped down at the meadows of Clyde, Sire. At Chapelhaugh."

James turned to look at his supporting lords. "You hear? Glasgow. He has gone this day to Glasgow. But will be back. Will he have taken Janet Kennedy with him?"

"Why should he?" Drummond asked. "Unless . . . ?"

151

"To have her wed him? Could it be? By some priest there?"

"There will be priests nearer than Glasgow, Sire."

"Perhaps to bring back a priest here, to wed her in his castle?" Bothwell put in.

"Would he not *send* for such a priest? Not go himself?" David wondered.

"Not if he wanted some lofty cleric to wed him. As so he might. But it may not be this of a wedding." James raised his voice again. "Is the Lady Janet Kennedy in this hold?"

There was no reply.

"Answer me, sirrah. It is your liege-lord who so asks. Demands!"

Still no answer.

"That means that she *is*," Bothwell jerked.

"Who are you, who refuses answer to your king?" James cried.

"I am Sir William Douglas of Cavers, keeper of this castle, Sire."

"Ha! And *I* knighted you, if I mind aright! On your knightly honour, is the Lady Janet here?"

"Ye-e-es." That came out reluctantly indeed.

"So! Then raise that portcullis, Sir William. We will come within. And await my lord of Angus."

There was a pause, and then, "As you will, Sire."

They waited, eyeing each other. There was some risk in entering that stronghold, even with the royal troop left outside. They could be held in, detained, imprisoned. But would any man dare to imprison the King of Scots in his own realm?

The metallic clanking of the chains of the portcullis being raised sounded. James ordered Sir Rob Bruce to line up his royal guards on either side of this drawbridge, and to keep them there, some to follow him in under the portcullis and within the gatehouse arch, to hold that also. He and his companions rode in.

152

A youngish man, finely clad, came down from the parapet walk to greet them, bowing to the king, silent.

"I recognise you, Sir William," James said, dismounting. "As well that you obeyed my command. My guard will see that you continue to do so. Now, take us within. And bring the Lady Janet Kennedy to me."

Without a word the other bowed again, and turned to lead the way across the wide courtyard to the great keep door.

They followed him inside, mounted the stair to the huge, vaulted great hall on the first floor, and there saw a woman waiting, no doubt the Lady Douglas, who promptly disappeared.

They waited, themselves silent now.

They had to stand for quite some time, eyeing all the splendour wonderingly. Then the door through which the lady had vanished opened, and within it Janet appeared, Sir William behind her. She halted and stared, as indeed did they all.

She was as lovely as ever, whatever fate had befallen her, flaming red hair loose, eyes flashing, full lips open, as her gaze darted from one to the other of the waiting men.

"James!" she cried. "David!" And she launched herself forward, to run and throw herself into the king's arms.

It made a dramatic scene for all there, Janet gasping out her relief, joy and thankfulness, James holding her close, kissing her hair and murmuring endearments, David gripping an arm, Douglas of Cavers quietly left the hall.

When some order returned and the principals were able to voice their emotions, thoughts and queries coherently, it was Janet herself who drew back and controlled herself and the situation, looking from the king to her brother.

"I knew that you would find me, come for me," she declared. "I knew it. I told him so. But . . ." She shook her red head.

"You . . . he, he misused you?" James got out.

"Oh, yes, he took me, raped me. But I gave him no pleasure in it, believe me!"

"Dastard! He will pay for this!"

"He declared that I was his. By law, by custom. Bought! All his . . ."

"I will teach him the law!"

"He is gone to Glasgow. I think to arrange marriage. But he will return . . ."

"Aye. Then we shall give the wretch his deserts . . ."

"Sire, wait you, I beg." That was the Lord Drummond. "I say that we should not await him. Linger here. Cavers will send to warn and inform him, that you may be sure. And he has many men, nearby. We could be trapped here. Angus will not come back alone. He will bring his people. We will be faced with fighting. Outnumbered. Is that the way? I say that we should leave, while we may. With this lady. Deal with Angus later . . ."

"That is best, yes," Bothwell asserted. "We could be endangered here. Play into his hands by waiting."

David thought the same, and said so. His sister could be the loser.

James, eyeing them all, frowned, and then nodded. "Perhaps. Yes, it may be best to go. Now Angus can wait – without Janet Kennedy! So be it. Out of this hold with us. Back to Stirling. And then . . . !"

So it was all haste. Janet did not delay them, having little gear with her anyway. All trooped out for their horses, the king taking the young woman to ride on his own beast, within his arms. There was no sign of Sir William Douglas.

Outside, the royal guards were probably well enough pleased with this development, sparing them all from having to do battle with the Douglases. Forming up, they left Bothwell Castle, to head northwards. What if they met with Angus on his way back? Would that perhaps solve some problems?

Once they were past Airdrie, however, that possibility could be dismissed.

It was dark before they reached Falkirk; but the road on to Stirling was not difficult and well known to all. It had been a long and memorable day.

In the royal citadel, after a very necessary but hasty meal, well after midnight, all sought their beds – and there was no question now as to which bed Janet Kennedy would occupy on this occasion.

In the morning, the king consulted his familiars, including David, as to what should be done about Angus. It was scarcely a matter for the Privy Council. Bishop Elphinstone was still at the castle, and his advice was usually wise. What could James do without provoking civil war with the House of Douglas? Also, without possibly offending Henry Tudor, who obviously had an understanding with that earl. James's personal feelings had to be tailored to fit the national weal. Yet something had to be done to express the royal displeasure.

The bishop it was who suggested a token and temporary banishment, one that would not be humiliating enough to cause the feared upheavals, indeed could only be a gesture in fact, but would make the king's authority and disapproval both known. Angus was known to have some properties on the Isle of Arran. Tell him to go and immure himself thereon for a period. Make this known as a degree of royal reproof, but insufficient to produce any major backlash. Angus might refuse to comply, but that would not be enough to endanger the realm's peace.

For want of any better proposal, James acceded. With his marriage approaching and so much hanging on it, the last thing that he wanted, on due reflection, was turmoil in the land. He would issue a banishment order to the Isle of Arran.

Janet was well enough content with that. She would never forgive Bell-the-Cat, but had no wish to be the cause of national disorder. At least her relationship with James Stewart seemed to be back on a basis acceptable to her.

David was able to return to Cassillis with a reasonably easy mind.

15

Whether the Earl of Angus did go to immure himself on Arran was not to be known, save by those close to him, but at any rate he did not engage in any public outcry over the Bothwell Castle affair; and the king's gesture was noised abroad sufficiently to indicate that even a Douglas earl could taste the royal displeasure.

It was not long after David's homecoming that Agnes announced that she too believed that she was pregnant, this to her husband's satisfaction, although he promptly began to worry about his dear one's physical well-being. He did want them to have children, yes, but not at any possible risk to his wife. He had it pointed out to him that women had been delivering offspring since Eve bore Abel, and possibly before, and few indeed ever suffered more than bearable birth-pangs. And these she was prepared to put up with. There were months before she would be in any way restricted in her wifely activities. Fear not, husband! Janet – when was *she* expecting?

David thought in about four months now, although she was showing little signs of it. And this of timing was going to be distinctly significant. For it looked as though it would approximately coincide with the arrival in Scotland of the king's young bride from London, which was hardly the ideal welcome for Margaret Tudor, especially if James intended for the birth to take place at Stirling Castle as seemed to be assumed. And, it was now reported, Margaret Drummond also was due to give birth within the next few weeks. James Stewart's potency could prove something of an embarrassment in the circumstances.

Agnes shook her fair head over the monarch, and

indeed menfolk in general, She hoped that her husband would not be smitten by similar desires and the falling for temptresses.

Whatever the royal concern with dates, Scotland enjoyed a period of comparative peace for those involved, such as had been notably lacking of late, with no hostilities with England, no internal disorders on any major scale, other than clan feuding, and no Douglas demonstrations, wherever Angus might be. David was happy to get on with a normal life at Cassillis with his beloved. There was no lack of activity, much of his seigneurial duties having been neglected, inevitably, for long because of his national and royal commitments.

Word reached them in due course that Margaret Drummond had been delivered of a daughter, at Drummond Castle, James not present at the birth but visiting her thereafter, fairly briefly. Janet, who sent the tidings, declared that all was well with her at Stirling, and the king duly attentive and caring.

Soon thereafter they heard news that must have come as some relief to James Stewart and those close to him. The coming north of the twelve-year-old Margaret Tudor had been put off for some months, on account apparently of some unspecified ailment of her father. The arrival and marriage would now take place in the later summer. So there ought to be no clash of dates relating to Janet's child-bearing.

Marriage, child-bearing and domestic developments seemed to be the preoccupation that winter and spring of 1501–2, the most surprising perhaps, at least for those concerned with national affairs, being the revelation that Archibald, Earl of Angus, wherever he had been hiding, had himself plunged into unexpected matrimony for the third time. He had married a young woman called Katherine Stirling, daughter of a little-known magnate of southern Perthshire, Sir William Stirling of Keir. What was behind this sudden change in marital intentions was not clear; it could hardly have been a matter of falling headlong in love at this stage of his life; and links with this Stirling family provided no obvious boost to his power, influence and wealth. But at least it seemed to imply an end to Bell-the-Cat's pursuit of Janet Kennedy, for which she and others gave thanks. It would be interesting to see what would be the position regarding Bothwell Castle now. He was not likely to let it remain in Janet's name – not that she had the least desire for this.

It was in May that David received a summons to Stirling, to attend a parliament called to deal with a crisis across the Norse Sea, where Sweden had rebelled against the overlordship of King Hans of Denmark and Norway, James's uncle, and with whom Scotland was in treaty of support. This was an unfortunate time for such to take place, but James felt that he had to do something, and Janet's child due any day. At least David's forthcoming fatherhood was not likely to make any complication.

At Stirling Castle he found Janet hourly awaiting her delivery, and the king in much concern over it, worried about her well-being and alarmed that the birth might take place while he was attending this parliament. He wanted to be present with her; but if he left the session it would no longer be a parliament, merely a convention, and this of the Danish situation demanded parliamentary authority. Janet herself was not greatly anxious, smilingly declaring that she had doubts whether she would be able to hold back her son's arrival – for she was quite sure that it would be a boy – until her liege-lord could be present. The night passed without the hoped-for genesis, although Janet had had to endure considerable pain, sleepless. James was reluctant indeed to leave her; but at least the parliament was held in the great hall of the castle close by, and he could be informed in a matter of minutes.

The word of it all spread around all attending, of course, and everyone sat prepared for unusual developments. However, that knowledge did have the effect of limiting talk and discussion, few long speeches made and motions passed or rejected briskly – one of the briefest parliaments on record. It was decided that only a token gesture of armed support for King Hans should be made, this made more acceptable by the news that France was sending a quite large force. Unfortunately the powerful Hanseatic League was backing the breakaway Swedes, and the Scots did not want to offend that huge trading organisation, which could affect their own trading ventures; but the French intervention might well have a major impact there. Sir Andrew Wood would transport the Scots contingent of, say, two thousand; and they were discussing how many and which ships should be sent, and whether there was time for other vessels based at Dunbarton on the Clyde to sail round the land north-abouts to take part, when the Lyon King of Arms came forward to the throne, to bow and speak into the king's ear. The immediate lightening of the royal features, all but with a grin, told all that it had been good news, and the Chancellor brought proceedings to a hasty end and James was out of his seat and off, almost before all were on their feet for the royal exit, the trumpets sounding belatedly.

David Kennedy was one of the first of the parliamentarians to win out of the hall and to head for the royal private apartments.

He found the monarch kneeling beside the great canopied bed and alternatively stroking a wearily smiling Janet's red hair and the pink hairless head of a small creature in her arms. He was uttering endearments, blessings, congratulations and praise, somewhat disconnected and involved, but fervent enough. And when he realised that David, as well as the royal physician were standing at his side, he gained coherence, and pointed.

"See you, there, there is James Stewart, Earl of Moray!" he declared. "There, my son! I make him Earl of Moray. And Janet – Janet will be well repaid. God be praised!"

"I ask no payment, James," the new mother said thickly. "Save to have and to keep this your child, and mine. That is enough. It is well, well, praises be!"

"*You* are well enough?" David demanded. "Was it . . . very ill? Hard to bear? Pain? I . . . we were thinking of you. All the time." He shook his head at his own male helplessness.

She smiled at him and nodded, wordless, and drew the child the closer to her breast.

He and the physician withdrew to leave the pair to themselves, and to Scotland's new earl.

The child proved to be sound in body and mind, and most certainly in lungs, with no complications, the mother quickly recovering her strength and able to feed him adequately. Soon James was proudly showing him off to all at court, as though this was a unique production on his part, although young Alexander Stewart, Mariot Boyd's son, was being reared down in Stirling town.

David lingered for another day at the castle, to be assured that his sister was indeed making good recovery and feeling fulfilled. Before he left for home, thankful that he had not been commanded to provide any Carrick men for the Danish task-force, he learned that the king had bestowed on Janet, for her son, the lands of Darnaway in Moray, with its castle; also the lordship of Menteith none so far off, for herself. The former was to remain in her care and possession so long as she did not marry, a significant provision, which seemed to imply the assurance of the monarch's continuing affection and association. Janet was, in fact, to control one of the great earldoms of Scotland until her son came of age, a notable conception.

Well enough content, David set off back to his Agnes to tell her all — although he did rather wish that Darnaway was not quite so far off, over two hundred miles, he reckoned, even from this Stirling, and all those mountains to cross. However, it occurred to him that the giving to his sister of Menteith also might well be James's way of ensuring that *he* continued to see a deal of his lady-love, for that was only a score or so of miles from Stirling, and Janet might in fact spend much of her time there, rather than in Moray. That thought was a comfort.

16

That summer, as David and Agnes waited for their own marriage's fulfilment, most shocking news reached them. Margaret Drummond and two of her sisters, Euphemia and Sibylla, had all died suddenly at Drummond Castle, poison assumed to be the cause, since no one else in the household had been affected. Fortunately the royal child, also called Margaret, did not suffer likewise. The nation resounded with astonishment and alarm, also theories as to who and what was responsible. Who might do such a thing, and why? Had it something to do with the king's little bastard? If so, why the other two sisters? Could it have been arranged by Henry Tudor, as warning to the king, about to be married, over producing children by other women? In which case, then Flaming Janet and her son would be in dire danger. Or could it be anything to do with Angus, whose son was married to a fourth sister? Lord Drummond might have enemies, who resented his closeness with the king; but he had two sons as well as these daughters – why slay *them*? It was all a mystery, but a grim one.

Agnes thought that it might well be less dastardly than was generally assumed, grievous as it was. Something bad, noxious, in what they had eaten might be the cause, although admittedly this might have been expected to affect others at Drummond Castle also. She could see no sense in murder, if such it was.

The impact on James himself was forceful and immediate. After attending the funerals of the three sisters at Dunblane Abbey, he promptly took Janet and her baby, not to Menteith, but on the long journey north to Moray, to instal them in the stronghold of Darnaway Castle, and to ensure that every possible safety precaution was there established, guards warned that if her life, or that of the infant, was forfeited, theirs would be also. Presumably he judged that the remoteness of Darnaway would be a factor for safety. He promised frequent royal visits.

This dire affair was succeeded by a very different kind of upset. The Danish expedition had proved to be a fiasco, arriving too late to be of any effect. They had reached the Kattegat to find all more or less over, Queen Christina of Denmark captured by the insurgent Swedes, and King Hans surrendering his authority over the rebel nation to win her back. Admittedly this meant that there had been no casualties or serious trouble for the Scots force; but it was all distinctly humiliating for it to have to return without a blow struck, especially as England had chosen to support the Hanseatic League and the breakaway Swedes, in theory at least, although not in arms; so their trade would not suffer, whereas Scotland's probably would. It was all most unfortunate, and many blamed James for belatedly going to the aid of his late mother's brother, Hans.

Much preparation had to be made for the forthcoming wedding, and other preoccupations shelved in national affairs – save for the traders and merchants. This marriage was to signal peace with the Auld Enemy, a prospect difficult to take in for most folk, for the English had been trying to subdue and take over the northern kingdom for four centuries, since Canute's time. Margaret Tudor was to arrive in Scotland about the beginning of August, and the arrangements for her reception, and the marriage to follow, were to be suitably splendid and impressive, to ensure that Henry and his proud folk could not criticise the Scots as feeble and impoverished, as they were all too apt to do, the fact that there were ten times as many English to Scots ever a point emphasised.

So a notable reception was planned for the young princess when she set foot on Scottish soil, and much celebration thereafter, culminating in the wedding at the Abbey of the Holy Rood in Edinburgh. Undoubtedly she would be accompanied by an illustrious company of the English notables, and it was these who had to be impressed rather than the girl herself. The king would not go to the border to greet his bride; more dignified to have her met by his representatives and brought to him at Edinburgh or nearby; otherwise he would be faced with the situation of spending nights in her company but not in her chamber on the way north, a matter which, in the circumstances, had to be considered.

When the word came from London that Margaret would be arriving at Berwick-upon-Tweed on or just after the first day of August, arrangements fell to be finalised. The young Duke of Ross, who was now Archbishop of St Andrews in name also, would head the welcoming meeting, supported by the Earl of Montrose, the Earl of Bothwell and a great company of the nobility and senior clergy. It would depend on what time of day the English party arrived at the border as to where their first night in Scotland would be spent. No fast riding would be suitable for such a train, and Edinburgh being some fifty-five miles from Lamberton, two days a-horse could be called for. That eastern Borderland, the Merse, was very much Home territory, and that proud house would take ill out of any night's hospitality being offered to the visitors in other than a Home establishment. Home Castle itself was too far west to be convenient, and Ayton had been destroyed by Surrey, who almost certainly would be amongst those there with the princess, so the first night might be best passed at Coldinghame, the priory of which was a wealthy and prosperous institution, its priors always Homes. Swinton would be convenient also, but it was not a Home place, and to take the future queen there would cause much Borders upset.

David Kennedy, not his father, was sent for to join the reception cavalcade, dressed in his best.

He had, inevitably, a long ride of it to meet up with the

distinguished company, right across Lowland Scotland, as he had had to do to reach Ellemford, for this very different occasion. But this time he went alone, not with a great troop of men-at-arms, and could ride the faster. He covered the one hundred and seventy miles in two days, spending the night at a hospice in Peebles, and reached Coldinghame Priory in time to spend a comfortable evening and night, with the main welcoming party not expected until the next afternoon.

The priory was an extensive and prosperous establishment, well known as such, lying in what was almost a dean where burns joined, not far from the coast, ancient, the first church there having been founded as far back as the year 830, and dedicated to the renowned borderland St Cuthbert. It became a priory in 1094, and was much favoured by the Margeretsons, especially King Edgar. Its wealth had been largely built up on the important trade of wool from the vast sheep-runs of the Lammermuir Hills, and since most of that wool was exported to the Low Countries, the monks had established a colony of Flemings at Berwick, to aid in the commerce, as early as 1250. The Home family had quickly perceived its value, and had become its hereditary bailiffs, and usually provided its priors also. The church itself was large but oddly constructed, or reconstructed, for it had suffered much in the cross-border warfare, being rebuilt many times; and the monastic premises extensive.

The monks treated David handsomely.

In the forenoon he went, on the advice of the sub-prior, to explore the nearby coastline, especially the stupendous St Ebba's Head cliffs. Ebba had been an Anglian princess who, in the seventh century had established a nunnery up on the summit of this mighty outthrust rock bastion, this to escape the attentions of the Norse raiders who had been terrorising this Northumbrian coast, like so many others. Even here, however, the women had not been safe, the Vikings following and assaulting them to the extent that they were said to have cut off their own breasts, some

166

said lips and noses also, to make them less attractive to their molesters. St Cuthbert himself had visited the nuns in his day. The headland, known as the fist of the Lammermuirs shaken at the Norse Sea, certainly impressed David Kennedy, brought up as he had been on cliff-top Dunure. These precipices and rock-stacks soaring hundreds of feet above the foam-spouting reefs, with their dizzy gulfs and cavernous rifts, made an awesome sight, and, with the screaming, wheeling seabirds competing with the crash of the breaking seas and the moaning of the seals in the deep inlets below, left the visitor all but dazed, and cautious not to venture too close to the edges of it all. David found the remains of the nunnery and its chapel only yards from the jagged cliff rim. Noisy as it was on this comparatively calm July day, what it would all be like in a winter's easterly gale was almost beyond imagination. Those nuns must have slept but uneasily on many a night.

Back at the priory, he found that other members of the reception company had arrived, from Dumfries and Galloway Maxwells, Johnstones, Herries and Agnews, although as yet the main party from the north were not come. Clearly it was going to be a numerous assembly.

It was. The Duke of Ross, the king's brother, presently appeared with over one hundred fellow welcomers, all attired as David had never seen them before, handsome garb not being normally a Scots preoccupation. The prince-archbishop was a slender, delicate-seeming youth, quiet and diffident compared with his brother, seeming very ill at ease in this situation and in the company he was keeping, Bothwell tending to take charge. Now they did not delay at Coldinghame, the enlarged company pressing on for Lamberton another ten miles, going parallel with the cliff-girt coast.

Lamberton Kirk, famous as the name of the bishop who had been Robert the Bruce's long-term friend and adviser, was situated some three miles north of Berwick-upon-Tweed, a mere hamlet, but significant as

167

now marking the border with England, however ridiculous this might seem, with nothing of importance there to mark the spot. But this was where the English had insisted on establishing the bounds of Berwick common when they had taken over the town and fortress in 1333, following the Battle of Halidon Hill, annexing it to England. So all south of this was now theirs in name, however much the Scots might deplore it, asserting of course that Berwick was the county town of Scots Berwickshire, never in Northumberland.

They found a further accretion to their numbers awaiting them there, Homes these, with their lord and his uncles the Homes of Ayton and Fastcastle. No fewer than seventeen Home lairds were present, to emphasise that this was their territory, very much so. They had news from Berwick. The princess's company were already there, having arrived the night before, and were remaining at the town all this day, being entertained and feted by the Captain of Berwick Castle, with sporting events and banqueting, even staging a fight to the death between bears and boar-hounds. They would not cross into Scotland before the morrow.

This information annoyed the Scots company, since it meant a lengthy waiting, and there was nowhere at Lamberton to accommodate all this gathering, high-born as it was. Why had the Homes not sent to Coldinghame to warn them? Nothing for it but to return whence they had just come, to the priory, and come back again in the morning, an irritating situation.

So it was for monkish hospitality again, welcome as this was, Lord Home, bailiff of the priory and one of his cousins, the prior, assuring that there would be no lack of provision. This of the English deliberately keeping the Scots waiting was, all agreed, typical.

David had to accept more humble quarters than on the previous night.

In the morning, it was back to Lamberton – and only just in time, for the outriders of the English host were already in sight; whether starting thus early also was intended to embarrass the Scots was not known, but suspected.

A host it proved to be when the princess arrived, over four hundred of an escort, illustrious indeed, with their old foes the Earl of Surrey and the Prince-Bishop of Durham, the Archbishop of York, no fewer than six earls, a score of lords, and knights innumerable. Also two ladies-in-waiting. Henry Tudor was intending there to be no doubts as to the honour being conferred now on Scotland.

His daughter herself scarcely matched up to all this magnificence, a plump, indeed stodgy, round-faced girl of no beauty nor grace, but with an obstinate Tudor chin. The welcomers eyed her, seeking not to look askance, but wondering what their liege-lord would make of this his bride. Meantime the Duke of Ross had to play the part of host to her.

And now, since Lamberton was no place to linger, they were faced with another problem. They would be back at Coldinghame in just over the hour, early forenoon. It had been intended that the princess would spend her first night in Scotland at the priory; but arriving thus early, although a day late, was unfortunate. The whole company could have proceeded on for another score of miles, at least; but as it happened there was no suitable place, short of Dunbar, to put up this large and distinguished entourage. It would look bad to take the princess as far as Dunbar on her first day; but what would they do with her and her lofty following all day at the priory?

It was Sir Patrick Home of Fastcastle who offered a solution. Let them all ride on northwards for another ten or eleven miles to his seat, and there deposit the princess for the night, with her ladies. It was no large hold, however strong, and there was not room for all this company; but these could return to the priory and pick her up again in the morning. His wife, who was the sister of Andrew Forman, Bishop of Moray, would look after Margaret Tudor adequately.

This was agreed, although some of the Homes exchanged glances a little doubtfully.

Before a move was made from Lamberton, Bishop Fox of Durham presented the Duke of Ross, in lordly fashion, with a pack-horse bearing, he declared, ten thousand gold angle-nobles, the final instalment of Margaret's dowery, which her husband-to-be had been wondering about for some time.

All thus arranged, they set off along the cliff road for the Eye Water and Coldinghame, David seeking to be companionable to a trio of English lords.

They did not wait long at the priory, after informing Prior Home of the situation, and rode on up on to and over the extensive Coldinghame Moor, scarcely the most attractive flourish of Scottish landscape for the newcomers, a sort of high heathery plateau devoid of features save for reedy pools and lochans and low hummocks, which was in fact the easternmost extension of the Lammermuir Hills, sheep its only denizens. No doubt the visitors decided that they had brought their monarch's daughter to a barren land as well as a barbarous people.

There were some eight miles of this before they reached its northern limits, and quite suddenly the prospect changed, and notably. Ahead of them the land dropped in green folds down to a widespread vista of fertile country and a picturesque coastline, hills to the west and all the Norse Sea to the east, far to the north the cone of North Berwick Law, and out in the mouth of the Firth of Forth the great columnar rock of the Craig of Bass. The contrast with what they had been seeing was striking, and even some English appreciation was expressed.

But soon they turned away from this, to follow a track through slightly lower moorland, seawards, the visitors clearly surprised. Not that Margaret Tudor evinced much reaction to anything that she saw; she was evidently less than impressionable. Three undulating miles of this and

170

they came to a minor ridge. The drop beyond this appeared to go on to emptiness, only the sea's far horizon marking any limit. No castle nor house was in sight.

Astonished, all but very few present stared. Whither were they bound?

With a wave of the hand, reassuring or otherwise, Sir Patrick Home, in the lead, dismounted.

"Highness, and my lords and ladies," he called. "Beyond is no good going for horses. Here leave your mounts. I shall send my men to see to them. Save for the princess and her ladies. We will lead their beasts. Fear not, it is none so far – and none so ill on the feet!" And he smiled grimly. "My house is one not taken readily, see you!"

The staring continued from under eyebrows raised or frowning. At first most there were reluctant to dismount, but when the other Homes left their mounts, and Sir Patrick himself went to take Margaret Tudor's mare by the bridle-rein and to lead it forward, they realised that this was not some extraordinary kind of diversion but their intended design. Most there probably seldom walked anywhere afoot, save in orchards or pleasances. The Duke of Ross, looking apprehensive, began to follow, then remembered the pack-horse laden with gold, and went back to take its halter and lead it on with him.

So the long, illustrious and bemused column set off for the void of what was presumably a cliff-top, comments loud, and not only on the part of the English.

In a few hundred yards they reached the cliffs, and the quite narrow path had to turn right-handed along the edge, dizzy drops on the left. Still there was nothing to be seen ahead but more precipices. Even the princess was looking bewildered and anxious now.

Apart from the four horses being carefully led along that winding track, through short heather and blaeberries, all had to walk in single file now. Surely never had so magnificently garbed a company paced its heedful way along that lofty but muddy course. These cliffs were as high as those David had wondered at at St Ebba's Head, dropping sheerly to the waves. And so far as could be seen, they went on thus for miles.

Then abruptly there was again a different prospect, at least for those at the head of the column. A minor promontory projected before them, towering high, and halfway down this a semi-detached stack of reddish rock rose, its base in the sea at one side, the other part of the cliff itself, with a sizeable gap at its head. And on top of this, between waves and sky, perched Fast Castle, scarcely believable as it was to behold.

Exclamations filled the air, above the seafowls' cries and the constant roar of the breakers. To be going *there*! And how to get to it? Never had all but a very few present ever seen the like, used as they might be to hilltop fortalices, including David Kennedy.

Home waved all on, and it became all the more apparent why the mounts had been left behind; for to reach the level of the cliff opposite the hold meant a steep descent, partly steps, no route for horses. So the princess and her ladies had to be assisted to dismount, wide-eyed, and their steeds with the pack-horse left behind, the last very much under guard.

The cautious downwards progress commenced. The young duke was looking more anxious than ever, not only about leaving the gold behind.

Why, David asked the Lord Drummond at his side, had this hold ever been built thus, on this wild, menacing coastline, and in such an inaccessible position? He was told that it had originally been for an objective as grim as its situation: to lure shipping on to the rocks and reefs below, to their wrecking, so that they could be plundered; indeed the name Fast was but a corruption of the French *Faux* or False. Allegedly horses were led along the cliff-top track by night, bearing lit lanterns, this to give the impression that here were habitations, havens and shelters from storm, whereas all in fact was savage threat. He agreed that it seemed a strange place to be bringing the king's bride for her first night in

Scotland. Had the Homes some present-day objective in this?

Down the difficult approach they picked their careful way, although some held back to wait on less awkward ground; after all, since only a limited number could get into that eagle's-nest of a castle, and most would have to climb back up here, little sense in going further. Some senior clergy thought that way, apparently, although Bishop Fox went on down with his charge. Also the Earl of Surrey.

When he could take his eyes off his footwork, David saw that the castle had three towers, a circular one at the gatehouse, a massive rectangular keep behind, and, at a lower level of the stack-platform on the seaward edge, another of odd shape, following the contours of the rock. A high wall, itself necessarily of irregular configuration, enclosed all.

Reaching what was little more than a wide ledge, they faced the gap between the cliffside and the stack, a gulf of well over a score of feet. A drawbridge was lowered for them to cross this, no passageway for those suffering from vertigo, with an awesome abyss below, and the gangway narrow and lacking handrails. No need for moats and ramparts here, with cannon unable to get anywhere within range.

Sir Patrick took the princess's arm to escort her across this walkway. Perceiving the alarm of one of her ladies, David Kennedy stepped forward to do the same for her, advising her not to look down. Heedfully the others followed.

Once within the uneven bare rock courtyard, there was little space available for their numbers; but the keep itself was more commodious than it might have seemed, four storeys and a garret in height, with a fair-sized hall and three bedchambers on each of the upper floors. However, even with the rooms in the two other towers, there was no capacity for any great number of the visitors.

The Lady Home, a friendly and motherly woman,

welcomed them kindly and took charge of Margaret Tudor, her husband having sent a messenger to inform her of this invasion of her strange abode.

In the circumstances, although there was ample provision and refreshment available, no large proportion of those who had got thus far elected to remain, preferring the ride back to the considerably more comfortable and spacious quarters at Coldinghame Priory. About forty all told remained, David included, and the rest took rather thankful departure.

The remainder were well entertained in that eyrie of a place. After an excellent repast in the hall, the princess and her attendants being catered for apart in the private withdrawing-room off, David for one went out to explore and examine. The atmosphere of the establishment was as extraordinary as was its situation, the sense of being suspended between sea and sky, the constrictions, and yet the awareness of space all around; and the incessant noise, this last not only the roar of the waves breaking below but the screeching, yelping, quavering and whistling of the birds, hundreds upon hundreds of them, which swooped and wheeled, dived and plunged all around the castle endlessly, every variety of gull, fulmars, petrels, skuas, kittiwakes, guillemots, puffins and the like, this their own world, indeed the smell of them and their droppings strong in the air. Those not thus in flight could be seen roosting on every ledge and cranny of the cliffs, some so near as almost to be touched, beady-eyed, watchful. As well as all his din, there was another strange sound which at first David thought might be the moaning of seals, but which he decided was too deep and regular for that. A servitor told him that this was the surge of the tides in a great cavern below the castle, this deep and long and high, into which boats could be rowed, and which had a wide shaft in its roof which communicated with the building above, allowing access by ladder from the water, for the knowledgeable, no doubt of use during the old wrecking days. One more astonishing feature of this Fast Castle.

The views along the cliffs left and right were dramatic, with crags and pinnacles and deep clefts, spray spouting up from the breakers, and the whole shoreline white with tortured water. Only seawards was there placidity, the empty ocean.

That night, as David shared a bedchamber with Lord Drummond and an English knight, and listened to the noises which had not ceased with darkness, particularly that menacing growling and groaning from the cavern just below, he wondered what Margaret Tudor was thinking of the country that her father had consigned her to, and if this was typical of it? He did not particularly like the youngster, and she did not seem to be of an imaginative frame of mind, but he did feel sorry for her in this.

Their Englishman was, it seemed, a Howard, kin to Surrey. He expressed his wonder at it all, and the two Scots were at pains to assure him that Fast was by no means normal.

In the morning they had to wait until the main company returned from Coldinghame before the climbing up the steep ascent to the main cliff-top was tackled, the ladies having to lift skirts high, amidst much pausing for breath. One of Margaret's attendants did thank Lady Home for her hospitality. Thereafter there was much relief when at length they reached the horses and the rest of the party, and they could resume their journey, now going northwards by west.

Soon they were down to the levellish ground that they had viewed the day before, and easy riding conditions. Following the now pleasant coastline, notable for its bright red rocks and sandy beaches, they went by Colbrandspath to Dunbar, there seeing another extraordinary castle, this built out on a series of stack-tops into the waves, the various towers linked by covered bridges, much larger than Fast but its cliffs comparatively minor. Here they turned due westwards for the Tyne valley at Prestonkirk, inland now, making up-river for Haddington, a thirty-mile ride but nowise taxing, the visitors exclaiming more

175

moderately over the dramatic isolated eminences of the Bass Rock, North Berwick Law and Traprain Law, tales anent which they were told.

At Haddington, quite a major town, they were to lodge at the famous nunnery in its riverside meadows, founded by the mother of Kings Malcolm the Maiden and William the Lion three centuries before, markedly different from the previous night's venue, all comfort and ease. Here they learned that King James was to meet them, not at Edinburgh itself but at the small town of Dalkeith, seven miles to the east. So their route would be somewhat changed, to cover the eighteen or so miles up Tyne by Pencaitland and Ormiston and Cousland, again easy riding.

There were no complaints. After the Fast experience, all seemed completely normal and acceptable.

Dalkeith was a Black Douglas place, but the links with Henry Tudor ensured co-operation, and indeed the Earl of Morton here was prominent amongst the royal party awaiting the princess's arrival. The narrow streets of the town were packed with folk, and outriders had difficulty in clearing a way for the travellers through the cheering crowds to reach the fine church of St Nicholas, before which James Stewart, clad in cloth of gold and a vivid lion rampant tabard, waited, mounted, to receive his bride, backed by the Lord Lyon King of Arms, the High Constable, the Earl Marischal and other dignitaries.

The actual meeting was somewhat confused. No one seeming quite sure as to procedure, the thronging press of cheering townsfolk scarcely helping. Surrey and the Archbishop of York led Margaret's palfrey forward, on which she sat gazing around her and not particularly at the monarch. The archbishop began to speak, but in all that din no one could hear his words.

James, eyeing the girl, evidently decided that it would be suitable to greet her with more of a flourish, whatever he thought of her appearance. He jumped down from his horse to go over to hers, which meant that all others, who knew how to conduct themselves in the royal presence, had to dismount also, none to remain in the saddle while their liege-lord stood, although this did not apply to the English there evidently.

With the princess showing no sign of dismounting either, the king reached up to grasp her round the middle and to pull her bodily down to him, she less than co-operative. With some difficulty and a flurry of skirts, he got her down, to hold her at arm's length and stoop to kiss her brow, she turning to look back at the archbishop enquiringly.

James, holding her, made a brief speech of welcome, gained no reply, and taking her by the arms turned and gestured from her to the waiting magnates, in some sort of presentation. Most of them bowed. Then his brother, the Duke of Ross, led forward that pack-horse laden with the dowery gold, thankful no doubt to be rid of the responsibility, even though this was perhaps scarcely the moment to hand it over. James waved it and him away, and all those dismounted stood for a moment or two, at something of a loss to know what to do next.

Bishop Forman of Moray, Lady Home's brother, with Bishop Elphinstone, took the lead, these two stepping forward to bow again, and then reach for the princess's hand to kiss it. This example was taken up by the rest of the waiting group, Margaret accepting these salutations somewhat doubtfully, her English escorts sitting their horses watching, the crowd still cheering.

The king evidently considered that sufficient had now been done to mark the occasion. Taking Margaret's arm again, he led her back to his own horse, not hers, mounted, and stooping from the saddle, with quite a major effort, lifted the girl up somehow, to place her on a side-saddle strapped behind his own, to her obvious bewilderment. Settling her thus, and telling her to hold on to his tabard, he waved to his supporters and her former escort to follow him. He reined round, to head for the road to Edinburgh. There was a hasty mounting and getting into some sort of order, the crowded street no aid, and the move was commenced, David Kennedy well to the rear now.

By Sheriffhall and Gilmerton they came to the capital, having to skirt round the southern and western sides of the mighty mass of Arthur's Seat, this, especially the challenging escarpment rock columns of Samson's Ribs drawing much comment from the visitors, if none from James's passenger. They entered the walled city by the St Leonard's Gate, and so rode in procession down the Cowgate, heading not up for the great fortress-castle but for the Abbey of the Holy Rood on the north side of Arthur's Seat. The streets here too were thronged with folk out to see the monarch's bride, people at all the house windows, these hung for the occasion with coloured rugs, plaiding and even clothing, some citizens actually with flowers to toss towards the royal horse. Margaret Tudor surely would not forget her welcome to Scotland however little reaction she presently demonstrated.

At the splendid abbey under the heights of what the visitors were already referring to as the mountain, the now multitudinous company at last reached journey's end, to dismount and place themselves in the good care of the abbot and his monks, assured of ample hospitality. James gestured towards the new palace he had started to build here beside the monastic quarters.

Large as these were, there was insufficient accommodation at the abbey for so numerous a company, so James took quite prompt leave of his bride-to-be, and led a large part of the Scots contingent off up the Canongate for Edinburgh Castle for quarters, in accordance with the custom that bride and groom should not spend the night before the wedding under the same roof, David going with this group. He forbore to ask the king, later, what he thought of their future queen, but judged that Janet would have no cause for female jealousy.

On the morrow it was back to the abbey for the nuptials in the great church still called after the fragment of Christ's true cross, the Holy Rood, which that other

178

Queen Margaret had brought from Hungary when she wed Malcolm Canmore, even though Edward Plantagenet, the Hammer of the Scots, had stolen it, and where it was now none knew.

The wedding was a tremendous and colourful affair, with no fewer than nine prelates taking part, two of them archbishops, three if young Ross was counted, Primate as he was but not in holy orders, he officiating after a fashion as groomsman. Surrey represented King Henry in giving the bride away, she showing little sign of bridal excitement, much less elation. Much ado was made of the presentation to the king of a sword and diadem wrought in flowers of gold, the gift of Pope Julius the Second, and handed over by his Protonotary, Bishop Forman.

Thereafter it was all festivity and feasting in the palatial abbot's establishment, no cost spared. At the banquet, a wild boar's head was presented to the new Queen of Scotland on a silver platter, the boar having been the symbol of the ancient Celtic monarchy, claimed to be the oldest royal line in Christendom. As well as this there were no fewer than fifty-five other dishes of meats and sweets, from swans, herons, geese, ducks, even peacocks, and salmon and trout and shellfish, to sweetmeats of every variety, even a jelly in the form of the arms of Scotland. And, of course, wines, ale and whisky unlimited. James was determined that the English notables should not go back to Richmond reporting the Scots as beggarly.

As an ultimate gesture to mark the occasion, the king created no fewer than forty-one new knights, some of them Englishmen, and made three new earls. And it was announced that there would be five days of entertainment, contests, jousting, tourneys, horse-racing and parades to places of interest, and miscellaneous pageantry. Church bells were to be rung continuously, and a fountain of wine to spout for all at Edinburgh's Mercat Cross.

Listening to all this, David, anxious to get home to Agnes, with fear of a premature birth, decided that it all was not for him. James would have a sufficiency of

179

courtiers, companions and attendants for his celebratory activities without the Master of Kennedy, surely. He would beg permission to retire from court.

It was noted by all that bride and groom did not retire together for that night, Margaret and her ladies leaving the almost entirely male gathering at no very late hour, James merely leading her to the refectory door, kissing her hair, and returning to his seat.

It was well after midnight before he rose again, by which time many of his guests were asleep at the table, noisy as the occasion had become. Few anticipated that he would be heading for the fourteen-year-old's bedchamber. No doubt he had made other arrangements.

Late as was his own bed-going, David was on his way south-westwards next early forenoon, with much to tell his love.

17

It was mid-September before Agnes was delivered of a little son, not premature and with no complications, a bundle of joy for his parents, and to be named Gilbert. For so small a creature, Gilbert dominated the Cassillis household for the next few months, his doting parents well content that it should be so, however many heads were shaken over them. Fortunately no royal calls came to Carrick meantime, and David was thankful to hear of the newly wed monarch's doings only by report. The word was that Queen Margaret, after an initial tour round palaces, towns, great houses, hunting-seats and cathedrals and abbeys, introducing the girl to her new people, high and low, was apt to be left on her own at Linlithgow Palace, the dowery-seat, most of the time, with the Countess of Surrey, who had come up to act as her chaperone and mentor, such as was undoubtedly needed. It was known that her husband had twice paid visits up to Moray before Christmastide, few doubts expressed as to the reason therefor, this despite winter travel conditions through the snowy Highlands.

David himself was anxious to see his sister, of course, and wanted to present his splendid small Gilbert to her, difficult as this might be to contrive so long as she remained up at Darnaway Castle. And since this isolation had been arranged by James Stewart precisely so that no reports of his co-habiting with his mistress would be sent to London and seem to make a mockery of his marriage, it seemed unlikely that southern Scotland would be seeing much of Flaming Janet for some considerable time. However, an understanding Agnes announced that, all being well, *they* could do the visiting, and before overlong. Once the spring was upon them, and no very long days' riding was involved, it was quite possible for a mother and baby to travel a-horse, even those two hundred long miles. And to demonstrate her contention, she began to ride abroad frequently, with the child in her arms, saying that her own mother at Borthwick had done the like and met with no ill effects. David was doubtful but wanted to believe her.

That festive season was the more joyful for the new arrival's burbling participation, even the Lord Kennedy showing some slight interest in his first grandchild, and the other members of the family appreciative. Agnes was anxious to try to repair bridges in this disunited household.

So the months passed, and whatever the success or otherwise of the royal marriage, the Scots as a nation were thankful for the peace with England, and the end of constant raiding and invasion. That is, except for the West March area, the so-called Debateable Land, where it seemed nothing would stop the cross-border feuding and pillage of Armstrongs and Nixons, Johnstones and Robsons, Irvines and Forsters, Carruthers and Croziers. This ages-old raiding and ravaging was not really warfare so much as a way of life here, and death, for these wild moss-troopers. It was in this connection, however, that David's period of peaceful living was interrupted. He received a summons to attend a Privy Council meeting at Stirling. His membership of that august body had not, on the whole, caused him as much inconvenience as might have been expected, its meetings comparatively infrequent. He hoped that this occasion would not prove otherwise.

The business, it turned out, was this of the West March. King Henry was complaining that the terms of the peace treaty were being blatantly broken by the Scots Marchmen, and that this must cease. He had ordered his West March Warden, the Lord Dacre, to take all necessary steps to ensure this, and hoped that his good son-in-law would effectively co-operate.

James, at the meeting, sought Bothwell's advice – he was still Chief Warden of the Marches. But the Hepburn declared that, well aware as he was of the lawlessness in the West March, he did not see what he could usefully do about it. These Border clans were a law unto themselves, and, secure in their inaccessible territory, were able to ignore all authority. And, of course, the English clans were equally to blame. Unfortunately the Scots West March Warden, the Lord Maxwell, was of scant help, his Maxwells by no means themselves innocent in the matter.

James suggested a replacement for Lord Maxwell, but had it pointed out that there was no one in a position to overbear Maxwell, quite the most powerful man on the West March. Any new warden would find his task difficult indeed.

In that case, the king said, since something must be done in this matter which was endangering the peace with England, he himself would go down to that March and seek to introduce law and order. Maxwell could scarcely ignore *his* authority.

Some doubts were expressed around that table over this. If in fact the royal will was flouted, as it might well be, it would do the crown and nation no service, and possibly lead to insubordination elsewhere. Yet to take a full royal army down there, strong enough to enforce his will, would amount to civil war and raise much of the south-west against the monarchy.

David put forward a suggestion. Let His Grace go, but not make a military expedition of it, if he was set on a gesture, but make it more of a royal excursion to these parts, where hitherto he had not gone, something in the nature of a progress; but while there, in Eskdale, Liddesdale, Dryfesdale and the rest, make his royal will well known to the moss-trooping clans, meet with the English warden, and have Maxwell join him, which ought to have the effect of hedging that lord in considerably, and should impress King Henry.

This was accepted as good policy by all present, including the monarch. He would do just that, and very soon.

The other item before the council was regarding the Earl of Angus. Whether he had ever gone to Arran was doubtful; but now that he had married this Stirling woman and was living quietly on his various properties, it seemed the time, according to Bishop Elphinstone, to make some peaceable gesture towards him, the accord with England now limiting his capabilities for making trouble. He was, after all the Red Douglas, and better to have as the king's supporter rather than his foe lying low. Some appointment that evidenced this, but in which he could do little harm, seemed to be advisable.

This also was agreed, although no actual role for Bell-the-Cat was put forward there and then.

The meeting broke up, with James telling David that he would be calling on him, as Bailie of Carrick, to aid in this projected visit to the West March. After all, it was his suggestion; and Carrick itself was none so far from that March. He also mentioned that he had seen Janet recently and that she was well content with her life up at Darnaway with their little son, and quite active in managing his earldom of Moray for him.

James was as good as his word in the matter of the West March venture, arriving down at Cassillis with Bothwell, and, to make it seem the more unmilitary, with Bishop Forman of Moray and quite a train of falconers, minstrels, even cooks, to ensure the right appearances of almost holiday. He had sent word to Lord Maxwell to attend him at Dumfries, and informed the English warden, Dacre, that it would be helpful for the due peace of the Borderland if he would meet him at some suitable spot along the March.

But he also asked David to assemble a modest array of his Carrick men to accompany them, just to let the warring clans know that there was some steel behind the velvet glove. Almost casually he added that he was appointing him, David, as Deputy Warden of the West March.

This last had that man in all but dismay. He had no desire for further appointments, especially one that might well entail considerable and difficult work dealing with those moss-troopers. And being deputy to the hard Lord Maxwell, with whom he had never been friendly, presented no anticipatory pleasure. But it was a royal command and not to be rejected.

So he went off to recruit some four score horsemen, while Agnes had to act hostess to their unexpected visitors. At least they had the minstrels to entertain them.

They rode away next day southwards for Dumfries, by the Doon Water and its loch, and over to the upper Nith, halting for the night at Drumlanrig, a Black Douglas place, where the king made a point of asking amiably after the Earl of Angus, and the laird was notably careful as to his answers. He did, however, commend all efforts to keep the dalesmen in order, and provided the royal party with a morning's hawking before they set off again down Nith. They called on the way at Lochmaben Castle, on the parallel Annan Water, a notable royal seat and former home of Robert the Bruce. James emphasised that they were in no hurry.

They arrived at Dumfries town at darkening, where they found Lord Maxwell awaiting them, and with quite a large following, his welcome cool. When he heard that he had a new deputy warden he was cooler still, scowling at David. He was a handsome man of middle years, of proud bearing. But he could not say nay. He and Bothwell did not get on together either, so it could have been an uncomfortable evening at the Greyfriars monastery in the town, had not Bishop Forman introduced a local celebrity, Dumfries's crookbacked vicar, who was noted for his tuneful voice and rendering of Border ballads and tales of the past, as well as his ready wit, he making a dramatic story out

185

of the Bruce's slaying of the treacherous Red Comyn in this very monastery two hundred years before, and Kirkpatrick of Closeburn's "making siccar", an event that made necessary a speedy coronation for the king-to-be before excommunication for the killing, before an altar, could reach Scotland from the Vatican, after which no bishop could have anointed him. The provost and bailies of the town, much affected by the royal visit, provided fair hospitality.

In the morning, word came from Carlisle that the Lord Dacre would meet the king at Rowanburnfoot, near to Canonbie in Eskdale two days hence, if that suited His Majesty. James sent back affirmation, and emphasised that this was to be a happy occasion, in celebration of the peace, and that friendship and cheer should be the order of the day.

They had a wait, therefore, and James was in no doubt as to what they should do with it: make an example of one or two of the malefactors, so that when the Englishman arrived he could be shown that they at least were in earnest in fulfilling the peace treaty. He asked Maxwell whether he had any law-breakers at present awaiting sentence.

That man shrugged. "Always there are offenders, Sire," he said. "Cattle-thieves, ravishers and the like. I hang them in due course, to be sure."

"Ah, yes, my lord. But I am here concerned with cross-border outrage, of which this Dacre may complain. Have you any of such for me?"

"None of these care aught for the borderline, Your Grace. Their raidings and depredations could be on either side, or both. I make little of distinction."

"Save for Maxwells, perhaps!" That was Bothwell.

The other glared. "What mean you by that, my lord?"

"Only that this Lord Dacre may be apprised of names. And it would be unfortunate if he judged that we were making . . . exceptions!"

Bishop Forman intervened, seeking to avoid a clash between these two in the royal presence. "This Rowan-burnfoot and Canonbie, Sire, where is it? Near to this Dumfries? My lord of Maxwell will know it?"

"Canonbie is a village in Eskdale, but a mile from the border," they were told. "Near to the Armstrong tower of Holehouse. Rowanburnfoot is on the borderline itself, a mile on."

"How far from here, these?" James asked.

"A dozen miles, east by north. Across the Lochar Water and the Kerr heights to the Esk."

"And are there any scoundrels awaiting execution thereabouts?"

"Always there are, yes." Maxwell shrugged again. "Armstrong country, as I said: I have prisoners in Langholm tolbooth who are to die, for reivery and murder."

"They wait there?"

"I have much other tasks demanding my attention in this March, Your Grace, than dealing with Armstrongs, even in insurrection. They can bide my convenience!"

"So! Let us go there, then. To this Canonbie. Hang two or three of them. To show this Dacre that *we* at least seek to maintain order and peace. We come back here? Or spend the night in Canonbie?"

"That is but a small place, Sire. Your Grace would do better at Langholm, where there is a religious house."

"Very well. Langholm let it be."

So they rode eastwards, over green, grassy hills, min-strels, cooks and all, with the Carrick and Maxwell escorts, making a company fully two hundred strong, to cross the Lochar Water and over into Eskdale, the country growing ever wilder and higher, but with its own beauty. At Langholm, where the Ewes and Wauchope Waters joined Esk, they were warned that they would find an Armstrong fortalice; but with such a large company and the king's presence there ought to be no trouble. When Maxwell visited there, he always went in sufficient strength. This information gave them some indication of conditions in the Debateable Land.

It was not exactly trouble that met them at Langholm as something of a slap in the faces of the Wardens and the monarch. For, apprised of their coming, the royal visit and its probable objectives, Armstrong of Gilnockie had that very morning raided the town's tolbooth and gaol, freed four Armstrong prisoners there, and only the Armstrongs, leaving others, and carried them off to his stronger hold of Holehouse Tower. Presumably the remaining ill-doers could be dealt with as the wardens thought fit.

Maxwell, a great shrugger, shrugged again. Apparently he was quite used to this sort of behaviour. But James was angry, as was Bothwell, the Chief Warden. This was insufferable! These Armstrongs must be shown who ruled in Scotland, and that the laws were not to be flouted. Where was this Holehouse?

It was a few miles to the north, he was told.

They would go there, then, and at once. Maxwell pointed out that it was a strong place, not large but not easy to take without cannon. The king was not to be put off.

So they all rode up Esk, Maxwell again warning that their coming would not go unobserved, over two hundred of them. Gilnockie would know of their coming.

When they arrived at Holehouse, or Hollows Tower as it was pronounced locally, it was to find a typical Border peel-tower set within a high-walled courtyard, with a stone beacon-holder set on its gable-top, for the sending of messages, by flame or smoke, to other such holds of the clan, all within a moat drawn from a burn entering the river nearby. A column of smoke was indeed rising from that beacon already.

It was Bothwell who rode forward to the edge of the moat beside the raised drawbridge. "I am the Earl of Bothwell, Chief Warden of the Marches," he shouted. "The King's Grace is here, in royal person. He would have speech with Armstrong of Gilnockie."

He was answered at once. "Gilnockie is not here. He has gone."

"Gone? Gone where, man?"

"He did not inform me. I am but keeper here."

David, for one, had heard all this before elsewhere.

"He had prisoners with him? From Langholm tolbooth. His Grace requires these."

No reply.

"Are these men in this hold?"

Still no answer.

James had ridden up to Bothwell's side, with Maxwell and others. He raised a royal arm.

"I am James. Your liege-lord, King of Scots. I want those men," he called. "And will have them! I have cannon at my castle of Lochmaben, none so far from here. I can have pieces here by the morrow. They will knock this hold stone from stone! Unless you, sirrah, render me these men forthwith. You hear?"

There was still no vocal response to that, and the king was beginning to shout again, when Maxwell touched his arm and pointed. An iron portcullis at the gatehouse was beginning to be raised.

They waited, and presently a group of eight men issued out from under the arch, and two of them began to turn the great handles which lowered the drawbridge.

On to the middle of the bridge they came, and stood, silent.

"Are these the men?" Bothwell demanded.

"These are," a thick-set, grey-haired man said.

"And who are you?"

"I am Armstrong of Enthorn, keeper here."

"These men are to hang. Lord Maxwell, your warden, has found them guilty of reivery and pillage. They were awaiting their fate at Langholm."

"If Armstrongs are to hang, Armstrongs will hang them!" he was answered briefly.

Bothwell frowned, Maxwell hooted, but it was James who spoke.

189

"Very well so," he said. "If that is your custom. So long as they hang for breaching the realm's law and the realm's peace. *You* hang them, sir. Now."

The Armstrong inclined his head. "As you will." And taking one of the men by the arm, he turned back towards the gatehouse.

"Wait, you!" James cried. "You will hang them now. Here before us. I, the king, will see justice done. See you to it."

The other paused, and looked back. "I have not . . . the means, Sire."

"A rope and a tree are all the means necessary! Here." James reached into the pouch at his belt and drew out a handful of small coins. These he tossed contemptuously on to the drawbridge timbers in front of the men. "To pay for your rope! Fetch one." He turned in the saddle. "Yonder tree will serve." And he pointed.

The eight Armstrongs eyed each other. Then he who claimed to be keeper gestured to one of them to go back into the courtyard.

All waited, silent.

It was not long before the man returned, with a long coil of rope over his arm. The money on the bridge was ignored. The eight men came slowly forward. Which four were the doomed ones was not clear.

None speaking now, the king, still mounted, led the way to the nearest tree growing beside that burn entering the Esk. He pointed again, wordless.

The man with the rope went over, inspected the branches above, and selecting one, tossed the rope-end up. The first throw did not catch on, and the end fell to the ground. He tried again, and this time the loop he had tied in it did go over, and he pulled the loop down. All watched, witnesses and victims alike.

Maxwell then added to this silent drama. He gestured to one of his own men to dismount, and made a mounting signal towards the Armstrongs. The keeper understood well enough, and tapping one of the moss-troopers on the shoulder, pointed in turn. Set-faced, that man went over and climbed into the empty saddle, there to sit. The horse's owner, at another nod, led his beast forward to the tree. Clearly all these Marchmen knew the process.

Under the tree the horse was halted, and the man with the rope handed the noose-end up to the rider without ado, that unfortunate taking it and putting the loop over his head, carefully ensuring that the knot was placed exactly at the back of his neck. Then he sat expressionless.

The keeper brought the three remaining culprits forward to take the rope in their hands, the other end of it. They too knew what was required of them. They all gripped the fibre firmly, with the man already there, and waited, to take the strain.

Then, at a nod from Maxwell, his man abruptly wrenched the horse's reins forward. The beast half reared and then plunged onwards – and after a yard or two the victim was jerked bodily out of the saddle by the rope and noose. The men on the other end of it pulled hard, and after almost hitting the ground, the doomed individual was hoisted high, twisting and swinging, head tugged over to an unnatural angle. And there, dangling, rotating, limbs twitching, eyes protruding, he hung.

All watching, probably few enjoyed the sight. David certainly did not, Bishop Forman beside him tense-faced. After a few moments, the latter, pulling round after turning away, rode forward towards the victim and, from the saddle, raised an arm to utter a brief prayer and benediction for the departing soul.

James forced himself to gaze. But when the bishop had finished and reined round again, the king called, "Cut him down. It is enough. He is . . . gone. And, and there are three others!" He turned to Maxwell. "See you to it. This is *your* duty. We will await you at Langholm." And he kicked his horse into motion, and away.

Most there were glad enough to follow him, having seen a sufficiency. And it would take quite some time to complete the other three hangings. The hoisters would

191

require replacements from amongst Maxwell's men as their own turns came.

Few had much to say to each other as they rode back to Langholm. It occurred to David Kennedy grimly that if he was going to be deputy warden of this March, he would have to get used to this sort of scene.

It was a while before Lord Maxwell rejoined the rest of the leadership at the Whitefriars monastery near Langholm. He reported that he had had all four miscreants hung up again on that tree, on extra ropes, so that they would be a lesson to others, and something to show Dacre when he arrived. They spent a reasonably comfortable night at the moderate-sized monastery, at least the king's party did, while the men-at-arms camped outside. And in the morning all rode down to Canonbie and beyond to Rowanburnfoot, where they settled to wait for the Englishmen. The actual borderline was unmarked, so whether they waited on the Scots or the English side was uncertain. But presently they saw quite a company coming from the south-west, rivalling their own in size. Dacre was not going to be outshone, evidently, by the King of Scots.

Actually he proved to be something of a character, a lively man of a sort of dry humour, anything but obsequious, but neither arrogant nor defensive. He had brought with him the Bishop of Carlisle, so they had two prelates to help in the proceedings. His party also came laden with cooked venison, oatcakes and wine, so that obviously it was intended that a friendly atmosphere should prevail, if possible. This suited James Stewart, and he reciprocated, all amiability, however little Lord Maxwell contributed, he and Dacre, of course, being apt to be confrontational.

The Englishmen brought tents, to encamp on the meadowland of the Rowan Burn, and presumably Dacre anticipated that their meeting should take the form of a conference there. But James had other ideas. He wanted to prove to Henry's representatives that he was taking all suitable and practical steps to ensure the peace at the borderline, and suggested to Dacre and the bishop that they should accompany him up to Canonbie, where he would have sundry malefactors from Langholm tolbooth hanged before them as evidence of this. Maxwell said that there were five more prisoners awaiting execution there other than the four Armstrongs.

The Englishmen were quite agreeable, and after a pause while the tents were being pitched, and refreshment consumed, the move was made, James and Dacre riding side by side and exchanging pleasantries, the two bishops behind with Bothwell, Maxwell and David. The last was certainly not looking forward to witnessing another execution of justice.

At Canonbie they waited at the monastery while Maxwell went on to organise the hangings, the king ordering his minstrels to entertain them meantime with fiddle-music and song.

Then Maxwell came back to announce that all was ready, and they moved on, superficially at least in good spirits.

At the village they found everything prepared, two trees with five noosed ropes hanging from branches, and the five unfortunates lined up, under guard. The same procedure as formerly was gone through, but this time simultaneously, horses used to mount all the victims together, but no jerkings forward until all five were in position. Then Maxwell gave the signal, and at least the initial stages of the gallows work took place duly regimented, although the actual dying was less so, some expiring more quickly and with less bother and display than others.

Dacre seemed duly impressed by the expertise of it all, and the Bishop of Carlisle left it to Forman to perform his valedictory requiems.

Thereafter they rode on up to Holehouse, where they viewed the four dead Armstrongs swaying slightly in the breeze. No sign or demonstration came from the fortalice.

James judged that this was all a sufficiency of proof of his will for peace, and they returned to Rowanburnfoot. Dacre, it seemed, had no plans for any similar gestures on his own part, while assuring that he would be equally active against English transgressors. Instead, in his tent, he produced a young woman, from Carlisle apparently, with a notable voice, to sing for them, and dance an accompaniment, while they ate and drank, the Scots minstrels joining in the entertainment. Then he challenged the king to a game of cards, at which he won £2–6–8 from the royal pouch, skilful at this evidently. He claimed that his gain would be accepted by him as compensation for having been shut up in Norham Castle that time, when James besieged it – something they had not known of, this producing the desired laughter.

Getting on so unexpectedly well with this Englishman, the king suggested a trip up to his royal castle of Lochmaben, twenty-five miles, set amongst lochs, where the hawking for wildfowl was particularly good, and they could pass a more comfortable night than in these tents. And, he hoped, he might recoup himself over his losses at cards. Dacre accepted the invitation with evident pleasure, his bishop not objecting, and, taking only a small proportion of his escorting company with him, set off in the late afternoon with the royal train north by west for Annandale, all in excellent spirits; all, that is, save for Lord Maxwell, who made no secret of his disapproval of this fraternising with the Auld Enemy, with whom *he* had to cope all the time. His air of coolness resulted in his not being invited to Lochmaben; and at Lockerbie he and his men left the royal party to head westwards for their own territory at Caerlaverock. There was little of regrets expressed at the parting, but James ordering him, as warden, to enforce sentence of outlawry on sundry North Liddesdale Armstrongs whom Dacre was complaining of for persistent raiding and havoc over into the Byrness area of Northumberland.

So, on to Lochmaben and a lively night, where James

lost more money at cards, and Dacre promised to make suitable examples of some of his own transgressors, Croziers and Robsons in especial.

In the morning, it was dispersal, the king heading north for Edinburgh, Dacre south-east for Carlisle, and David west for Carrick, much mutual appreciation expressed on all sides, and the peace process much advanced.

Before he left the royal presence, David was informed that, to repay him for his new responsibilities as Deputy Warden of the West March, he was to receive the barony of Leswalt, in the Galloway part of that March; also the forfeited properties of Balgray in Lanarkshire and Foulwood in Cunninghame. Quite overcome by this generosity, which would make quite a rich man out of him, David headed homewards. What would Agnes say to all that he had to tell her? And was this sudden increase in wealth and importance worth the extra concerns of the West March?

18

Agnes was less than happy over the West March situation, and especially over her husband having to be a party to and witness of those hangings. She hoped that this was not a foretaste of things to come, and that he would not be expected to behave as a hangman and executioner hereafter. David said that he had been thinking about it all on his way home, and believed that he saw glimpses of hope. Lord Maxwell, to be sure would not be eager for him to be active on the March, who had never wanted him as deputy; so he could probably restrict his activities, and to the sort of ones that he would not find too objectionable. The king would never get to know of this, and if he did, and was critical and rebuked him, or even relieved him of the office, so much the better. There could, obviously, be handicaps as well as benefits in being Flaming Janet's brother!

This of Janet, Agnes said: she was quite sure that young Gilbert could now be taken on the long ride up to Moray in this summer weather, if they did not attempt to go too far in any one day. It was time that they visited Janet. Nothing loth, David agreed. Two hundred and fifty miles from Carrick. How many days riding with the child? Agnes said that they could surely cover forty in a day, without overdoing it. Their son would sleep most of the time, lulled by the horse's movements, so she had discovered. So six days? David wondered whether that was practicable; but they would see how it all went.

A day or two later, then, they set out, the infant wrapped before his mother in a plaid. They had a young woman attendant and two servitors with them. The weather was dull but not wet nor windy. Their route was the usual one as far as Stirling, by Cumnock and the Clyde, west of Glasow to Cumbernauld and Falkirk. The first day they did even better than Agnes had foretold, reaching a monkish hospice at Strathaven for the night, forty-five miles, young Gilbert no trouble even though he slept less than anticipated, only crying when he was hungry, and Agnes able to feed him from the saddle. Proud of themselves and their son, they had the monks making a great fuss over their unusual visitor.

Next day, crossing Clyde, they had thought to get as far as Falkirk, but reaching there by early afternoon, Agnes said that they should press on to Stirling, which they did, and were able to pass the night in quarters that David had often occupied in the castle. The king was not present, having gone somewhere northwards they were told; it would be rather comic if they found that he too was up visiting Janet. They paid their respects to the girl queen, who received them with her usual lack of warmth or even interest, even when Agnes presented the child. James was obviously saddled with a less than exciting wife.

Now they had to face territory new for Agnes at least, once across Forth. They were making for St John's Town of Perth, another forty miles, up the Allan Water vale and into Strathearn. Actually they covered this in excellent time, so that again they would have been halting fairly soon after midday. David suggested that they went on the few extra miles to Scone, where they could put up at the famous abbey, and Agnes could see the coronation place of the realm's kings and the Moot Hill where the oaths of fealty were sworn. This they did, the young woman duly impressed.

David reckoned that they were now about halfway to their destination, in three days' riding. But ahead of them lay the Highlands, with very different country to cover, by drove-roads and difficult tracks, through high passes, with rushing torrents to ford and steep ascents to climb. Agnes declared that she was looking forward to this, having always wanted to see the like.

They went up Tay, easy going at first, but by Birnam Wood, of MacBeth fame, they were into more challenging country; and after Dunkeld, early college of the ancient Celtic Church, they were into its first passes, the mountains beginning to soar above them. At Killiecrankie, Agnes saw the torrents and cataracts she had heard of, deep in fierce ravines, and, for that serene young woman, was strangely excited. Emerging from the string of passes into the more open country of Strathtay, with high mountains on either side, they were able to make better time of it, and indeed got as far as Pitlochry, past where Tay swung off westwards, and they had to follow the Garry northwards, well pleased to have reached another hospice run by the Church. What would travellers do without the monks' so valuable services? Young Gilbert was not proving to be any problem.

Now they had Athol ahead of them, their drove-road ever rising through heather-clad hillsides alive with vast flocks of red deer, David on the look-out for wild boar, which could be dangerous, in that charging the horses, these could bolt and possibly throw their riders. But none such were seen, although eagles were spotted circling high, the first Agnes had ever seen.

Still climbing, they came in late afternoon to one of the highest passes in all Scotland, they had been told by the Pitlochry monks, that of Drumochter, and they must get through this quite lengthy defile to reach the first hospice or shelter for many a rough mile at Dalwhinnie. David was worried about this stretch of the journey, probably the most taxing day of all. But they won through to their goal without any undue stress, if a little later than their usual halting time, he thankfully, Agnes for her part exclaiming at the spectacular and farflung vistas suddenly opening before them as they emerged from the pass, all Strathspey ahead, flanked by tremendous ranges of mountains, David praising

God that they were not seeking to make this journey in winter.

At the Franciscan hospice they sought guidance from the brothers as to their ride on the morrow, for they had been told that their north-going road divided hereafter through Moray, this ahead of them the Badenoch district thereof, one branch going more or less straight on, for Inverness, the capital, and the Great Glen, the other swinging eastwards for Elgin, the episcopal seat. It was this last they were to take for Darnaway, the monks informed, following the Spey as it headed for the distant sea. Cromdale was recommended for the next night, a Cistercian establishment, for they would not make Darnaway till another day. So it looked like seven days of travel, not six.

The ride down Spey, with its great flooded marshlands, lochs and islets, and dramatic peaks on each side, the Monadh Liath or Grey Mountains on the west, and the Monadh Ruadh or Red Mountains on the east, the latter the highest they had ever seen, was an experience that they would never forget. This was a different world from their own southern uplands, of scenery spellbinding and distances immense, the eye challenged on every hand. Often the pair and their companions drew up their horses just to gaze and wonder. And the people they saw were strange also, for the land was far from empty, dressed in tartan plaiding, bearing themselves proudly but nowise hostile, indeed often bowing towards them with a sort of innate dignity.

As the day wore on, they were more and more into forested land, that is on the lower ground and quite a distance up the mountainsides, open scattered woodland of great ancient pines usually growing out of heather and juniper bushes, none of their own elm and beech, but with some birch. They had never seen such massive pines as these, trunks of reddish brown as thick as any oak. Great birds such as they had no knowledge of, larger than any geese, even peacocks, burst out from amongst

199

the trees, and deer were everywhere. They looked and marvelled.

Cromdale proved to be quite far enough for that day, and they continued to bless the churchmen. Some of the senior clergy might be proud and concerned with power and riches; but these hospices and the care for travellers were a godsend, invaluable. Without them, long-distance travel would be all but impossible for such as themselves.

They learned now that Darnaway Castle lay another score or so of miles almost due north. They must continue to follow Spey for five more miles, the turn off by Knockandu for Dallas, then on towards the town of Forres, from which Darnaway was distant only three miles, this in the valley of the River Findhorn. They also learned, incidentally, that the king himself had spent a night here on his way to the distant shrine of St Duthac at Tain, in Ross, but a week before. Neither David nor Agnes had ever heard of St Duthac, but the monks informed that he had been the Chief Confessor of all Ireland, who had come to Scotland five centuries before, on pilgrimage, and was buried at Tain, on the Dornoch Firth, where in fact he had been born, before going to great things in Ireland. There seemed to be some doubts amongst the brothers as to the facts of this saint's life, but their visitors had little doubt as to James's concern therefor.

The last stages of their journey were less demanding, through picturesque country still, with much woodland but less mountainous, the Findhorn a noble river, coming down from the Monadh Liath, whereas Spey had come from a deal further. So it was a more rushing torrent, which made for difficulties in fording.

They found Darnaway between Forres and Brodie, the castle arising on an eminence out of woodland, and with magnificent views in all directions. Here there was no off-putting approach of raised drawbridge and lowered portcullis; indeed the little party rode in under the gatehouse arch without challenge, into the courtyard, this at midday. Dismounting at the keep door, it was a maid who met them as she came out, a basket over her arm, to ask them in friendly fashion and a lilting Highland voice how she might help them, eyeing the child with interest. David said that they sought the Lady Janet Kennedy. Was she at home?

They were told that her ladyship was in the orchard, whither she herself was bound; they were gathering plums. So leaving their attendants with the horses, they followed the young woman out through a postern door and down a quite steep track to a level grassy area dotted with fruit trees. There they saw Janet, her vivid red hair gleaming through leafage, for she was up a ladder picking plums. At the foot, in a basketwork cradle of sorts, a small child crowed, red of hair also if more moderately so.

At her brother's call, Janet all but fell off the ladder in her surprise, delight and haste to descend, and came running, to throw herself into David's arms.

"Davie! Davie!" she cried. "*You*! Come! Come all the way to see me! My dear David, here is joy! How, how . . . ? Oh, brother dear, how come you here?"

"By that long road, lass," he said, clasping her to him. "A fair ride indeed, but worth every mile of it to see you, lass. It has been long, in time as well . . ."

"Yes, long. How I have missed you! But . . ." Freeing herself, she turned to Agnes. "And you – *you* to come, also! So far. And with your child, Agnes. Oh, my dear, the wonder of it!"

"We had to come," Agnes said simply. "Missing you as we have done. You left a great gap, Janet!"

"Yes. For me, also. Oh, I have missed you, longed for you both. And now – now this one!" And she held out her arms to take little Gilbert.

"Gibbie and his aunt!" David said. "Another Lord Kennedy to be! And here is your James. Another James son of James!"

Agnes went over to pick up the other child from the

cradle. "My dear, what a fine boy! Ah, heavier than Gibbie. He will be one year now? Son of a king – and looking it! Is his father proud of him, my lord Earl of Moray?"

"Oh, yes. He dotes on Jamie. He was here only a few days back. He has gone on to Tain, in Ross, on pilgrimage to the shrine of St Duthac. He will be calling in again shortly, on his way back to Stirling."

"This Duthac?" her brother asked. "I had never heard of him. Who was he? I thought that the king's favoured saint was Ninian, at Whithorn in Galloway. On his pilgrimages there, he used to call in at Cassillis, going and coming. But now . . . !"

Janet smiled. "He finds this new observance . . . convenient! He rode here, from Stirling, unattended. In one day, changing horses twice, so urgent is his new devotion! This Duthac, he tells me, was born at Tain, around the millennium. A ruined chapel marks the site. He went to Ireland, and became noted there, dying at Armagh in the year 1065. His bones were brought back to Tain, and buried there. He is much revered hereabouts. This chapel is a girth, or sanctuary, for sinners and fugitives. So James feels that his concern over his father's death may be atoned for there."

"There are other sanctuaries a deal nearer to Stirling or Edinburgh than Tain in Ross!"

"Perhaps. But this one has royal connections. Here Queen Elizabeth de Burgh, the Bruce's wife, was seized by the traitorous Earl of Ross and handed over to Edward of England, sanctuary or none. And other monarchs have visited it. So . . . ."

"Our liege-lord is a very dedicated monarch," Agnes observed. "So you are likely to see him not infrequently?"

"That is my hope," she was told. "So long as the new queen does not restrain him."

"I think that there is little likelihood of that!" David assured her. "Margaret Tudor is scarcely bewitching! Nor will ever be, I would judge. But you like it here?

Find living up in Moray not unpleasing? Far from your homeland, as it is?"

"I miss you, and Cassillis, greatly, to be sure. But, yes, I find this Darnaway, and my life here, not unpleasant. It is very different from Carrick, but rewarding also. I have much to occupy me, much to cherish and see to for this small son of mine. His earldom is a large one, all but the largest in the land. I find myself to be its keeper meantime. A royal fief, it has been neglected for long, and much needs attention. I must do my best for its year-old lord. And for James."

"It is a strange role for a woman," her brother said. "To oversee a whole province, much of it mountains and occupied by the Highland clans. James has thrust a great responsibility upon you, lass."

"It does not displease me. So long as I see him frequently. I have stewards and bailies to aid me. And the churchmen are of great help, the good Bishop Forman sees to that. The see of Moray is very powerful; that is why James had him, his chaplain, appointed thereto. So I do none so ill with it all. But, see you, come within. You will be glad of refreshment. This Darnaway is a fine house, although it was much in need of care when I arrived. It was built by Randolph, Earl of Moray, nearly two centuries ago, but in a fair place."

So the visitors settled in at the castle. They found it echoingly large for one woman and a child, despite servants in plenty, Janet in fact occupying only one tower and wing of it all. The principal seat of a great royal earldom, it was rather extraordinary to have fallen into the care of the daughter of no very great Lowland lord, however spirited a female.

David found what followed a strange interlude in his life, he one man linked to two mothers with small infants, the care of which was so very important to them, so much so that life was all but dominated by the little creatures and their needs. Not that he found this irritating; indeed he enjoyed the spell of it, although he would not have wished it to continue indefinitely.

Their stay at Darnaway was not all baby-caring, to be sure, for Janet was eager to show them something of the domain for which she had become responsible. She too had accustomed her son to being carried long distances on horseback, although she usually employed a maidservant to ride abroad with her carrying the child, she only taking him to breast-feed as required, but delighting to have him with her. So the next day she conducted her guests on a tour round the burgh of Forres; what its townsfolk thought of two infants-in-arms being paraded through the streets was not to be known. They paid a visit to a quite renowned leper colony, of the Order of St Lazarus, a mile outside the walls; and then out to Kinloss on the all but landlocked bay of the Findhorn, great haunt of wildfowl. From there they rode along the coastline to Burghead where, under the ancient Norse name of Torfness, had been the operative base of the Earl Thorfinn Raven-Feeder of Orkney, King MacBeth's half-brother, who had cut such a wide swathe in eleventh-century Scotland; MacBeth himself had been Mormaor of Moray. Here, on a thrusting, rocky peninsula jutting out half a mile into the Moray Firth, they visited the vitrified stonework and ramparts of a Pictish fort of major significance, all but the Picts' capital, with the great battle of Mons Graupius fought in the fertile plain inland. They admired bull carvings in the rocks, and a notable underground bath-chamber cut in the solid rock, thought to have been a baptismal well of the early Christianised Picts, fed by a spring in the living stone.

Janet told them that the earldom, which included the large bishop's diocese, extended to many thousands of square miles, although the majority of these were anything but square, mountains and glens, moors and lochs, although the lower ground, known as the Laich of Moray, was some of the most fertile in all Scotland: all a mighty responsibility to place on any young woman's shoulders. Especially as the occupants of the Highland areas looked upon the Laich as a legitimate area for raiding; indeed it was called by the clans "the Moray-land where all men take their prey". There were, to be sure, keepers of the royal castles of Elgin, Inverness, Cawdor, Nairn, Auldearn and the like, but these wielded only local sway, whereas she had overall authority. Her father had called himself King of Carrick; but she, it seemed, was queen of an area many times the size.

Only when the infants were abed that evening did David Kennedy become the focus of attention, a humbling experience for a privy councillor and deputy warden of a March.

The day following, Janet took them to see Elgin and its great cathedral, known as the Lantern of the North, which the Wolf of Badenoch, son of Robert the Second, had burned merely because the then Bishop of Moray would not grant him a divorce. They saw the Panns Port, or Bread Gate, where the local lepers, who were not permitted to enter the city proper, were given their sustenance, this causing David to wonder whether that dire disease was particularly prevalent in these parts, more so than in the south. Janet admitted that she did not know. Then on to the episcopal palace, a magnificent establishment built on an island in a shallow loch, really an arm of the sea, this beginning to silt up by blown sand. The building was six storeys in height, and fortified, as apparently it had required to be in the past to withstand the assaults of such as the Wolf of Badenoch and the Highland raiders. David saw all this as not unlike the situation of the West March of the Borders.

Agnes wanted to see at least something of the Highland area of the earldom, beyond this Laich, so next day they were taken south-westwards up Findhorn, through forested land until they were into the skirts of the mountains, by Ferness and Dulsie, reaching Mackintosh country, although they did not get as far as the chief of Clan Chattan's Loch Moy, Janet conceding that she found this chief helpful. Then they turned south for

Lochindorb, wildly beautiful territory now, dominated by the heights which somehow managed to combine serenity with savagery. At Lochindorb, a large expanse of water in the lap of the mountains, the theme was scarcely serenity, they were told, for on an island in the loch was the now ruined castle of that ferocious prince Alexander, Earl of Buchan, the aforesaid Wolf of Badenoch, whose savageries were scarcely believable, his favoured sport the hunting of the people of the forested lands, like deer or boar, on horseback with hounds and spears, men, women and children – and he a son of the King of Scots. This castle was his chosen seat for this activity, although it was in Moray, not Buchan, and Janet declared that it had witnessed scenes of horror unparalleled in Scotland despite the loveliness of its surroundings, this the king had told her. That one of his own ancestors should have perpetrated such was perhaps the greatest stain on the fame of the royal house. That their own small Jamie was also a collateral descendant of this fiend was a dire thought.

When they returned, by the headwaters of the River Lossie, past Glenerney and the Darnaway Forest, it was to find that the king himself had arrived at the castle on his way back from Inverness and Tain, alone still. He greeted the visitors in friendly fashion, duly admiring little Gilbert, and marching about with his own small son in his arms, loud in his praise. His continued appreciation of Janet was made very evident, her hold on his affections nowise diminished by the child-bearing and her preoccupation with the infant. They all made a domestic little party, with no least air of royalty about it.

On the morrow, David felt that it was time to be gone, much as they would have liked to linger. By the time they got back to Carrick they would have been away for almost three weeks, and his duties there called, not to mention those of his wardenship, which James only briefly referred to. He, the king, would stay another couple of days with Janet and Jamie, but even so, he would be back at Stirling well before the Kennedys were that far, at the rate he rode with his changes of horses.

It was parting then, but with promises of a return before overlong, and the so demanding journey southwards to be faced. But by now little Gibbie was so used to whole days in the saddle that he seemed to look on it as normal living, and his parents felt no sense of guilt. Indeed, when they got home, he might well demand a continuance of it all.

19

It was late autumn when David received the royal order which he had been uneasy about for some time, this to fulfil his duty as Deputy Warden of the West March. However, the command was not one such as he had most dreaded, that of carrying the sword down amongst the Marchmen, punishing, hanging and the like, nor even trouble with the Lord Maxwell. It might well be difficult and demanding of his powers of tact and judgment, but ought not to involve him in bloodshed and violence at least. It was not pertaining to the actual borderline at all, but to Galloway, and of all things, was concerned with the bishop thereof, although what this had to do with the wardenship was unclear. George Vaus, Bishop of Galloway, had appointed the small but famous town of Whithorn, site of the king's pilgrimages to the shrine of St Ninian, as a free burgh, a new conception, as he claimed was within his power so to do. Formerly it had been a burgh of barony; but this new status gave it additional privileges. And the royal burgh of Wigtown, county town of that shire, was protesting to the crown. The Whithorn merchants, including the priory thereof, had started to export commodities, wool and woollen goods, hides, salted meats and suchlike, to Cumberland, Ireland and the Isle of Man, and this was damaging the trade of Wigtown, which had hitherto enjoyed this monopoly in Galloway. The bishop apparently would not listen to the provost and bailies of that royal burgh, and so they appealed to the monarch, who passed it on to the deputy warden.

David was not well versed in the matter of the privileges

and rights of the various burghal communities, royal burghs, burghs of regality and burghs of barony, and had never so much as heard of a "free burgh". So, for once, he had to go and consult his father, whom he knew had created burghs of barony at Girvan and Ballantrae. Lord Kennedy was scarcely welcoming, but did gain some satisfaction in being able to inform his unfilial and ignorant son. Burghs of barony, which could be instituted by earls, lords and bishops, had certain rights, licences, freedoms; they could hold markets and fairs, and deduct duties, charge tolls where the king's highway passed through their bounds, hold common grazings, require corn to be ground at their mills, all a source of income for them and their lords. But no, they could not export goods overseas. Royal burghs had that right, along with being able to send representatives to parliament, appoint their own magistrates, hold head-courts, exact duties on foreign imports, and have their own provosts and town councils. Burghs of regality were somewhat less important, had bailies not provosts, and were not represented in parliament, but otherwise had similar privileges. Wigtown, being a county town and having its own sheriff, would certainly be a royal burgh.

Thus informed, David perceived that in this dispute the scales seemed to be weighted in favour of the royal burgh. His father had known nothing about free burghs. But since it was the bishop who had set up this new entity, presumably for his own advantage, some negotiations with the said prelate were probably called for. Why had the king placed this matter on *his* shoulders, instead of on those of another prelate, such as Forman or Elphinstone? Or even the Archbishop of Glasgow, who was presumably Galloway's superior, he did not know. But undoubtedly there would be some reason.

Agnes advised clerical guidance in this his first real task as a warden, little as it seemed really a warden's duty. But who could he approach? He could hardly go to the court at Stirling to see Forman or Elphinstone. Archbishop

Blackadder was unsuitable, going to him seeming to make of it an inter-clerical issue, which it was not. It occurred to him that James Stewart had perceived all this and had elected to offload it on to himself.

For clerical guidance, Crossraguel Abbey, always in Kennedy possession, lay just two miles from Maybole, its present abbot a younger brother of Kennedy of Bargany. David went there that very day.

Abbot Kennedy, the sub-prior and ten brethren occupied the large and rich abbey in style and comfort, amongst wide and well-tended lands, Holy Church ever an example of good living. The abbot was helpful. Bishop George of Galloway was a man of parts, he said, which David took to mean that he would have to be handled carefully. His diocesan seat was at Whithorn, that town entirely his; indeed the bishopric had been known as of Whithorn originally, only being changed to Galloway in later years. This of free burghs had been established by the king's father, James the Third, at the instigation of his mentor, the late Archbishop Sheves, and there were only a few of these created, and all held by churchmen. They were not quite on a level with royal burghs and did not send representatives to parliament, but they had almost all the other advantages, more so than regalities, and some that were unique to them, including freedom from sundry forms of taxation, and the right to levy tithes on fisheries, very valuable for coastal communities. Yes, they had the right to export and import without limit.

What then, David wondered, was the point of his mission? With all these privileges, what was Wigtown's case? Why appeal to the king? The bishop sat secure, surely?

The abbot tapped the side of his nose. Douglas, he declared. The power of Douglas. The Black Douglases controlled Wigtownshire, from their castles of Threave and Haugh or Urr, of Corsock and Gelston. No doubt the trade from Wigtown and Stranraer was important to them. And the monarchy had ever to be heedful of the power of Douglas.

What then was he to do, David demanded, if it was now an issue between this bishop and the Douglases? Not a question of rights and privileges, but of power. Why was the king sending him on this mission? He was only Deputy Warden of the West March. This seemed to have nothing to do with the March.

The other could only suggest that His Grace had some especial reason for sending him. Was he not a privy councillor? And close to the monarch through his sister? Perhaps he saw him as an able and personal envoy?

David did not see himself that way. What could he do? The bishop – was there anything about him that he should know, to advantage?

George Vaus was in a strong position, it was emphasised. He had a large diocese, and was all but independent of other Church authority. It was doubtful if Archbishop Blackadder had any sway over him. The king's much-used pilgrimage shrine at Whithorn put him in an especial position. The bishopric was unique in traditionally owing allegiance, like Carlisle, to the English Archbishop of York. So he was not a man to treat lightly. The abbot could only suggest that the king had chosen him, the Master of Kennedy, for this task for personal reasons.

Much concerned, David went back to Cassillis.

Agnes, hearing of it all, thought that James was sending him because he could really effect nothing in the matter, and merely wished the Douglases to know that he was not ignoring their interests. David would not be in a position to effect anything of major value, but he would at least give the impression of royal concern. Let him go, then, without any expectation of success. It was all but a gesture, she judged.

Only moderately comforted by this assessment, David set out next day for Galloway.

It was quite a lengthy ride, for Whithorn lay at the very southern tip of the central of three peninsulas of the province of Galloway jutting out into the Solway Firth; seventy miles, he reckoned. His best course, he judged, was to go to see the bishop first, and then return to Wigtown and report there on his efforts, however unsuccessful they were likely to be, and to express the royal concern. What better could he do?

He went by Girvan, turning inland there, and on by Barrhill and Bargrennan to Penninghame, where he forded the River Cree, thus keeping well west of the Douglas country of Threave and Loch Ken. Thereafter he came to the head of Wigtown Bay, not really a bay at all but a twenty-mile-long arm of the sea. Down the western side of this he had to pass the quite large town of Wigtown, but he did not halt there meantime, pressing on by Kirkinner and Callieston, another fifteen miles, to Whithorn. The October dusk was falling as he reached his destination. He was very much aware of the sea here, at the very tip of the peninsula, salt water on either side of him.

David had never been this far before, and was interested to see that there were actually two Whithorn communities: the main one, which was quite a town, housing the priory, the church of which was the diocesan cathedral, and also housing the episcopal palace, this all taking up most of the built-up area; but there was also the Isle of Whithorn, a seaport village, the most southerly in all Scotland, with a good harbour, sited on a rocky promontory which had once been an island. It was on this that St Ninian had founded the first church of Christ in Scotland, in 397, which he called Candida Casa, this later sacked by the Norsemen, who built a fort nearby.

David entered the priory and recognised at once that it was a handsome establishment, signs of wealth and abundance on all hands, the cathedral clearly ancient but impressive although not large, the great house built alongside, presumably the bishop's palace, equally so, the monastic premises extensive. He enquired thereat for Bishop George.

A monk conducted him to the prior, a haughty, dark-avised individual who named himself James Beaton, and conceded that he had heard of the Master of Kennedy, this in no very regardful fashion. When told that it was the bishop that he had come to see, and the prior declared that he would enquire of the prelate whether he would grant audience, David raised his own head a little higher and announced that Bishop Vaus would indeed see him, since he came on the king's command. This produced a level stare, then a shrug, and Beaton went off leaving the visitor standing. It was scarcely a propitious start to the mission.

It was not the prior but a more civil character who appeared presently, introducing himself as Gavin Dunbar, the bishop's secretary, who would conduct him to the episcopal presence. David, used to easy relations with Bishops Forman and Elphinstone who, if they had secretaries did not flourish them, nodded, and was led out and over to the palace building.

He was taken into a splendid chamber, hung with tapestries and handsomely furnished, where a big, heavy-built man, overweight and richly clad in no clerical garb, received him. Despite his jowls and fleshy features, his eyes were keen, shrewd, and they examined the caller searchingly.

"I am told that you come in the king's name, although unannounced, Master of Kennedy," he was greeted carefully. "For what am I . . . honoured by this visit?" The secretary remained in the background.

"His Grace sends me to you, Bishop, on a matter that he knows that you will wish to promote, being spiritual father and guardian here. That is the peace, goodwill and prosperity of this Galloway region of his realm." David had been rehearsing this opening gambit for much of the journey. "He sends me, a member of his Privy Council, with his good wishes."

"Indeed, sir. Peace and prosperity are my concern, yes. But I am not aware that such are in any way endangered hereabouts. Does His Grace so judge them?"

Thus swiftly and without preamble brought to the

purpose of his visit, David coughed and chose his words heedfully.

"The spiritual and ruling concerns of the realm should play in harmony, for the benefit of all, His Grace most rightly holds," he said. "You will agree, he knows. But here in Galloway there is a danger of some disharmony. In the matter of trade and the people's well-being. You will not be unaware of this, he believes."

"Trade and well-being? Is the king concerned with these? I would have thought that he could have other . . . interests!"

"Anything that affects the kingdom's weal and national accord is our liege-lord's concern, Bishop." He paused. "And this of Wigtown's trade difficulty is such."

"Then let him tell that to the Douglases!"

Again David coughed. "It is the provost and magistrates of the royal burgh who make complaint," he said. "*Their* trade and wealth that is being affected."

"Douglas!" the other repeated flatly. "The Wigtown merchants and shippers would never appeal to the crown. Only Douglas would do that. Or cause them to do it. And the king fears the might of Douglas."

David, in no position to deny that, shrugged.

"Where think you, sir, that the Black Douglases win their wealth?" he was asked. "To maintain their hosts of armed men, greater forces than any other in the land? Not from cattle and sheep on their hills, and oats from their farms. They win it from the trade shipped out of Wigtown and the like. All there are in their pouches! And they would keep it all to themselves. Debar others, who have the right. As this free burgh of Whithorn has the right."

Thus swiftly they came to the crux of it all.

"You, or your Whithorn merchants, are challenging the Wigtown traders, Bishop? They did not do so previously. This is a new venture. Is it necessary? Or wise? When it could cause much . . . ill."

"It is our right. Whithorn has an ages-old link with

Whitehaven and Maryport in Cumberland, dating from when the two sees were founded together, from York. We trade in hides and boot-leather and saddlery. In salted beef also, this being cattle country. Theirs is not. From Cumberland we gain wool and mutton and ironware. This is important, and part of the revenues of the bishoprics of Carlisle and Galloway, always has been. Handling it all by pack-horse train the long road by Dumfries and over the border at Gretna, as had to be done in the past, is toilsome and wasteful. Also costly, for the wretched Marchmen of Eskdale and Liddesdale and the rest waylay and loot and steal. It is no longer to be endured! This free burgh has the right to export by sea. We shall so do."

"As has Wigtown, Bishop. You created this free burgh for this purpose? Knowing of Wigtown's right . . ."

"Wigtown, or the Douglases' people, used to trade with Ireland and Man. Now they are shipping to Cumberland also. It is insufferable."

A thought formed itself at the back of David's mind. But first he ventured otherwise. "Will reason, agreement, not serve, Bishop? Trade in more than goods? I am told that Whithorn is shipping also to Ireland and Man now. Could not a bargain be struck? You to leave these last to Wigtown, Whithorn only to trade with Cumberland?"

"They, the Douglases, would never so agree. They are greedy as they are arrogant! Holy Church will not submit to their graspings, be impoverished by these robber-barons!"

David glanced about him at all the signs of wealth and abundance there. But he did not voice his thoughts. Instead, he said that he would go on to Wigtown hereafter, and urge agreement and fair exchange.

"It is not Wigtown that you should go to, Master of Kennedy, but to Threave Castle and Castle of Urr, and the others."

"Perhaps it is so. But . . ." He brought out the other notion from the back of his mind. "See you, I am Deputy Warden of the West March, Bishop. I have some authority with the Marchmen. And some Carrick men to aid in that authority. If I was to see to the guarding of your pack-horse trains, would that not help your trade with Cumbria? After all, shipping has its limits, has it not? Vessels can only carry so much. And wild weather can delay and halt."

The bishop was eyeing him now differently, assessingly. "The Lord Maxwell, Warden, has never aided us," he said. "Indeed his Maxwells are, I judge, scarcely innocent in the plundering!"

"I take my orders from the King's Grace himself, Bishop, not the Lord Maxwell. And the king's wish is for peace and goodwill."

"You would do this? Protect the Whithorn train?"

"I would, yes."

"M'mm. I would see that you were rewarded for so doing, sir."

David raised his brows. "That is not my aim in this, Bishop. It is peace between Wigtown and Whithorn."

"Then see you to it, Master of Kennedy. That would aid in the matter, I grant you. But still we would ship to Whitehaven and Maryport. On occasion."

"But not to Man and Ireland?"

"If that would better the cause of peace and prosperity that you speak of. And please His Grace – yes."

"That is well, then. I will go to Wigtown and tell them there. Also inform the king. And, when you next send a horse train over the border, if you will have me told at Cassillis, I will see that it is guarded well."

"So be it. And you will not be the loser thereby, Kennedy."

An agreement of sorts thus reached, Bishop George did not develop any more friendly attitude. Nor did he suggest hospitality for the visitor in this his palace, merely observing that David would find overnight accommodation in the priory.

They parted without cordiality, even though the secretary was somewhat more so as he conducted David out.

216

He could not complain of monkish hospitality that night, although he saw nothing of Prior Beaton.

In the morning, it was back up the bay shore the fifteen miles to the Cree and Wigtown. There he sought out the provost, one Glendinning, who proved to be a leather-tanner, his establishment not large but clearly prosperous. His reception of the Master of Kennedy was other than that at Whithorn, very respectful, especially when he learned that he was the king's emissary.

"His Grace is concerned over your appeal to him, Provost," David told him. "He recognises your problem over this of the rivalry of Whithorn, in trade by sea, and would resolve it. I have been to see the Bishop of Galloway and made him aware of the king's concern. We have come to some . . . accord. Do you wish to summon your bailies, magistrates, to hear of it?"

"If we have accord, Master, then that will not be necessary, I think. So long as I may tell them of it."

"Perhaps it is the Douglas lords whom you have to tell?"

The other looked down, but did not deny it. "What is this, this accord, Master?"

"The Bishop asserts the right of his free barony to export and import by sea. But he will limit such activity by the Whithorn merchants. He will confine their shipping trade, so as not greatly to contest and harm the Wigtown commence. Their ships will trade only with Cumberland, with which the bishopric has especial links, the ports of Whitehaven and Maryport, and leave Man and Ireland to you. And will resume pack-horse carriage of goods overland, guarded by my men. I am deputy warden, as you may know, and can see to this."

The provost drew a long breath. "That is guid, guid, Maister," his speech suddenly thicker in his relief. "Very guid. I will so report, yes. It is well ordered, och aye, well ordered. I will tell them all so. We will a' be right grateful to you, Maister. And to His Grace. Now, you'll hae some

217

cheer? Refreshment, just? While I tell one or two o' my bailies."

"I thank you, but no, Provost. I was well served at Whithorn Priory. And I have a long ride back to Cassillis. I will leave you to inform and assure your . . . friends. Let us hope that this will all make for peace and goodwill. As His Grace desires. Tell them that."

Brief as was this exchange, David felt that it was sufficiently effective. Indeed, as he rode home northwards, he found that he was quite pleased with himself. He had, he judged, fulfilled his mission to James's probable satisfaction, managed to bring about a degree of at least surface harmony within this Galloway; and not only that, but had made some sort of sense out of his appointment as deputy warden, given himself a role to play. He did not think that his Carrick men would find occasional convoying duties on the border in any way grievous, especially if, as the bishop averred, they would be rewarded for their services.

He wondered what Maxwell would say. He could scarcely object, since it was all done in the royal name. And Agnes? He looked forward to that last.

20

David did not have to go all the way to Stirling to report, for the word was that the king was at Edinburgh superintending the construction of the semi-royal wing of the monastic quarters of the Abbey of the Holy Rood, to make of it more seemly lodging in the capital for a married monarch with a court where women, not merely mistresses, were more in evidence; this allegedly on the advice of Don Pedro, who was now seemingly more or less permanently attached to the Scots establishment. The object, it was thought, was that King Henry would expect his daughter not to have to spend much of her time skied up in a rock-top fortress.

To Edinburgh, then, with the news from Galloway, Agnes and little Gibbie going with him as far as Borthwick to see her family, she quietly proud of her husband's success on his first diplomatic errand.

At the abbey David found much activity, not all of it concerned with building construction, hunting in the royal park around Arthur's Seat, hawking at Duddingston Loch, banqueting, masques and dancing in the abbot's quarters, the queen left behind at Linlithgow, but no lack of feminine company for the monarch so appreciative of such. But there was concern also, for it transpired that the king's brother, Alexander, Duke of Ross, titular Archbishop of St Andrews, was seriously ill at Stirling. He had never been a robust and active character like James, but reclusive and studious; and now he had more or less taken to his bed, and with signs of the same listlessness which had preceded the death of his younger brother John some years before. James and he had never been really close; but he was the heir to the throne, until the king had legitimate offspring, and that did not look like happening soon, with a wife in only her sixteenth year.

When James had time to see David alone, he was relieved to hear of the Galloway situation, and expressed his praise and gratitude. In this matter of acting guard on the Whithorn pack trains through the Debateable Land, he was well pleased. This would offer a frequent presence of strength, representing the crown and the rule of law, so badly required there, Maxwell certainly not providing it; he never had done. Unfortunately, as the situation stood, that man could hardly be displaced as Chief Warden, the office being all but hereditary in the Maxwell family, and none other thereabouts sufficiently strong and powerful to challenge it; otherwise David himself could have been made Chief Warden. This of an escorting body for the Whithorn traders, indeed others also, would serve to demonstrate that the Marchmen were not immune from the realm's authority, as they appeared to consider themselves. And it would give him, David, the authority to show himself along the border without seeming to usurp Maxwell's position. Occasional leading of the convoys, therefore, would be helpful in this.

David did not linger at Edinburgh. He had never visited two of the properties, those of Leswalt and Foulwood, which James had given him on his appointment as a warden, with Balgray, presumably to help him pay for his services. Leswalt was far distant in the Rhinns of Galloway, that is the furthest west of the three great peninsulas of the province, fully fifty miles from Wigtown, a remote holding indeed, but at least not near to Douglas dominance. That, inconvenient of access however valuable it might be as a lairdship, could await inspection. Balgray was in the Cunninghame district of his own Ayrshire, a barony, between the River Irvine and the Annick Water, none so far from Cassillis, a mere score of miles, which he had visited and found to be good fertile land. Now he would go and see and survey Foulwood, in Lanarkshire, near Lanark town itself, before returning to pick up Agnes and Gibbie again at Borthwick.

Lanark lay some forty-five miles south-westwards from Edinburgh, going by the northern skirts of the Pentland Hills, by Balerno, the empty moorlands of Tarbrax and Yardhouse to Carnwath and Carstairs. Foulwood, he was told, lay in upland country on the Mouse Water, this in an area belonging to the ancient family of Lockhart of the Lee, one of whom had accompanied the Good Sir James Douglas, with the Bruce's heart, on that crusading venture nearly two centuries before, and, unlike Douglas, had survived to bring the heart back. Another of the survivors had been Sir William Borthwick, an ancestor of Agnes's. He, David, would call on the Lockhart.

Due west of Carstairs he crossed the Mouse at Cowford, and in five miles thereafter reached Foulwood, which he found to be a broken-down tower-house on a mound, probably once a motte and bailey castle, fallen on evil days and uninhabited. However, it was surrounded by well-doing farms, six of them, with a mill, all now his property. He visited all these and interviewed the tenants, and also the miller who acted as steward for the lairdship; it was not a barony, like Balgray and Leswalt. He made arrangements for the better transmission of rentals and revenues to Cassillis. He spent the night in the millhouse in fair comfort, the wife there in some trepidation at entertaining so seemingly lofty a guest.

Satisfied with what he saw and heard, David rode on next morning to Lee Castle, a bare three miles, where he was welcomed by Sir James Lockhart, an elderly man of some presence, whom he had met at parliaments. He told him of his accession to the Foulwood property, and learned that it was formerly owned by the Graham family, who had lost possession through implication in the murder of King James the First, and had their lands forfeited to the crown by James the Second. They spoke of the long past connection of the Lockharts and the Borthwicks, and Sir

221

James showed David his precious relic from that notable occasion, the Lee Penny. This proved to be a red jewel, presumably a ruby, set in a silver coin. To this curious memento was attached a strange story. On that crusading venture, although the Douglas had been slain, Lockhart's ancestor, in the fray, had captured a Saracen emir of some importance. This man, held prisoner by the crusaders, had somehow gained an approach for ransom, this by a woman, wife or mother, she offering jewellery of much value in exchange for the captive. In the bargaining process she had hastily sought to withdraw this ruby and silver item, which had been amongst the pouchful. Noting her concern, Lockhart had demanded to see it, and learning that she deemed it more precious than the rest, wanted to know why. She had revealed that it was of especial worth, a talisman, with miraculous properties. Dipped in water, that water developed healing qualities of great benefit, including stopping bleeding and reducing fever. Sir Simon had insisted that this was to be the ransom for the emir, and reluctantly the woman had acceded. So the strange token had been brought back to Scotland, and was much treasured by the succeeding generations of the Lockhart family, who claimed that it had indeed demonstrated its healing powers on not a few occasions. Much intrigued, David handled it, and said that he would remember this, if occasion required.

He also noted that the banner flying from the topmost tower of Lee Castle displayed a crimson heart within a fetlock, a heraldic play on the name and fame of the Lockharts.

Seeing him off on his way back to Borthwick, Sir James showed his guest another extraordinary feature of the Lee. This was a tree near the Castle, highly unusual in more ways than one. For although it was an ancient Caledonian pine, it rose nearly seventy feet in height, and was so wide of trunk at six feet above the ground that its girth was no less than twenty-eight feet, a marvel indeed.

David rode back eastwards much more impressed and

interested in what he had seen at the Lee than the accretions to his purse gained at Foulwood, and with much to tell Agnes.

David was not long in being required to fulfil his commitment to escort one of the Whithorn trading trains over the borderline. He found a message awaiting him when he got back to Cassillis, declaring that a portage would be going to Carlisle in one week's time, and would look for the promised protective guard. He sent back a courier forthwith to say that he would join the column at Dumfries, in person, with the required manpower to ensure safe passage.

He had no difficulty in collecting a band of Carrick men at this season, early November, with all harvest work over and beasts brought down from the higher ground for the winter. He reckoned that one hundred would be about right for this gesture, enough to present a deterrent for any marauding Marchmen, he recognising that a large pack-horse train would demand a sizeable escort to protect its necessarily extended length. They took the road southwards, two days later, with Kennedy of Culzean to act as David's deputy, with a view to taking over future convoys when he himself was unable to be present.

At Dumfries they had to wait at the Nithside meadows for another day before the slow-moving column of pack-horses arrived, lengthy indeed and heavy-laden. David realised that he had by no means brought over-many men as escort, for he reckoned that there were over one hundred and fifty pack animals, in addition to the mounted men leading them, one to every three horses. He wondered where the Whithorn merchants and monks had got all these beasts, until he learned that there were groups from Creetown and Gatehouse with them also, to take the opportunity of this protected passage.

Spacing out his men down the length of the procession,

223

which, at only two abreast, extended for a considerable distance, he led the way for the borderline.

They went by Dargavel and Rockhall to avoid going anywhere near Caerlaverock Castle, the Maxwell seat, and on to Annan and Eastriggs. But nearing this last, what David had feared happened; the Lord Maxwell came after them, having presumably been informed of this large procession coming through his territory unannounced. At sight of David he did not become amiable, even though they were in fact distant relatives by marriage; but he could not interfere when told that this was being done at the king's command. He turned back, without any good wishes.

They were not far from Gretna and the Esk crossing when they met with their next encounter. They had been aware of horsemen observing their passage from a distance, and guessed that the moss-trooping lairds had not been left unaware of their presence and progress. And here, on a slight ridge ahead of them they saw a fair-sized party of riders, possibly thirty or forty, barring their road. Ready for something of the sort, David blew on his hunting-horn to summon forward the bulk of his Carrick men from their positions down the train, and, with them, rode forward to the waiting band. At his side Culzean bore a banner with the Kennedy arms of a golden chevron on a white shield between three cross-crosslets.

He blew another blast on his horn. "I am the Master of Kennedy, Deputy Warden of this March," he called. "Who are you?"

The Marchmen carried no banners. Nor were they in a hurry to answer him. But at length one spoke.

"This is Eskdale, and we are of this dale. We look to our rights."

"And the rights you look to now? To whom do I speak?" David demanded.

"I am Armstrong of Mossknowe." He did not specify the rights.

"Then, Armstrong of Mossknowe, I greet you. And let

224

me assure you that the wardens are aware of your *rights*, and will sustain all such. But not . . . otherwise."

There was silence. Then David turned in his saddle, to wave forward the long train behind him, and heeled his mount into motion, his Carrick men, hands mainly on sword-hilts, closing ranks behind him.

The moss-troopers, outnumbered three to one, did the reverse, parting right and left to allow the pack-horse column past. Just to ensure that there was no last-moment snatching by the Marchmen, Culzean turned some of his people back to help line the passageway, to glowers.

So, safely, the travellers moved through and onwards, leaving a sullen company of horsemen behind, who were not long, however, in reining round and spurring away northwards.

David was not the only one who heaved a sigh of relief as he glanced back.

They continued on their slow way, to Gretna, where they forded the minor River Sark, and crossed into Cumberland.

What, David wondered, would be next? The lawlessness was not confined to the Scots Marchmen, the Croziers, Robsons, Fosters and the rest equally ungoverned. Would the fact that this large consignment of goods was destined for their own Carlisle carry any weight with them? Or would all booty be grist to their mills? Anyway, readiness for trouble was nowise relaxed.

Presently, it seemed strange to be having to ford the Esk, very much a Scottish river, but with its outfall in England.

They were not long past this when, near Rockcliffe, they saw ahead of them another company of horsemen. David braced himself and his men for a second encounter. But as these drew nearer he saw that this troop at least sported banners, three of them, devices at this distance undecipherable. Also they came trotting on towards the Scots in good order.

When they were close enough to distinguish details,

there was seen to be something about this company that spoke of discipline and authority, not enmity or threat, although they carried lances as well as flags. Then two men came spurring forward, one under a banner bearing six gold rings on blue, these well dressed. David held up a hand to halt his train.

"You are the Lord Bishop of Galloway's people?" one of these called as they came up. "We are sent by the Lord Bishop of Carlisle to welcome you, sirs. Bishop George sent us word."

"Then I greet you kindly, friends. I am the Master of Kennedy, Deputy Warden of the March, acting on the King of Scots' orders. Well met!"

"You have suffered no interference, no troubles? Bishop George feared that you might do so."

"We met with some Marchmen, yes. But they wisely did not seek to hinder us. To whom do I speak, sir?"

"I am Sir William Musgrave." He was a good-looking man of about David's age. "Kin to my Lord Bishop. He was concerned for the safety of this company of my Lord Bishop George's."

"It is scarcely the company of the Bishop of Galloway," David declared. "However much of the goods carried may be his. And, Sir William, in Scotland we do not call our bishops lord, as you do. *I* act in the name of the king, King James."

The other shrugged, and wheeled his horse around. "We take you to Carlisle, Master of Kennedy," he said. "I fear that it will be dark before we get there. Eight miles or so, by Kingmoor and Stanwix."

As they rode on south-eastwards, side by side, and the two parties formed into one extended column, Musgrave observed that this was the first pack train to have come unharmed over the border for long, and that it was a notable sign of the peace which King Henry had hammered out with the Scots, through the Lord Bishop and Lord Dacre. David said that he had met both of these, but gently mentioned that King James had personally forged

226

the said peace process with them, as well as wedding King Henry's daughter. This Musgrave, although no doubt a pleasant enough character, clearly required to be instructed as to facts and accuracy.

It was indeed dark before they reached Carlisle. The Scots found themselves being led not to any market-place or warehouses with their goods but to Carlisle Castle itself, a great citadel, all but a city in itself within its walls, and which, it transpired, was the seat of the bishop, who, it seemed, was the ruler of Carlisle, and very much concerned with the trade and prosperity of this, the greatest town in the north-west of England, rivalling evidently the Prince-Bishop of Durham in the east. In Scotland, the great prelates had their importance, other than merely spiritual, with seats in parliament and holding offices of state on occasion; but here they appeared to be the leaders of the communities, something David had not realised. Bishop George of Galloway might well be seeking to emulate.

They all were conducted to a large storehouse within the citadel walls, this torchlit, where many men awaited them, and the pack animals were unloaded and the goods therefrom stacked and sorted and recorded by monkish clerks, all in the most businesslike fashion. David was interested to see the contents of all the luggage he had been escorting. As well as much salted and smoked beef and the tanned hides of cattle, leather goods of many kinds, doublets, jerkins, boots from thigh-length for riding to ladies' slippers, belts, saddlery and harness, pouches and purses, even waxed buckets. The tanneries and craftsmen of Galloway had been busy indeed, all presumably under the direction and for the wealth of Holy Church. There were other items also: dairy produce, cheese, butter and lard, also basketwork and horse-hair products.

And in neat rows, at the other side of the warehouse, waiting to be sent back in exchange for all this, was the Cumbrian merchandise, woollen goods and clothing, iron-ware, pots, hooks, knives, even swords and daggers.

227

A particularly bulky and heavy load was a selection of grindstones and querns for crushing and grating corn, from some especial quarry.

All this, it seemed, would be prepared and ready for loading on to the horses in the morning for a first-light return journey. Meanwhile David and Culzean would be ensconced in the bishop's quarters of the castle, while their men were led off elsewhere. It was all highly organised.

The bishop granted them a brief interview that evening. David asked after Lord Dacre, and was told that he was presently at his principal seat of Naworth. During the negotiations with King James over the peace terms, that lord had been very much in charge, the bishop subsidiary; but here it seemed that the prelate was the more important.

They spent a comfortable night, well catered for.

In the morning, it was an early start – although earlier for the others, it seemed, for they found the pack train all drawn up and waiting just outside the citadel walls. However there was some delay, for they had to wait for Sir William Musgrave and his men to arrive from Edenhall to escort them back to the borderline, little as David deemed this necessary. But it was apparently bishop's orders.

The journey homeward passed without incident, no marauders in evidence, even though no doubt their progress did not go unobserved. A quite friendly farewell was taken of Musgrave. And once across Sark into Scotland again, the same freedom from attention was experienced. Undoubtedly the Marchmen had taken due note of the new situation. It was to be hoped that this would continue to apply hereafter.

At Dumfries in due course, David and his Carrick men took leave of the pack-train people, with whom they had developed good relations. These were by no means lessened when the monkish leader thereof handed over one of their leather pouches containing quite a substantial amount of silver coin by way of recognition of services

228

rendered, and which David passed on to Culzean to distribute amongst their force. It seemed probable that this role as escorts might well become quite a popular one hereafter.

So it was home to Kennedy country, duty done, and none so unpleasant. Bishop George of Galloway might be judged less critically perhaps.

21

That Christmastide passed congenially at Cassillis, with no royal orders coming for the Bailie of Carrick. They wondered how Janet found the festive season up in Moray, and wished that it was not quite so far away. They would visit her again in the spring, but doubted whether even James Stewart would get up there in mid-winter, with the snow-covered mountain passes to be negotiated. But Flaming Janet, a sociable creature, had probably made new friends in those her northern territories.

It was late January when the news reached them that the Duke of Ross had died, the heir-presumptive to the throne, and Primate of Holy Church, aged only in his early twenties. This was serious, as well as grievous for the king, for the succession to the monarchy must be ensured, and there was no legitimate member of the royal family nearer than John, Duke of Albany, who lived in France, a grandson of James the Second, son of a French countess, and who allegedly spoke only French, no suitable king for Scotland. And James's queen was of only fifteen years, scarcely able to produce the required offspring for some time. The problem was inescapable, for all concerned with the rule of the land. If James was to die, or be killed . . . !

The king had there and then appointed his son by Mariot Boyd, Alexander, to be Archbishop of St Andrews and Primate, aged eleven, to the raised eyebrows of more than David Kennedy.

In March David paid a visit to Galloway again, this time not in connection with Whithorn or its traders but to inspect the third of the properties given to him, Leswalt.

This, although situated on the western of the three great peninsulas, that of the Rhinns, he had always thought of as remote indeed, and entailing a long journey to reach. But on reflection he realised that in fact it was less distant than was Dumfries, or even Wigtown if he went directly south down the Ayrshire and Galloway coasts, past Girvan and Ballantrae and Glenapp, to reach the long bay, almost an estuary, of Loch Ryan, on the far side of which lay Leswalt, some fifty miles.

Strangely, he had never been south of Ballantrae itself, fifteen miles beyond. This was because his father and the laird here, Kennedy of Bargany, were at feud of a sort, cousins although they were, and Bargany's lands and castle of Ardstinchar were to be avoided. David, as Bailie of Carrick, was concerned to be on better terms with this powerful member of the clan. So he would take the opportunity to visit him on his way southwards.

He found Ardstinchar, a fine tall hold on a cliff-top above the quite major River Stinchar, and, after a somewhat doubtful reception by its laird, was able to come to terms with the elderly John Kennedy, who, it seemed, had quarrelled with David's father over the heiress, Elizabeth Montgomery, whom he had wished to wed, and allegedly, she him, but had lost her by what he considered were unfair means – this being David's own mother. However, that was an old story, actually one that his visitor had never so much as heard of, and he was soon prepared to let bygones be bygones, and to be friendly towards the son if not the father.

Well content over this, David went on his way. He was going to be Lord Kennedy one day, and wanted no family difficulties.

Almost as soon as he crossed Stinchar, his road turned inland from the cliff-girt coast, to cross uplands of no great height, empty sheep country this, to reach another large river, south-flowing, the App, which rose out of the flanks of a prominent summit of these hills, Beneraird. Reaching this, he rode down Glenapp, a steep-sided valley, all but

231

a lengthy ravine, until it opened to salt water again at the mouth of Loch Ryan. This sea loch was almost two miles across. Unfortunately there was no ferry over this, no fishing-haven to provide a boat, so he had to go on down the east shore of it for another eight or so miles until he came to the town of Stranraer at its head. Here he was told that Leswalt lay less than four miles up the other side of the loch, easily found, in Agnew country.

This of the Agnews concerned David a little. He had never met any of this quite important Galloway clan, but knew that they were influential in these parts, indeed that the chiefs of the family were hereditary sheriffs of Galloway. Their main castle was at Lochnaw, and if this was near Leswalt, it would be politic to call there to see the sheriff before inspecting his new properties. Agnew might well be involved in Wigtown's affairs, and could have views on the Whithorn position. Also, these powerful local magnates could be somewhat hostile to new proprietors coming into their areas.

Riding from Stranraer, parallel with the shore, up to Leswalt, he found the countryside pleasant, rising inland to green slopes and moorland, very much cattle country. Leswalt itself proved to be a village set on a stream at a meeting of roads, set inland about a mile below quite a major hillock crowned by an ancient Pictish fort. There was a church and a mill but no castle or hallhouse to be seen; yet this was a barony and must have a seat, surely.

However, first to see Sheriff Agnew. Asking at the mill, he was told that Lochnaw Castle lay a mere two miles westwards, at the White Loch, in a fertile vale south of the Garchrie Moss. This he judged to be unfortunate, too close at hand. He might have to tread warily here, even though his estate was of the king's giving.

Lochnaw he found a quite extensive establishment, the usual square keep within a courtyard larger than usual, with its subsidiary buildings, this on the edge of a sizeable loch in picturesque wooded country. It was now early evening, and David hoped that he might find the sheriff at home.

He did. Quintin Agnew was a gravely dignified man of middle years, who turned out to be less guarded than the visitor feared, and nowise hostile. He had heard of the Master of Kennedy, and of his famed sister Flaming Janet bearing the king's son, the Earl of Moray. Also he had been impressed by the handling of the Wigtown–Whithorn dispute, which might have blown up into quite serious conflict. In fact he was glad to see the new Baron of Leswalt, for properties with absent lairds could be troublesome, with the folk lacking oversight and authority, and wrongdoers ever apt to misbehave; and he had enough peace-keeping to see to as Sheriff of Galloway without having problems on his own doorstep, this complicated by the fact that Leswalt was a barony and its baron having magisterial powers, even of pit and gallows.

David, promising to try to ensure good behaviour at Leswalt, found himself getting on well with this Quintin Agnew, so well indeed that he was invited to share the evening meal and stay the night, a very welcome convenience.

He asked where was the seat of the Leswalt barony, and learned that it was at Carmagill, about a mile from the village up the Sale Burn, no very large house and in a distinctly derelict state. The barony had been held by a Douglas, who had lived elsewhere, a far-out kinsman of the Earls of Douglas themselves; and at the fall of that great line in 1452, when James the Second had actually slain the eighth earl with his own hand, like so many other Douglas properties, Leswalt was forfeited to the crown.

David was scarcely heartened to learn that his new holding had been taken from the Douglases, who might well still resent this and prove difficult. He certainly wanted no problems with the Black Douglases as well as the Red. But Agnew declared that Leswalt had been an isolated property of that great line, the only one in the Rhinns area; and they had shown no interest in it since its forfeiture fifty years ago.

They talked at some length about the Whithorn free-barony situation and Bishop George, and the sheriff confessed that he was relieved that David had found a workable solution to this competition over trading rights, which had looked like developing into serious strife, in which he, as sheriff, would inevitably have been involved, and in a difficult position indeed. The last thing he wanted was to be embroiled in hostilities between Wigtown, the Douglases and the Bishop of Galloway. This of escorted convoys seemed to be an excellent solution, especially under the warden's authority.

David learned that the parish church was the one at Leswalt, and this was the burial place of the Agnews of Lochnaw and Galdenoch, as well as their worshipping place. The sheriff praised the local priest, who was in fact a good influence for law and order in the barony, as distinct from his spiritual duties. He happened to be an Agnew also, which perhaps helped and had its conveniences.

Out of all this, David voiced a thought that had been simmering in his mind for a while. He felt that it was time that he did something about his brother, Alexander, who was now of full age and at something of a loss at Dunure. He might offer him this Leswalt. He could not be the baron but he could live here and act the laird, keep the property in order, pass on most of the revenues, as deputy. Agnew thought this a worthy suggestion.

So, in the morning, David went to inspect his barony. He called first on the priest, Father Andrew, whom he found to be a young man of character and who, like the sheriff, was grateful for the Whithorn arrangements, the dispute there concerning him also, the bishop being his ecclesiastical superior. He in fact conducted David around the property, the farms in especial, presenting the people to him. There were no fewer than nine farms here, and more apparently at the coast, David remembering the

234

names of only two of them, the easiest to grasp, strange Celtic names, Meikle Larg and Culmore. They were all used for cattle-rearing, crop-raising only for winter feed for the beasts. There proved to be another mill, as well as the one he had called on, this up the Sale Burn about one mile, near to the hallhouse of the barony. This surprised David, for the farms he visited did not look as though they would produce sufficient grain to require two mills to grind it. But he was informed that there were other farmeries along the coastal strip, lower ground and more fertile, this between Salchrie and St Mary's Well. He would visit these on his homewards way.

The hallhouse itself was indeed empty and in poor state, although the tenant of the adjoining demesne-farm attended to it in some fashion. It was not large, as such places went, a semi-fortified manor rather than any castle; but David judged that it could be refurbished and improved to make a comfortable enough home, certainly good enough for Alexander his brother. They ended up the circuit by returning to the church, where Father Andrew showed him quite proudly the many tombs of the Agnews, his ancestral line, which went back for as far as twelve generations.

David took his farewell of the young priest, having gained a favourable impression of the Agnews. He thought that Alexander would find them good neighbours if he agreed to come here to Galloway as laird.

David had a look at the four more farms along the levels near the shore, and admired the little shrine of St Mary's Well, which he had not heard of. He then turned for home, well satisfied that James Stewart had given him a worthy addition to his lordship. He would bring Agnes down here one day to see it all. He liked the Rhinns of Galloway.

22

The return to Cassillis revealed that soon after David had left for Galloway, a request had come for another escorting company from Whithorn. Agnes had not known for how long her husband would be away, so she had taken it upon herself to send to tell Kennedy of Culzean to arrange and lead this. There was no need for David to go with every pack-horse train, was there? He very much agreed; he had no wish to spend over-much of his time riding safe-conduct to traders over the border.

They were planning their spring-time visit up to Moray again, when a summons to a parliament arrived from the king, this to be held at Edinburgh on 11th March. David, these days, did not seem to be allowed much time at home with Agnes and Gibbie at Cassillis.

At Edinburgh the accommodation at least was better than at Stirling, the Abbey of the Holy Rood providing excellent hospitality. The king summoned David for a brief discussion on the subject of burghal and baronial rights before the session opened, he determined that there should be no more dangerous confrontations such as the Wigtown–Whithorn one elsewhere in the land, as was being rumoured.

This parliament was held up in Edinburgh Castle's great hall. There was a surprise for most, including David Kennedy, even before the monarch made his official entrance. For who should prove to be the new Lord High Chancellor in charge of proceedings, in place of the late Argyll, but Archibald Bell-the-Cat, Earl of Angus. This, it seemed, was James's way of allaying any possible Douglas trouble, and giving Angus a fairly lofty position where he could do no great harm, duties only formal and entirely public. He had been behaving unexceptionally for over two years now, settled quietly with his new and uncontroversial third wife, Katherine Stirling. But he had begun to rebuild the damaged Tantallon Castle, that great stronghold so difficult to reduce, and the king felt it wise to receive him back into approximate favour.

In fact, Angus acted Chancellor very well, authoritative without being aggressively so. David doubted whether he was indeed a reformed character, but James's judgment was probably wise.

He commended the business with this of burghal trading rights, source of considerable possible disharmony in the realm, the king himself initiating the discussion. He cited the Wigtown–Whithorn situation and praised the Master of Kennedy for his excellent solution of that particular problem. But there were other possible troublespots throughout the land, and parliament must seek to regulate the matter, to prevent further upsets. It was necessary to make clear and unmistakable divisions between the rights of royal burghs, burghs of regality, these new free or civil burghs, and burghs of barony. He proposed for a start that, while civil burghs should not be abolished – they had been an innovation of his late royal father and Archbishop Sheves – no more of them should be formed, since they could obviously clash with the royal burghs which must remain supreme.

David glanced over at the bishops' benches where Bishop George of Galloway sat amongst the others. That man did not rise to contest this suggestion. In fact it was Bishop Elphinstone who agreed, and put the royal proposal in the form of a motion. Bishop Forman seconded. With these two prominent ecclesiastics supporting, and the civil burghs having been set up by prelates, no one else chose to contest it.

Angus declared the motion passed. No more civil burghs.

The various privileges of the other burghs were then

debated. Again it was Elphinstone who led off. He declared that he judged that only royal burghs should have the rights of foreign trade save, with a glance at Galloway, existing civil burghs. That burghs of regality should have similar rights, save for that last. But that burghs of barony, although less powerful and privileged, should be greatly increased in numbers. These were the basic centres of internal trade of the realm, and as such were vital for the well-being and prosperity of the people at large. But there were too few of them. For instance, the shire of Peebles in the borderland he knew, although some thirty miles approximately along its four sides in the central Tweed area, had only the one burgh of barony, the town of Peebles itself. Which meant that the folk therein could only buy and sell goods lawfully, hold markets and fairs, at a centre often a full day's journey from their homes. The same applied elsewhere. In his own diocese of Aberdeen, he could identify at least four townships that ought to be burghs of barony for their areas.

Men all over the hall jumped up to support this, calling out the names of communities innumerable that should be raised to burghal status. Angus had to bang his chancellor's gavel for order. But with the issue so obviously important to many, a committee of the estates was appointed to go into all claims and cases in detail.

Elphinstone made one final suggestion. To distinguish towns and burghs that were raised to this status, each should have erected a burghal or market cross, mounted on a platform of sorts, as symbol of their authority. Such structures should also be used as places from which official announcements, royal proclamations and orders of council could be made, something much required in many towns. This also was accepted.

This matter of trade and burghal rights disposed of, however important to the representatives of the people and the churchmen, a deal less so to the lords and nobility, was the main business of this parliament. But what *was* of concern to the many magnates present was the pluralism, as it was named, of many of the prelates and senior clergy, this frequently impinging on their own rights and privileges as landowners and lairds.

Hearty James, Earl of Buchan, introduced this matter, looking at Bishop Forman. His own spiritual diocesan, the said excellent Andrew Forman, was also Abbot of Dryburgh in the borderland and Prior of Pittenweem in Fife. He proposed a limit on such pluralities of office, with their benefits. The Sinclair Earl of Caithness rose to second, pointing out that the Bishop of Caithness was also Abbot of Kelso, again in the distant borderland, and Abbot of Fearn in Ross, and with lesser holdings far removed from his see.

Again Angus had to call for order as other lords made similar assertions.

The Archbishop Blackadder of Glasgow declared that this was not a matter for parliament to consider. If there was any need to review it, that would be the concern of the College of Bishops.

The king intervened, with Angus seeking to quell the protesters. The last thing he wanted, at this stage, after the trouble between Wigtown, the Douglases and Bishop George, was disharmony between lords spiritual and temporal. He urged the College of Bishops to look into the matter. He introduced a non-controversial subject of his own, to, as it were, calm the waters.

It was the matter of woodlands, he said. For long, trees and forests had been felled, all over the kingdom, and with little or no replacement and planting, the wood burned without heed to the future. Now they were growing short of timber. Sir Andrew Wood, here present, was finding it difficult to win sufficient timber to build his ships. Smiths were short of fuel for their forges, builders requiring material for houses and barns. This was grievous, as all must know, even the poor folk's household fires telling them so. There must be replanting. If every baron, laird and landlord was to plant a few acres each year, this would greatly help for the future. And every tenant farmer planting even one acre of worthy trees – oak and beech and ash and rowan – with hedges to protect the young trees from deer and rabbits – would greatly benefit the land. Also it would improve the sport.

Coming from the monarch himself, this, put into a motion by the Chancellor, was not contested, and passed without discussion.

A politic note to end on, James rose from his throne. Angus, seeing it, declared the session adjourned as all got to their feet. Sufficient unto the day . . .

The Kennedys were not long thereafter in making their second visit to Moray. Young Gilbert, no longer a mere baby, was actually less placid a passenger on horseback now, and David took turns with Agnes in carrying him, still in front of them, not old enough to ride behind of course. Not that the child objected to the travelling, but he was more restless, more interested in all that he saw, wanting to examine and point, sleeping but little. So they did not improve on their timing for the journey.

They found Janet and young Jamie in fine fettle; but she confessed that she had found the winter long indeed. James had managed to visit her only in November and late February, because of the snow-filled passes, and they had decided that this must be amended. She should not spend mid-winter at Darnaway in future, but somewhere more accessible. Yet somewhere that would not be too obviously a mere mistress's lodging, with young Queen Margaret and her English courtiers to consider. And there was this child Earl of Moray to think of also, infant as he still was. It would not look suitable for him to be cooped up in some modest and minor establishment. So they had decided on Bothwell Castle, in Lanarkshire. In theory, Janet was still Lady Bothwell, for Angus had put this lordship in her name as part of her dowery payment, and this had never been rescinded or cancelled despite the changed circumstances, although never actually appropriated either. So James used this odd

240

situation to their advantage. As part of his agreement with Angus to raise him to be Chancellor of the realm, he had gained consent that Janet should indeed possess Bothwell Castle, although not all the lands of the lordship. So this was where she would spend the winters in future, where James could visit her and their son readily and without arousing undue comment. Eight months of the year, then, at Darnaway, and four at Bothwell.

David was amused at this monarchial arrangement and provision; but it would allow him to see more of his sister also, Bothwell being less than fifty miles from Cassillis.

They spent a pleasant week at Darnaway, visiting many places of interest, both in the Laich, or low-lying country, and in Braemoray, as the highland parts were named. Janet took them to see Bishop Forman at his palace of Spynie again. She had found him to be a good friend, when he was in residence, and even when he was not, for he spent much time in the south on national affairs, his archdeacon, at Elgin, was a great help and support for a woman seeking to manage a great earldom. But the bishop was at Spynie at present.

David had always got on well with Andrew Forman, and enjoyed this visit. He greatly admired Spynie Castle, for it was that rather than any episcopal palace, a stronghold required in the past against raiding Highland clans – and not only these. But it was quite the most luxurious and splendid fortalice he had ever come across, much more so, although smaller, than the royal holds of Stirling, Edinburgh and Linlithgow. Forman all but apologised for this when the visitors expressed admiration for what they saw, declaring that his predecessors in the see had been concerned to emphasise the power and dignity of Holy Church in a land where the sword had ruled, when the Prince Alexander, the Wolf of Badenoch, terrorised this whole area, when the castle was first erected. A previous Earl of Huntly had also threatened to "come and pull the bishop out of his pigeon-holes," so Spynie had required to be a place of strength. Admittedly that did not account for all the handsome carved stonework and heraldic decoration, but David did not comment on that. Nor did he refer to the recent parliament's discussion on the matter of episcopal pluralities; but Forman himself did, mentioning that were it not for revenues derived from his abbacy of Dryburgh and priory of Pittenweem, much wealthier areas than this Moray, the Church's labours for the weal of the folk hereabouts would be much restricted. It made good sense to have the richer help the poorer, as Christ had taught. Was David to take due note, and act thereon? He supposed that with his Cassillis and the three new properties given by the grateful monarch, he might be looked upon as one of the rich now?

An aspect of this transference of not only moneys and wealth but of the means of actually generating such was demonstrated when Forman took them to see his new Saltcotes, as he called them, down at the bay-side. This was something that he had learned from his Fife priory of Pittenweem. Salt was an essential commodity, required daily by all, and especially by those preserving meats and fish, much of Fife's trade and export being such. And at Pittenweem the monks had provided the salt for the folk by heating the sea water in great pans or baths, turning it into steam and depositing the salt. He had brought two of the monks north here and they had advised on the building of similar salt-works at Spynie, smiths beating out great iron cisterns under which fires burned to boil the sea water. These were proving to be a great success and were being copied elsewhere, providing salt for the entire Moray Firth area, improving trade and creating wealth.

David was much interested and impressed by this venture, and took careful note. It came to him that here was something that he could emulate at Leswalt, and in due course perhaps at Dunure. Salt-pans on his coastal strips could be a source of revenue and prosperity not only for himself but for the local folk. The idea of turning sea water into wealth was a notable one.

The bishop also took them to see the sheds nearby where the farmers' and fishermen's products were being preserved in the salt for keeping and for export elsewhere, all an admirable development. Holy Church, they were learning, had more kinds of good living than the one to teach its people.

Janet conducted them on other visits also, notably up the Findhorn River, a headlong stream which, she said, could rise as much as fourteen feet above normal levels with melting Highland snows, causing severe flooding in the lower ground, which she was trying to control with dykes of stone, gravel and turf. The river cut a dramatic course, near Darnaway, through solid rock, forming narrow gorges and ravines where the water boiled and thundered in cascades and falls sending spray high. An especial point they were taken to, called Randolph's Leap, was where it was recorded that Alastair Ban Comyn, in the days of the Bruce, had managed to leap across the chasm to safety when pursued by Randolph, Earl of Moray, Bruce's nephew, after seeing his father and five brothers slain for treason. Why it was not called Comyn's Leap, Janet could not tell them. It seemed an almost impossible jump for any man, but fear of cold steel could evidently outweigh fear of death on rock or in roaring waters, and spur a fugitive into an extraordinary feat.

When they eventually took their leave of Janet, it was in the knowledge that it would not be so long before they saw her again, at Bothwell or Cassillis.

23

It was soon after their return home that Agnes announced
that she believed that she was pregnant again. This pleased
them both, for they wanted a brother or sister for Gibbie,
their only regret that it must restrict their travelling
together, although not for some considerable time, she
assured.

Brother Alexander proved to be happy to accept
the Leswalt stewardship, and was quite eager to go
there to inspect his new responsibilities. Agnes said
that she would wish to go to see this new acquisition
also. Indeed the other two brothers, John and William,
expressed a desire to accompany them, life at Dunure
growing ever more restrictive for young men, with Lord
Kennedy an ageing and ailing man, now become all but a
recluse, but proving no kinder, and making poor company
indeed.

So it was quite a family party that set out southwards,
in May, only Helen left behind with their father.

They all liked Galloway, finding it strangely different
from Carrick and Ayrshire, although so comparatively
near at hand, the folk different also in this land of
the southern Gael, as the name implied. The Rhinns
in especial they admired, seeming nearer to Ireland, a
mere twenty-five miles, than to Dumfries, double that,
and the scenery quite dramatic.

Leswalt pleased them all, and young Father Andrew
a welcoming guide and friend. They all roosted in the
hallhouse, assessing what must be done to make of it
a fit home for Alexander, and possibly for his younger
brothers on occasion, who much approved of this new

situation and expressed the wish to spend at least some of their time here.

David left the others to it, and went down to the coastal strip of his barony, to plan for the establishment of salt-pans. In this venture he found that Sheriff Agnew was interested; indeed he accompanied David on the second of his inspections, saying that if it all proved successful he might consider setting up a similar endeavour on the other, western, side of the peninsula, which belonged to Lochnaw. There was a fishing community at Portpatrick, which might well prove to be a suitable location for salt-making.

They held a conference with the fisherfolk of Soleburn, and managed to arouse interest, even some enthusiasm, for the project there, the locals perceiving some profit in it, both in preserving their catches and in selling the salt to others. There was plenty of local timber for the necessary fires, and David would get smiths from Stranraer to construct the metal pans. And Alexander would be at hand to supervise all. David suggested that once the pans were working and salt produced, they might find a ready market for it at Whithorn, where the monks and traders could no doubt use it to effect in their exporting. It could be transported there by the fishing-boats easily enough. Agnes said that David was in danger of becoming a merchanter himself, a salt baron!

After a week of this, leaving the three brothers to see to the advancement of the Leswalt projects, husband, wife and child returned homewards.

They found exciting news awaiting them at Cassillis. Some Italian adventurer and navigator, named apparently Christopher Columbus, had found a new world far beyond the western ocean, a seemingly great continent, with strange, dark-skinned people and rich lands. There had always been talk of such a place existing, allegedly reached by some early Vikings, but this had been considered to be something of a myth and legend. Was this Atlantis . . . ?

An order from the king for David to attend a Privy Council meeting at Edinburgh was also awaiting them, business unspecified, so he had only two nights at home before having to be off again. As well that Carrick did not seem to demand a deal of governing these days.

The council, it turned out, was to consider the means of raising new revenues for the purpose of building a fleet of warships, by Sir Andrew Wood, partly to control the still unruly Western Isles and Highlands but also to counter the continuing activities of English armed pirate vessels which, despite the peace between the realms, was actually getting worse, and gravely damaging Scots trade, especially with the Netherlands, their principal customer overseas. Protests made to King Henry had proved of no avail. Wood, there present, declared that only warships escorting the merchanters would solve the problem. But the building of such great vessels was costly. His pride and joy, the *Great Michael*, was now all but completed, and he invited the councillors to come down to Leith to inspect it. But funds had run out, and much money would be required to build the necessary new craft for trade protection.

The king and his lords all looked at the bishops present, as the authorities on gaining wealth and revenues on any major scale. Elphinstone said that the traders themselves, who would be the main beneficiaries, ought to provide the essential funding; but it was difficult to raise the money in advance for the slow process of shipbuilding. Some increase in harbour-dues would be insufficient. He suggested that if all justiciars, sheriffs and magistrates were to be instructed to *fine* transgressors, in moneys and goods, instead of always imprisoning and even hanging them, considerable funds could be raised if all such fines were transmitted to the Treasury – and he looked round the lords of council significantly. These were all judges in some degree as holders of baronies and jurisdictions of one sort or another; and fines were well known to be apt to stick to lordly fingers.

246

There was some clearing of throats, but the thing was agreed in principle and Patrick Paniter, Abbot of Cambuskenneth, the king's secretary, was instructed to draw up a suitable scale of fines for various offences.

Bishop Forman proposed another source of revenue: the changing of many of the larger tenancies of royal lands into feus, this carrying certain privileges and perpetual occupation, with security of tenure, but at a price. Major revenues could be raised thus.

James agreed to consider it.

But all this of collecting moneys was not really what was preoccupying the monarch, but something much more to his taste. This was the matter of the printed word, something scarcely known in Scotland. There apparently had been a great advance in this extraordinary development, this starting at Mainz in Germany. One Johannes Gutenberg had invented a printing press, and using it had produced a bible and a psalter, these able to be reproduced in any quantity required merely by pressing moulded metal letters in ink on paper, a most wonderful device which could all but change the world, making the written word available to all, not only the Scriptures and sacred themes but laws, chronicles, poetry, legends, orders and the like, such no longer needing to be written out laboriously by hand by monks and clerks. It was even said that pictures and designs could also be printed; there was no end to what could be achieved by this invention. Gutenberg himself was dead but his work had been continued and improved by one Johann Fust, in Strassburg. Scotland could, and ought to, be to the fore in making use of this. He, James, was determined on it.

Most there admittedly did not share the monarch's enthusiasm, but the clerics were obviously much interested, Elphinstone and Forman particularly. They asked for details and how this wonder was to be brought to Scotland.

James waved towards Abbot Paniter, who it seemed had learned of it all in Paris where he had been studying.

He had passed on this information to one of his own clerks, Walter Chepman, here in Edinburgh, who was eager to learn more, and if possible to establish a printing-work here in Scotland. He, James, proposed to send Chepman to Strassburg, to discover more, and try to bring back expert craftsmen who worked at this art. Here was something notably worth pursuing, no?

Since clearly this of printing on paper for books and documents was much concerning James Stewart, none present could pooh-pooh it, however unimportant it might seem to some. Many of the lords could not even write their names, using seals and crosses for signatures. But the clergy saw it differently, and voiced support for the project.

Apart from one or two formalities, that concluded the business, and James declared that he was going to accompany Andrew Wood down to Leith to inspect progress on the *Great Michael*, urging others present to do the same. Most agreed to do so, and they rode the two miles down to the port.

This great ship, the largest and finest that Wood had ever designed – indeed he claimed it to be the largest in all the world by his information – was quite extraordinary, and far in advance of any of his previous efforts, not only in its size. And costly, to be sure, which was why some of the councillors were not enthusiastic over the project. But even these could not but exclaim in admiration when they saw the vessel at the quayside, dominating all around, not only other shipping but buildings and warehouses.

They were informed that it was no less than two hundred and forty feet in length, by fifty-six wide. Above the main deck it had five more soaring in the bows and four at the stern, all with gun-ports for cannon. It had no fewer than four tall masts, each with high crow's-nests, as they were called, circular roosts for men with light guns and crossbows to assail any vessels able to approach sufficiently near, such as might have managed to survive the cannon-fire – for thirty-five full cannon were planned for, beside three hundred smaller artillery, culverins, double-dogs and the like. Its sails, they were told, were as large as the rest of it, enabling it to outsail almost any craft it was ever likely to meet. Wood was a genius in the design of shipping, and this was his triumph, James having supported him in it all, despite the expense. Once this was patrolling the seas, few pirates and privateers would think to run the risk of countering the *Great Michael*.

They all went aboard and met the Barton family, experienced shipmen whom Wood had enlisted to man, or at least captain, his ships, and were shown much of detail, although all was not yet completed. Loud was the admiration expressed for all that they saw. Few cannon were yet in position, and the forging of more might well be a delaying factor in eventual putting into service; but the vessel itself looked sufficiently ready to sail, and with ample men aboard, to have the impetuous James suggesting a trial run there and then. In this, unexpectedly, he was supported by Bishop Forman, who seemed to have infected the king, as well as David Kennedy, with an interest in the salt-making process, with its advantages for trade and wealth. Why not sail across the Forth estuary in this great craft and visit the pans at Pittenweem Priory, where he himself had learned of it all? It was only early afternoon, and Pittenweem less than twenty miles away.

But Wood shook his greying head. He would be happy to give His Grace and the others a short voyage to demonstrate the *Great Michael*'s excellences, but not yet. Various items were still not in order; and much better to sample his proud achievement when it was in full state of completion. At the disappointment expressed, he declared that if they were anxious to go over to Fife, he could take them in his own private craft, the *Columba*, moored nearby, which he used almost daily in coming to Leith from his house of Largo, none so far from Pittenweem. It was not a large vessel, but big enough to take the present company, he judged.

Not all of the councillors were eager to go inspecting salt-works, which they tended to see as the concern of tradesmen and the like, not for earls and lords, however clerics might see it, so most there called off. But James and Elphinstone were very ready to go, and David Kennedy also. So a move was made, most returning to Edinburgh, but the monarch and these others making along the quayside for a modest, single-masted open boat, with long oars and a square sail, which they were assured would have them over at the Fife shore in well under two hours in this south-west breeze. The crew of six had to be routed out of a dockside tavern, but drink-taken as they might be, they proved efficient enough at handling the *Columba*. James confessed that this was a new experience for him. Rowing-boats on lochs, for fishing, he knew; otherwise he had been only in large ships. He took a real interest in all that he saw, especially the scenery, exclaiming at the great stack of the Craig of Bass and the chain of lesser islets leading to it, all backed by the green cone of North Berwick Law. But soon he was pointing further ahead. There was a much larger island, all cliffs and precipices by the look of it. Would they pass near to that?

This was the Isle of May, Wood told him; and, if he mistook not, it was Bishop Forman's property. It was of especial interest to him, as a shipman, for it had an essential feature, a beacon or lighthouse to mark the entrance to the Firth of Forth and to warn seafarers, making for the Fife ports, of the danger of running on to these rocks and cliffs, for the isle was a mile long, and on a wild night could be a menace indeed.

This was the cue for Forman, who admitted, yes, it was his property, or rather that of his priory of Pittenweem, the monks of which maintained the beacon, ferrying fuel out to it almost daily, timber from the mainland woods. It had been, in fact, the first lighthouse in all Scotland, founded by St Ethernan, one of Columba's disciples, who had set up his cell or chapel at Pittenweem, and learning of the wrecks that could occur there in the mouth of Forth, had made it his diseart or private refuge where he could commune with his Maker. There he had established the mighty beacon, a notable gesture and ambitious task, this to be fully recognised when it was understood that there were no trees on the island and the wood had to be brought from the Fife shore on rafts towed by coracles. A major benefactor was Ethernan.

The king admitted that he had never so much as heard of Ethernan, and was told that this was because an ancestress of his own, the Blessed St Margaret, queen of Malcolm the Third, Canmore, who had brought the Roman Catholic faith to Scotland from Hungary to replace the ancient Celtic Church, had changed the name from Ethernan to Adrian, in honour of the then Pope of that style. His Grace would have heard of St Adrian?

James thought vaguely that probably he had. But, obviously intrigued by this account, declared that he wished to visit this island, since they were clearly going to pass near it. Was that possible? Despite those fearsome cliffs? After all, this Ethernan had landed there.

The bishop said that it was entirely possible, if Sir Andrew agreed, for there was indeed a minor priory on the May, a subsidiary of Pittenweem, and it had a haven of sorts at its southern end, where the wood for the fires was still landed. No large vessel could use it, but this *Columba* would not find it difficult, he thought. Wood agreed. He had been on the isle more than once as a young man.

They did not have to alter course greatly. Approaching the May they all gazed with something like awe at the tremendous cliffs, these circled by wheeling, diving, screaming birds. David was used to cliffs at Dunure, but none so lofty as these, so jagged, and of a strange, greenish rock, such ledges as there were festooned with seafowl. Forman said that the name had nothing to do with May-month or May-blossom but derived from the ancient Norse *má-eye*, the isle of the sea-mews.

When they rounded the southern tip of the island, they

251

realised how narrow it was in proportion to length, a mere ridge thrusting up from the sea, a mile long but perhaps no more than a quarter of that in width. At this end it fell sharply to a grassy stretch of no great size and a rocky shore, this including a bight-like bay, little more than an inlet, one side of which had been built up to form a rough quay. Here the *Columba* edged carefully in, with little room to spare, and they were able to land.

They were met by a group of six monks, whose duty was to service the beacon, apparently the Pittenweem brothers taking it in turn to perform this task. These no doubt had been watching the vessel's approach for some time, for visitors to the May were a rarity indeed. When they discovered that it was the King of Scots himself, and their own bishop, their wonder was almost beyond words. Nearby was the little monastery, if that it could be called, a very modest and low-browed establishment, as it would have to be to withstand the winter's gales beating on this so exposed site. It seemed that it had been founded by Queen Margaret's youngest son, David the First, he who had built so many abbeys up and down the land, including the Holy Rood and Forman's Dryburgh, sixteen monarchs back from James. And not far off were the scanty ruins of the chapel built in the sixth century by the hands of St Ethernan himself.

James was for climbing the steep and rocky slope up to the long summit ridge, to the site of the beacon on its highest point, although the two clergy and some of the older visitors thought better of it. David and Secretary Paniter went with the energetic monarch, and they remarked on the problem of hoisting heavy loads of wood up here. Those monks must be tough characters.

Up there, distinctly breathless, they could hardly hear themselves speak for the noise of the thousands of seafowl filling the air in such clamour as to make them dizzy, their droppings unfortunately unavoidable. Very quickly, having viewed the cairn and its beacon, they had had enough of this. They were told that innumerable different

252

breeds of birds, not just the sea-mews for which the ancient Norsemen had named the isle, haunted the place, some always, some seasonally, gulls of every description, oyster-cathers, sandpipers, redshanks, divers and terns. The visitors reckoned the May was a different world from their own.

But interesting as it all was, they did not linger. How the monks put in their days when they were not ferrying logs and carrying them up to the fire, they knew not. But they certainly were rendering an important service for seafarers; and of course they would only have spells out here, in between normal monastic land-based activities.

So it was cast off and heading for Pittenweem, five miles, this a fishing village near the priory on a rock-bound and cave-yawning coast – cave being what the name weem meant. The monastery was a large one, with every sign of prosperity, providing a most useful halting place for travellers, and they were many, to and from St Andrews, the metropolitan see, and one of the most important places in the realm.

The sub-prior, intrigued by the monarch's interest in salt-making, took them down to a sheltered cove east of the village and harbour, where they viewed extensive works, much larger than those of Spynie, or for that matter than David had planned at Leswalt, the visitors seeing the steam from the evaporating pans rising from some distance off, many men working there. There were five of these great baths raised on iron pillars, three with fires blazing beneath, and the other two being scraped with hoe-like implements to detach the deposited salt, to be further dried and then packed into sacks. Nearby there was something that David had not seen before, built-up ponds to contain large quantities of salt water, these being kept filled by relays of pannier-horses bringing up a constant supply from the shore, this so that storms and tidal problems should not interfere with constant production. These ponds were used also to ensure that impurities, such as sand, weed, clay and ground-up shells,

253

sank to the bottom, enabling only pure sea water to be led off to the heating pans.

They spent some time examining all this lengthy, interesting and clearly profitable endeavour, and thereafter partaking of the priory's hospitality, before they realised that it was high time to be sailing back to Leith, with the wind now in their faces. They left Pittenweem and its busy monks with many expressions of esteem.

Aboard the *Columba*, James Stewart observed that it had occurred to him that instituting a monopoly and tax-raising on salt production might well be something to consider in the realm's need for moneys. Neither Forman nor David Kennedy expressed any enthusiasm for this suggestion, and the king said no more.

24

The following year was a momentous one for the Kennedys; and for more than them, for England, and therefore to some extent for Scotland also. Agnes was delivered of another son, whom they named James, like so many another, this without problems other than the normal discomforts. And John, Lord Kennedy, died, no great surprise, for he had been ailing for long. So suddenly David was Lord Kennedy and King of Carrick – not that this made any great difference to his life, for he had more or less acted the part for years.

Then the next year news reached them that King Henry Tudor had died; and though this, on the face of it, might not greatly have concerned Scotland, it did at least pose questions and doubts for those who ruled the land, for he was succeeded by his son, the Prince of Wales, now Henry the Eighth, and he was known to be a very different man from his father, hot-headed, arrogant, unscrupulous and rejoicing in the style of the First Knight of Christendom, this implying a military disposition. What this might mean for Scotland remained to be seen.

And only a month after all this, young Queen Margaret, now in her twentieth year, was delivered of a son. Great were the rejoicings. There was now an heir to the throne, legitimate. One more James Stewart.

The king's delight was unbounded. He showered gifts on the somewhat bewildered mother, who became less of a sort of hermit in Linlithgow Palace. There was to be a great ceremonial baptism at Holyrood Abbey, at which all of any stature in the kingdom would attend. This new little Duke of Rothesay would be paraded through Edinburgh and shown to the people as their monarch-to-be.

David received a special invitation, or order, to attend the christening, which surprised him; all magnates were to be present, and he would have gone anyway. He seemed to have been attending religious ceremonies of one sort or another recently, for Lord Borthwick had also died, and he had taken Agnes to the funeral. Then their small James had to be christened, and the Lord Kennedy buried in the family crypt at the Collegiate Church of the Virgin Mary at Maybole. Now he set off for Edinburgh less than enthusiastically.

He found the city in a great stir, its population possibly doubled by incomers, all in a state of holiday and celebration, James's generosity, despite empty coffers, being boundless towards all, visitors and townsfolk alike. There were pageants and tournaments, street games and sporting events, open-air feastings, wines and ales for all at the Market Cross, the Tron, the Tolbooth, at St Giles High Kirk and at the entrance to the citadel. David had obviously come late on the scene; in fact, when he entered by the West Port and headed eastwards for the abbey by the Grassmarket and the Cowgate, he had to push his way through thousands awaiting the sight of the monarch parading the streets and actually carrying the new heir to the throne in his arms to show him off to all. And in due course James appeared at the head of a splendid and illustrious train, child cradled high and every now and again raised higher still to all but brandish him from side to side in pride. Amongst the many great ones at his back, David noted none other than Archibald Bell-the-Cat, the Chancellor. There was no sign of the young mother.

David followed the cavalcade down to the abbey, quite prepared, in all this throng, to be sent off to some accommodation elsewhere, the monastic quarters obviously full to overflowing. But no, a sub-prior was on the look-out for him, and conducted him to a small chamber at the east end,

256

where, washing and tidying himself after his journey, he was further surprised to be informed that His Grace would send for him for audience in due course. This all seemed rather extraordinary treatment in the circumstances, and he wondered what was behind it.

It was almost an hour before he found out, and he was getting hungry and wondering whether he could summon victuals, for he had eaten nothing for long, and he felt almost like a prisoner there. Then the sub-prior came back and led him through crowded corridors and passages, busy with servants hurrying with cauldrons and platters and laden dishes, and he recognised that he was approaching the main refectory and dining-hall of the abbey. He was cheered by this, at least.

But it was not to a seat at one of the long tables that he was taken, but to a chamber behind the top end of the hall, behind the dais platform, and there ushered in, past a guard who, bowing, announced, "Your Grace and my lords, the Lord Kennedy, at Your Highness's command."

James stood there with only three of his closest associates, the Bishops Elphinstone and Forman and the Earl of Bothwell. "Ha, my lord Kennedy, greetings! Late as you are!" he was welcomed.

"I had a father to bury, Sire. May I congratulate you, and Queen Margaret, on the birth of an heir? Here is great blessing for yourselves and your realm." That was scarcely original.

"To be sure. I celebrate it. We all do. And in many ways. But one of which, my lord David, is to summon you to my side this day."

"*Me*, Sire? How can I serve in this? I rejoice, yes. But . . ."

"You have served me, and the realm, passing well, my friend. I would have done this before, but *now* is the time." James went over to a table and picked up a scroll of parchment, which he handed to David. "There it is. I here and now create you Earl of Cassillis!"

David gasped and stared. "Earl . . . !"

257

"Aye. An earl of Scotland. You deserve it well. I would have done this before now. But it is unsuitable to raise a son above his father when such is alive and a lord of parliament. And he was to be no earl! Here is *your* celebration!"

As David stood dumbfounded, the two prelates came forward to shake his hand. Bothwell, never a demonstrative man, merely patted a shoulder.

"Tomorrow you will attend the baptism in the abbey-church," the king went on. "Sitting on the earls' benches. Meantime, dine at my table tonight, my lord."

David took that as his dismissal, and bowed himself out.

Scarcely believing that he was not dreaming, he found his way back to his modest quarters.

So that evening he sat at the dais-table amongst the great ones, between Elphinstone and Forman, scarcely aware of the magnificence of what he was partaking.

The baptismal celebrations next day were extraordinary. A great procession, under banners and decorations, preceded by minstrels and musicians, was led by the monarch, infant in his arms, queen at his side, and backed by all the magnates of Church and state – even forty new knights created for the occasion – and set out from Holyrood to make a complete tour of the walled city, all inhabitants ordered to be out on the streets to greet their future king and cheer him on his way. They rode up the Cowgate, almost a mile of it, right to the Grassmarket and the West Port, then turned up the West Bow's hill to the Lawnmarket where wine was served from rows of casks to all, the king himself dispensing some of it. But not the queen, who hardly gave the impression of enjoying the proceedings. Nothing, not even proud motherhood, would make Margaret Tudor other than a rather stodgy onlooker at events.

Then down to the Market Cross, the Tolbooth and the High Kirk of St. Giles. where the provost and town council welcomed all, before joining in the procession, all having practically to force their way through the packed streets, flags, colourful sheets and plaiding hanging from the tenement windows.

The second mile brought them down the High Street and Canongate to the Abbey Strand, and Holyrood again.

Thereafter it was into the great church for the so important ceremony. In theory, the heir to the throne should have been baptised by the Primate of Holy Church, the Archbishop of St Andrews. But since that was now the mere boy Alexander, and no priest, moreover the infant's half-brother, he merely stood beside the Archbishop Blackadder of Glasgow, who performed the christening, the proud parents, and presumably Margaret was that, close by. Considering all the build-up to it, and the significance of the occasion, the actual proceedings were very brief and quickly over, with a few howls from the child contributing. No doubt it was sufficient.

There was more banqueting and festivities of various kinds thereafter; but David sought royal permission to retire. His presence was of no importance in it all, and he was eager to be back at Cassillis, to admire his own new offspring and to tell Agnes that she was now a countess.

James made no objection. In parting, he asked about the name Cassillis. Since it was pronounced as though it were "castles", a number of folk who had not seen it written had asked how anyone could be made Earl of Castles unspecified? It seemed a folly. David was able to tell him that the word came from cashel, an ancient Celtic word for a fort or fortified township; and there were three Pictish forts in the Cassillis area. That had to serve.

Agnes's reaction to the earldom for her husband was that it was well deserved indeed, and overdue. Being a countess would make not one whit of difference to herself. But young Gibbie as now Master of Cassillis might take some getting used to. She hoped that it all would not mean David's involvement in increased affairs of state. A happy home and family life were her priorities.

David endorsed that wholeheartedly. He promised that he would seek to limit his commitments. But James could be pressing . . .

25

The new baby Jamie, the Cassillis one, suffered a series
of minor problems that late summer, involving the
bringing up of his mother's milk an hour or so after
being fed; and even though a wet-nurse was resorted to,
this still continued, resulting in some restriction of his
growth, although otherwise he seemed healthy enough
and sufficiently lively. This prevented his parents from
making their annual visit up to Moray to see Janet, a
disappointment. But they would surely be able to call
on her at her new winter lodgings at Bothwell Castle in
due course, and so sent her word.

As it turned out, however, Janet it was who did the
calling. She arrived one day in August at Cassillis, with
her small boy, to much acclaim, announcing that James
had brought her south with him after one of his visits
to Darnaway and Tain, to take her to Bothwell agreed
for her forthcoming winter-time residence. He would be
taking her north again in ten days' time. But meantime
she was supervising the furnishing and making habitable
of one of the towers of the great castle to her taste
and comfort, James lavishly generous in the matter.
Incidentally he had created her Lady Bothwell, which
gave her some acceptable status, as distinct from being
merely the mother of the Earl of Moray. It carried no
especial privileges and was not hereditary. It was as well,
perhaps, that the Hepburn Earl of Bothwell was a widower,
or his countess might have had cause for complaint.

Janet congratulated David on his earldom; and he
confessed to her that he had wondered once or twice
how much the king's relationship with Flaming Janet

Kennedy might have contributed to this appointment. She disclaimed any hand in the matter, truthfully, he hoped.

She stayed for two nights and then returned to Lanarkshire. David and Agnes would have accompanied her, but she said that with the place in a state of refurbishing, as it was at present, she would prefer them to see it when she came south again in late October, by which time she could welcome them to some comfort.

David asked his sister how she felt about all the excessive celebrations of the birth of the young prince and the adulation displayed towards this offspring compared with James's attention towards her own child. Janet expressed herself as unconcerned. This was just relief on his part over the dynastic situation, which had been worrying him ever since the deaths of his two brothers. The succession had to be secured; a throne without a legitimate heir was a grievous position for the incumbent monarch. As to *her* young Jamie, she had no doubts that he was beloved of his father in a way that it was unlikely that this other child would be, for James had no deep affection for Margaret Tudor, whereas she knew that he was still in love with herself. And his behaviour with her son when they were together left her entirely assured as to his abiding affection. She asked no better.

David had a refurbishing project of his own to see to. Dunure Castle was now his; and although he and Agnes had no intention of leaving Cassillis for that cliff-top hold, it was the ancient seat of the Kennedys, and during the last years of his father's life had become somewhat run-down. It was his brothers' and sister's home and should be kept in order.

Then there was the Leswalt situation to see to. That far at least they could risk taking the new Kennedy, Jamie; there seemed to be a plethora of infants so called, all part of the celebratory situation inevitably.

They found all in reasonably good order beside Loch Ryan, although Alexander was actually away when they arrived, on one of his Whithorn escorting duties; and the other two brothers returned to Dunure. Fortunately, the young priest, Andrew Agnew, was taking an active interest in the salt-works process, which he saw as of advantage to his parishioners, and salt was being produced at Soleburn, although not yet in large quantities. With the new information David brought from Pittenweem, greater headway was to be looked for. Sheriff Agnew was interested to learn of this also, for he had founded his own pans at Portpatrick by now, and finding that other fishing communities on the Irish Sea coastline were eager to emulate.

For her part, Agnes perceived considerable improvements that she could initiate at the Leswalt hallhouse, so she made herself equally busy – to the major satisfaction of brother Alexander when he got back from his Carlisle task. He declared that he was quite enjoying his life in Galloway, where he was being accepted as *Deputy* Warden of the West March in place of his brother, and Lord Maxwell making no complaints as to his activities, indeed probably preferring him to David in that position, as impinging less on his own authority. Indeed, now that he was an earl, and so superior in rank to Maxwell, David decided that he would ask the king to relieve him of the wardenship, and appoint Alexander in his place, since it made an uncomfortable relationship in the circumstances. Moreover, he had a sufficiency of other responsibilities to occupy him – too many according to Agnes.

They spent a worthwhile two weeks in Galloway, before learning from the sheriff that the national mood of celebration over the heir had become distinctly deflated. The infant prince was proving less than healthy, indeed there were considerable anxieties developing as to his condition, and James was much preoccupied. And to add to this, there was trouble with England.

It had not taken long for Henry the Eighth to prove himself a very different monarch from his father. He was only of eighteen years admittedly, but was intent on establishing himself as a force to be reckoned with. Pope Julius and France were presently in a state of war over the Republic of Venice, and Henry took the opportunity to ally England with the Pope and cancel his father's latterly favoured arrangements with France. He sent a request, all but a demand, for the Scots to end their long-enduring Auld Alliance with France, this in the interests of peace and harmony between the two realms, he said; this because until he, Henry, produced lawful offspring of his own by his late brother's widow, Catherine of Aragon, his elder sister, Margaret, Queen of Scotland, was heir-presumptive to the English throne.

James could by no means agree to this, and a Privy Council had to be held to decide on reaction. So David had to make another journey to Edinburgh. The decision there taken was to send Bishop Forman as envoy to London, to assure Henry that the Scots friendship with France implied no military co-operation against England, any more than against the Vatican and Venice; that James greatly valued the goodwill of his brother-in-law, and peace and harmony between the two kingdoms, and would use every effort to ensure that such continued and indeed was strengthened. He could hardly add that he had no least desire that his small son should become, for the time being, heir at one remove to the throne of England.

David did not envy Andrew Forman this embassage.

Whatever he said to the bishop, the pugnacious Henry Tudor was swift to demonstrate his dissatisfaction with the Scottish reaction. Forman was barely home, with no very satisfactory report of his meeting, when deeds replaced words. Sir Andrew Barton and his brother were playing their role in providing escorting warships for the Scots trading vessels sailing to and from the Low Countries, Wood's *Great Michael* not involved on this occasion, when, off the English coast, their convoy was attacked, not by pirates or privateers but by none other than the Lord High Admiral of England, the Lord Edward Howard, and his brother, the Lord Thomas, in force. Despite putting up a valiant fight, the two Barton ships, the *Lion* and the *Jenny Perwin*, were boarded and captured, Sir Andrew himself being slain, along with large numbers of his crews, the damaged vessels being taken into the port of Blackwall-on-Thames.

James was furious. His especial concern with ship-building and the creation of a powerful fleet, as well as his eagerness to develop trade and national wealth, were thus assailed; and as Wood was now an old man, Sir Andrew Barton had become his principal aide in these important concerns. To have him slain and his ships captured while protecting convoys, and by Henry's Lord High Admiral himself, was not to be borne, the need for peace between the two kingdoms notwithstanding.

But to take adequate action was difficult without precipitating actual warfare. James decided to invoke the terms of the treaty made with Henry the Seventh, that if an Englishman killed a Scot within the English Marches, or vice versa, the relevant wardens must produce the murderer at a joint Wardens' Court for trial and punishment. Admittedly this referred to land-based assault, but James judged that the principle was good for other slaying also. So he sent a demand to London that the English admiral and his brother should compear before a Wardens' Court to answer for their actions. And since Lord Dacre was the English Warden with whom he was on best terms, he stipulated that it should be the West March court, especially as the Howards had strong links in the Carlisle area, at Greystoke.

And so David found himself involved. He and Lord Maxwell were instructed to visit Dacre at Carlisle and set this judgmental process in action, however unlikely it seemed that it would in fact come to any satisfactory fruition.

With his aim of now passing his wardenship to his brother, David could not refuse this mission, unlikely to have any success as it might be; but he requested that it should be looked upon as his last regarding the West March. James acceded.

David had not had any direct contact with Maxwell for a considerable time, and this peculiar duty was not such as to enhance their relationship. The older man did not refer to the grant of the earldom, save only in the most casual fashion, and clearly intended that it should not affect the fact that *he* was Chief Warden and Alexander only deputy. He made no comments on the Whithorn escorting project, and the fact that it was now being joined by traders from other communities, although David did extol his brother's efforts, and saw them as a very real contribution to the peace of the Borderland. Maxwell's views on peace were left unexpressed. Needless to say, the pair were accompanied to Carlisle by quite an impressive force of Maxwells.

Presumably the Marchmen's system of news gathering and dissemination was working effectively, as ever, for they did not have to wait long at Carlisle Castle before Lord Dacre put in an appearance, affable enough towards David if less so to Maxwell, even asking after King James's and his wife's weal. But when he heard of the object of their visit, he all but hooted. The motion that the Lord High Admiral of England and his brother would come up to the border to place themselves before any sort of court, warden or other! That King Henry would sanction it was beyond all. Were such to be treated like reiving moss-troopers?

The envoys pointed out that it was part of the treaty agreed with the late King Henry. Offences committed against the other realm's nationals should be dealt with so, and the slaughter of Sir Andrew Barton and his men by the Howards came into that category, even though it took place at sea. Clearly, however, it was not the location of the killings but the personages involved which made Dacre see it all as impossible. But he promised to send and inform King Henry of the charge and demand, whatever might be the result.

With that the envoys had to be content, and they returned whence they had come.

David's report to the monarch could not have greatly surprised him; but at least the gesture had been made and Henry would have to produce some response.

That response came quickly. A senior English churchman, Nicholas West, arrived at Edinburgh to announce that it did not become one prince to accuse another of breaking a treaty merely because he had done justice on a thief and a pirate; and that if he had done further justice instead of shown mercy, all Barton's men would have been dead as Barton himself. There would be no trial of his admirals, whether on the border or anywhere else.

This curt communication produced such anger in James Stewart as none of his close associates had ever before seen. But there was nothing that he could effectively do about it. He sent West back with a demand that the two captured ships should be returned to Scotland forthwith, with their remaining crews.

Relations with England had not been so low since James the Second's days. The possibility of war began to be discussed amongst all sections of the population.

To add to the feelings of anxiety and gloom, the ailing infant Duke of Rothesay died, making a mockery of all those celebrations. James was devastated. However, Margaret Tudor was pregnant again. Her husband had prayers said in the churches for a successful delivery and, God willing, for another son.

26

In all this apprehension and despondency, David and
Agnes, with the two children, paid a visit to Janet at
Bothwell Castle, none so very far off in the middle Clyde
valley. They found it a major strength indeed, although
some part of it in a state of delapidation, set on a steep bend
of the river, its unusually lengthy courtyard dominated
at one end by an enormous round donjon tower rising
to almost one hundred feet in height. It had four other
lesser towers, all built in the round, which was unusual,
and was reputed to have been constructed that way by
the Douglases as a copy of the great castle of Couchy,
in France, home of Marie de Coucy, the mother of
King Alexander the Third. It had originally been a
main Douglas seat, but when that line of great earls fell
and suffered forfeiture sixty years previously, it had come
to the crown, and been little used since. It was, in fact,
a distinctly unsuitable occasional residence for a king's
mistress. Janet had not attempted to do anything about
refurbishing the huge donjon tower, nor indeed the later
single-storeyed hall within the courtyard at the opposite
end, nor yet the handsome chapel, but had contented
herself with making the lesser south-east tower habitable
and reasonably comfortable, with the few servitors James
provided occupying the adjoining courtyard wing.

James was visiting her frequently here, and finding
consolation over his various problems and anxieties, such
as his young wife could not give him. Janet saw her role as
of some value to the distracted monarch, giving him relief
and comfort and even aspects of a family life which clearly
he did not have with Margaret Tudor. His pleasure in her

company, and that of their small Jamie, was a sufficient fulfilment for her strange love affair, she declared. She had no regrets.

This little Jamie Stewart was a lively character, as sturdy as the legitimate one had been feeble. He got on well with Gibbie Kennedy, and these two at least made full use of the vast, rambling castle, exploring, clambering over its battlements, ramparts, turrets and stairways, particularly intrigued by its courtyard well, so deep, and tapping an underground stream. Down to this there was a series of steps cut in the walling, fortunately with a knotted rope hanging beside them for safety. The young Earl of Moray was well warned about this favoured activity, his avowed aim being one day to explore that undergound stream.

In fact, the king turned up the day before the Kennedys were due to leave for Cassillis, an anxious man. Henry, he reported, was sending up troops in considerable numbers to reinforce the garrisons of the border fortresses of Berwick, Norham, Wark and Carlisle, these facing all three Marches. Indeed it was said that Dacre had been moved to be Captain of Berwick Castle, which was strange, perhaps ominous, for Carlisle was his base. James thought that possibly his comparative friendliness towards the West March Scots had told against him, and he had been moved eastwards accordingly.

It was a worrying situation. If he, James, was to order more men down to the Scots holds of Ayton, Birgham, Roxburgh, Jedburgh and Hermitage, facing those English ones, then the least spark of cross-border hostility, so apt to prevail anyway, could set off full-scale war. And not only was war against all his wishes and aims, but the nation was not ready for it.

So the brief remainder of the Kennedys' visit to Bothwell was less than happy. David realised that at any time he might well be called upon to muster the full armed strength of Carrick and Ayrshire for battle.

One item of especial interest to Agnes they did learn. James had appointed her cousin, Robert Borthwick of

269

Ballencrieff, to a new position, that of Master of the Ordnance. He had long been interested, apparently, in metalwork, and had set up a great forge at Ballencrieff in Lothian, using local coal mined at Tranent to fashion weaponry, especially small brass cannon, some iron, but brass his favoured metal. This, although it had been known to the Romans, had been little used in Scotland, or indeed elsewhere; but Borthwick saw great advantages in it, especially for artillery. It was produced as an alloy of iron, copper and zinc, and required great heat to forge it, far hotter than any fire produced by burning wood. Hence this use of Tranent coal, the furnace fanned by bellows. The king had great hopes for new pieces thus formed, and he had brought over from the Low Countries two expert gun-makers, and allotted these to Borthwick, with orders to construct much larger cannon, greater than any so far founded in Scotland. They had started on a series of heavy pieces, partly founded in brass, rivalling even Mons Meg in size, which Borthwick was calling the Seven Sisters. James believed that these would be superior to anything that Henry Tudor could field if it came to war.

Agnes scarcely knew this cousin. David was interested, especially in the use of coals for the forges instead of wood. Could this be utilised for the salt-making process? According to James coal produced much fiercer heat than could timber.

The new Earl of Cassillis, it is to be feared, was much more interested in pursuing industry, trade and communal wealth than in warfare.

Indeed, when he got home to Cassillis he was not long in seeking to make possible use of this new information that James had transmitted on the use of coal, not for brass-founding or cannon-making but for his salt-works. The heating of the sea water in pans demanded great quantities of timber, and the cutting down of a sufficiency of trees to fuel the projects was not only a major task, using up much more time and energy than the actual salt evaporation, the transporting of the heavy wood in the necessary quantities itself demanding the labour of many men and horses. But not only that: woodlands, once felled, took a lifetime to be replanted and renewed. This was the greatest problem of the salt manufacture. But if coal could be used to produce even fiercer heat . . . ?

Coal, then. He knew little about it or its production, like most other folk. He could go and see this Robert Borthwick to discover the necessary information. But where was the coal available? Was it to be found readily? In large enough quantities to be worked? Was there, indeed, any of it in his own lands of Carrick? He had never heard of it being used locally, but that did not mean that it did not exist. Who could tell him? As ever, it would be the clergy who would know, if anyone did, the extracters and developers of the nation's wealth and resources. He would go to the Kennedy abbey of Crossraguel to enquire.

Abbot Kenneth was helpful. He said that he knew that coals had been dug at various areas of Carrick, certain blacksmiths using it for their forges. He had seen them working bellows to increase the heat of the fires, these, as he recollected, at Coylton, Tarbolton and Riccarton. Coylton was the nearest at hand, no more than six miles from Cassillis. The smith there had made sundry ironwork objects for the abbey, altar rails, candlesticks, even a weather-vane for the chapel gable. And of course, the usual shoes for the horses.

So David rode to Coylton, a village inland on the Water of Coyle, this a tributary of the River Ayr. He found the smith at work, Wat Dryden by name, beside his forge, shoeing a farm-horse, and greatly put about to be visited by the Lord Kennedy himself; he had not got round to thinking of him as the Earl of Cassillis. On the subject of coal he was very knowledgeable; in fact he said that he dug his own supplies from a riverside quarry or heugh nearby, as his father had done before him, and would never dream of using wood for his forge. He demonstrated the use of great bellows for blowing the fire into white heat. But when asked about the use of such for increasing the heat

271

of outdoor salt-pans, he did not see that these would be effective. But would the boiling of sea water require such strong heat? He judged that the ordinary breezes which blew would fan the coal fires sufficiently, surely?

David conceded that this was probably so. The main requirement was that coal should serve in place of wood, and last longer. He was assured that this was certainly so. Coal burned much more slowly than wood, while producing possibly twice the amount of heat.

Much heartened by this, David wondered about supplies of coal available. Was there a sufficiency here at Coylton to fuel his salt-pans, without depriving the smith, and others, of their requirements? Although he understood that there were other coal-heughs elsewhere in Carrick. He was assured that the whole riverside bank, all but a hillside, was made of coal, so far as they could tell, and that so far, Dryden imagined, they had only scraped the surface of it. Although his lordship might well find other places to produce the fuel nearer to his salt-works.

Well pleased with all this, David returned home. Coylton was actually on Cassillis land, although only just, so there would be no problem about taking supplies. This all was a matter that he thought he would place in the hands of the Crossraguel monks. These might even consider the setting-up of a salt-works of their own on the nearby coast, for they had their fishing community at Maidens. The entire area could benefit. Agnes supported him in this, and was glad that a far-out kinsman of her own should have brought it all to their notice. But was there any need to go to see this Robert Borthwick? Probably not. His concern was with making cannon. He might have improved bellows and furnaces than had any smith, but for evaporating water such would not be required, would it?

Although the sense of threat and fear of invasion was prevalent in the land, that Christmastide did produce some easement for the Scots. The news from the south was that Henry Tudor had actually demanded of Louis of France that the province of Aquitaine be handed over to him, as rightfully his. His predecessors, the Plantagenets, had so claimed, Eleanor of Aquitaine, daughter of the last duke thereof, having married Henry the Second of England – even though before that she had been wife to Louis the Seventh of France. So there had long been dispute over this. Now the Tudor was doing more than disputing. He claimed more than Aquitaine of course, he, like his father, still quartering the lilies of France in his English standard. But that was a more general and non-specific challenge. This new requirement was direct and forceful; sufficiently forceful for him to send a fleet and six thousand men across the Channel to reinforce his claim, under the Howard brothers. Thomas, the older brother, although not the admiral, was now calling himself Earl of Surrey. Their grandfather, the aged Duke of Norfolk, had died, and their father was now duke, Thomas his heir, as Surrey.

So there was at least a lessening of tension north of the border. If Henry was involving himself in what amounted to war with France, he was the less likely to engage in military aggression against Scotland at the same time – or so it was judged.

James and his councillors were allowed a breathing-space.

Sadly, however, the monarch's relief in international affairs was not matched in the personal and dynastic. For Margaret had her second child, delivered early in the new year, safely enough, another son, whom they named Arthur, but who, from the first, was sickly and frail, so much so that the clerics advised that he be baptised promptly, to ensure his entry to the better world to come, which they feared would not be long delayed. So this time there was no celebration and public rejoicings, only a private christening – and this only just in time, for the infant died ten days later, to major woe. Was the queen not going to be able to produce the heir which the throne demanded? James was devastated.

This sad situation produced an unexpected development, in that Janet, recognising the impact of this on her lover, and wishing to offer him all possible comfort and caring, decided that she could best console him by remaining at Bothwell, instead of departing for the north in late spring, much as she preferred Darnaway and its surroundings. Which meant, of course, that not only the king but David and Agnes could see much more of her, to their satisfaction. Margaret Tudor could not but be aware of her husband's frequent excursions to Lanarkshire and elsewhere, but no doubt accepted that monarchs were ever apt to seek satisfaction from mistresses, and that queens' functions were to produce heirs rather than carnal and personal delights. After all, her own brother was notorious for his amours and bed-mates; nor had her father been innocent in the matter. Margaret had her dowery palace of Linlithgow, and with her own little court to support her; and since there was no pretence of love between the royal pair, she probably was content enough.

Agnes more than once demanded to be told why kings and princes should always be expected to marry only women of equal rank, however little they might fancy them. After all, they did not always bring alliances and international accord, as now with England. Surely a union with one of their own people, whom they could love and with whom they could create a happy family, would be sufficiently good for the realms as well as themselves?

David could not answer that satisfactorily.

Oddly enough it was a visit from Janet that sparked off a further endeavour on David's part in the sphere of community development and the creation of prosperity, which had become so important to him. She told him that James had recently been at Bothwell, and had mentioned that Master Gunner Borthwick had learned of a new use for the debris of his furnaces. As well as ash, charcoal would be left if all the coal had not been fully consumed.

Charcoal had long been obtained from burned wood, but this of winning it from coal was new, at least to him and his like. And charcoal was a very useful product, it seemed, with all sorts of worth; but it was especially important in the making of explosives. When ground down into black powder, it was, James said, the main necessity for gunpowder. The firmer the charcoal the better the explosion. Hence Borthwick's interest. He had learned of the possibility of making charcoal from coal ash or embers from a Hollander visiting one of his two colleagues at Ballencrieff, a kinsman. This man had said that the Arabs had known of it for long. Janet thought that it might be of interest to her brother, in view of his new coal-digging activities for salt-making.

David stared at her. "Charcoal! The very word!" he exclaimed. "Why have I never thought of it? Charcoal. Coal! Always they had thought of it as coming from wood. Did the Arabs dig and burn coal? Certainly the Saracens had used cannon of a sort, as the crusaders had found out. This is something I must indeed look into."

Agnes had a word to put in. "Might it not be of more value to *you*, David, than to my cousin? Is he not using much hotter fires for his cannon forging than you are for the salt-water heating? So his coal will be much more completely burned, no? With his great bellows. Leaving less behind, less cinders and charcoal. Your salt-pans could produce more, no?"

"You are right, lass – right! There is much ash and cinders and the like left to cast away. Here is something that I must know more about."

"I thought that you would be interested," Janet said. "I said so to James . . ."

Nothing would do, then, but that David must pay a visit to this Borthwick cousin, to discover details and facts. And Agnes, needless to say, wanted to accompany him. The children were now old enough to be left with nursemaids. So they could ride fast, and reach eastern Lothian in a day.

A week later, then, they set out to cross Lowland Scotland, by the Cumnock muirs, the Douglas Water, Biggar and the Morthwaite Hills to the Lammermuirs. Ballencrieff lay in Haddingtonshire a couple of miles seaward of the county town itself, on level ground at the foot of a minor range of low, grassy hills called the Garletons. There, in the Vale of Peffer, they found a lairdship, with a small tower-house and a large farmery attached, the steading and barns of which were no longer used for cattle, hay, grain and the like, but turned into a manufactory, a busy establishment of forges and furnaces, coal-stacks, even a grinding mill of a sort. It was dusk when they reached there, but even so the red glow of damped-down fires and a pall of smoke over all greeted them, a strange sight amongst all the spreading farmlands and pastures.

They were well received at the tower, Robert Borthwick proving to be a big, burly man with a rumbustious sense of humour, hardly to be looked for in an enthusiast for cannonry and warfare, his quiet and patient wife in marked contrast. They had a small son; and the two Low Country assistants, named Hans Gunmare and Georg van Erisling, appeared to be permanent lodgers.

Inevitably the evening's converse was all about coal and charcoal and brass-founding, more of the last than David was interested in; but he did learn much about improved bellows, which could be operated by water wheels, on the principle of mills. Also the need to grind the charcoal sufficiently finely if it was to be used for gunpowder. This had previously been done by pestle and mortar; but Borthwick had devised small water mills to do it much less laboriously and more efficiently by using the same water source, from a tributary burn of the Peffer, to drive the grindstones. David was particularly interested in this. He learned that there was an almost unlimited demand for this black powder, mainly for gunpowder, not only in the cause of warfare, especially ships' cannon, but for blasting stone from quarries and, for that matter, coals from the heughs.

Meanwhile Agnes and Susannah Borthwick were glad to discuss very different topics.

In the morning they went to inspect the forge-yard and mills, where they found no fewer than thirteen men busily employed. It was all an impressive experience, quite apart from the useful information gained, the sight of the fiercely glowing furnaces worked by sweating men stripped to the waist, the heat which kept the visitors at a distance, the roar of the flames and the continuous strange creaking, wheezing, pumping of the different bellows, causing Agnes to observe that this must be what hell was like! Not that the workers seemed to deem it so, for they grinned and waved and seemed content enough.

David was especially interested in the milling process, the use of water, running water, to drive the mill wheels that produced the power. Grain mills, of course, he had known all his life; but this of adapting the principle to smaller, power-driven devices was new. He did not have to remind himself that at the various salt-pans there was no lack of water. Somehow they must use that to good purpose, and possibly not only for grinding charcoal. Could they grind salt itself into finer particles than the flakes that they normally produced?

Well content with their visit, they took their leave. Borthwick told them that he was in fact not exactly transferring his activities to Edinburgh Castle but creating a somewhat similar establishment up there on the rock-top, this at the king's urging, James being greatly interested and eager to watch the processes, and, of course, demanding ever-increasing supplies of ammunition as well as the cannon. There would be difficulties, to be sure, in arranging supplies of coal to come up to the castle rock; but that was the king's affair; and at least there should be no lack of water available for the milling, the citadel being provided with deep wells down through the mass of rock, as was necessary for the castle garrison. His Hollanders were even suggesting erecting small windmills up on the heights, such as they apparently used in their Low Countries, to pump up the water, which could then be cascaded down over part of the cliff-face to drive the grinding mills on a fairly broad ledge to the north-east of the tourney-ground approach.

The Kennedys made their return journey partly along the nearby Lothian shore towards the town of Musselburgh, to call at Salt Preston, where the Abbot of Newbattle had set up possibly the first salt-pans in all Scotland, and from whom, indeed, Bishop Forman had learned of the enterprise, and so was responsible eventually for David's concerns. The abbot was not present when they called, being up at his great abbey near Dalkeith; but the monks in charge were much surprised to have an earl and his countess visiting them. Never before, apparently, had the like occurred, the nobility but little interested in such activities. David did not learn much that was new to him at Salt Preston, save in the sheer size and extent of the workings, no less than ten pans producing, he was told, between eight hundred and nine hundred bushels of salt each week. But he was able to gain some information of use on possible developments, in especial the sackcloth-making sheds where they made coarse material bags for the transporting of the salt to all destinations, this instead of using creels, lined baskets and returnable leather bags, for carriage on pack-horses.

Finding all this a challenge and satisfaction, David certainly did not shut off his mind to further efforts in trade and manufacture. Why should the churchmen corner it all? It was not the actual wealth produced that urged him on, for as the principal landowner of all Carrick now he did not lack for substance. It was the notion of bringing and spreading prosperity to many, and using the gifts God had given them, much so long neglected and unrealised, that appealed to him. He would be the gainer also, of course. That Agnes encouraged him in it all added to his satisfaction. There ought to be more to the nobility and knightly ones than the possession of lands and the mastery over their fellow men, with their swordery, castle-building, hunting and tournaments.

27

That year of 1511 did not lack its events, developments and tensions for Scotland, its king and its people, David Kennedy included, although war with England remained only a threat, even if an ever-present one.

In March, two envoys arrived from the Continent, the first from France, the second from the Vatican, an unfortunate coincidence to have them both appearing at court at the same time, in view of their missions. De la Motte, the Frenchman, made a dramatic arrival, for he came by sea, and his ship entered the Firth of Forth in an easterly storm, all but wrecking it on the Craig of Bass and sweeping it on past Leith, its destination, for another score of miles, right to the harbour of Blackness near Linlithgow, before it could dock, this beside the *Great Michael* which lay there with other ships-of-war, James's fleet now filling Leith haven to overflowing. So that the first that the king heard of his visitor was that he was in Linlithgow Palace, of all places, in the company of Margaret Tudor, pregnant again, the sister of the man whom he had come to fight against and if possible subvert. He was in fact sent by King Louis to demand from James what he would do, under their Auld Alliance, if Henry of England personally led a large-scale invasion of France, as was being rumoured, as distinct from these raids by the Howard brothers. Needless to say this put James in a difficult position when De la Motte eventually arrived at Edinburgh, for almost the last thing that he desired at this stage was to have to commit himself to actual invasion over the border, as Louis desired as the required distraction. He was forced to temporise, which was not like James Stewart.

His discomfort over this was not helped by the second arrival, a few days later, of Octavian Olarius, a papal delegate, who had not had problems caused by sea conditions, since he came overland, through England, with Henry's blessings. *His* demands were even more upsetting. Pope Julius, ailing man as he was, required from the King of Scots a promise that he would give no aid to France and its allies who had joined Louis against the Holy League, as it was being called, of the Vatican, the Emperor Maximilian, Venice and Aragon. If he, James, did, then excommunication would follow.

This, of course, was a dire threat indeed, since not only would it imply personal condemnation, if not damnation, but would have the effect of Holy Church in Scotland being unable to co-operate with the monarchy, and his close friends and advisers such as Bishops Forman and Elphinstone placed in a position in which they must shun James Stewart or else suffer dismissal from their dioceses and replacement from Rome.

Temporising, in this situation, was even less easy than with King Louis. The king had to try to keep the two emissaries apart while he worried over his reactions.

At least he still had the advice of his two favourite clerics. Forman and Elphinstone agreed that delaying tactics were advisable. Send his own emissary to Rome, have his interview and representations, requesting details as to this Holy League and its aims and prospects, claiming ignorance but emphasising no hostility. To get back to Scotland with the answers would take two months probably, if travelling, as this Octavian Olarius had done, by land. And much could change in two months. The word was that Julius was a very sick man, and seeking to dominate Christendom from his bed. And Giovanni de Medici was preparing to succeed him, a very different man with quite alternative policies reputedly.

This at least would offer another breathing-space, and James was grateful, especially when Andrew Forman volunteered himself to be the envoy to the Vatican. If he went thither with the returning Octavian, then he would travel by land, down through England, which would of course take much longer than going by sea, increasing the desired delay. James blessed the Bishop of Moray, not for the first time, this even though certain clerics whispered that Forman had his own concerns at Rome, wishing for his future advancement, and to establish links with the next pontiff. He would be seeking the Scots Primacy in place of the unsuitable youth Alexander Stewart, or even hoping for a cardinalship. Churchmen could be back-biting and envious equally with other men.

So Forman departed with Olarius, however distant their relationship, and James sent De la Motte back to King Louis with questions also as to what France would expect of the Scots in the event of the feared invasion by Henry. Would the presence of a strong Scottish fleet, based on some of the French ports, be a useful contribution? This would at least be less dangerous and demanding than any actual invasion over the border. Actually, apart from this French requirement, James would not be too unhappy over Henry personally leading an assault on France; it would probably mean that it would much delay, if not rule out, any invasion of Scotland.

In such fashion were international policies and strategies hammered out.

Barely was all this over when another crisis was upon the royal household. The queen went into premature labour, at Linlithgow, to her husband's concern and frustration. After much difficulty, more than in her other birth-givings, however, one more son was born, James with little expectation that the infant would survive, small and frail as he was. So once again there was a hasty christening of another James, with much head-shaking and gloom. But the child did survive and made progress, although the mother made but a slow recovery on this occasion. James spent most of his time at Linlithgow, unusual as this was for him, watching and all but overseeing the daily state of this new Duke of Rothesay, debating whether to change the wet-nurses and the child's care, affairs of state for the time being left to others. Was there this time going to be success, fulfilment, an heir to the throne? It is to be feared that he paid less heed to Margaret Tudor's well-being.

Those concerned with the monarchy practically held their breaths.

Janet, anxious for James, was in a difficult position. She could hardly visit him at Linlithgow, in the queen's own house, yet she wanted him to know of her caring and good wishes. She came to Cassillis and persuaded her brother that he should go and tell the king of her feelings and solicitude. He could find an excuse so to do, surely?

David thought that Robert Borthwick was the answer. Anything to do with cannon-founding and artillery was of abiding interest to James Stewart, and this of the production of the necessary black powder related. If he and Borthwick could go and visit the port of Blackness and there inspect the installing of cannon on the *Great Michael* and other warships, this only a few miles from Linlithgow, then they might go on to the palace and report progress, and David could seem to seek guidance on how much of the powder was required from his various salt-works, a sufficient reason for the visit.

So he journeyed over to Ballencrieff again, found that the Master Gunner was at Edinburgh Castle, and proceeding on thither had no difficulty in getting Borthwick to co-operate, he wishing to inform the king of progress anyway, and glad of the earl's association, he being a little unsure as to what authority the status of Master of the Ordnance conferred on him when it came to calling unsummoned on the monarch, especially at such a time.

The pair rode the eighteen miles to Blackness, then, and David was indeed much interested in all that he saw there, boarding the various ships and inspecting the different types of cannon and their placings, having explained to him the properties, capacities and ranges of them all, and why the brass element was so important, as distinct from cast-iron. The supply of cannonballs also was a major concern, and most of the ship captains were somewhat anxious about this, with possibly insufficient available for an emergency. Borthwick agreed to look into it. The forging of the balls was not part of his duties, although he had to have it ensured that they were made to the exact sizes and weights required for the various pieces.

Thereafter, then, they were able to ride over the low green hills of the Binns to Linlithgow on its quite large loch, with the handsome red-stone palace rising close above the water. They had no difficulty in gaining access to the king, who seemed to be spending much of his time fishing from a boat on the loch. Far from questioning their visit, James, in his pride, brought the infant prince in his arms, from his cradle, to show them, and to demonstrate the child's fitness, health and lively state. Admittedly it was a little difficult to turn the converse to matters of artillery.

Still more difficult it was to come to the real object of David's presence. He could scarcely mention Janet's loving care for the monarch in front of Borthwick, however much that man knew of the situation. So he had to devise a ruse whereby they took their leave of the king, and then he told the other that he had recollected something regarding his Carrick that he had omitted to mention, and must go back and deal with it, making it evident that he would go alone.

James, in fact, was clearly glad to receive his message then, admitting that he had not been able to call on Janet for some time; but happily he would be in a position to do so soon, very soon, his anxiety over this child now more or less shed. He had missed seeing Janet. Tell her so. And missed seeing his little Jamie of Moray also. But now, his mind relieved, and all going well, it would be different. And he expressed his appreciation of the kind wishes being sent.

David could return to Cassillis with these tidings.

*   *   *

284

The Kennedys had a surprise indeed in early summer when they had a royal visitation. They had never expected to see Margaret Tudor at Cassillis, but there she arrived, and the infant Prince James with her. The king had decided to demonstrate his thankfulness for the safe production of an heir, at last, by conducting a pilgrimage, and taking mother and child with him. And it would be to his old shrine of St Ninian at Whithorn, since he could hardly take them to St Duthac's at Tain, up in Ross, on the way to which they could not fail to call at Darnaway where, he revealed, Janet and her son had now returned. So southwards it had to be, not northwards this time, and Cassillis was a convenient halfway house; convenient for James, that was, if less so for David and Agnes, who had to entertain a large train of magnates and courtiers, the queen's as well as the king's, taking part in this celebratory excursion. And, no doubt, they would halt again at Cassillis on the way back to Linlithgow in due course.

The queen proved to be an unresponsive if undemanding guest, keeping herself to herself and her ladies and English chaplain, Agnes soon giving up attempts to be the entertaining hostess. James, however, was in excellent spirits, and made much of Gibbie, Master of Kennedy, and his young brother, indeed knighting the former, child as he was. He commanded David to accompany them on to Whithorn, where he had successfully come to terms with Bishop George of Galloway. And he could present his brother Alexander, Deputy Warden of the West March.

So David joined the royal train, and was able to show the king the Crossraguel Abbey's salt-pans and powder-making plant at Maidens *en route*, although the Leswalt establishment was much too far out of their way, in the Rhinns, for any call there. The queen was supremely uninterested, as indeed were most of the company.

Bishop George was not present at Whithorn, apparently

being over the border in Cumbria with his English friend and colleague there, the Bishop of Carlisle. James wondered about this. Was this association between the two prelates a good thing, or was it not? Could it be useful in relations with England? Or the reverse? Did Bishop George's strange adherence to the Archbishop of York offer advantage or danger?

The pilgrimage ceremonial at Candida Casa was simple and brief, considering the long way all had come to perform it, the Prior of Whithorn less than expansive in his conducting of the service, and almost certainly unhappy about having to provide shelter and sustenance for the great company at his priory. But this did mean that the visit was not prolonged, and a return made northwards fairly promptly. Whether Agnes was glad to see them all back at Cassillis again so soon was another matter, for the company stopped there for a couple of days. As well that David's commercial enterprises were adding to his own wealth as well as that of the various communities.

In the event, it was not long after the royal entourage departed that David got an unexpected summons from the king to attend a Privy Council meeting in Edinburgh, no reasons given, and this forthwith. Taking Agnes and the children to Borthwick Castle on the way, he duly presented himself at the Abbey of the Holy Rood, to find it thronged. De la Motte had arrived back in Scotland from France, and the assumption was that this suddenly called council was not unconnected with the fact.

It indeed proved to be so, James Stewart distinctly agitated. King Louis was in sore trouble. His army had been defeated by the joint forces of the Pope, the Emperor and Venice, this Holy League, at Nevarra in Italy, with grievous losses; and Henry Tudor had now based himself at Portsmouth where his admiral's fleet was now assembled, an ominous development. Louis required Scottish aid, and swiftly. No temporising on this occasion.

The councillors were divided. Some of the nobility were in favour of a gesture of support, a military gesture. An attack on Berwick-upon-Tweed was suggested. It should belong to Scotland anyway. And Dacre was captain there now, was he not? And he was not so hostile towards the Scots as were some. Others favoured sending the fleet to Louis's aid, only the fleet. Still others to take no action at all, telling Louis that conditions here prevented any effective moves meantime.

James himself had a point to make. Now that he and his queen had a son and heir, until Henry Tudor produced such son of his own, as seemed unlikely with Catherine of Aragon, Margaret was heir to the English throne. And the English had never had a queen-regnant, and were known to be against a woman on their throne. So, in fact, their young Duke of Rothesay was meantime heir-presumptive to Henry, he who would one day be King of Scots. This could mean the union of the two kingdoms, extraordinary as it might seem. If Henry did lead an invasion of France, as Louis feared, and was slain in battle . . !

All round the table men eyed each other. Here was a situation hard to take in. The Auld Enemies could then become one realm, and under a Scots monarch, James acting regent for his son.

The king went on. "In these circumstances, any Scots invasion of England at this stage could grievously endanger such coming about. Prevent Henry from himself going with his army to France. Turning his eyes northwards. Louis may wish that, yes; but looking to the future, France would be the gainer, with no longer any threats from England. We tell De la Motte so. Catherine of Aragon has had two children, both stillborn. That is an ill omen for the Tudor. If there should be another such, then . . !"

Elphinstone spoke. "Henry is now in his twenty-second year. But his queen older, his former brother's widow, the Prince Arthur. She produced no child for him either. It may seem that no heir to the English throne

287

is likely, other than your royal wife, Sire. King Louis must see it."

"Yet he requires action, under our treaty," Bothwell said. "We must do something."

"Send the fleet, or part of it," Forman advised. "To different French ports. That will endanger us less, yet temper Louis's demands meantime. The French fleet itself is large. With ours added, it could give Henry pause. The pity that Queen Catherine is aunt to the Emperor Maximilian, the present Pope's ally. But that may change, before long."

"Yes," James agreed. "I say, send De la Motte back with that word. I shall send John Barton with a number of our ships. To different ports is wise. That will lessen the damage, yet make their presence the better felt."

David made his one contribution, glancing at the bishops. "We shall not pray for this Pope's death, but hope that he may be . . . replaced!"

There were murmurs of agreement round that table.

28

Agnes provided David with a third son that late autumn, to much rejoicing, for her husband was very much a family man. They named him Thomas, and were thankful that they were not called upon to suffer miscarriages, stillbirths and early deaths, like so many others were. Agnes made a serenely competent and devoted mother, and Cassillis Castle was a happy home. This birth did, however, prevent any journey up to Moray that summer. So they had to wait until November before they could see Janet, at Bothwell.

She it was who told them that Queen Margaret was pregnant again, and that James was hoping for another son, to confirm the succession situation. This matter of procreation seemed to be a paramount concern in their lives. Yet Flaming Janet was not thus herself involved, although that the king was no less interested in her was evident, which was not to be wondered at, for she was quite the most strikingly beautiful woman that her brother had ever set eyes upon, and far from frigid by nature. Doting on her young son, no longer just a child, and ruling for him the great province of Moray, she felt that she had a role to play for his father, a role of some value. She had no complaints with her rather peculiar life.

The nation's situation meantime was in precarious balance. One happening that caused no mourning in Scotland was the death, in a battle with French warships, of England's Lord High Admiral Howard. Unkindly, most could wish for a similar fate for his brother Surrey.

There were repercussions over this battle, for in his wooing attempts towards Scotland, King Louis sent De la Motte back, but this time he arrived at Ayr, not in the Forth, and came with some captured English merchant-ships as gift, and in them a strange cargo, vast numbers of eighteen-foot-long pikes or lances, these to aid the Scots soldiery in the hoped-for invasion of England. According to the French officers who brought them, these were quite the most effective weapons, especially against charging cavalry, keeping ordinary spears and lances well out of range, and swordery of course still more so.

They learned also that Henry had indeed sailed with his army from Portsmouth, to Artois, just across the narrows of the Channel, near the Flanders border, and was laying siege to the French fortress-base of Therouaine, leaving Surrey in command of forces in England.

As a precaution, however, the Tudor had sent his own message to Scotland, to avoid any assault on his rear meantime, and this by none other than Dacre, or at least Dacre's emissary, one Beverlaw. The gist of it, if indeed the truth, was extraordinary. It was that Louis of France had announced that Henry was an impostor, and that the true King of England was Richard de la Pole, the brother of the imprisoned Earl of Suffolk, of the Yorkist line, as distict from the Lancastrian Tudors, and that Louis was recognising this Richard as monarch and urging his allies to do the same. This, of course, if somehow put into effect, for instance by a defeat in France for Henry's army, would cut out any succession for Margaret and the young Duke of Rothesay. Clearly Henry considered this to be sufficient to drive a wedge between James and his French alliance.

But was it to be believed? And if indeed Louis had so declared, was it merely a ruse, sufficient to cause internal upset in England, possibly a rising of the Yorkist supporters while Henry was abroad? There was major questioning in Scotland. De la Motte told James that he knew nothing of it all, and thought that it could all be an invention of the Tudor's to ensure Scottish inaction. James sent the man Beverlaw back to Dacre at Berwick asking for clarification, confirmation, and De la Motte back to France for the like information. If it was all an invention, which of the two warring monarchs was responsible? James Stewart was said to believe that it was all a lie, a device of Henry's – or so said Janet Kennedy.

While the nation waited and wondered, the queen gave birth once more, this time to a daughter. And again it was tragedy. The child lived barely a month. James had to cherish his small and blessedly healthy son the more.

David received a summons to Edinburgh, not for a Privy Council meeting this time, but for James to saddle him with a special mission connected with this vexed question as to the authenticity of Henry's allegation about France's support for the Yorkist claim to the English throne. Dacre had sent back word merely reiterating that this was the message that he had been ordered to transmit – which took them no further forward. He, David of Cassillis, might be in a position to discover more. He had performed a notable service, those years ago, in the matter of establishing the overland trading links between western Scotland and Carlisle, which escorting arrangement still went on successfully under his brother Alexander. Many had reason to be thankful for this, in especial the Bishops of Galloway and Carlisle. And the churchmen were ever the knowledgeable ones on all matters of importance in the realms, their information transmitted apparently by their system of so-called wandering friars, travelling priests who took the Church's services to all parts of the land, this enabling them to learn and convey the facts of national matters with notable speed and presumed accuracy. It was so in Scotland, and no doubt worked equally well in England. So James imagined that if anyone knew the truth of this matter, it would be the English prelates. And the Bishop of Carlisle had reason to be grateful to the Earl of Cassillis and his brother. So David was to go to Carlisle and seek to learn whether it all was a canard of Henry's devising, or if in fact King Louis

291

was indeed declaring Richard de la Pole to be King of England.

David was scarcely happy to have this mission thrust upon him, with grave doubts that he would have any influence with the Bishop of Carlisle, or enough to gain the information wanted, even if the bishop had it. But he could not refuse the royal command, and had to agree to attempt the task.

So it was back to Cassillis, and then on to the West March. Agnes said that if Lord Dacre believed it all to be the truth, she did not see how this bishop would know any better, David saying that the king thought that Carlisle's special links with the Archbishop of York might well have him well informed.

He rode south next day then, with two of his men, south by west actually, for he decided to go to Leswalt and collect his brother who might have more pull with the prelate than himself, being a frequent visitor to Carlisle. He wondered whether there would be any benefit in seeking to contact Bishop George of Galloway at Whithorn, but decided that this was unlikely to be worth while.

Alexander Kennedy, at Leswalt, was as doubtful as was his brother over the possibilities of this mission, but admitted that he frequently saw Bishop John, and was on good terms with him; indeed had interested him in setting up a salt-work at his priory near Silloth. They went on for the border together, Alexander declaring that they had no trouble with the Marchmen these days, although he still maintained a strong guard for the trading convoys, north and south. He was, in fact, not long back from leading one such.

They duly entered the Debateable Land, and crossed the line at Gretna. They saw no signs of moss-troopers, even though their progress probably did not go unobserved by some of those ever-watchful characters.

By Mossband ford and Rockcliffe they reached the Cumbrian capital, and experienced no difficulty in entering the walled city, Alexander well known nowadays to the gate guards. They made their way through the narrow streets to the cathedral and bishop's palace, both splendid examples of the power and wealth of Holy Church.

Bishop John, elderly and hawklike, was scarcely of an amiable nature, but unbent to some extent when he saw Alexander Kennedy and was introduced to the Earl of Cassillis. He assumed that their visit was to do with the trading convoys, declaring that these were indeed of major value to all save the moss-trooping rogues and scoundrels; also adding that his good friend and colleague, George, Bishop of Galloway, was to be congratulated on the matter – which was not quite appropriate, since that prelate had had no hand in the matter, save that he demanded some action. However, David let that pass.

Alexander asked how the salt-pans were faring, and was told that they were being sufficiently successful to have the bishop considering establishing another similiar enterprise at Allanby Bay, further south.

On the way there, David had been pondering how best to introduce the distinctly delicate object of their visit, and had decided that the best opening would be to declare that King James was much concerned over peace with England, and that he and his Privy Council, in especial the Bishops Forman and Elphinstone, believed that Holy Church could do much to ensure this. Could there be co-operation between the churchmen in Scotland and England, active co-operation, in this so vital matter? He did not see that this query could cause any upset.

So, when he said as much, Bishop John loftily declared, "Holy Church is always working in the cause of peace and goodwill, my lord. This your king and council must know."

"To be sure. But it is felt that if the two Churches acted in concert, much might be achieved." He took a chance. "This of the Holy League could be supported."

"Let your James tell that to his friend Louis of France!" the other jerked.

This was the reaction that David had hoped for. "His

Grace would do so," he said. "But considers that the King of France would heed him more surely if he was assured that the Churches of Scotland and England were at one with King James and King Henry over this folly of the assertion that Richard de la Pole is the rightful King of England."

"Folly indeed! Worse than folly – shame!" the other exclaimed. "So evil a malediction against His Majesty Henry!"

"If there is indeed truth in it! Not in the allegation itself, to be sure – that is folly as I said. But in whether indeed King Louis ever announced it? That it is not merely some lying whisper put about by the supporters of the Yorkist faction in England?"

"Those traitors! No, Louis of France himself declared it. At Tours in June at a meeting of his Estates-General. It is no whisper but the shameful shout of a wicked prince! And at the very place where the blessed St Martin brought Christianity to us all!"

Thus suddenly, unexpectedly, easily, David had the answer to what he had come all this long road to learn. Louis *had* made this rash and unwise announcement; it was not an invention of Henry Tudor to damage relations between France and Scotland. Scarcely good news for James Stewart; but at least he would now have the truth.

David could scarcely leave it thus and take his departure; this dialogue had to go on further to seem to be authentic. He took another chance.

"Has the Yorkist cause any real support in England?" he asked. "This de la Pole, has he a following of any size?"

As expected, this had the bishop frowning. "No, my lord, he has not. Nor has his brother, the imprisoned Earl of Suffolk, deranged as he is. Traitors both."

Clearly now they had reached a point where Bishop John could be left, without suspicion that he had been questioned as to his special knowledge over the Louis assertion, he no doubt assuming that this query as to

294

Yorkist support in England was the real reason for this Scots' visit.

"Then, my lord Bishop," David went on, "can I tell His Grace that the Church in England is anxious for peace with Scotland, and will, if need be, work with the Scottish churchmen to that good end?" he asked.

The older man stroked his chin and inclined his greying head. "The Church is ever for peace on earth and goodwill towards men, as I said." That was carefully non-committal.

The visitors felt themselves able to bow themselves out, with suitable good wishes. It had been a curious encounter and assignment, but presumably James would now have what he wanted to know. What he might be able to do about it was another matter.

29

David was not long back from giving his report to the king when the news reached Scotland that the Pope Julius had died. James decided forthwith to send Bishop Forman, as envoy, to the Vatican to see the new pontiff, and if possible get him to have the threat of excommunication lifted; and on the way, to call on King Louis and to declare to him that if the Auld Alliance was to continue, this declaration of support for the Yorkist de la Pole must be withdrawn and proclaimed. Forman was to sail in James Barton's flagship. The embassage would take some time, inevitably, and it would be well into the winter before Barton and the bishop got back.

So a mercifully quiet and uneventful period could be looked for north of the border, leaving Henry and Louis to fight it out in France.

David and Agnes were not alone in being thankful to be able to live a normal life, in Carrick and the Rhinns of Galloway. And Janet came south from Moray to Bothwell again. No council meetings were called meantime.

Gunpowder, however, continued to be in demand, especially for the ever-growing fleet, to be produced at the salt-works and elsewhere. And the monks of Crossraguel devised a method of grinding charcoal with circular mills driven by oxen pacing round and round endlessly, working the grindstones. There was an increasing recognition of the uses of coal, keeping the heughs busy, this encouraged by David in his concern for the dire cutting down of trees which was threatening to make the Lowlands landscape bare.

He had another interest to occupy him as well, again

brought to his notice by those busy monks at Crossraguel. This was drainage. There was some boggy ground near the abbey, and by digging ditches they had not only drained and dried up this area, making it usable for planting and growing crops, but were using the water produced to good purpose, forming ponds for storage in dry spells, for the washing of the cloths they spun, even for duckponds. David perceived the possibilities of this, on a much larger scale. Like all other landholders he had, in the lower ground below slopes and hills, great tracts of marshy territory. If this, or some of it, could be thus drained, how much more valuable farmland and good pasture could be produced, the poorer ground even used for the planting of the much-needed trees. Here was a new conception, which might prove productive indeed on his wide lands.

It was February 1514 before Forman and Barton got back from their extended mission. They had been reasonably successful with King Louis, but not with the new Pope, Giovanni de Medici, now styling himself Leo the Tenth. Louis had agreed to withdraw his nominal support for De la Pole; he had only announced this in an effort to worry Henry into a return to England, with fears of a Yorkist rising. He regretted any upset to King James; and to emphasise his apologies he sent a contribution of fifty thousand francs to assist the Scots military preparations, and said that if more Scots warships would come to French ports, he would be responsible for equipping and re-victualling them. Also when such fleet returned to Scotland, it would be accompanied by a number of French galleys. He particularly urged James to send the *Great Michael*, the fame of which was now widespread. And he pleaded for some further action against Henry, to make him retire from French soil.

The Vatican visit had produced less satisfactory results. The threatened sentence of excommunication was only to be held in abeyance, not entirely lifted, so long as Scotland remained in alliance with France and against the Holy League and its ally, Henry Tudor. Although before his ascent to the papacy de Medici had indicated large alterations to Julius's policies, once installed he amended little. He condemned the appointment of the teenage bastard son of James as Primate of Scotland, no priest as he was, and indeed declared that Forman himself was to be suffragan Archbishop of St Andrews, this no doubt in an effort to cause a rift between the King of Scots and his ablest adviser and envoy. It was not to prove a successful device, but it did indicate that James had little to hope for from the new Pope.

Oddly, Forman came back with a second archepiscopal dignity. For Louis of France had appointed him to the all but honorary position of Archbishop of Bourges, a position which carried no real authority but was endowed with certain revenues.

All this left James Stewart less than certain as to his advisable procedure. Relations with France were now back on an even keel, but Louis was expecting some demonstration of the Auld Alliance support. Henry was still campaigning in Anjou, but not making notable progress. A policy of inaction meantime seemed to be wise for Scotland, but for the French requirements, and these, as it were, paid for in advance by Louis's favourable gestures.

David was not surprised to be summoned to a council, this to be held at Linlithgow, not Edinburgh or Stirling, where the king was now passing much of his time, not because of his queen's presence there but that of his so precious small son and heir.

At this meeting, with Forman present, both he and Elphinstone strongly advocated caution, a masterly inactivity. But since something had to be done to seem to aid Louis, and if possible to bring the Tudor home from France, the new nominal archbishop suggested an armed demonstration, but less than invasion of England. The Irish princeling, O'Donnell, Earl of Tyrconnel, had twice requested Scots aid in freeing his land from the hated invader. So, despatch an expedition to Carrickfergus in Ulster, the main English base, and eject the aggressors. This would be a signal to Henry without actually setting foot on his soil.

All there agreed that this was a notable and excellent suggestion, which none of the others had thought of, James sufficiently enthusiastic to wonder if he should lead this sally himself. Both the prelates were against this, however, pointing out that he should await results and Henry's reactions. If it was not a success, James could deny personal involvement. At this stage careful balancing was essential.

So the *Great Michael*, with no fewer than fourteen trained gunners aboard, and ten other ships-of-war, left the Forth to sail north-about round Scotland for the Irish Sea, these under James Hamilton, Earl of Arran, the king's distant kinsman, since Barton was already gone with Scots ships for Louis and Sir Andrew Wood was now too old for campaigning. It all left James with few ships indeed, this on the twenty-seventh day of July.

All waited and wondered.

It took only two weeks for Arran to get back, sailing in the *Great Michael* to the Clyde at Dumbarton, while the rest of the fleet went on to French ports. Their heavy cannon had battered Carrickfergus into submission successfully, and the English garrison had surrendered, with O'Donnell's Irish now enheartened enough to expel most of the other invaders from the land. The gesture had been a tactical success, yes. Now to learn of its impact on Henry and on Louis.

Scotland did not have long to wait for word of this, either. De la Motte arrived once again, in one of the promised French galleys, to declare his monarch's gratitude and to beseech more help. For Henry had gained Therouaine, and now held all of Anjou, and was advancing eastwards. And in his triumph, and possibly in reaction to the Scots–Irish venture, had issued a declaration to the princes of Christendom, including the Pope, that he was now King of France and Suzerain and Lord Paramount of Scotland, as well as King of England, and would attach his three realms to the Holy League.

At this announcement by De la Motte, James Stewart's fury knew no bounds, those in his company at the time at Linlithgow all but fearing for his sanity. The Tudor, Suzerain of Scotland! He beat his fists on the panelling of the palace-hall walling in a paroxysm of rage, and kicked over a small table laden with flagons of wine. Until he cooled a little, De la Motte did not risk completing his message. When he did, it was to present the king with a scented letter, a woman's glove and a gold ring from the finger of Anne of Brittany, King Louis's attractive and beguiling queen, beseeching James to advance but three feet into England, and break a lance for her.

Whatever Louis's own urging on this subject might be, his envoy did not add there and then. For James became a man all but transfigured. The fury of moments before was replaced by shining-eyed rapture and exultation as he took the ring and raised the scented glove to his face. He would do it, he swore; before God in His high heaven, he would do it! The die was cast. They would cross the border, in fullest strength, and the Tudor would discover who was Suzerain of Scotland, and heir to the throne of England. And Anne of Brittany learn that her appeal was not in vain, by all the powers, she would!

That Frenchwoman must have known of James Stewart's devotion to the opposite sex, although she had never met him, known of his enthusiasm for the tournament's lance-breaking as well as his romantic nature. And she was not known as Amorous Anne for nothing.

All royal resolution now, James ordered a council meeting at the earliest to translate his vows into action.

All this David Kennedy learned from Bishop Forman three days later.

At Linlithgow, the atmosphere of excitement and anticipation was very evident, however doubtful David, for one, was over the cause of it all, doubts he shared with the two prelates at least. Although it was a Privy Council meeting he had been called to attend, the palace and town were thronged with others who were not councillors, half the nobility and chieftains of Scotland seeming to be present, whether summoned or of their own accord. The land indeed was ringing with it. England was to be invaded at last, the Auld Enemy taught its lesson.

That council was unlike any other that David had attended. James was usually good at taking or at least listening to advice, heedfully hearing all points of view and permitting, encouraging debate. But not on this occasion. It was a council-of-war, not a conference, the king in very evident command. They were there to discuss the details of the national mustering to arms, not the whys and wherefores. Forman and Elphinstone saw that advising caution, delay and half-measures would be dismissed, would serve nothing, and sat mainly silent throughout. They did suggest that on so major a matter as this, a parliament would be suitable as well as advisable, to test the nation's feelings and support, but the king dismissed that as not only unnecessary but impracticable. A parliament demanded forty days' notice, six weeks. In six weeks Henry might well have gained further victories in France and be the more secure in his position of dominant arrogance. There was no time for that. He must be shown that the Scots were a force to be reckoned with. Suzerainty! That word had become like a red rag to a bull for James Stewart.

It was numbers of men, how soon to be able to strike, and where, which constituted the business of this council. And admittedly most of the lords present were supportive, even if David Kennedy, for one, was less so.

There was competition, indeed, amongst the magnates as to the numbers each could field, given time, how many horsed and how many afoot, ancient rivalry evident. When David was eyed, he shrugged and suggested two hundred from Carrick. He could hardly say

301

less, but clearly others there thought that he could say more.

It was decided that they would aim to cross the border on the East March at the end of August, mustering on the Burgh Muir of Edinburgh in fullest strength. They would not proceed far into England, just sufficiently to emphasise their threat, slightly more than Amorous Anne's three feet.

James let it be known that next day, the Eve of St Christopher, there would be a special service of petition, praise and prayer for the success of their venture in St Michael's Kirk, near this palace, at which all his leal supporters would be expected to attend.

That night, in that crowded establishment, David noticed that the king appeared to have found himself a new lady to his taste, Mirren Livingstone, daughter of the lord of that name. He did not think that Janet would be concerned. She had come to accept that James required a plenitude and variety of women, but believed that although these might come and go, her own position was secure in his love, deeper love.

St Michael's-by-the-Palace was a large and handsome building, almost a small cathedral, and next day it was packed for the occasion. Bishop Elphinstone conducted the worship, however unenthusiastic he might be over the enterprise that this was intended to bless. The king sat, and knelt, at a small desk or faldstool just before the chancel steps, not, as was usual, up in a throne in the chancel itself, presumably to emphasise the petitionary and supplicatory nature of the ceremony. It was noteworthy that the queen was not present, as indeed it was scarcely to be wondered at, her brother being the target of the entire proceedings. Scotland, surely, had never had so unpopular a queen.

The bishop was but halfway through his office when there was an unlooked for, indeed extraordinary, interruption, or rather an intrusion, since the actual service went on, even though the singing of the choristers faltered

302

momentarily. Out from the right-hand, westernmost transept of the cruciform building a figure came stalking, with a long crooked stick, a strange figure, a tall, old man with long white hair to his shoulders, wearing a blue robe, girded round the waist, walking with dignity. Ignoring the bishop, priests, acolytes and choristers, this apparition came pacing on, straight for the king at his faldstool.

Looking up, James stared. Most others present who could see it stared also.

Standing in front of the monarch, this oddity spoke in a level but stern voice, which because of the continuing singing, could be heard only by those nearby.

"Sire, I am sent to warn you not to proceed with your present undertaking. You hear me? Not to proceed. For if you do, it shall not fare well. Either with yourself or with those who go with you."

Straightening up from his kneeling, James eyed the creature wordless.

"Furthermore," the stranger went on, "it has been enjoined on me to bid you shun the familiar society and counsels of women, lest they occasion your disgrace and destruction. Hear you, I say!"

James found words, of a sort. "Save us, who a' God's name are you? What . . . ?" For the king to be addressed thus, whatever the message, was beyond all belief.

He got no answer to that. "Heed!" the old man said simply but strongly, pointed an admonitory finger, and stalked on past, and into the crowded nave. James got to his feet, to gaze after that weird character. "Wait! Stop! Stop, you!" he exclaimed. But the old man made no pause in his pacing, and using his stick to aid him, pushed his way into the staring close-packed throng.

David Kennedy, who was standing not so far from the monarch, amongst the earls, quickly lost sight of the oddity. That densely crowded assembly swallowed him up.

James shook his head, part bewildered, part anxious, part angry. "A, a madman! Or a, a spectre!" he got out. "Which?"

And still Bishop Elphinstone continued with the service, although few there, save those in the chancel, now paid any attention to the worship.

David was not the only one who went forward to the royal side, most of the lords and courtiers present seeking to do so, all exclamations, questions, discussion, all but disbelief. Some declared that it was a maniac, some a fanatic, some a bogle, some the devil himself in human form, a visitor from the Other World.

Bishop Elphinstone could no longer ignore that noise of talk and argument from the body of the church. He brought the ministration to a premature end, pronounced a brief general benediction, and came down to join the others round the king.

"Your Grace is pleased to dispense with further seeking of God's blessing!" he accused, frowning.

"Scarce that! You saw? This, this creature? What he did? You may not have heard, but . . ."

"I saw another old man pass me. Who might be more lacking in his wits than even your servant, Sire! Was that sufficient to interrupt this holy office?"

"He miscalled the king!"

"He spoke against this great endeavour."

"He threatened all!"

"He was beyond all belief – insolent fool!"

The chorus of outrage continued.

When he could make himself heard, the bishop said simply, "I think to heed Almighty God the more, before the altar in this house of His."

"Aye, well, enough of this meantime, my lords. Back to the palace," James ordered.

David, walking thither, found himself beside another David, Lindsay of the Mount of Lindifferon, who had been appointed guardian and tutor-to-be of the child Duke of Rothesay.

"What think you of this extraordinary affair?" he asked.

"I judge that it was a piece of clever play-acting, a

mummery," Lindsay said. "To seek to turn the king from invading England."

"You judge that it was no spectre, then?"

"I have never seen a spectre. But would one such lean upon a stick?"

"M'mm. So – a ploy! A device. Who would so devise? Use a mummer?"

"Who, my lord, but she most concerned? The queen, I would say. To spare her brother this of invasion."

"Ha! I had not thought of that. Yes, it is possible . . ."

"I was near enough to hear," Lindsay added. "That word about shunning familiar women. There, at a remove, spoke a woman! And who but the queen? And she much misliked this of Queen Anne of France sending her glove and ring."

David nodded. "I dare say that you have the rights of it. Yes, it could be her."

Soon most in the palace were thinking similarly, although not all. Some saw it as a dire warning.

David went home next day, to raise Carrick for the king, fairly well convinced that Margaret Tudor had indeed more of her brother in her than he, and others, had calculated.

30

The Burgh Muir of Edinburgh, traditional gathering place
for Scotland's armies, had never seen such a sight, so
great an assembly of men. Some said that there were
as many as one hundred thousand there, although that
could have been something of an over-estimate. Never
had the nation responded so fully to the royal command
to muster in fullest strength, this a token of James's
popularity, for he was well loved of all classes of his
people, a dashing, handsome, romantic figure. From
Caithness to the Mull of Kintyre, from the Isles and
the far north-western Highlands to Tayside and Fife
they had come, the earls and lords with their followers,
the Highland chiefs with their clansmen. And the East
March and Border folk, the Homes and Swintons, the
Haigs and the Wedderburns and the Nisbets, were to
join them *en route* to the border. And it was not only the
men and horses that filled the moor but the artillery, the
waggons and the sleds, laden with cannonballs and sacks
of gunpowder, with tents and pavilions, food and drink,
and those thousands of eighteen-foot-long French pikes
and lances sent by Louis. Edinburgh's common grazings
were extensive, but two weeks after that extraordinary
demonstration at Linlithgow, it all was overflowing.

David Kennedy had far more than his suggested two
hundred with him, the Carrick men having volunteered in
unexpectedly large numbers, as seemingly had happened
elsewhere. However much the senior churchmen were
against this great venture, the nation at large clearly was
not. William, Lord Borthwick, at his brother-in-law's
side, had provided over one hundred, and that from an

area less than one-fifth the size of Carrick. David had left
Agnes and the children at Borthwick Castle meantime,
promising to be suitably careful, with no rash bravado,
and to return before long. After all, they were only going
to penetrate a short distance into England, not make any
deep invasion. It was to be a mighty gesture, yes, but
ought not to take overlong. Janet, up in Moray, if she
knew of it all, would be equally anxious.

With the numbers involved, a large proportion, of
course, were afoot, especially the Highlanders who seldom
used horses for their fighting. But even so, there would be
perhaps fifteen thousand horsemen, a great array. James
was going to go on ahead with these, cross the Tweed, and
on Northumbrian ground await the slower-moving foot,
the cannon and the stores, with those French pikes and
lances. The occupying wait would in itself be a notable
challenge.

So, in due course, with the furthest-to-come contingents
arrived, the move was made, the mounted force, a gallant
sight with hundreds of banners flapping in the wake of
the royal lion rampant standard, with horn-blowing and
cymbal-clashing to spur them on their way, James seeing
it all in the nature of an outsize tourney such as he so
greatly favoured. All Scotland's great ones rode with their
monarch, the officers of state, the justiciars, the sheriffs,
the Earl Marishal, the Lord High Constable, the Lord
Lyon King of Arms, the High Chancellor, he the now
elderly Earl of Angus, the Red Douglas, no fewer than
ten other earls, also the young Alexander, Archbishop of
St Andrews, although not his suffragan, Andrew Forman.
The realm had never seen the like.

They rode by Musselburgh and Haddington, to pass
through the Lammermuirs to Ellemford, where they
picked up the first of the Borderland parties, from Duns
and the Whiteadder and Abbey St Bathans area. Then on
into the Merse where, at Swinton, the Earl of Home and
all his many lairds awaited them. They were not going
to cross at Berwick, where its strong castle and fortifed

walled town could have held them up to no purpose; let Dacre come after them, if so he felt inclined. They would ford Tweed between the strongholds of Norham and Wark, where the Till entered from the south, or nearby, possibly at Coldstream. No laying siege to fortresses on this occasion.

They camped that first night all along the side of the great river, England only a matter of yards away. If news of their coming had reached Northumberland, there was no sign of opposition as yet.

James planned to advance perhaps a dozen miles into England, and there wait for the foot and the cannon to catch up with them. Thereafter to form a sort of parade east and west, parallel with the borderline, to make entirely clear the Scots presence on Henry's land to as large an area as was practicable. Whether they had to break a lance or two for Anne of Brittany in the process remained to be seen. But at least they were going to advance her three feet, or more, which she pleaded for. One day perhaps he would visit her and tell her so. Would Louis be a jealous husband?

In the morning, they crossed Tweed at three points, still entirely unopposed, although surely their presence and numbers must have become known to the English borderers by now. Up Till they proceeded, and if they were being watched by other than the inhabitants of the little communities they passed, it was not evident.

In a couple of miles they came to Castle Heaton, just beyond Twizel, the first stronghold they had to do something about, for it would be dangerous to leave this intact between them and their following foot army. But they had no cannon as yet. However, here they gained proof of a sort that their advance was known by the Northumbrians, for two white flags flew from its towers as they approached, symbols of surrender, this before a shot was fired. Its owner had departed, leaving only a steward to hand over to the Scots, beseeching that, in such circumstances, the hold should be spared from damage and destruction. James accepted this, his main concern that this must have been decided upon at least the day before. So if Swinburne of Heaton knew of their coming, others would also. Dacre? How prepared were the Northumbrians for this invasion?

Up Till another three miles was Etal Castle. But two miles beyond it was another castle, Ford; strongholds and tower-houses and peels proliferated thus near the border, as they did on the Scots side also, and necessarily so, with raiding a constant menace to both. Etal was a much stronger place than Heaton, or Ford either. James did not want to get involved in siegery, as yet without artillery. But Ford, now? It might be wise to bypass Etal meantime and visit Ford, visit, not necessarily capture.

For Ford, of the Heron family, was known to James Stewart. He had visited here long ago, seventeen years back to be exact, when in his early twenties, with his East March warden, in an attempt to settle what had become an ongoing feud between the Homes and the Carrs of Etal, Sir William Heron then being the English warden. And he, James, had been much impressed by Elizabeth Heron, the warden's young wife, a lively and good-looking creature, then barely twenty years old and much younger than her husband. And she had had a beckoning eye, which did not go unnoticed by the royal visitor. They had got on notably well, and if Sir William had not been so very much present, they might have got on better still. James had often thought of Elizabeth Heron, especially of late, oddly enough, when a strange circumstance had developed involving Heron. Sir Robert Kerr, the Scots Warden of the Middle March, had been murdered in most shocking circumstances by John Heron, bastard brother of Sir William. He had been ordered to give himself up by a joint Wardens' Court to stand trial, but had refused and fled. According to the Marches law, when such as this occurred, a hostage had to be yielded up until the murderer was caught; and Sir William himself, as warden, was the only Heron available. He had submitted himself, however reluctantly, to the required procedures and had been immured in the Home stronghold of Fast Castle on the Berwickshire coast. And he was still there, for the Bastard Heron had never been found.

James, aware of all this, thought that a visit to Ford Castle might be informative and possibly productive in more ways than one.

There were sizeable villages at Etal and Ford both, and these would serve as well as any other to base his horsed array while they awaited the arrival of the thousands of foot and the cannon, as planned.

While most of the force was left at Etal, surrounding but not actually assailing the strong castle, David, along with most of the senior lords and chiefs, went on with the king to Ford, its castle a fine and extensive establishment, if less highly fortified and strategically placed than Etal. Here, James with his magnates presented themselves, but not in any threatening way. He informed that he knew Lady Heron, and hoped that she was at home, this to the interest of all.

Whatever the lady thought of this invasion of her home, she did not seem greatly surprised, eyeing James not unkindly. And the king's interest was promptly understood by all, for she certainly was an attractive woman, well-made, comely and vivacious, now just short of forty years but looking a deal younger. She apparently had no children or family there. And her welcome to James was almost as though his call had been expected. If she was troubled by the presence of all his lofty companions, she did not make it evident.

So, about a dozen of them, including David and the young Archbishop Alexander, settled in meantime, in comfortable quarters. It was not how David, for one, had visualised armed campaigning, even on this distinctly unusual invasion.

James was not long in disappearing in Elizabeth Heron's company.

When he eventually reappeared, he had much of interest

and importance to tell them all, if scarcely personal details. First and foremost, their coming had been known to the English for at least a couple of weeks; no doubt Margaret Tudor had found means of sending word of his plans to Lord Dacre at Berwick. And that man had taken due precautions. He had assembled something like fifteen thousand men from Northumbria – which accounted for the ease with which they had taken Castle Heaton – and he had sent warning hot-foot to London, to Surrey in command there during Henry's absence in France. And, according to Lady Heron, Surrey had sent orders back for Dacre not to attempt any assault on the Scots host; he would come up with a suitable force and see to that himself. Dacre was to go with his men to Newcastle, there to ally himself to the Earl of Northumberland's Percys and the Bishop of Durham's men, to wait for further orders.

This of Surrey's coming had its impact on all, although it had been more or less anticipated since he, as Earl Marshal of England, could hardly ignore the Scots move. How large an army would he bring with him? And when would he reach here? There was much debate over the position. Was their sally over the border a gesture, to warn Henry and perhaps bring him back to England? Or was it a challenge to armed conflict? Differing views were expressed over this. Some were for returning, the gesture made. Some for at least going back over Tweed, to face Surrey there, with the English having to cross the river, under fire, to get at them, David agreeing with this. Others, mainly the younger lords, declared scornfully that this was craven folly. With the enormous host they had coming, to run back to Scotland before the English could reach them would undo any good that this invasion could achieve.

James himself tended to take this view. Would not a retiral now, when reported to Henry, merely seem to turn this great venture into feeble play-acting?

They had two days to wait at Ford Castle before the

311

foot arrived, Highland bagpipes heralding their approach, thousands upon thousands of men. The entire Till valley became full of trudging, chanting soldiers. The cannon were still to come, oxen-drawn and slow.

The Highland chiefs, the Mackintosh, Cameron of Lochiel, Maclean of Duart, MacIan of Ardnamurchan, had brought their tartan-clad legions, and were at one in advocating confrontation with Surrey. They had not marched all this way merely to turn and march back again. Some of the others with the footmen did say that crossing Tweed and waiting there would give the greater advantage. But admittedly it would not be the same as meeting the enemy on their own soil.

The matter was more or less settled next day, in unexpected fashion. A messenger arrived at Ford Castle from none other than Surrey himself, no less than the Rougecroix Pursuivant, a senior herald. He declared that the Earl Marshal of England would meet with the King of Scots on Friday, the ninth day of September, at noon, to show him that English ground was not to be trodden with impunity by Scots or any other without invitation. Unless King James preferred a retiral to a meeting?

That, to be sure, could have only one answer. No doubt Surrey well knew of James Stewart's character. The herald-pursuivant was sent back south with no uncertain message. His Grace of Scotland would meet the Earl Marshal of England on the ninth day of September, and on English soil.

So there could be no more argument and discussion. They had eight days to wait and prepare. James used those days to good effect, as well as sending off his parades east and west to, as it were, show the flag, to send out scouts over the surrounding territory to prospect siting for battle, the best places to confront Surrey. And when the cannon eventually put in an appearance, they were promptly used to batter the walls of the strongholds of Etal, Norham and Wark, so that the entire area resounded for days with the boom of gunfire. It was to be presumed that her kindnesses caused Lady Heron to appreciate that they were sparing Ford Castle.

The investigating scouts reported that, in all this territory of the upper Till, there was one undoubtedly advantageous site for the Scots army to take up position. That was Branxton Hill, a wide eminence of lofty ground some four miles south of Ford, with an east-facing escarpment known as Flodden Edge. Up there was the base for them, a difficult place to assail, with every tactical advantage, and backed by ample space, on the high ground, for all the men and thousands of horses.

With two days to go until Surrey's proposed meeting, the move was made. James said farewell to Elizabeth Heron meantime, and the entire Scots force, save for roving scouts, made for and occupied Branxton Hill and Flodden Edge. Pavilions and tents were erected, and all organised in as orderly fashion as was possible, food supplies gathered from nearby farms, fodder for the animals, all a major undertaking for so vast an assembly of men and beasts. The cannon and oxen had to come up also, of course, although Flodden Edge was no place for artillery fire, in that at such height the pieces' muzzles could not be depressed sufficiently to aim at anything below. All that they could be used for here was perhaps to demonstrate welcome over the heads of the English on the low ground. The long French pikes were duly distributed.

Then, on 7th September, in thin chilly rain, Rougecroix Pursuivant arrived again under a white flag, with Surrey's salutations, and to announce that the Earl Marshal would meet the King of Scots and his people on the plain of the River Till at Milfield, in two days' time.

This had James disturbed, although few of his supporters were, who saw it as confirmation of their choice of position. Milfield was low and marshy ground, some two miles south-east of Flodden, flanking the Till, which Surrey no doubt intended to use to his advantage, as so many had suggested that the Scots used Tweed. They at least had the benefit of being here first and choosing the best strategic site.

But the king was in two minds about this. Surrey and his men would have to climb up this very steep slope to assail them, a grievous handicap, which he probably would not attempt. What would result, then? Would it become a sort of siege? The Scots up here, the English surrounding them on the low ground, neither side able to fight. But eighty thousand men, as was now reckoned the army to number, not to mention the horses and oxen, could not remain indefinitely on an open hilltop, without supplies, food, water and fodder; whereas the English could encamp around comfortably enough and use the countryside to supply them. And they would have cannon down there, usable if the Scots descended. It would be like starving out a besieged castle. It would therefore be an impracticable position to maintain, as well as seemingly cowardly and unknightly in avoiding battle, and his force almost certainly the more numerous.

There was much debate about all this as they waited.

David Kennedy wished that they were safely back on the north side of Tweed, leaving the enemy to face the problems, not themselves.

31

Friday, the ninth day of September, dawned wet and chill, unpleasant conditions for all idling there on the high ground of the exposed ridge. And the visibility was very poor, distant areas vague. Surrey had said that he would meet the Scots at noon. If he kept to his word, and with a large force, he could not be far away by now. He might come early, or late. James had his army stand to arms early.

They waited. They seemed to have been waiting a lot of late. And in these poor conditions morale was scarcely at its highest; although that would improve, no doubt, once the enemy was there to confront. The Earl of Home's men, moss-troopers, knowing the area from much raiding and making ideal prickers or scouts, were covering all approaches.

The Earl of Angus was no help to morale. He kept telling all who would listen to him that they ought to be six or seven miles north of here, on the other side of Tweed – and there was still time to make the move, although they might lose a few cannon if Surrey came on time. For once David agreed with the Red Douglas, but did not say so.

The hours passed, the scouts reporting no enemy presence. Were the English having second thoughts? Were they merely delayed? If they were going to be present by midday, their outriders ought to be in evidence by now, even in this rain and poor viewing conditions.

Then, Home scouts came with the news, at last. The English *were* present, but not where they were expected to be. They were miles to the east, a great army, having left the upper Till, and were heading north by east, by Doddington Moor and Barmoor and Lowick, almost parallel with the coast and only three or four miles inland.

Surprised, the Scots wondered. Was Surrey seeking to get between them and the Tweed? Cut off their possible retiral to Scotland. If so, he must be arrogantly sure of victory. The Homes said that others of their kind were keeping watch on the enemy's progress.

It was well past midday before further information arrived. The English had swung round westwards now, and were approaching Till again, and crossing it, much nearer Tweed, fording near Castle Heaton indeed. So – an encircling move. Surrey must know that the Scots waited here on Flodden Edge; he would have his own scouts out. Was he intending to get behind them, not at Milfield at all but making for the western and lesser slopes of this Branxton Hill, to seek to assail them in the rear? Where he would not have this steep escarpment to face? James might have to turn his people around to face the other way.

The next word to reach them was that the English cannon were crossing Twizel Bridge. Perhaps that ought to have been demolished? That was still nearer Tweed than was Heaton. What was Surrey's intention?

And then they learned the truth. Surrey was holding to his word, making for that Milfield area, but from the north not the south. Why, they knew not. Perhaps he had feared some sort of ambush by the Scots in the hilly Wooler area, and had avoided it?

Soon thereafter, they actually saw the foe, a great host heading due south now, coming directly towards them, or at least below them, as though making past for the Milfield rendezvous. Did the Howard think that they, the Scots, would accept his challenge to meet them there, on the marshy ground? Leaving their strong position on the hill?

But, no. The long columns of the enemy array, how

many thousands it was hard to estimate, came to halt directly below, there to form themselves up into divisions, phalanxes and sections, all very orderly, the cavalry dismounted, the foot in their squares and companies, all in clear view now of the Scots above, despite the rain; just as the Scots, or some of them, would be equally evident up on the escarpment.

Thus the two armies waited, inactive. Waiting for what? Neither could assail the other, placed where they were. The English cannon had not yet arrived, but even when they did, they could be no more effective than the Scots ones, since they could not fire steeply upwards any more than the others could fire steeply downwards.

It looked like stalemate.

James kept watching their rear, in case another part of the enemy force was meantime working round westwards to engage in a pincer movement, to surround them, or seek to mount these lesser slopes to attack from behind. But there was, so far, no sign of anything such.

It was inaction, confrontation at perhaps only some four hundred yards, but at levels differing by as many feet. Waiting. What for?

The Scots sought to assess the enemy strength. It was difficult, fairly tightly packed as the English were. But the general judgment was that, large as the opposing force was, it probably numbered less than half of their own. And that was a challenging thought.

For how long that mutual waiting went on it would be hard to say, until at length the situation that James and the others had feared did develop. A large force began to appear to westwards, from the Branxton direction. The English had indeed divided into two great cohorts, and Flodden Edge was now faced from east and west. And while the enemy force to the east, presumably the main body, might do no more than wait down there and cut off any Scots attempt to move in that direction, for the Tweed or elsewhere, the western array could mount these easier slopes and assail them from that side.

James made up his mind, the waiting over. To turn and face this westwards threat could give Surrey the opportunity to climb the steep slope unassailed, and attack their rear. Much better that the *Scots* used that abrupt descent to charge in fullest force down upon the foe, with all the impetus that would give them, than either wait on their high position, or leave it to face westwards to join battle with the other array.

Not all agreed with this choice, in especial Angus, who there and then accused the king of continuing folly, not mincing his words, saying that they should have gone to put Tweed between them and the enemy long since, as he had urged, but asserting that this was still possible. They should at once head northwards along this lengthy ridge, and descend it at that end. Their scouts said that there were just the two English divisions, one below here and that other western one. An escape from this position, then, northwards, and make for Tweed while they could. He declared this in no respectful fashion.

That word escape had James Stewart the more decided, and hotly so. He had not brought his eighty thousand to *escape* the English, who were almost certainly fewer than themselves. If the Red Douglas desired to escape, let him do so. Him and his be off, back to Scotland, if that was their desire! Afraid, let him go home!

Bell-the-Cat cursed, and stamped away from the royal presence. But his two sons did not follow him, heads shaking. The Master of Angus declared that the Douglases did not flee on any field, even this ill-chosen one; they would fight, whatever their father did.

The Earl of Home put in that while this of seeming flight was not to be considered, there was something in what Angus had pointed out. If the northern flank of this edge was indeed free, as his prickers said, then part of their force, a mounted party, should use it to get them to the lower ground and threaten the enemy in their rears, either of the two arrays, or both. The Gordon Earl of

Huntly agreed with this. James acceded. No flight, but a diversion.

So the final decision was made. Home and Huntly, with a sizeable cavalry force, to head northwards along the ridge, and down. The remainder of the army to make its dash down the steep eastern slope upon the enemy there, with all strength and fury, afoot necessarily since horses could not charge down that awkward, uneven and slippery descent, the beasts, such as Home and Huntly had not taken, to be left on the escarpment meantime. Thousands of men, hurling themselves down upon the inactive enemy, would make an overwhelming impact. They would shatter the foe. Then a rearguard could bring the horses north-abouts to them, before the western English force could win up to the ridge. That was the royal decision. No more delay. Ready themselves to move.

The Highland chiefs at least approved of this strategy; that was their kind of warfare. Others were less happy, but all agreed that they could not just remain idle up here any longer, all but besieged as they now were.

So all formed up along that lengthy edge. The Highlanders would form the van. James himself would lead the centre, with the Earls of Crawford and Montrose. Lennox and Argyll to lead the right, Bothwell the left with his Borderers, the Carrick contingent with them. Home and Huntly to ride off northwards. Angus could remain with the horse, if so he chose. It was now late afternoon.

With everyone at least eager for action, whatever the outcome of it, wet and chilled after hours of waiting idle in the rain, they were ready. The western English array was still the best part of a mile off.

David Kennedy, with Bothwell and Rothes and Morton, found himself on the left of the long line, the northern portion. For these lords, it would be strange fighting, on foot. But then it was a strange enterprise in every way.

Presently, horns braying from the centre and bagpipes sounding their high challenge, it was action at last. Over the edge of the escarpment they surged, in their thousands, banners flying, swords drawn, axes raised, and those lengthy French pikes, three times the height of a man, over less than welcoming shoulders.

Within moments, David knew that they were into trouble, trouble other than that of battle. Once over the first lip of the ridge, which was less abrupt, the slope steepened acutely into bare rock and thin soil. And both were slippery, with all the rain. Men's feet, his own also, began to slither and slide. It was difficult to maintain a balance, at the run, but infinitely worse for his men, bearing those eighteen-foot-long pikes. Excellent as these might be for using in defensive hedgehog formations to keep cavalry at bay, for men seeking to bound down a broken, tilted and treacherous hillside they were a disaster, their bearers packed tightly in their hundreds and thousands. The pikes fell from shoulders and men tripped over them or were struck by them, tumbling headlong. In that stumbling, sliding disarray some of the lances broke and splintered, wounding, tearing flesh. Their bearers began to cast them away, this creating a menace for those behind. It became an all but complete shambles, the already difficult charge developing into a disorderly rabble, the falling, cursing men in front colliding with each other before being overrun by those following.

David himself, with no pike, but sword in hand, fell three times before he was halfway down the quarter-mile of descent; and even as he picked himself up, he perceived that the same was happening all along that hillside, few of the lances having got that far.

And then it was not pike-shafts, splintered or otherwise, that constituted the menace now, but arrows. The enemy below them had formations of archers in position there, in groups amongst the footmen, probably Welshmen with their long-bows, which unlike the cannon, could shoot uphill, weapons that the Scots had never used in warfare, only for sport. A hissing hail of arrows now met the stumbling, careering mass, and packed close as they were, none could miss a mark. Everywhere men fell, transfixed, for their fellows to trip over. David felt a searing pain in his left shoulder, although this shaft merely struck him a glancing blow. The hail of death was continuous and widespread.

But sheer weight of numbers carried the Scots host onwards, downwards, in whatever confusion, and at last into the English massed ranks they collided, these disciplined, drawn up and awaiting them with banks and hedges of spears and halberds, axes and maces, swords and daggers. The very weight and impact of the descending Scots dented the front ranks and lines of the enemy, and to some extent the chaos was communicated to them also.

Hacking his way through the smiting, milling, yelling press, his wounded shoulder forgotten in the excitement, David found himself detached from his following of Carrick men, such as had got to the foot of the hill on their feet. Indeed he became surrounded by Englishmen. But most of these were paying no attention to him in the turmoil, one man, while so many were descending upon them, however disorderly; in fact most with their backs to him, few if any probably recognising him as a Scot. He had not realised that battle, hand-to-hand fighting at least, could be so unbelievably confusing, for friend and foe alike.

Sword out before him, bloody now, he reached a slight rise in the uneven ground, on which one man was trying to direct others, some sort of a leader possibly. But, drawing a great breath, David thrust him through with his blade. The man pitched forward – and took the sword with him. David had to stoop and tug, indeed putting a foot on the unfortunate's neck, to give him leverage. The weapon freed, he gazed around him, panting. None attacked him. He himself could not distinguish Scots from English now. There was no recognisable line of battle. To the right, the south, some distance off, he saw banners actually still upraised. Presumably there was some order there, even though, as he looked, flags and pennons swayed and went down. The quality fighting there, then? And as he stared, he recognised the red lion rampant on gold amongst the others: there was James! The king had got thus far. Then the royal flag, in its turn, went down. Gulping, David started to battle his way through the surging throng towards where he had seen it.

His progress was not so difficult as might have been expected, for he was now deep into the enemy, and none was looking for assault there, not perceiving him as a foe, one of their own lords no doubt. And *he* did not attack any now, intent on getting over to the area where the banners were; just why he did not ask himself. David Kennedy was little less confused than all around him. It was, probably, some urge to get near his liege-lord.

Then he saw the lion rampant was raised again, presumably successive bearers replacing those who had fallen.

As he drew nearer it, David was stumbling frequently, this over bodies, some still, some jerking and twisting. Recovering himself from one such stagger, and looking down, he was shaken to see that it was none other than the Lindsay, Earl of Crawford. So he was amongst his own fellow Scots here, the fallen ones at least. He himself seemed to be one of the fortunate. Was he going to survive this catastrophe? Oddly, it came to him that Agnes would be urging caution, heed, care.

Soon, instead of stumbling over bodies he was trampling on them, clambering over them, as he neared where the royal banner reeled. He was past looking for identities now, but he did see Sir William Douglas, Angus's second son – at least he thought it was him, although the features were horribly slashed, blood all but hiding them.

Picking his way, he had to fend off the occasional blow; but there was such an entanglement of friend and foe that it was not any recognisable attack or defence. That is, until he reached that central area of the lengthy former line where determined and decisive fighting was taking place, this around that royal standard.

And there was James Stewart, right arm hanging limply, his doublet slashed, blood on his brow below the golden circlet which served as crown. He was wielding a mace with his left hand, prominent, standing on top of a heap of slain, with just behind him his son, the Archbishop Alexander, he seeking to hold the lion rampant aloft, sword in the other hand. Bothwell stood near, if standing it could be termed, lurching drunkenly, *his* sword being used to keep him upright.

Even as David stumbled towards his monarch, he saw an arrow strike Alexander Stewart, piercing his throat just above his breastplate. Staggering back, he fell, and the standard with him.

That flag, somehow, in those grim moments, was all-important to David Kennedy. It seemed to represent not only his king and country but all that he held dear, all that he had lived and worked for. Somehow he had to win to it, save it. Agnes would not decry that, surely . . . ?

Lurching, tottering over the slippery slain, he slashed at a spearman who was aiming at the king, felling him. Arrows were showering over and amongst them, the deadly Welsh cloth-yard shafts. One passed so close to his head that he felt the wind of it. Then, at last, he reached the king's side, or close behind him, avoiding that swinging mace, whether James realised it or not. It was the great flag that he sought, where it lay, its staff across the body of Mariot Boyd's son. Dropping his sword and grasping the wood, he raised the standard aloft, in something like triumph. An arrow pierced the cloth almost at once, but he managed to keep it approximately upright, at the monarch's back. Bothwell had pitched forward on his face, and lay still. Just beyond him was Atholl, on hands and knees, head drooping. It was astonishing that James himself remained on his feet, shouting his defiance.

The King! The King of Scots! He to whom David had sworn fealty, as they all had. Scotland still lived! And he,

David Kennedy, stood at his shoulder, as he had vowed, that time, to do. And in his grip the symbol of the nation's pride, the king of beasts in *its* pride. Here was fulfilment, culmination, a man's destiny! If he achieved no more, fell like these others, he had this, this . . . !

He saw it coming, recognised it, one of those long French pikes, the man behind it grinning in hate, in menace, an Englishman who had somehow won it. This, then, was it, the testing, the end. Or, the beginning . . . ?

David Kennedy was hurled backwards, still clutching the standard's staff. He knew no pain, impact only, the irresistible force, the completion. Then darkness, darkness – but kindly darkness. And a light ahead, a warm, beckoning light, gleaming. When he reached that, all would be well, well. He was on his way . . .

EPILOGUE

Flodden Field was the greatest disaster in all Scotland's dramatic story, thousands upon thousands slain, including the king himself, the flower of the nation's manhood. Most of his lords, twelve earls, even two bishops and two abbots as well as the young Alexander. And yet, as the early dark fell, in the driving rain, the Earl of Surrey did not know that he had won an inglorious day even though the King of Scots had fallen. For the Earls of Home and Huntly and their mounted men had defeated the western wing of the enemy, although thereafter they were not able to affect the main battle, if battle it could be called. In Surrey's opinion the English host had not aquitted itself as it should have done, its confusion only a little less than that of the Scots; indeed, as the fighting tailed off, with the light, he summoned his captains and berated them for incompetence and poor fighting. It was only the following morning, in daylight, on a field of only death, that he realised that he had, in fact, won a notable if scarcely gallant victory, the Scots threat removed; and he celebrated by knighting no fewer than forty of the captains he had reprimanded the evening before.

Over ten thousand Scots died. They were buried in two great pits. The English losses were less than half that.

So David Kennedy never returned to his Agnes.

The Earl of Home was much criticised for not returning to the aid of his king after his western victory, Whether or not he deserved to be is hard to decide. The word brought to him may have convinced him that it was too late to effect anything. But even today, at the annual Selkirk Common Riding celebrations, they sing:

325

Up wi' the Souters o' Selkirk,
And down wi' the Earl o' Home!

This referring to the return to the town of a single survivor.

It is said that no single community of Scotland was not plunged into mourning by the catastrophe.

But at least Surrey did not proceed to invade the northern kingdom, his losses and prudence sufficient to make him return southwards there and then.

King Henry came back to England shortly thereafter.

The young Duke of Rothesay now became James the Fifth; and the pregnant-again Queen Margaret produced another son, Alexander, Duke of Ross. With the queen as regent, and the Privy Council now largely composed of senior clergy, so many of the nobles leaving only under-age heirs, the Scotland of James the Fifth faced a very uncertain future.

Flaming Janet Kennedy, Lady Bothwell, brought up her son, James, Earl of Moray, to be a worthy young man, even Lord Dacre, in 1519, decribing him as a "springkeld", a fine youth. He became a great support of his half-brother the king, and in 1532 was made Lieutenant-General of the realm. Three years later he went to France to negotiate the marriage of James to the King of France's daughter. He died in 1544. When his mother died is not recorded.

Young Gilbert Kennedy became second Earl of Cassillis in turn, and in due course a member of the Privy Council and a noted ambassador. His descendants still hold that earldom, now incorporated in the loftier title of Marquis of Ailsa.

Archibald Bell-the-Cat, Earl of Angus, having left Flodden Edge before the battle commended, retired, a broken old man, his sons dead, to the Priory of Whithorn, where he died a year later.

But Scotland and the lion rampant survived.